THE PASSION OF SAINT-JABLONSKI

THE PASSION OF SAINT-JABLONSKI

ANDREW MONDRY

ISBNs: 979-8-9990422-6-2 (paperback); 979-8-9990422-7-9 (ebook)

Library of Congress Control Number: 2025946752

First Printing: 2025

Printed in the United States of America

PRAISE FOR ANDREW MONDRY

Andrew Mondry's brilliant, knowing, and wildly funny first novel *The Passion of Saint-Jablonski* is a book for and about America—not the country we want, or pretend to have, but the one we've got: mad, poor, rich, hustling, suffering, and trying for it all with a mix of hope and desperation. Mondry is the real deal—like Russell Banks meets Carl Hiaasen. Think of the tender, comic songbook of John Prine, the dreary kindness of the New England soul, and that one friend who kept threatening a move to Florida. A great novel by a great writer.

— DAN BEVACQUA, AUTHOR OF *MOLLY BIT*

For Danielle, Raelyn, and Ava with all my love and laughter.

CHAPTER ONE

EVERYONE HAS A THEORY, a hot take about what happened down there. Not even the semen-retainers and pee-keepers can agree on the facts. The crypto-bros—currency and zoology alike—have their stories, too, but regardless of what they witnessed, they all testified. Some posted until their fingers turned to knuckled bark, while others sat before obscure subcommittees commissioned to understand what happened that summer at the Royal Palm Condominiums (which for reasons of national security will henceforth be known as "the association").

No one cared much about the truth. The facts were reduced to red threads on a corkboard, a feathery Rorschach blotch. Convenient, sure, but definitive? Ick. With everyone entitled to their own truth, it proved to be a cheap commodity. No, everyone was simply looking to arrange the rubble of tragedy into something meaningful.

The only party yet to be heard from is Saint-Jablonski himself, who has been missing ever since; but each testimonial, whether online or IRL, always starts with the night he and Al found Gator.

They were smoking a joint and watching reruns of *John D.*

Wolf: Bounty Hunter when there was a knock at the door—the two birddogged. Stosh felt as though his father was about to burst in and ring him one.

"You expecting someone?" Al asked.

"Do we ever?"

Another knock.

The couch was an old sectional that Stosh had found at a thrift store upon his arrival in Florida. It enveloped the small living room, each day seeming to take up more space; the TV so close they could nearly feel its warm glow on their faces. Al's spot was closest to the bathroom, just far enough away from the mold to avoid the noxious funk, and Stosh's seat was beneath the front window. He tried to lift the broken blinds and peer out without being noticed, but Birdie's face was nearly pressed against the glass.

"She saw," he said.

"Tara-Lynn?"

"Worse."

Al took the joint, said, "Good luck," and retreated to his room.

Stosh sprayed some Febreze and answered the door to find Birdie standing in the corridor with Misty, or whatever her dog's name was.

"There's a gator in the pool," she said.

A large jet screamed off somewhere in the dark sky as the dogs down the street exchanged grievances about the noise. *Surely this is not real*, Stosh thought before he could arrange the stones in his head.

"That's a new one," he coughed. "What'd Tara-Lynn have to say?"

"I don't know. I tried her cell, but she didn't answer."

"We should probably call animal control, or the cops, right?"

"You're the Vice President," Birdie said. "But that seems like a good place to start."

A nervous heat rose in the back of Stosh's throat.

"Maybe I can take a look after dinner," he said.

"I made lasagna," Birdie added. "Want me to make you a plate?"

Stosh waffled, his empty belly willing to do the talking if his mouth couldn't, but he refused. "Oh, thanks, but I think we're getting Jocko's tonight."

"Stuff's no good for you," Birdie smirked and walked out the door. Misty didn't move until the tension of her leash yanked her from a dream.

Stosh may have been the VP, but it was in name only. Tara-Lynn was the only authority. That was the deal. She got the power and his vote, and he got the loan. He called her, but it went straight to a voicemail box that was already full.

He thought about calling Tara-Lynn's daughter, Bambi, but he knew she'd ask about the paperwork again and probably see the call for what it really was—an excuse to talk to her. He hadn't heard her real voice in almost a year. Occasionally, he'd listen to old voicemails from her when his usual remedies for loneliness didn't work, but there was no use in panicking her over what was probably nothing and exposing his own desperation in the process.

Alligators, Stosh whispered to himself, chewing on each syllable as if they belonged to a foreign language. He was from up north. The only critters he'd had to deal with were pugnacious squirrels and the occasional gopher. The hell did he know about reptiles? Amphibians? Whatever.

Al cracked his door and peered out.

"Birdie's gone. Just me," Stosh said. "Got a gator in the pool."

"Tara-Lynn's gonna love that."

"Can't find her."

"Sucks to be you then."

"You're gonna send me out there to deal with an alligator by myself?"

"Hopping on *Call of Duty*. Sorry."

Stosh had taken his duties as the VP pretty lightly, often looking the other way at what he thought were silly infractions of the by-laws—people walking on the grass, folks throwing paint cans and other debris in the dumpster; that strange old man, Fred, messing around with the sprinkler heads. It wasn't a job, Stosh figured; he wasn't getting paid, so what did he care? But he supposed an alligator in the pool was something he should deal with—a matter of public safety.

Woefully underprepared, Stosh stepped into his slides and headed for the pool, a nine-iron in his hand.

The air was thick, almost pulpy. The palm trees still sagged with rainwater from the earlier storm as the manholes gurgled and glistened in the streetlights. The condos had been off-base housing for airmen stationed at Jackson Air Force Base next door, but were sold to developers after the fall of the Soviet Union. There were four main buildings, each with twenty units in them—little particle board dorm rooms adorned with fist-size holes in the walls and smoke-stained popcorn ceilings. The sun had bleached the buildings' siding many years before, and the moisture had long been busy eroding the brick frames, but they were affordable at a time when nothing else was.

Stosh pulled one of those gaudy red GOOP signs from the muddy lawn and threw it in the dumpster as he made his way to the pool. He figured the signs would've disappeared after the election, but it appeared the campaign to return us to the Glory Of Our Past didn't end at the White House.

The girl from 78 D was outside smoking a cigarette as he turned the corner toward the pool. He thought her name was Amy, but he wasn't confident enough to say hi. Instead, he nodded politely toward her. She did little to recognize him other than flick the ash from her cigarette in his direction.

It wasn't until she saw the nine-iron that she asked, "What's the trouble?"

"I think there's an alligator in the pool."

"I'll take the gator over your club," she chuckled.

"I have no words, my sword is my voice," Stosh said, brandishing the club.

"What?"

"Macbeth."

"Which one does he live in?"

Maybe someday Shakespeare will be a good wingman.

"Could be the Skunk Ape," Amy said.

Stosh looked to the pool. He'd heard the stories, even had some of his own theories about the cryptid, but a community pool seemed like a silly place for an apex predator to prowl. Then again, what did he know? He was just a dumb Yankee.

Amy stuck her nose up in the air, said, "Smells like skunk to me."

"Maybe there's one stuck in the filter again," he said.

"Nah," she said, "Skunks don't make the hair on your ass stand up."

"Oh," he said, clenching his cheeks.

He continued toward the pool, steam rising from its concrete apron in milky tendrils. Despite growing up Catholic, Stosh had always been drawn to the paranormal. As a teenager, he spent his summers working for the parish, cleaning mossy toupees from the cemetery's ancient headstones, taking time to record the names so he could look them up online later. No witches. Just the victims of smallpox and typhoid, but that's how he discovered his favorite YouTube Channel—Apeus Dei Cryptozoology. He'd never had an encounter himself, but he believed if God could reach into our world, then the Anunnaki certainly could.

As he got closer, he saw a figure standing by the fence—a long, slender thing, like a scarecrow that had been blown from its field. The stench got thicker. He wiped his sweaty palms on his already damp shirt and tightened his grip on the nine-iron. He said a quick prayer to the patron Saint of Cryptids and swallowed hard, but it was only that strange old man, Fred. He'd been banned from the pool for smoking weed there, so he was standing outside the fence, leaning against his walking stick with what seemed like the same joint he'd been fined for some months ago still hanging out of his mouth.

"I don't see it," he said as Stosh approached.

"Maybe it's gone," Stosh said.

Fred turned to Stosh, lowered his head so that his glasses slipped down the bridge of his nose, and peered at him from beneath the brim of his planter's hat.

"You Jablonski?" he asked.

"Saint-Jablonski," Stosh corrected him. "I'm on the board."

"Nice of one of you to show up."

Stosh's face got warm. He apologized.

Fred scoffed.

"I better get on with it then," Stosh said.

Fred mumbled something beneath his breath and walked away.

Stosh had felt better with Fred nearby. He seemed like the kind of guy who could handle himself against a gator or Skunk Ape, even though he couldn't have weighed more than a hundred and ten pounds. But now, it was just Stosh and his nine-iron. He entered the key code and opened the pool's gate. He could tell there was nothing in the pool, though the water was dark, almost black, and glossy. He heard rustling from the shed. With his phone's flashlight in one hand, he used the nine-iron in the other to open the shed's door. He could feel the blood drain from his cheeks, and something hard drop into his lower intestine, but what he found wasn't a gator, but some kind of pig. The thing squealed and thrashed. He put the nine-iron down and tried to get to where it was. He climbed over the lawn mower and the various power tools that seemed so old they'd grown out of the mossy walls of the shed. The little pig was boxed in by a bag of ancient fertilizer and a pile of even older bags of grass seed.

Stosh picked the hog up and held it at arm's length, doing his best to shield himself against its thrashing blows. He carried it out of the pool area and brought it over to the patch of woods beyond. He thought it'd scurry right off, but it just stood there.

"That's no gator," Amy said, walking over. "Poor little guy's kind of cute."

"Strong for something so small," Stosh said.

"Too bad they're overpopulated," she said. "Somebody'll probably shoot it by morning."

"You're kidding."

"There's a TV show about a family that hunts them in Pensacola."

"Really?"

"Same family that had that bounty hunter show," Amy said.

"John D. Wolf!?" Stosh said. "I love that show."

Amy nodded, said, "They hunt *these* fuckers now."

"What do we do?" Stosh asked as the thing sniffed mindlessly at the ground.

"You two can do whatever you want," Amy said, crushing her cigarette butt beneath her flipflop and walking away without a suggestion.

After a few minutes of trying to shoo the thing into the woods, Stosh called the sheriff's department and was all but laughed off the phone. Next, he called animal control, who said that he could do one of two things: wait until the next day when an officer could come out at a time yet to be determined, or kill the animal, as he was well within his rights to take its life.

"The third option?" he asked.

"Bring it home," the officer laughed.

Stosh hung around for a bit to see if it'd leave, but it just kept sniffing around, using its snout to dig at the loose ground. Stosh tried again to call Tara-Lynn, but she didn't answer. No doubt she would have the little thing executed, but at least the blood wouldn't be on his hands.

There was no gator; the community was in no more danger than it typically was during hurricane season. Satisfied he'd met the minimum requirements of his official duties, Stosh shrugged and walked away, but the hog took notice and followed. He'd heard one should run in a zigzag to evade alligators, but the tactic didn't seem to work with wild boars, as the thing matched Stosh's bumbling jukes and weaves.

By the time he got back to his unit, Stosh had tried everything short of a stiff-arm to elude the hog, but there it remained, sniffing and snorting at his heels like an annoying little brother. Maybe Al would get a kick out of it, though he was prone to strange bouts of OCD, but Stosh had no other options.

"The hell is that!?" Al said, sitting on the couch with the bong in his hand, as Stosh walked inside.

"A wild hog," Stosh said. "Can I hit that?"

"I know, but the fuck?"

"Can I just hit that first, and then I'll get into it."

Al handed Stosh the bong. He drew the lighter to the bowl and gurgled up a fat one. He held the smoke until it all but ripped his lungs apart.

The hog took inventory of the place. It roamed from room to room, snorting and giggling in its hog way until it finally returned to the living room. Life in the Saint-Jablonski/Bertolucci condo was one of routine. They preferred such excitement to be on TV or on their phones, not IRL. They had both accepted their fates as observers, welcomed to comment but always free to scroll by.

"Here, boy," Stosh said, snapping his fingers at the thing.

"It's a boy?" Al asked.

Stosh shrugged.

"You didn't check?" Al asked.

"Do you want the honors?"

"Not my farm, not my pig."

"It seems masculine enough," Stosh said, looking at the thing moseying around the living room with a certain entitlement.

"It's small."

"Maybe it's one of those teacup pigs or whatever."

"That's a myth."

"What's a myth?"

"The 'teacup' pig. It's a pig-myth," Al said.

"A 'pig-myth'?"

"Yeah," Al said. "No such thing as a teacup pig. They don't exist."

"Dude."

"What?"

"You cool with it—him—staying here for the night?"

"Not my pen, not my problem."

"You said that already."

"Did I?"

"Must you?"

"All I'm saying is that when we moved in here, you made me get rid of Ziggy," Al said.

"We can't have pets."

"But we can have livestock?"

"It's totally different. You wanted to keep the cat—we're gonna get rid of the pig."

"I mean, Birdie has her dog, we have our pig, but there are no pets allowed—got it."

"I had no say about Ziggy," Stosh said. "That was Tara-Lynn."

"Loosen up," Al said, with a knowing grin. "I'm just kidding."

"You know how my blood gets."

"That Catholic guilt of yours. Just too easy."

"It's this pot you get. It's no good for my head," Stosh said. "And speaking of guilt, didn't you think you gave your father skin cancer after you used all the sunscreen to..."

"We don't talk about that," he said. "Where'd the pig go?"

The hog was at the back door, just standing there, staring at it as if there was someone on the other side. Stosh filled a bowl of water and placed it on the floor in the kitchen.

Al went to bed, and Stosh was ready to do the same before he realized he hadn't eaten dinner. He popped a frozen pizza in the oven and turned on the TV. The news was on, and though he drank from the daily firehose of doom that was social media, he left the tube on if only for the noise, but a name caught his ear—Cletus Wriggle. Stosh wasn't close with any of his neighbors, but he knew Cletus from across the street. Stosh had always been impartial toward cops, but Cletus's face appeared so frequently on the nightly news since all that business with J'Davious Wallace went down that Stosh tried to avoid the galoot.

Everyone has their plotki, Stosh thought before changing the channel. He stared at the hog and wondered if there were more "pig-myths" he was previously unaware of. He went over to it and scratched its chin, and with a strange curiosity, he lifted its hind leg and confirmed that they had a boy.

Stosh had never owned a pet. Not a hamster nor a fish. Sure, he'd had Tamagotchis, a couple of them, but they had all expired, chirping away in the junk drawer until their batteries died or were dissected for use in the TV remote. Despite his excess, Major prohibited pets in the house and even banned Stosh from watching *The Dog Whisperer* because that commie Cesar Millan worried too much about the pack and not enough about the individual dogs.

Gator, Stosh smiled at the hog—a proud and happy moment.

CHAPTER TWO

STOSH HAD FALLEN asleep on the couch, half the frozen pizza still sitting on the coffee table, when he woke up. He'd barely eaten any of it, but Gator was hot to grab himself a slice. He wiggled around the table, crying for a bite, and Stosh thought about giving him one, but it was pepperoni, and Stosh wasn't a cruel man.

After his usual orchestra of hacking, Al came out of the bathroom—"Better get ready quick if you don't want to be late again."

Stosh looked at the cable box that was blinking 4:22 AM. He lived by the cruel Florida sun, measuring the days by his own shadow and the number of sweat rags he went through. He went to his bedroom, threw on an old polo, then came back into the living room where he picked up Gator.

"You bringing him to work?" Al asked.

"I was thinking I'd drop him off somewhere on the airfield."

"Their natural habitat."

"Always something to say," Stosh said.

They only had a few minutes to spare. Al was the Lead Groundskeeper at Palm Ridge Country Club and was the first laborer to ever return to the course for a second consecutive summer, so he rarely caught any flak if he was late. That's how Al was—dependable, solid as a seven-iron, whether on the mower or working Stosh's bag. They'd grown up together, chasing dreams on and off the course. Al was the only person there for Stosh after his father was locked up and Bambi left. He agreed to move to Florida without so much as a question. As close to brothers as either would ever have.

Stosh, on the other hand, was just lucky to be working at Palm Ridge. He was an Assistant Pro and had spent the last two summers working the youth camps. He spent his downtime taking inventory of the luxurious pro shop and caddying for the locals who lived at the course. It was a decent gig. He got to play whenever he wanted to, but working there was a constant reminder of his own failure. Unlike Al, he was expendable, considering central Florida was full of guys just like him, guys who'd once dreamed a big dream and now just needed to make rent.

They piled into Stosh's decrepit *Ranger*. Stosh noticed that old lawyer, Ray Limon, was getting into his *Corolla* and thought that if an attorney could only afford a Toyota, then he surely would never see anything nicer than his little pickup truck.

A few units down from their own, Stosh and Al saw something they'd never seen before at the association.

They stared at the woman in the gazebo in a way that made Stosh feel old and gross.

"That's not the girl from across the street, is it?" Al asked.

"Amy doesn't strike me as the yoga type."

"Sure has been a while for me," Al said.

"You wouldn't know what to do with a woman like that if she came with a manual."

"And you would?" Al retorted, smirking with a raised brow.

"I'm not the one with my tongue hanging out."

They laughed, each corralling whatever fantasies they were designing in their heads.

"We're already late," Stosh said, turning the engine over and crawling up the main road.

"Doing it for the 'gram," Al scoffed.

Stosh looked over at the woman. She had set up her phone on a tripod and seemed to be recording herself in the bruised glow of dawn.

"You know what this world needs?" Al said. "More shame."

"I guess so."

"As a Catholic, wouldn't you agree? Isn't anything private anymore? Isn't anything sacred!?"

"And what is it that you hold so close to your heart?" Stosh asked. "What secrets and multitudes does Al 'Little Bert' Bertolucci contain?"

"It's too early for your shit."

"You started it."

"Whatever."

JACKSON AIR FORCE BASE was the only thing standing between them—the hardworking people of the association—and the beautiful estates of Palm Ridge, but even though the Air Force was in the process of decommissioning the base, they wouldn't allow anyone to cut through it. Instead, Stosh and Al had to drive around the base, turning a five-minute commute into a twenty-minute slog, full of stoplights, bus stops, and the vagrants that accompany the hourly-rate motels on the strip.

Stosh stopped to let a few of them cross the street. He recognized one of them from the association. The guy didn't live there, but Stosh had seen him walking through the property and assumed he lived down at the brook where there was some encampment. He skulked across the street, his long arms swinging like an ape. He craned his neck and smiled at Stosh. Stosh waved. Still a stranger down there, he accepted what pleasantries he received.

Stosh pulled into the base but stopped short of its gate, which was once highly secured by large men in uniform but had since been swallowed by a fleshy green plant that was far more exotic than anything Al had ever had to chop or whack back up north.

Al huffed and crossed his arms when Stosh got out of the truck and put Gator on the ground. Stosh said goodbye and drove away carefully, so as not to run the little guy over. But as he did, he noticed a figure out on the tarmac, a man in what appeared to be neon green Bermuda shorts and a pair of rather large Mickey Mouse ears. *Just another day in Florida*, Stosh thought, a Disney Dad who'd wandered a little too far from Magic Kingdom. Stosh threw the car in drive and pulled out of the base.

Al had to be mowing by about 6:00 AM, before the first tee-time went off, but there was really no reason for Stosh to be at the clubhouse so early. He spent the first hours of his day sipping his coffee and evacuating his bowels, but Ketch, the pro, demanded he be there early. Stosh figured it was so that the residents didn't have to see the help coming in.

They were late, but like every other morning, they drove up to the gatehouse and were greeted by Henry, who only peered at them from above his newspaper before raising the gate.

They drove up the service road behind the Magnolia-lined terrace that runs up to the clubhouse. Stosh parked the *Ranger* by the maintenance shack. Al exited and walked off to his mower, while Stosh headed to his golf cart, parked in the other direction.

"Take the Ranger home when you're done. I have a late lesson," he hollered to Al.

"See you at home."

"Have a good one, sweetie."

"Fuck off."

Stosh drove his cart up to the clubhouse and went through the service door in the back of the building. He went to the break room, clocked in, then made his way back to the men's locker room, but Ketch was there, sitting in front of his locker.

"Let me guess, something about a pig?" he said.

"How'd you know that?" Stosh said.

"This girl I've been seeing lives near you," Ketch said. "Amy."

"No shit," he said, though still new, he found coincidences unnerving. His world had become so small—the association, the ridge, and the liquor store in between. It was a far cry from the life he'd imagined for himself even a few short years before, but it was insulated and predictable. Safe in a way that would've bored him as a teenager.

"Anyway, your punishment for the day is camp," Ketch said.

"Come on, man, I thought I was done with those."

"I could be a real dick and start writing you up."

Stosh sighed and laced up his cleats. There is nothing more tedious, frustrating, and, quite frankly, dangerous than conducting a golf camp for five-to-eight-year-olds. Jesus, Stosh might as well play Russian roulette, with all them little ones swinging what is the equivalent of a lethal weapon like it was nothing but a pool noodle.

All the students lived at the Ridge. They knew little of the world outside of the resort. Even at such a young age, they understood Stosh and the other employees were only there to serve them.

The driving range sat up on a ridge behind the clubhouse. If you face the course, you can see the sunrise over Kissimmee, over the first hole, and the most dedicated players the club has as they make their way off the first tee in the pubescent hours of the day, hoping to get 18 holes in before most finish their lunches. That's how Stosh grew up playing, as early and often as possible. Major would get him up and out to the course for nine holes before going to work on whatever project Major had lined up for the day. And late in the season, Major would pull Stosh from school in those last freak days of a New England fall, when it felt like winter in the morning, summer in the afternoon, and something ethereal in the evening. They'd race the sun, Major and Minor, each playing as quickly and carelessly as ever, neither really caring where their balls went. They just kept swinging, and Stosh thought they could actually keep the sun from setting. That's how Stosh tried to train Christian—early and often—when his family sent him to Florida, but Christian played his practice rounds well after noon, always working out the sweats and itching for his next high while he struggled to finish nine. But even stoned, Christian was a better golfer than Stosh and any of the hacks the Ridge housed.

The morning was idyllic. The Oompa-Loompas were busy popping out of the woods, replacing divots and grooming the bunkers behind the early players. The humidity was low, and thin, wispy clouds shredded the sky. The orchestra of sprinklers across the course flashed and spun, the water catching the sun's rays and reflecting them into little fleeting rainbows.

It was quiet, too, until the birds started. Years before, someone had complained about the absence of songbirds on the course, so management installed speakers to blast fake chirps and tweets. Now, every morning around the first tee time, the system kicks on with a flurry of squawks and whistles. Occasionally, the system malfunctions, causing a cacophony of bird calls to erupt all at once, as if there were some great unknown bird massacre happening on the back nine.

That morning, Stosh barely heard his phone ringing over the noise of the Jurassic hour. He hoped it was Tara-Lynn, but no such luck. He answered the call and was greeted by the same old robotic voice asking him to accept the terms and conditions of the call. He hesitated, as he always did, then accepted.

"Minor!" Major said in his bubbly voice.

Stosh had to give his old man credit—even in prison, his optimism could not be corked.

"What movie was it this week?" Stosh asked.

"*The Last Man Always Carries an Automatic Weapon,*" Major bellowed in his best voiceover impression. "Heston in his prime. You remember that one, right?"

"Yup, it's quite the flick."

"What's the matter?"

"I just got to work."

"Keep at it, Minor. It's only a matter of time until you're back out there on tour."

"I'd settle for a raise."

"Can't wait to play a round with you."

"Still got about three years before we can do that," Stosh said.

"That's where you're wrong, Minor. I talked to my lawyer yesterday, and we have an appeal hearing next month."

"Another one?"

"This one might be it, I'm telling you!"

Stosh gnawed on a fingernail, said, "Have you talked to Tara-Lynn since I moved down here?"

"Don't get me started on that one," Major said.

"What's that supposed to mean?"

"Nothing, Minor," Major chuckled. "You know she was never a fan of mine. Last time I talked to her was when she agreed to help you move."

Stosh kicked at a few broken tees on the ground. It was a long shot.

"Times up!" Stosh heard someone say to Major.

"Call you Saturday," Major said.

"That's a busy day for us."

"Talk to you then," Major said before hanging up.

He always called first thing in the morning. Said it was the only time of day he could really talk, really get his thoughts in order. He used to wake Stosh up early on the weekends to help on the job. Mom left before Stosh could remember her—found someone better, Major always said, which Stosh couldn't imagine was too hard. Major was in construction until he started his own venture flipping old houses into so-called "eco-friendly" housing. He had a little nest egg and bought his first house on what is now known as Quabaug Heights, on the north side of Cold Springs.

He flipped his first house for twice what it was worth, and from that little enterprise came the birth of Saint-Jablonski and Son Green Contracting. He flipped most of those houses on Quabaug. You'd think you'd be able to go up there now and see his handiwork, but there's a reason he's in prison. Stosh didn't know much about the scheme—a scheme he was unwittingly a part of as a kid helping his dad hang drywall on the weekends—but he had inspectors and appraisers that he always used, guys who said they could navigate the tax incentives and rebate programs. Guys he'd pay off for favorable numbers or to look the other way on his shoddy electrical work—guys who would eventually testify against him in a rather publicized trial.

But his reckoning came later, after he'd made his first million, after he'd bought and developed the whole street. They had all kinds of cars back then, too, the most prized of which was a red Mustang supposedly used in some Charlton Heston flick. However, most importantly, they had memberships to Stoney Hill Country Club, the premier course in the area, and Major always ensured Minor had the newest clubs.

As usual, Stosh had to shake Major's voice from his head. He took a minute from setting up the driving range and looked out at the course. That old ache returned to the place between his belly and his chest. He was supposed to be out there playing the course, not cleaning it up. It was like watching someone else's dream.

He still remembered when he got the job. He'd done what he could to doctor his application. Previous employment—Associate Partner at Saint-Jablonski and Son Green Contracting (translation: helped father on the weekends) and Dream Facilitator at Dreamy's Mattress (translation: salesman at national bedding chain). But the most pathetic part came when he had to write down his golfing accomplishments—Stoney Hill Junior Club Champion (2008); Course Record (65), Stoney Hill Country Club (2009); Second place, Polish National Credit Union Invitational

(2010). And that was it. Looking back, no matter how pathetic his resume was, he'd performed no labor that would have prepared him for the soul-crushing work of coaching five-year-olds for just above minimum wage.

Stosh went back to it. He finished setting up and left himself barely enough time to hit the head before the students started arriving. He wasn't just tasked with teaching the kids the great game of golf, but he also had to help them out of their parents' cars as they arrived. Caddying was not supposed to be a demeaning job. You're essentially a golfer's attorney, Major once told Stosh, but there was something belittling about caddying for a kindergartener.

They showed up in waves. Mostly mothers, but the occasional father, drove up the main road, circled the clubhouse's cul-de-sac, parked their cars, and waited for Stosh to hustle over. The residents of Palm Ridge were as traditional as they come—neat houses, clunky foreign SUVs for the wives, and sleek luxury sedans for the husbands. The women didn't work, and Stosh couldn't blame them. When you're married to a seven-figure salary, why bother? The men, well, Stosh didn't really know what they did to afford the lives they had. It confounded him. As much of a cheat as Major was, he did work. Stosh saw it and labored alongside him. But these guys? Who knows what they did. They all had degrees and titles that required acronyms—CFO, CEO, POS—all the same.

Most of the parents were punctual. They had appointments to get to and meetings to attend. The kids were typically on the range and ready to go by 7:30 AM, but Cecilia was always the last to arrive. She was the only resident of Palm Ridge that Stosh knew personally. She was married to Christian and still lived on the resort with the money she'd inherited, not from Christian, but from her grandparents, who had made their fortunes in tape, but not in scotch or duct. They owned a company called *Stick 'Em Up Tapes and Adhesives* that manufactured specialty tapes, such as crime scene and evidence tape used to secure seized drugs and the like. They'd made money in all sorts of ventures, but tape was what made them Palm Ridge rich. And that irony wasn't lost on Christian, who never missed an opportunity to tell anyone who'd listen that the only official charges he'd ever faced were thrown out because of his relationship to the people who made the tape that secured the so-called evidence found in his car.

But that morning, Cecelia only showed up five minutes late. Stosh knew it was her pulling up the road, not only by the speed at which she drove but because she was the only woman on the resort who still drove American—the early morning sun shining off her white Lincoln Navigator.

Stosh thought that he saw Christian in the passenger seat, leaned back in his usual swagger, but it was just a trick of the light. It was a big passenger seat to fill, and Stosh wasn't sure if anyone could ever do it.

"I thought you were done with camp," Cecelia said, pulling up to the clubhouse.

"Me too."

"Trying to play with us later? Cara and I are gonna try to get nine in after she gets out of work."

"I have a late lesson, but I'll catch up with you when I'm done."

"OK," Cecelia said. "You guys behave for Uncle Stosh."

"He's not my *real* uncle," Sasha said.

"He was daddy's best friend," Quentin said from his booster seat.

"That doesn't make him our uncle."

"Close enough," Stosh said, grabbing their bags from the trunk while Cecelia sat in the front seat, texting so fast he thought her fingers might catch fire.

Stosh remembered the countless times he had to lug both his and Christian's bags to the clubhouse while Christian was busy checking his hair or getting fixed before a round.

Christian was a brilliant player, a true natural, but he spent more time hustling pills than he did working on his game. It was Calvin, Christian's brother, who called Stosh to ask if he'd take him in. Tutor him, were Calvin's exact words. Christian had a shot at a scholarship to OSU, one of the best college programs in the country, but they wouldn't take him because of his numerous extracurricular activities. The idea was to send him to Stosh, under whose sober watch and tutelage, he'd right the ship and play as a Cowboy for OSU.

Cecelia moved down shortly thereafter, though Christian preferred she hadn't. Theirs was not a relationship conducive to stability and sobriety. They lived off the fat cap of life—those wholly unhealthy but scrumptious bits of young love. Their relationship was a canvas on which mosaics of broken beer bottles and burnt foil were assembled to create stained glass windows into their troubled souls.

Stosh often found himself in the middle of their fights, answering phone calls in the middle of the night, and throwing an extra blanket on the couch, leaving the door unlocked just in case Christian needed a place to crash. He did what he could, and he still was.

The kids lumbered behind Stosh. He set them up on the far end of the driving range and kept a close eye on them. Like their father, they got frustrated easily.

All was going smoothly until about an hour in, when Stosh had to stop Quentin from taking his driver to another kid's head.

"I want to hurt him!" Quentin hollered.

Stosh carried Quentin off to the side of the range and tried to calm him down.

"He said Daddy was a thief!" Quentin said.

"Who said that, Trevor?" Stosh said.

"Yeah," Quentin said, the hate still boiling his cheeks.

Stosh had never thought much about having kids, but now it was a hard no. Who the hell would want to do this for free?

"I hate Trevor!" Quentin yelled before shaking in a full-on tantrum—fists flying, little arms raging. Thankfully, Stosh's thighs took the brunt of the boy's anger, unlike the last time, when he caught Stosh square in the goonyachts.

Stosh let Quentin have his moment, trying to hold him the way Cecelia had taught him to. Even though Trevor was a spoiled little shit who probably deserved a good crack on the head, he was right about Christian. He went on a rampage just before he died, robbing a handful of houses in the Ridge.

Stosh gave the other kids a new drill and took Quentin down to the very end of the range, giving him time to cool down.

And that's how it went that day, even at lunch. Quentin wouldn't eat the Kale and Quinoa salad the chef prepared, so Stosh took the little guy down to Jocko's. Stosh wasn't all that upset—he was thirty and the last thing he wanted was Kale or Quinoa, so smashburgers and milkshakes it was.

Jocko's was nothing but a little shack on the side of the road that Stosh stumbled across his first weekend in Florida. He'd never learned to cook. He was raised in clubhouse restaurants, places with names like Mulligans, Bogey's, and the 19th Hole, so Jocko's became his caterer for a while, until some influencer did a review of their famous Volcano Burger and turned the shack into a viral sensation, flooding the small parking lot with self-described foodies trying to get a fix of the porn IRL. But that didn't keep Stosh from enjoying it when he could.

Stosh and Quentin were in the middle of their double-doubles when the strange man who'd been holding a sign that said "Jocko's is People" in the parking lot approached them.

"To eat here with your son is an abomination!" he hollered.

Quentin laughed.

"Don't you know what this place is?" the man said, spit flying out of his mouth. "It's the epicenter of evil! A stop on the cabal's depraved underground railroad!"

"Get out!" one of the employees yelled at the man. "I've told you before. We don't even have a basement here! You're crazy!"

The crazy man limped away, opting instead to stand across the street with his sign.

"I'm so sorry about that, folks," the employee said. "Please, see me at the counter for coupons for your next visit."

"He was funny," Quentin said as they finished their lunch.

It appeared to Stosh that the village idiots had returned with a vengeance ever since the last election, but in his experience, they mostly existed online, on Facebook feeds and message boards, but occasionally, they cracked through the screen. It was somewhat refreshing to experience an analog looney; vintage, you might say.

"I want to play golf with Daddy in heaven," Quentin said on their way back to the Ridge. "I bet I could beat him," he said.

"My money's on you, buddy," Stosh said; however, he couldn't help to think Quentin was better off with his father chipping around the Elysian fields than he would be if Christian were still playing on this earthly course; because as a boy who'd experienced it, he could say there is no pleasure in a son beating his father in a game they both loved. Major spent a lot of time and money on making Minor a better golfer, but when Minor finally beat him, it was as if Minor had clipped his old man's nuts. Stosh could never understand it. Isn't that what you want of your children, for them to have a better life than you, to be better than you? Major could be cruel, but Stosh had tried to prune all that bad fruit, all that trauma, as Bambi used to call it.

The clinic wrapped up around three in the afternoon. Stosh cleaned up the range just in time for his lesson with Dana Van Ronk.

She always scheduled her lessons late and always with Stosh, even though she didn't work and had all day to play if she wanted to. Stosh was not, nor has he ever been, accused of being much of a looker. If you were to ask him, he'd say he was 140 pounds of personality, though many would disagree with that, too. He was a skinny Polack with arms like a pair of elongated kielbasas, and a name that sounded like something you'd cough up after a long night of drinking. But the way Dana insisted on taking lessons only from him, and the way she looked at him, suggested that he was just her type.

The course charged Dana a substantial fee, but Stosh was paid only his hourly rate. Such is the life of an assistant pro, and that's all he was—a caddy, a cashier, a looper.

But he didn't mind Dana. She was sweet and gracious, unlike many of the other wives in the community. He'd heard her husband died in a plane crash but didn't know much more about her or where she was from, though it was obvious she was not from Florida. She moved too quickly, talked too much to be a native.

It was nice to have some female companionship on the course, to show off a bit. Bambi rarely came out on the course with Stosh, especially when he started getting serious attention from colleges in their senior year of high school. She had no intention of going to college but went with Stosh to Eastern Carolina University. She hoped to get a job bartending at one of the many bars in the area. That was until they realized she could go to school for free if they were married. Bambi was hesitant at first. They were only nineteen years old, even younger than when Major had Stosh. But they jumped into it. Major insisted on a Catholic wedding, but Bambi had only grown up with that vague Christianity that manifested around the major holidays but largely remained absent from daily life. Stosh, however, though not devout, considered him as Catholic as he was Polish or American. It was a part of his DNA, whether he liked it or not. Major offered to pay for the entire ceremony if they'd just get married in the Church, but what did it even matter? They were just kids. They got married at City Hall as soon as they arrived in Greenville, just a week before the semester began, so that Bambi could start classes right away.

By the time they were done with the lesson, Dana had gone through two sleeves of Stosh's Pro-Vs.

"Can you actually drop me at the clubhouse?" she said as they drove through the parking lot. "I'm gonna get my clubs regripped."

"Don't waste your money," Stosh said. "I can do it at some point this week."

"I couldn't, not after losing your balls," she said.

"Throw me ten bucks and buy the grips. I'll take care of it," Stosh said. "I'd rather take your money than let you give it to the club."

Stosh dropped Dana off at her car just as Cara and Cecelia were driving up in their cart. The ladies exchanged pleasantries, with Cara introducing herself as Cecelia's sister, though only because she lacked the appropriate title to express their strange bond—they'd both been with Christian at various points in the months before he died and learned of each other only afterward, when each appeared at the hospital, but instead of finding an enemy, found what could only be described as family.

Stosh still needed a Venn diagram to keep track of those on Christian's roster.

"Dana Van Ronk, huh?" Cecelia said after Dana left.

"She lives here?" Cara asked.

"The corner unit by the gym. Her husband was on that Malaysian flight, the one that went missing," Cecelia said.

"Jesus, Stosh—you really have no shame," Cara said.

"She was just taking a lesson," he said.

"Sure," Cara joked.

The sun was setting over the Ridge, but they had enough daylight to finish nine. Whenever Stosh played after work, he played barefoot. It made him feel as though he was a member, not an employee. Brought him peace. They played quickly that night. There was almost no one on the course. The place nearly emptied out at dinnertime, with families filing into the club's dining room for a meal or returning home for the same.

"Wanna come for dinner?" Cecelia asked Stosh after their round.

"I should probably get home. Strange things are going down at the condo," he said.

"Al in his feelings again?" Cara asked.

"The President's missing," Stosh said, and with those words, it became real. He still hadn't heard from Tara-Lynn, and by now, she certainly would've called, if only to gossip or review her most recent list of violators.

"So?" Cecelia said.

"I'm the Vice President. I should probably be around, just in case."

"And what are you going to do if something happens?" Cara asked.

Stosh shrugged, said, "Do you think I can get a ride home? Al's got the truck."

"Get in," Cara said.

It was full dark when he got home. The humidity had been cracked open by a brief storm that swept through earlier in the afternoon, but he could feel it building back up again, swirling up from the swamps and wetlands that surround the association. He decided to walk over to Tara-Lynn's place.

He was now worrying that she might be hurt, or in danger, but when he looked into her unit, it was empty—completely cleaned out. What the hell was she up to now?

Stosh sulked back to his place, where he hoped Al had cooked a frozen pizza or had some leftovers to share, but as he was walking back, he felt as if someone was following him. It was in those moments he remembered where he was—in wild, wild Florida. He remembered the first time he saw a water Moccasin wiggle across the lake; the first time he saw a gator creeping along the water hazard on the Ridge's par-three eleventh hole. Florida still belonged to the wild. It was everywhere, peering from behind every bush, and lurking just beneath the gentile water of every swamp, lake, and pool.

Those ancient nerves began to ignite, bringing the hair on his neck to full attention. He stopped and looked around, the gears of his prehistoric brain stuck between fight and flight, but before he could turn on his heels and run like hell, little Gator came waddling out of a nearby Azalea. He greeted Stosh with a jolly snort. Stosh could tell it was Gator by his cheerful disposition and the little tuft of white hair that started at his brow and crowned his head like a halo.

To hell with it, Stosh thought. "The Queen is dead, and I'm her heir."

Gator followed Stosh home. Al was passed out on the couch with no food to offer other than the crust of his grilled cheese. Stosh made some Ramen, and as the noodles boiled, he stole a look out the back window and saw that same beautiful woman, stretching in the ethereal glow of her ring light as if she'd been there all day.

CHAPTER THREE

THE RAIN KEPT the course closed the next day, which allowed Stosh some time to wrap his head around the past day's events. However, when he woke up, and saw Gator investigating the kitchen, snorting and buggering on at each corner as if looking for something to eat, he realized he'd need more than a day to figure out the acid trip he'd stepped into.

He tried one more time to call Tara-Lynn but was not surprised to get her voicemail.

"You know how big these things get?" Al asked, coming into the living room. "That thing is gonna gain about two hundred pounds before it hits puberty."

"When did you become such an authority on pigs?" Stosh asked.

"It's a long story," Al said, sitting down on the couch and lighting what was left in the bong from the night before, "but it ends with my sister in tears and my father buying a smoker."

Stosh opened the front door and walked with Gator outside. He whispered encouraging words, hoping the little guy would do his business, but after a few snarls, he took off back toward the brook.

The condo's office, where Tara-Lynn had ruled for as long as Stosh had lived at the association, was in the basement of the unit next to his. It was nothing more than a poker table, a safe, and a cabinet with files on each resident so thick they'd put J. Edgar himself to shame.

Birdie was already down there when he arrived. She only worked part-time and did the more menial tasks that Tara-Lynn couldn't be bothered with.

"Any word?" she asked him.

"I went by her place. Everything was cleared out," he said.

"Think it was the ANTIFAs from the BLM protest in Kissimmee?" Birdie asked. "Looked like things were getting hairy over there."

"I don't think ACAB stands for *All Condos Are Bastards*."

"She has her daughter listed as her emergency contact. Should we try her?"

Stosh blushed, said, "From what I understand, they don't have a good relationship."

"Well, we better find her fast because we bounced a check," Birdie said. "And there should be plenty of money in the account."

"Has that ever happened before?"

"Do you pay attention in our board meetings, Stosh?"

"I'm not really a numbers guy."

He had a degree in English, despite his father's objection. Major was a cynical pragmatist, and although the typical coursework for a promising but less-than-phenomenal golfer like Stosh included a degree in Golf Management from the Professional Golf Association of America, Major refused to let his son follow that track. To Major, a career in golf was all or nothing. Marketing, he believed, was a more practical contingency plan, or something similarly mind-numbing, like finance or business administration. But after a semester of coursework in those subjects, Stosh found only the writing to be of any interest and switched his major to English. He figured if he couldn't hack in on

Tour, he could become a teacher, or something noble like that. He even took a job in the university library. It was monotonous, but he loved it, though Major found it silly. He was like many Americans who believed in the virtue of "hard" work in the absence of a corner office, a white-collar job, and a large paycheck. Stosh was tasked with checking in the returns and filing them away on their respective shelves. He found it therapeutic, organizing the books by category and author and slipping them back between the other books on the shelves.

Bambi had bought Stosh one of those e-readers for their one-year anniversary, but there was something about it that he couldn't get used to. It was like the difference between porn and sex: sure, porn serves its purpose, but it ain't nothing like the real thing.

Books, neither digital nor analog, had been appreciated in the Saint-Jablonski house. Stosh didn't believe his father had ever read one cover-to-cover. He trusted whatever pundit was popular on Fox News at the time, relied on them to form his worldview, one in which he was the victim, the minority, a part of a demographic of Americans that was always under threat.

But reading and fiddling with books didn't seem to do Stosh any good, either. He stood there in the office, staring at a profit-and-loss spreadsheet as if it were some ancient tablet.

"How much money is usually in the account?" he asked Birdie.

"At least fifteen thousand," she said. "And then there's the reserve fund, which has about two hundred and fifty thousand, last I checked."

"Could someone have taken it?"

"The only person who has the authority to do that is Tara-Lynn," Birdie said. "You don't think..."

"I know she was shrewd, but stealing?"

"You weren't here in the beginning," Birdie said. "You know she was married to the old president, right?"

"That pastor guy?" Stosh said.

"Revered Killroy," Birdie nodded. "He was a good man. Liked to exaggerate, but still good. Used to run the church up there at the top of the street."

"That sad thing?" Stosh asked. "Tara-Lynn told me he was the pastor of a megachurch."

"He'd like to think so. It was a small congregation, mostly just us from the condos, but it felt like a community, that is until Tara-Lynn moved down here and learned that the megachurch preacher she met online was nothing but a parish pastor with a little condo and something a little less than the size of a flock," Birdie said. "And it didn't take her long to run for president. Won in a landslide that would've put Barry Goldwater to shame. There was a mutiny after she took control: the whole board resigned. She hand-selected the rest of you, filled the board with docile old women and incompetent morons. No offense."

Stosh averted his eyes, said, "I thought it would look good on a resume."

That was only partly true—he did naively think that being the Vice President would somehow propel him to the front of the hiring pool, but it made little difference in his hourly rate at the Ridge. The truth was, Major had talked Tara-Lynn into loaning Stosh the cash he needed for the down payment on his condo with the understanding that he'd serve on the board and vote according to her whim. He accepted the terms of the deal even though he knew it would only deepen the chasm between him and Bambi and forever entangle him with Tara-Lynn.

"Whatever happens, I'm sure this is gonna make the annual meeting a lot of fun," Birdie said.

"Should I go to the bank?" Stosh asked.

"And maybe call an attorney."

"Can we afford that?"

"Depends on what's left in the bank."

Stosh knew only one attorney—Calvin Kennedy, Christian's older brother, but Stosh thought better of getting him involved.

He didn't even know what kind of law Calvin practiced, though he learned it wasn't divorce after calling him for help when he first got the papers from Bambi.

Stosh didn't speak to Calvin for a while after Christian died. He felt like he had let Calvin and his family down. Felt ashamed, and maybe Calvin did, too, but can any of us save another, or are we solely responsible for our own redemptions? If that was the case, then there was probably little Calvin could do for Stosh's current predicament.

STOSH HAD to wait in the icy bank lobby for nearly an hour to meet with the Branch Manager, who was allegedly the only person who could help.

"Mister Saint-Jablonski?" He greeted Stosh, sounding out each syllable with confusion. It always made Stosh cringe when he heard a stranger say his name. How cruel his Jaju was to change the already silly-sounding "Jablonski" to "Saint-Jablonski" in a sorry attempt to better assimilate with the French-Canadian population he found himself living amongst after coming to America.

"I'm glad to see Tara-Lynn came to her senses," the manager said.

Stosh paused then said, "It happens so rarely."

"But I won't be able to give you your old rates if you want to reopen the accounts."

"Reopen?"

"She had us wire the funds from your accounts to a bank out of the Cayman Islands."

Something pulled at Stosh from a dark place beneath his gut.

"She didn't have the authority to do that, did she?" Stosh asked, unable to hide his ignorance.

"The accounts only required one board member's signature to move the money."

"Who authorized that?"

The young man checked his folder. "It appears you did."

Stosh turned red. He felt his lungs pucker.

"When you joined the board," the manager said, showing Stosh his electronic signature on the form. "You don't remember that?"

"I've signed a lot of things in my capacity as Vice President," Stosh said, clearing his throat and hiding his embarrassment with hubris, just like Major taught him.

"I'm truly sorry, sir." The man sighed and said, "I can waive the overdraft fee on the bounced check."

Stosh left the bank, failing to notice the man in the green Bermuda shorts and oversized sun hat he'd held the door for, and sat in his car for a while. His cheeks were flushed, his eyes felt like they were vibrating as he swallowed the sea urchin in his throat. He fanned himself and blasted the A/C. The feeling was the same he'd had when Major was arrested and innumerable times after Bambi left. He couldn't wrangle the racing thoughts, each one manifesting as a bead of sweat on his forehead. Could the police, or FBI, or whoever had jurisdiction over condo crime hold him accountable? Could the unit owners sue him for his incompetence and neglect? Jesus, could he be sharing a bunk with his father?

Stosh thought about calling Major for advice, but he wasn't exactly an ace at evading the authorities. The only person he had left to confer with was his only true confidant, his caddy, Al "Little Bert" Bertolucci.

AFTER EXPLAINING the situation over a joint on their couch, Stosh and Al agreed the only appropriate thing to do was to get piss drunk.

Al rolled another joint, and Stosh went to get a fresh bottle of vodka. Gator was waiting outside his condo when he got back home. Stosh knelt and scratched him behind the ears.

"Is that your emotional support pig?" someone asked from behind him.

Stosh couldn't place the woman, but she seemed familiar, even in the way she spoke.

"No," Stosh said, like a jerk.

"I was told we were only allowed therapy pets," the woman said.

"Oh, yeah," Stosh said. "Are you new here?"

"Just moved in a few weeks ago."

Stosh introduced himself as Vice President of the board, figuring that if the title didn't get him a better job, maybe it could get him a date. The woman said her name was Zyvalia, and she didn't seem impressed.

"I have a feeling there are going to be some changes around here," Stosh said with his chest, "and not just about the pets."

"Looking forward to it." She popped her earbud back in and continued walking up the street.

Zyvalia. Her name vibrated off his lips, felt like caramel on his tongue, especially compared to his own, but it wasn't worth thinking too much about. He had business to attend to.

Al took the bottle from Stosh when he got inside. They each took two shots in a row and smoked a cigarette in the kitchen. Stosh didn't usually allow smoking inside, but that day was a day of firsts, and he remembered Major often sitting at the kitchen table, smoking with his associates. He only smoked occasionally, but if he was celebrating a new deal or a good round, he'd sit at the table with one of his partners or whatever rando he'd been paired with at the club, smoking and sharing war stories.

It hit Stosh. "The influencer."

"What?" Al said.

"I just met the influencer."
"Is she single?"

CHAPTER FOUR

STOSH SPENT several days that week setting up the course for the Squib and Schuster Capital Fund Open at the Ridge. It was a three-day tournament in the middle part of the Old Dixie semi-pro tour season.

Stosh had spent two years on that circuit, but never even came close to winning. He always found new and creative ways to lose. By the end of his second year, it was clear that he'd lose his tour membership, so he officially retired in mid-July, with a large chunk of the season still ahead.

He had lost before, both as a student-athlete and as an amateur, but he'd never quit. After his last tournament, an invitational in Texas, he returned to North Carolina, where Bambi was still in school, working on her master's. She had excelled in her program and continued her education after earning her bachelor's degree. She was going to be a teacher, and Stosh was planning to do the same, but when he got back to her, things had changed. He'd spent nearly two years on the road, living out of his Camry, eating fast food, getting fat without her, and losing all the time. All the while, as he fumbled his career, she was busy building her own.

Because he wasn't winning, he didn't earn much, and what money he did make usually went back into his game, whether it was to pay for a local caddy or upgrade his clubs. He had one sponsor on tour, a tech startup that Major, acting as his agent, had found for him. The company was called Ascension, and they made HCM software.

"What does HCM mean?" Stosh had asked Major when he presented him with a polo and hat embossed with the company's logo.

"Human capital management," Major replied, sporting his own swag.

"Human capital?" Stosh asked.

"Human resource stuff," Major said. "Hiring and firing, that kind of thing. We didn't have this stuff in my day. We didn't need any wonks in human resources or an app to find employees. Hell, we used to pick up spicks right outside the hardware store."

"Jesus, Dad."

"You know how Workday sponsors Mickelson?"

Stosh nodded.

"Same kind of company," Major said giddily.

The shirt was itchy, and the hat didn't fit right, but by the time Major secured the sponsorship, Stosh had all but made up his mind that his career would be over shortly.

Stosh took some time off when he returned to Bambi, but then one month turned into two, and two months turned into six. He wasn't working. He wasn't golfing. He was just hanging around —a real NEET.

The whole time, he felt Bambi pulling away toward her career and a life without him. They'd only had sex once since returned, and it ended with her crying in the bathroom while he signed up for a free trial of HIMS. His days often had several false starts, waking up with Bambi only to return to bed, where he spent the morning scrolling through montages of Tiger Woods' historic 2000 run or videos about alternate histories, secret societies, and even some about conspiracy theories. He found comfort in their wild stories. They helped him associate himself with the world in a way he otherwise couldn't. They made him feel in on the take, like he was slowly solving a mystery with each video he watched. But the one that really freaked him out was the Mayan calendar apocalypse theory. The supposed date had come and gone, and the world was still standing, but the date had coincided with the end of his golf career, or at least kind of coincided. Close enough. He'd never thought about the end of the world before. He'd thought about death—as a Catholic, the theme was never far away. To the Church, the end of the world and the return of Jesus were something to celebrate. Through Catholic alchemy, death became life, but he'd been lapsed for long enough that the thought of a secular apocalypse left him feeling hopeless and scared. There was a time he believed that his long list of golf accomplishments would survive after he died, that his trophies would remain as relics of his works, but with his golf career snuffed out, and his marriage swirling ever faster down the drain, he was as lonely as the atheists said.

He groped around for meaning, for a system of belief that could comfort this newfound anxiety but could still reconcile the Catholicism baked into his DNA. He turned to the Apeus Dei YouTube channel and *Ancient Aliens*. Lucky for him, the latter seemed to play on an endless loop, beamed in from the great pyramids of *Amazon Prime* 24 hours a day. The theories were no more contradictory than those in the Bible, and he could watch them in 4 K! In the off chance the show wasn't on, he could always watch reruns of *John D. Wolf: Bounty Hunter* and get his fill of aliens online.

But Bambi's patience was running out. They occupied two different worlds, with Stosh's head firmly up an Anunnaki's ass, and Bambi's buried in her books, there was little tethering them together. He knew it was coming, but that didn't make it any easier when it came.

Divorce.

He tried to find the words to rebut her, to convince her that they were just going through a phase, a normal part of any relationship, especially one as long as theirs, but he didn't have the language. She was right, he was just meandering through life at a time when most people are finally figuring it out, the way she was.

When his logic failed, he turned to guilt-trips.

"After everything I've done for you, everything Major's done for you, you're gonna call it quits?" he said during one of their many skirmishes after the first big fight.

"You and Major both; you really think you can buy love. What has Major ever really done for you? Seriously, think about it. He made you get that ridiculous tattoo that everyone makes fun of," she said, pointing to the Polish eagle on Stosh's bicep.

"Who makes fun of it?"

"Come on, Stosh, it looks like a fucking chicken."

"So, I wanted to get it," he said, looking at the thing, knowing full well that it looked far more like a domesticated chicken than it did any bird of prey, but he was willing to die on that hill if only to spite her.

They agreed to live together long enough for Bambi to finish school, but the fights went on for some time. They teetered between amicability and anger. They picked at each other's insecurities and failures. She attacked his libido; he attacked her promiscuity. She said he lost his passion; he said she never had any. She called him childish; he called her boring. And in between insults, he apologized for everything. He wasn't sure if he meant any of it, or if he was just inviting her to apologize for her own transgressions, whatever she thought they were, but she just told him it was over, over and over again.

Her life had become what so many of us dream about. We hope, even pray for the moment when we turn the corner and crash into the rest of our lives, meet the people who will finally matter, who are worth all the time and heartache and loss that form naturally in the world and for which there is no escaping but can only be dulled by love and passion and the camaraderie of a tribe. That's exactly what happened to her, and in real life, for that matter. She turned the corner, met her partner, had a baby, made new friends whose weddings she would attend, whose kids would grow up with her own, whose birthdays and retirements and anniversaries she would celebrate, and whose funerals she'd mourn at.

Stosh had taken to the dating apps after their breakup but found only confusion. His love had always been analog. His relationship with Bambi the product of proximity, of growing up in a small town with the same group of friends, learning to love her through a series of adolescence hijinks and experimentation. He wondered if he could ever replicate that online, but his apathy was so great that even swiping right seemed to be too much work.

Bambi's luck was rare, and when Stosh thought about it, a voice in his head reminded him that if there were winners in these matters, then there were losers, too, and he was beginning to think he was one of the latter.

It pained him to admit she was right, and so he didn't. He refused to sign the divorce papers, even when Bambi became pregnant with her daughter. It was the only petty act of hope he had left to play.

And of course, she was right that he'd lost his passion (and that the Polish eagle looked a hell of a lot more like a rooster than an eagle). You'd hear tragic stories about athletes whose careers were ruined by injury or personal tragedy, but rarely did you hear about guys like Stosh, the quitters. Their names may have appeared on the scoreboards of obscure golf tournaments rebroadcast on the Golf Channel in the middle of the night, but they never stayed there. They disappeared, without a trace, as if the minutes, hours, days, weeks, and years they poured into the craft were for nothing but a hobby, a cruel pastime; as if all the grit, optimism, hope, and fear they had to muster or bury or conquer or swallow to compete meant nothing. Some blamed it on circumstances or a lack of opportunity. Some blamed it on family obligations, the chasing of other, more domestic dreams or loves—but some, like Stosh, had nothing, no one to blame: those who were no longer able to stand the constant loss and persistent failures of the sport; those who lost all hope of future victories and quit. Those were his people.

He moved back home shortly after Bambi left, and the conspiracy theories and alien fantasies became less useful. There was no story he could spin to account for what were solely his problems.

Major was little help when it came to heartbreak. For someone whose wife left without a trace, he still had an abundance of hope in the sanctity of marriage.

"She'll come around. After all we've done for her, she'd be a real bitch not to," he said to Stosh one night over a few beers in the kitchen.

"Jesus, can we please talk about something else?"

"I talked to Billy, over at Stoney Hill, said he'd let you do some per diem teaching, and might even have a groundskeeper position opening up soon."

"I really don't want to go back there, and who'd want a golf lesson from a quitter?"

"You didn't quit. You're just taking a break. I didn't raise a quitter."

"I just need a break," Stosh repeated as if it were a mantra.

"I didn't raise no commie, either, so take Billy's offer, or help me drywall the houses in phase two."

"I'm supposed to meet up with a friend from high school, says he has a job for me. Sales."

"Selling what?"

"Mattresses."

"Oh, come on. I don't know what your opposition is to hard work. I have plenty of jobs for you."

There was no winning with Major, but Stosh was just as stubborn. He wanted to build something on his own, even if it meant selling mattresses for Dreamy's.

Greg had messaged Stosh on Facebook, saying he was just trying to catch up, but there was something obviously suspicious about high school friends who used Facebook Messenger to reconnect with people with whom they had not had a strong relationship to begin with. It only took a few back-and-forths before he pitched Stosh the Dreamy's job. He assumed Greg got a small commission for recruiting new employees, though he had absolutely no sales experience and had never really worked a real job besides helping Major and the library gig in college. Stosh figured it was a racket, but with his resume, he didn't have much of a choice. Stosh agreed to meet Greg at the Dugout to discuss it further.

Stosh met him there after happy hour. The bar was populated by the ghostly faces of those Stosh had sat next to in Spanish class, in Western Civ, and Algebra.

"Holy shit. Stosh!" one of them said to him in that Marlboro tone known only to townie bars.

Stosh didn't have enough hat to pull over his face.

"It's a shame, man. I know a lot of people were rooting for you," Greg said after the fanfare subsided. He was wearing a cheap suit that swooshed and crinkled every time he squirmed in his chair. "They put up a kind of shrine of you in the high school, like all your trophies and stuff."

"They set the bar pretty low, huh?"

"I wouldn't say that, man. You were good."

Stosh shrugged as Greg filled him in on the past decade of his life. It was the usual trip, all the major talking points one posts on social media. Had a kid, shares custody, bought a car, got a DUI, rents the top apartment of a three-family.

"So, what's this job all about?" Stosh asked the first chance he got.

"We can get to that," Greg said. "Not sure if you've seen, but I started a podcast."

"Sounds fun," Stosh said, like most of us, bored at the thought of another white guy shooting the shit with his friends on the internet.

"You want to be a guest on it?"

Stosh grimaced.

"I mean, no pressure," Greg said, "but I figured it could be good for you and your story, you know, your brand."

"Sorry," Stosh said, "but I don't think my story is all that interesting."

"Compared to most around here?" Greg said. "Trust me, it is."

"What do you want to know?"

"We can talk about it on the podcast."

"Yeah, I guess that'd be cool," Stosh said.

"Sweet, man. I have a makeshift studio in my mom's basement."

"Cool," Stosh said, trying to keep his eyes from rolling out of their sockets.

Greg went on to explain the job. It was a draw versus commission, with PTO, and Greg even said the company would send him to headquarters to train, but Stosh reminded him that he'd never sold a thing in his life. Stosh looked around at the townies at the bar as Greg bragged about his commissions. *Never thought this is where it'd end. All that work on the course for a one percent match on a 401k and maybe a week vacation at Hampton Beach.* He looked around and noticed a small plaque on the bar in front of an empty seat in the corner. "In loving memory of Lucky. The only dog allowed." Maybe if he tipped well enough, he'd get a plaque in the bar too.

Stosh sat for three hours with Greg and his stoned friend that Saturday afternoon. He hated to admit that he enjoyed telling the war stories he had from life on the minitours.

The following Monday, he drove out to Framingham, where Dreamy's northeast headquarters were. They put him and the other recruits up in a Holiday Inn Express and gave them meal coupons for the hotel bar. They attended eight hours of class every day. Learned all about mattresses—the history of them, what they're made of, etc. Stosh took notes, passed all the tests, and got fall-down drunk at the hotel bar every night. It was kind of like a vacation.

After training, they assigned Stosh to a store out in Ware, Massachusetts, a little meth and Oxy town that was always the butt of regional jokes. The town's Mecca was a Walmart and the monolithic parking lot that buttressed it, and across that great sea of pavement was Dreamy's.

Stosh was a horrible salesman, not just because he didn't care, but because he didn't believe in the product. He thought the prices were too high and the quality too low. And Greg didn't quite explain how the pay worked—draw versus commission meant that, yes, Stosh got paid an hourly rate, but if he didn't meet or exceed his daily salary of one hundred and twenty-five dollars in commission, then he'd go negative into draw, which meant he'd need to sell double to make any real money. It reeked of scam, a real multi-level scheme the likes of which Major would have actually appreciated, but Stosh figured it was only a matter of time before they canned him. His District Manager, a swollen zit of a man, told him he had the lowest numbers in the district—a pillow to mattress ratio in the gutter—but that they needed warm bodies, so his job was safe for the time. It wasn't all bad. There was only one person per showroom, so he was left alone. There was little to do in the absence of customers, so he spent most of his days reading and playing games on his phone. It was the kind of mind-numbing job he needed at the time. But it was a torturous schedule—four days a week, eleven hours a day. He was losing touch with reality: working when he would have been playing golf, drinking when he should've been sleeping, and sleeping when he should have been living.

There were some days he didn't see any customers, and the radio cycled endlessly through a mix of early millennium pop songs and one-hit wonders. The radio was controlled by corporate, set on a timer to play the entire business day with only Dreamy's commercials to break up the music. At the end of each ad, Casper Sugarheard, the company's owner would say, "Thank you for shopping at Dreamy's. And remember, here at Dreamy's, your dreams are safe with us."

In addition to the mattress propaganda and the corporate-controlled radio from which it spewed, the company tracked how many times the door was opened to count "ups," or the number of customers and potential sales each store had daily. Stosh's "ups" were a point of contention for his manager.

"You've had ten door pulls and only one pillow sale," he'd say. "That's unacceptable, not in my district. I want you to close every up."

But what his manager and the company failed to understand was that data without context was useless. Those numbers didn't reflect who was coming into the store, like the local kids who liked to bum rush it and jump on the beds, or the homeless guy Stosh let use the bathroom whenever he needed it, or the solicitors and Jehovah's Witnesses who frequented the store and Stosh welcomed and entertained if only to stave off the boredom. But it was the surveillance state, and his life had been reduced to data points, numbers, and patterns trapped in the matrix of a digital shopping cart.

It was a special kind of torture. After all, they played Nancy Sinatra's *These Boots Are Made for Walking* on repeat outside the Branch Davidians' compound in Waco, and the army played Metallica and Van Halen outside of Manuel Noriega's room in Panama before they overthrew him. Perhaps, Stosh began to think, Dreamy's was a front for a secret CIA experiment, a psyop. He'd heard of such things, descendants of MK Ultra and the like, but in reality, it was just a shitty place to work.

The worst yet were the quarterly meetings, when the sales force was addressed by the Sultan of Sleep himself, Casper Sugarheard. Only then were they allowed to lock the store. They'd have to sit in front of their computers and watch the Sultan go on about the economy, about how the government was the enemy, taxation was theft, and that they were only one vote away from communism.

Stosh would've lost his mind if he hadn't misplaced it the year before.

Then Major was arrested and Stosh stopped showing up to work. Greg was a little pissed, sending him a series of slightly irritated messages about how, because he left before his one-year anniversary, he had to pay back his recruitment commission.

Stosh testified as a character witness on Major's behalf, but everything he said, though perhaps not a lie, was unnatural and something less than the truth. Testimonials, he'd heard many say in passing, were supposed to be powerful. To tell one's story and speak one's truth was supposed to bandage those wounds which cannot be seen but are worn internally, but Stosh's heart remained curdled, his soul in atrophy even after he testified. He was too loyal to his father to speak the truth and too ashamed to admit he should've known the folly of it all along. And for his sins, he sat in the courthouse every day of the trial and watched the prosecution peel back the particle-board veneer that was Major's kingdom. For all the preaching about faith, God, and hard work, Stosh learned Major had been nothing but a grifter.

Stosh had nothing. Everything Major had owned was repossessed to pay back the money he'd tricked out of his victims. The only person Stosh had left was Tara-Lynn, who, after some negotiation, offered to help him move down to the association, into one of the units she owned. Al was still floating around, working at

Stoney Hill as a groundskeeper. Stosh felt a little embarrassed asking his friend to move with him, but his father had just died, and he didn't have anyone either, so there they were, embattled again. A golfer and his caddy. A knight and his squire. Brothers-in-irons.

CHAPTER FIVE

STOSH HAD BEEN TOO busy at work to spend much time preparing for the annual meeting, but he asked a generative AI app to write an apology worthy of his neighbor's sympathy. The only good line it came up with was something about everyone being part of an "economic diaspora", though Stosh thought that might be a bit much for the residents of the association.

"You want me to come with you?" Al asked as Stosh got dressed for the meeting.

"No, but I might need bail money."

"Glad to see you haven't lost your sense of humor."

"We still have some of that Tito's?"

Al poured them each a shot, and Stosh followed with a second. He hadn't eaten much all day, and the vodka sat hollowly in his stomach like hot guilt.

The rest of the board members were gathered in the office when he arrived. All but Birdie resigned on the spot when they learned of Tara-Lynn's crimes, and Stosh didn't blame them. They did, however, agree to at least sit for the meeting as he gave everyone the bad news, then he'd pardon them.

They held the meeting in the abandoned church at the end of

the street. The place was eerie, with its clapboard walls and down-home horror vibe. It wasn't like the Catholic churches Stosh had grown up in. Those were impenetrable. This place felt like it'd blow away if they were a little closer to the coast. The building was still maintained and used by various AA groups who, despite having access to the entire building, continued to hold their meetings in the basement.

Not everyone went to the annual meeting. Most people at the association only cared about condo policies when they were personally affected by them, but the individuals who did attend were the most vocal in the community. Fred would surely be there, and Cletus Wriggle, too, who Stosh learned had been suspended from the sherif's department after his affiliation with the far-right Big Boys of the Bygone Day was made public in the wake of the police killing of J'Davious Wallace. With those two characters in the crowd, Stosh feared they might take physical action.

About forty owners were seated in the pews when the board arrived. Stosh, with his cabinet in tow, walked to the front of the church and took their seats in the aluminum chairs in front of the altar, just beneath the full-scale statue of the crucifix that hung from the ceiling. Stosh reviewed the notes from his AI-generated speech, but he didn't think there was anything he could say that would make the situation better.

After a few minutes, the congregation settled and went silent. Stosh could see Fred had come in and was standing at the back of the church, already shaking his head as if reciting his grievances.

Stosh stood up and walked to the pulpit.

The people were confused by his presence and the absence of their leader, and before he could say anything, someone hollered, "Where's Tara-Lynn?"

Someone else said, "I heard she left."

People started to mumble and look around the church in

hopes that Tara-Lynn would appear, the great Wizard of their own strange Oz.

"Please, folks," Stosh said. "I'll get to that in just a minute."

Everyone settled again, and Stosh began his ill-hearted attempt to tell the good people of the association that they were doomed.

"I was informed a few days ago that we bounced a check that was issued to pay our gas bill," he said, "and after going to the bank, it appears Tara-Lynn may have misappropriated some funds."

Gasps, mumbled curses, and a few pearl-clutches rolled across the audience.

"So, she finally did it," Fred said, walking up the aisle with the help of his mangled cane.

"I know many of you had issues with Tara-Lynn," Stosh said.

"We warned you," Fred said. "We told you she was up to no good, and what did any of you do to stop it? You fined *us*, but now the truth comes out."

"I can assure you that no one other than Tara-Lynn was aware of what she was doing," Stosh said.

"How was she able to take the money?" someone asked.

"She had set up the account so that only she could transfer or withdrawal funds," Stosh said, hoping the liquor's permanent hue on his cheeks hid his guilt as another round of gasps echoed forth from the crowd.

"Someone other than Tara-Lynn must have authorized that," Mrs. Bronski said. "We always had dual control measures in place to keep something like this from happening."

Stosh swallowed the rock in his throat and said, "You know how Tara-Lynn was, but I changed that, so now it requires two board members and a member of the community to transfer or withdrawal even one dollar from our reserve account."

"How much did the bitch get?" Fred asked.

"We only have about six thousand dollars left in total."

"How much did she get?" Fred asked again.

"Around one hundred and fifty thousand."

"Jesus Christ," Fred said.

"Watch your mouth. You're still in a house of God," Mariam Bronski said.

But Fred pointed his crooked finger at the board and started in with great fury—Cunts, bastards, liars, cheaters, monsters, devils, cowards, thieves. And all the board could do was sit there and take it.

Mariam Bronski clutched her chest, seemingly more disgusted by Fred's language than Tara-Lynn's crimes.

Stosh was ready to self-immolate. The heat rose up from his belly and rolled into his throat. He swallowed the vodka back down and wiped the sweat from beneath his eyes. His breath hitched. That's it, he couldn't do it. He knew well enough to quit, but then a young man in army fatigues stood up and whistled the meeting to a halt.

"Folks," he said, disarming the whole crowd with his down-home smile, "I'm new to the community. My name is David Anders. My wife and I just bought a place here. I only met Tara-Lynn once, at our orientation, so I don't have much of an opinion, but I was assigned to Jackson Air Force Base, and we've lived all over the states in places just like this. Democracy is hard, but I think we have to trust that we can come together in these times to fix whatever problems we have. All I care about is what's to come. Not what's happened."

Despite David's best efforts, there wasn't one un-furrowed brow still staring at Stosh. He wanted to run out of there, but he had nowhere to go. His face was warm from more than just the liquor—the shame, regret, and disappointment of the past several years converging on his chest, his breath a heaving column of stale, hundred-proof air.

"Fred's right. There was never really a 'we,'" he said. "There was Tara-Lynn and then there was the rest of us. Like everyone else on this board, I was played. She kept us in the dark, packed the board with people who didn't understand or, in my case, didn't care about what was going on. I have no idea what's going to happen to us, but I know that if you're like me, you have no place else to go. This place was my backup plan. It was actually the backup to my backup plan. I'm only here because I had no place else to go; had no one else to turn to," he said, now pulling out his AI-generated apology. "If you're like me, you washed up on this shore not by your own accord, but because you'd been ship-wrecked, and the tide happened to push you here, and it became home. Some of us lost love, others our jobs. How many of you lost houses during the recession?" Stosh asked and watched as the hands rose. "How many of you are here because your wife or husband took the house in the divorce?" Another wave of hands shot up from the crowd as he stole a glance at his notes. "I've seen the tow trucks, the repossession notices taped to your doors. We're all refugees of an economic diaspora. I lost everything before I moved in here, and I really don't have anywhere else to go, but I still care about this place, and I want to invite every one of you to become more active members of this, our community. We all have our plotki, as my father used to say, but we have an opportunity to make something better, something that serves us all and not just a few. I'm out of my element, and I know you don't trust me. I have no experience, but neither does the new guy in Washington, and so, I guess I'm a bit like him, or not like him at all, but I'm an outsider, and I know I need your help. So, you can either tell me to get lost or you can help me, because I'm gonna need it."

Stosh had moved himself to near tears. He could taste the vodka rising up his throat again, sitting like a bubble of syrup at the back of his tongue. He wasn't sure he meant what he was saying, but he didn't move from that pulpit. He didn't budge. He stared back at every angry eye in the crowd, and if they wanted his scalp, they could have it, but he saw their faces loosen, their brows soften. They knew they didn't have a choice. He was the answer to their decrepit prayers, and even Fred went silent, whether it was from the joint he'd lit in the back of the church or personal resignation, Stosh wasn't sure, but he'd have to take the wins when they came.

David stood up, nodded toward Stosh, and turned to address the crowd. "I think Mister Saint-Jablonski is right. It doesn't seem we have much of a choice, and I believe his intentions are good. I wish I could be here to help, but I won't be moving in until after the summer." He turned to Stosh. "But if there is anything I can do, I'm willing to help."

Mrs. Bronski then stood up and asked for a vote—should he, Stanislaus Lech Saint-Jablonski, be voted in as President, and all but two hands went up. Cletus and Fred abstained, but despite their protests, he was elected the fourth president of the association.

There was something invigorating about that moment, something satisfying that Stosh had only ever felt during a tournament. It was win or lose, and no matter how many caddies, advisors, or board members he had on his side, he had that enormous feeling that the play came down to him.

Ray Limon limped up to him after the meeting.

"I think we have an opportunity here to make something new, something really creative," Ray said with surprising vigor for someone his age. "I taught law for years—mostly labor and constitutional, cut my teeth in the free speech movement, but that was so long ago now," he faded for a moment into nostalgic bliss before returning to his point. "But anyway, I'd love to help out."

"I have a feeling we'll need some counsel."

"Especially with someone like him hanging around," Ray said.

Fred was standing next to Cletus, looking in Stosh's direction.

"And better keep an eye on that Cletus, too," Ray said. "I hear he runs with those Big Boys of the Bygone Day or whatever they're called. The people behind that rally in Carlsville last summer."

Stosh didn't know much about what trouble Cletus had been in, just that it had cost him his job on the force, but regardless, his confidence had swelled to a bulbous growth, so he walked over to Fred and stuck out his hand. "Let's start again," he said.

Fred looked at Stosh, his face all twisted with anger. Stosh kept his hand out for an embarrassingly long time, but he was now a man without shame.

Fred relented, placing a limp collection of brittle fingers in Stosh's hand. He could feel the old man's bones shift like soggy branches beneath his loose skin.

"I don't think we've met before," Cletus said. "Some kind of speech you gave up there."

"I was just speaking my truth," Stosh said.

"So that bitch really stole all the money, huh?" Cletus said.

"That's what it looks like."

"And you had no idea what was going on?" Cletus asked.

"Makes you either stupid or guilty," Fred said.

"Never said I was smart," Stosh said.

Cletus kind of laughed at that and said, "You're gonna have your hands full either way."

"That's why I was hoping you could maybe sit on the board."

"Me?" Cletus asked.

"Why not?"

"I think you and I might have a different idea of how things should be," Cletus said.

"Even better."

Fred scoffed and walked out the door.

"I guess I can help," Cletus said. "I *have* been pretty bored lately."

After everyone was gone, Stosh locked up the church and headed back home, his cheeks still warm with adrenaline. He felt drunk with victory. And to make his night even better, little Gator was snorting around his front door. Stosh knelt and scratched the wiry tuft of hair on his head. He snorted and rubbed his head against Stosh's shin, nearly knocking him over.

"All right, all right," Stosh said, then went inside his condo.

"Shit, you survived?" Al said, his cheeks bloated with weed smoke.

Stosh took the rig from Al and ripped a fat one. His blood was up. He took another shot and paced the room, relaying every detail of the meeting. After another shot, Stosh went out back for a cigarette.

It was another muggy night in central Florida, but it was clear enough to see some stars. For all his alien research, he didn't know Sagittarius from the Big Dipper. He'd been raised to believe a bearded man was sitting on a throne of clouds that would eventually judge him, and he hoped his recent act of faith would count toward his entry fee. He slipped into the thought a bit more: *Why are there clouds in heaven? Why did angels even need wings? One would think they'd just be able to fly, like, do they really need wings?* It was bestial, vulgar, really, but maybe those cute pictures of little cherubs with their cheeks hanging out were just cultural products, created to sell an image —a story in and of itself. Apeus Dei had several videos dedicated to the Nephilim, but those guys believed that they were aliens, not angels.

Stosh stood slack-jawed and stupid, looking at his fate amongst the stars.

"Economic diaspora?" a voice said from behind him.

Stosh braced himself against the sound.

"Didn't mean to scare you," David said.

Stosh exhaled, said, "Appreciate your help. I don't know what would've happened if you didn't say something."

"Sometimes it takes an outsider, like you said."

"The uniform probably helps, you know, in the credibility department."

"That too," David said. He looked up to the sky. "You can see Scorpio."

"I could never connect the dots."

"My wife is into that stuff. Always tells me it takes more than two stars to make a constellation," he said. "Whatever that means."

"I was raised Catholic. Thought all that stuff was witchcraft."

"But we love our witches."

Stosh nodded and tried to keep his mind from wandering back to the angels and their grotesque wings.

"Well, like I said, I'll be gone most of the summer, but here's my number if I can help with anything. I have a feeling that guy is going to be a problem," David said, nodding in the direction of the hedgerow that separated the two parking lots, where Fred was standing in the shadows, the ember from his pipe illuminating his face with each puff.

"So creepy," Stosh said.

David walked away. Stosh looked over to the hedgerow, but Fred was gone, having dissolved back into the darkness from which he had come.

* * *

The First Letter of Saint-Jablonski
to the People of The Association

Dear owners,

I'd like to thank you for your early support in our new administration. I would like to express our gratitude and invite you all to participate in the community, but we feel it necessary to first address the concerns regarding the pool. Unfortunately, we've had to delay its opening as a result of the sludge that has appeared in it.

We've made several attempts to test the unknown substance with what products are available at the local pool supply store but have been unsuccessful. With that said, given the current state of our finances, we're unable to afford the help of more sophisticated tests and will have to delay the pool's opening until further notice.

Luckily, this substance does not appear to be leaking from any of our systems and/or land but seems to be somewhat of a phenomenon.

Again, we apologize for the inconvenience; until we can determine what this substance is and its source, we must prioritize safety and keep the pool closed until further notice.

We thank you for your cooperation,
Stanislaus (Stosh) Saint-Jablonski, President

CHAPTER SIX

THAT SATURDAY WAS the second day of the Squib and Schuster tournament, and the residents of the Ridge were out in force. They moseyed around the grounds, roaming from one hole to another, drinking fruity drinks with little umbrellas in them. The kids ran around, being constantly stopped and hushed by the Oompa Loompas responsible for what the Ridge called "crowd cooperation." They'd pop out from behind trash cans and bushes with paddles that read "Quiet Please,", slapping the wood planks into their palms as a reminder that the instruments could also be used to beat those who failed to "cooperate" into compliance.

Stosh spent most of his day avoiding people, the young ones especially, staying in the clubhouse and helping Cara out at the bar, restocking the fridges and humping buckets of ice up from the freezer.

"Come here," she said after he brought her a case of beer.

He followed her into the kitchen, where there were no cameras. She poured them each a shot. They clanked their plastic cups then disposed of the evidence.

"You working tomorrow?" Stosh asked her.

"Only the morning shift. Ketch has his girl starting in the afternoon," Cara said.

"Amy?" Stosh asked.

"You know her?"

"She lives at the condos, across the street from me. She's an artist or something." Stosh said.

"What does that mean?" Cara asked.

"Someone told me she's a graphic designer. I don't know," Stosh said.

"But she needs to bartend?"

"I didn't run a background check," Stosh said.

"I'll look her up on Instagram," Cara said.

Stosh took another shot and went back outside, leaving Cara to do her sleuthing. He drove around in his golf cart, stopping at each hole to empty the overflowing trash and recycling cans, neither of which were segregated from the other's content. He emptied all the trash bags into the dumpster and went into the pro shop.

Dana was standing there with new grips for her clubs.

"Can't go wrong with Golf Pride," he said, noticing her selection.

"Ketch said the same thing," she said. "I'm just going to have him do it here. I don't want to bother you."

"I totally forgot," Stosh said. "I can do them. It's really no problem."

"You're busy with the tournament and all. I don't mind paying the extra money."

"It's the principle," Stosh said. "This place doesn't need any more of your money."

"I'm supposed to be playing tomorrow morning, and the ones I have on now are falling apart."

"I'm off in a little bit," Stosh said. "I can swing by your place and get them done in no time."

Stosh finished his work and took a shower in the locker room.

The only other shirt in his locker was an Ascension polo from his amateur days. He put it on and scrubbed the grass stains from his khaki shorts. He found an old bottle of Axe Body spray and doused himself in a fog, leaving his eyes burning and a regretful smell lingering above him like a pubescent aura.

Stosh took the short drive from the employee lot and pulled up to the gatehouse that separated the course from the neighborhood.

"Looking sharp," Henry, the security guard, said. "Where you off to?"

"Dana Van Ronk's place. Told her I'd replace her grips."

"Is that what you white boys call it?" he laughed.

Stosh blushed.

"All right, all right."

Henry checked Dana's list. There were no surprises at Palm Ridge. To get into the neighborhood, you had to be on a resident's list, or else Henry had to call the owner and get permission on the spot.

"And there you are. One Stosh Saint-Jablonski," he laughed. "What kind of name is that, by the way?"

"Polish, but my grandpa tacked the 'Saint' on so people thought we were French."

Henry gave him the same look Stosh always got when he explained his name. The truth was that his Jaju had first changed the family name from the Russian spelling of Jablonsky to the Polish, Jablonski, during a mini-Red Scare in their hometown of Cold Springs in the 1950s. But when that wasn't enough to evade his neighbors' suspicions, Jaju took it a step further and added the 'Saint' to the last name in a poorly researched attempt at assimilation.

"Whatever you say," Henry said and lifted the gate.

Stosh drove up the main road slowly, trying not to draw any additional attention to his decrepit *Ranger*, but every head turned as he approached Dana's place. He knew most of the residents who played golf, and he was friendly with them, but it was obvious that their cordiality began on the first tee and ended on the eighteenth. This was GOOP (Glory of our Past) country, and the signs still stood in the emerald lawns despite the election having long been over. But then again, they weren't there for political reasons. They were warning signs. A variation on "Beware of Dog," "No Loitering," and "Private Property." He was the help, always would be, but he knew he had it better than Henry, who, if he'd left that gatehouse and wandered up to the resort might be arrested or possibly killed by some vigilante who could always claim he was simply standing his ground.

Driving up the road, Stosh once again thought about Dana's husband and waffled for a moment. He thought about his own marriage and Major's many women, most of whom didn't hang around long enough for Stosh to remember their names. He hadn't been with anyone since Bambi, or before her, for that matter. He'd gotten a few matches on the dating apps, but nothing ever stuck. He found himself navigating a completely new world of sexuality he was not at all prepared for as a straight, white, Catholic guy.

Dana was sitting on her front porch when he pulled into her driveway. The evening sun draped her in blades of light. She looked beautiful, sitting there in her sundress, reading a book, with a pitcher of something refreshing on the table beside her.

"That was fast," she said as Stosh got out of his truck.

"Don't let me intrude."

"It's just trashy romance stuff."

"I don't find enough time to read these days."

"Want some tea?" she asked, looking up at him.

"Sure."

She froze, nearly dropped the glass of tea and asked, "Is that an Ascension shirt?"

"Oh, yeah, they sponsored me when I was trying to play professionally."

Dana trembled, her mouth agape. "That was my husband's company," she said.

"Really?" Stosh said, happily surprised at the coincidence, but then, putting everything together, said, "Oh, shit."

"I've never seen anyone but him and his partner wear those shirts," she said with a hint of paranoia in her voice, her eyes a pair of dull marbles.

"I'm sorry," Stosh stammered. "It was the only clean shirt I had."

Stosh kicked at some loose stones in the landscaping, a bubble of regret gurgling in his belly as he chased away his own paranoia. *What are the chances?* Would he ever be relieved of his father's shady business deals? He seriously considered turning heel and leaving, sparing himself further embarrassment and Dana any unnecessary heartache, but Dana composed herself, wiped what could have been either tears or sweat from beneath her eyes, and invited him to sit down.

"My husband's business partner thought they'd finally made the big time when he saw someone wearing one of those shirts on the Golf Channel," she said, shaking the memory away. "So, you like to read?" she asked, clearing her throat.

"I studied literature in college," Stosh said, happy to get back to humdrum conversation.

"Really?" she said, crossing her legs, the sunlight winking off their shiny skin. "I got my degree in marketing," she laughed.

"Smart move."

"That's what my parents thought, but my husband says artificial intelligence can write marketing copy as well as any college grad."

Stosh went silent.

"I mean, that's what my husband *used* to say," Dana said.

Stosh rubbed at the condensation on his glass.

"I thought about calling him my ex for a time, but that doesn't seem right either," she said.

"I'm sorry."

"No, please," she said. "My therapist says I do this. You know, blather."

"It's not blathering," Stosh said.

"It's not quite small talk," Dana said.

"Does this have vodka in it?" Stosh asked as he sipped from his glass.

"I call it Super Tea. Vodka and *Twisted Tea*. I'm no puritan, like some of these people," she said, nodding to the woman across the street with a planter's hat on. "I mean, they don't even try to be discreet."

Stosh chuckled and waved to the woman, who quickly turned and walked away.

"Want me to tell her I'm just here to change your grips?" Stosh asked.

Dana smiled and led him to the garage, where he went to work. He had the clubs stripped and regripped in under a half hour.

"Are you sure I can't repay you?" Dana asked.

"It's no worry."

"Are you hungry?"

Stosh felt the emptiness in his belly and said, "I could eat."

"I'll buy if you fly," she said.

Stosh waited for Dana outside as she went and gathered her things. He did his best to clean the ash off the passenger seat. He sprayed a little Febreze and wafted it around the cab.

"Just roll down your window, I don't have A/C," Stosh said as she got in the truck.

She pulled her hair back into a ponytail, and they drove down through the neighborhood, waving to Henry as they went through the gate.

"I could go for a burger," she said. "You ever been to Jocko's?"

"I'm a stoner," he said, "of course I have."

"You smoke?"

"I figured you knew."

"You fooled me," she said. "I haven't smoked since I was in college."

"It'll be legalized here soon."

"Do you have any on you?" she asked.

"No, but we can swing by my place."

"I mean, it'd be fun, right?"

Stosh didn't know why he smoked so much weed. He was only a casual user until he gave up his golf career. He told himself that it was about the ritual. It was something he did to end the day. To put a hard stop to it. He enjoyed breaking the buds, preparing the rig, and sharing in the tradition with Al. They weren't on their phones, and they rarely spoke, their reverence manifesting as dank folds of blue smoke above their heads like empty thought bubbles. But then he found himself smoking before work and on his breaks and whenever he had enough time to roll a joint or pack a bowl. He was regressing, living out an adolescence he never had. Sometimes when he smoked, he imagined he was a salamander, slowly wiggling back to the primordial ooze.

He headed toward the association, but as he did, he became nervous. The association didn't hold a flame to Palm Ridge. He was embarrassed, and as he thought about it, he felt that maybe Dana was just looking to go slumming for the night. He tried not to get sour, figured he could still have fun either way, but he had a hard time trusting anyone, considering how things ended with Bambi, Major, and now Tara-Lynn. Other than Al, he didn't trust hardly anyone, but he kept driving.

They pulled into the association and drove slowly through the neighborhood. Stosh eyed the grounds differently now that he was president—he noticed the blistered paint and mossy rooftops; the broken shutters and warped siding, but it wasn't all bad. There were children playing on the lawn, and owners sitting on lounge chairs watching them. Some boys played catch. Some girls etched hopscotch lines on the pavement. This didn't happen under Tara-Lynn's administration. People feared being fined. She had the ever-watchful eye of the Stasi—she breathed suspicion on every citizen, condemned otherwise law-abiding folks to lives of paranoid doubt. If she could've, she would've fined the birds for chirping too early. Owners stayed inside their units, doors locked, boiling in the heat. But now the locks were undone, the doors splayed open, and the community began to heal itself.

If there was one honest thing about his speech, it was that the association was the only home they had, and it deserved to be saved.

"This place is cute," Dana said.

What the hell does that mean? Cute sounded like just another word for poor.

"You should've seen some of the places I lived in after graduating from college," she said, looking out her window, gawking at the units with broken blinds and cracked shutters.

Stosh cleared his throat.

"That came out bad," she said, cringing.

"It's cool," he said, parking the Ranger. "I'll be right back."

Stosh got out of the truck and went inside. Al was on the couch with Gator at his feet. The pig had already put on weight since they took him in, and Stosh could see two pearly nobs starting to form at his mouth where his husks would soon appear. He greeted Stosh joyfully.

"Got any herb?" Stosh asked.

"I was just about to light up," Al said, pulling a joint from behind his ear.

Then the front door opened, and Dana was in the threshold.

"Sorry," she said, "but this weird old guy started talking to me. Kind of freaked me out."

"Sounds like you met Fred," Stosh said.

Al folded his arms across his chest.

"I'm Dana," she introduced herself.

Al grunted something indiscernible.

"Pardon the man," Stosh said, "but his name is Al, and he speaks something close to English."

"Do you work at the Ridge?" Dana asked.

"Groundskeeper," he burped.

"I thought you looked familiar," she said. "Wow, and what is that?" she said as Gator came back into the living room.

"He's friendly, so far," Stosh said.

"You're taking this Florida Man thing seriously, huh?" she said.

Al laughed at that.

"Do you mind?" Stosh said, reaching for the joint.

"Guess not," Al said.

Stosh and Dana went back out to the truck and headed off to Jocko's.

"He was interesting," Dana said as they passed Fred.

"He doesn't really like me," Stosh said.

"I can't imagine anyone not liking you."

"I'm kind of the president of the board here, and he has a problem with authority."

"A stoner golf pro who moonlights as a condo president. You don't hear that every day," she said.

"I kind of fell into the situation."

"Care to elaborate?"

"How about I spark this?" he said, putting the joint between his lips.

They smoked as they drove. Dana took gentle, hesitant drags and held the smoke in her lungs for only a second. She declined any more puffs after her third. Stosh took a long one and punched the joint out after that, just as they pulled into Jocko's.

"I think I need a minute," she said.

"You OK?"

"It's been a long time," she said. "That was just pot, right?"

"You're cool, but I wouldn't waste my stash of bath salts on you."

She looked at him as if he'd just told her the Malaysian government had found her husband's corpse.

"That was a joke," he said. "Seriously, are you OK?"

Dana shrank and rolled up her window as if that would somehow keep the paranoia at bay, but Stosh knew where she was. He still went there sometimes after smoking the Frankenstein bud that Al brought home—reality is as elusive as the smoke coming out of your mouth. Everything has eyes peering at you with an authoritative, all-knowing glare. Even the milkshakes have ulterior motives. The hamburgers are conspiring; the onion rings' scent, like the sirens' call, is luring you into a trap. He had to shake the same feelings from his gut to keep her grounded.

"Hey," he said, "this is Florida; a couple of thirty-year-olds smoking weed is the least of this place's problems."

She relaxed, and as if on cue, the crazy guy—the analog man from Stosh's last trip to Jocko's with Quentin—appeared, this time holding a sign that read: "Jocko's Burgers is people! Omega sent me!" Not far behind him, the man in the green Bermuda shorts and Mickey Mouse ears, whom Stosh wrote off as a fugitive from one of the many halfway houses in the area, was walking in the opposite direction.

"See," Stosh said, "crazier is never too far away."

Stosh typed her order into his phone, added a chocolate milkshake to it, and went to the window. After placing their order, he walked to the liquor store next door, got a few nips, and ripped one on his way back to pick up the food.

"How are we doing?" Stosh asked as he climbed back into the truck with their order.

Dana forced a smile, her knees tucked close to her body.

The sun had now completely disappeared. Jocko's neon sign buzzed and flickered like a grotesque astrological sign in the shallow sky. Stosh placed his hand on Dana's knee and squeezed it. A warm buzz came up the back of his neck. He hadn't touched anyone for any reason in longer than he could remember. Maybe it was just the pot, but he felt an attraction to Dana he had only previously been suspicious of, now manifest in a pocket of sweat on his lower back.

He felt the muscles in her thigh loosen. He turned over the truck and drove back to the Ridge.

There was another security guard on duty when they got back there. He was a young white kid who, from the way he tucked his pants into his combat boots, aspired to be not only a cop, but perhaps something even more menacing. He might as well have had "Big Boys of the Bygone Day" etched into his buzzcut.

"Never any surprises at Palm Ridge," Stosh said.

"They were never this strict before the break-ins," Dana said.

"I think I read something about that," Stosh said, thinking about Christian.

"It was so weird. They only hit three houses—mine and the ones on either side of me, but they barely took anything. They nearly cleaned out the other houses, but they only took one thing from me."

"Really?"

Stosh suspected Christian was hitting houses before he died but didn't know the extent of the damage.

"My husband's crucifix," she said. "He didn't even wear the stupid thing. It was a gift from his business partner."

"What'd he do for work?" Stosh asked, trying to pivot and hide his guilt.

"He was an engineer by trade but started the business with his college roommate."

"Ascension," Stosh said, "Human Capital Management, right?"

"Very good," she said. "He had just finished a contract with the DOD before the accident."

"What would the defense department want with HR software?" Stosh asked.

"It was some kind of algorithm. Real hush-hush stuff," she said as they pulled into her driveway. "Leave the joint, take the milk-shakes," she said as she got out of the truck.

Stosh smiled but couldn't stop thinking about Christian breaking into her home.

Dana's place was immaculate. Fresh flowers stood at attention in a crystal vase on the dining room table, and the place smelled like a hotel lobby—fresh and invigorating. But what really impressed Stosh was how all the appliances' clocks were perfectly synced. He felt ashamed of his condo, but then he saw what looked like a massage table tucked into the corner of the dining room with a bunch of straps on it. Some kind of sex thing? Na, she didn't seem like the type. Too mousy and proper. Someone with her money could afford a private masseuse, no problem, or better yet, a more clandestine kink.

They cast down their cache of burgers, onion rings, and fries on the marble countertop and got into it as if the other person wasn't there. They made a mess of the whole thing, too—ketchup, mayonnaise, mustard, and Jocko's special sauce speckled the counter like a Jackson Pollock painting by the time they were done.

"Is there anything left of that joint?" she asked as they finished their milkshakes.

"Yeah, but I'm not taking another trip to Jocko's, so take it easy this time."

"You're cute."

Stosh eyed the masseuse table and its straps. A prude at heart, he tried to hide his discomfort with performance.

"Ah shucks," he said.

Dana smiled and walked around the beautiful mess they'd made on her countertop and kissed him. He kissed her back. They pivoted. She moved him to the couch and sat him down before climbing on top of him. Now his body began to fail him—the milkshake's eyes were peering again.

He retreated inward. He began to think, his body denying him the pleasure of holding Dana as she ran her hands through his hair, her tongue doing far more work than his. He tried to think of Bambi, the way she used to touch him, the way she used to come home late, after closing the bar, and climb into bed, waking him up with her lips just inches away from welcoming him into her mouth, but even that failed him. He couldn't locate the file in his brain.

"Did I do something?" she asked.

"No, God no. It's just been a long time," he said.

Dana dismounted him and moved to the other end of the couch. She tugged at the top of her shirt, lifting it up and over her cleavage.

"I haven't done this in a long time," he said.

"Neither have I," she said.

"You're beautiful, and, like, I totally would, you know..."

"I wasn't gonna fuck you if that's what you were thinking," she said.

"I didn't mean it like that," he said, stealing a glance at the table with its black straps.

"I don't know what you meant, but I was just trying to have fun."

"I know, and so was I. My roommate says I'm a prude, and I grew up Catholic," he said, trying to lighten the mood, though she didn't laugh.

He was frozen and feeling stupid. Why was he even there? What the hell did he want? He wasn't some horny kid anymore. He was just fine with his five fingers and a library of tabs on Google, but of course, the porn industry wasn't what it used to be—there were no more hot nurses and well-hung doctors; instead, we get desperate stepsisters being bribed or blackmailed by their faceless stepbrothers.

He stood there boiling in his own guilt and shame until his phone's ringtone liberated him. It was a text from Birdie. A unit owner had a leak in her ceiling. He wasn't sure what the hell he was supposed to do about it, but it gave him a reason to get out of what had become an incredibly disappointing and awkward situation.

Dana had tucked herself into the corner of the couch with a blanket, mindlessly clicking through TV channels.

"There's an issue at the condo," he said. "I should probably check it out."

"No problem," she said, her eyes fixed on the TV, its blue lights blinking back at her with each change of the station.

"Do you want me to help clean up?"

"I'll take care of it."

"I don't mind," he said.

"I don't care," she said.

Stosh knew better than to push the issue. He bowed his head in contrition and showed himself out.

It was always easier to get out of Palm Ridge than it was to get in. He barely had to pump his brakes as he approached the gate. He drove in silence back home, his heart bloated, needing nothing but a fart after its long constipation. No, he was not in love with Dana, but she was as human as he was, if not more, and he hated feeling as though he'd authored any of her pain.

Birdie had texted Stosh the owner's number. The unit was just a few doors down from his. The owner greeted him at her back door.

"How's the pig?" she asked.

Stosh looked at her sideways. She was tall, her brilliant red hair pulled up into a wreath on top of her head, her copper earrings dangling like wind chimes from her dainty earlobes. It took him a second, but then he placed her—the influencer.

"Oh, fine," he said.

"The leak is coming in from the bathroom ceiling," Zyvalia said, leading him inside.

"I'm not sure I can be of much help," he said.

Her place was a replica of his own, except she had hardly unpacked anything, with most of the living room filled with boxes.

She showed him to the bathroom, where a bubble had formed in the ceiling, causing the paint to sag.

"You're in luck," he said, "the same thing happened to me. It's probably your neighbor's dishwasher. I'll go up there and let them know we have to shut the water off."

"See, you're handier than you think," she said.

"Happenstance," he said.

"No such thing," she said with a big smile, which was somewhat grotesque. It stretched, literally, from ear to ear—her eyes just as outsized and magnificent—but it only made her more attractive. It was as if her grace was too big for her features.

They walked back to the kitchen. Stosh eyed the handle of Tito's on the counter.

"You want a drink?" she asked.

"Would love one."

"OK," she said. "Close your eyes."

"I'm sorry," he said.

"Close your eyes and hold out your hand."

He did as he was told, his stupid heart thumping away. After a moment, he felt her presence return. She commanded him to open his eyes. She was standing before him, her arms outstretched, her fists closed.

"Pick a hand," she said.

Stosh couldn't control his smirk. He reached for her left hand but hesitated and tapped her right.

She turned her hand over and presented Stosh with what looked like a small red pill. He wasn't feeling *that* adventurous, but the way the night was going, he wasn't going to start saying *no* now.

"Mike and Ikes," she said with that big, vaudevillian smile. "A chaser."

She poured them each a shot and they chased the harsh bite of vodka with the childhood giddiness of his favorite Halloween candy.

CHAPTER SEVEN

STOSH SPENT most of that Monday helping Al pick up after the tournament. Al hated the tournaments. All the equipment and people trampling around really did a number on the grass, especially on the first cut.

A local guy by the name of Steve Volpe won the tournament by two strokes. He'd earned a few grand—most of which would have likely already been spent on lodging and a local caddy—and a spot in the Ridge's Club Championship at the end of the summer.

Birdie called Stosh at lunch. Assuming it would be more bad news, Stosh was pleasantly surprised to learn that almost everyone had paid their dues. He was proud of himself and the community for pulling together. That bulbous growth of confidence throbbed as he stood up a little straighter and lifted his chin a bit higher.

"But," Birdie said, "Fred's refusing to pay."

"What can we do?"

"Tara-Lynn used to fine anyone who was late twenty dollars a day until it was paid."

"Did she really?"

"Depended on the person, but with Fred, yes."

"Jesus."

"Want me to send him the fine?"

"Let's hold off. I'm hoping I can get through to him."

The course was pretty empty, with most of the residents being hungover from the tournament, so after restocking the beer and merch in the pro shop, Stosh spent the afternoon on the range, trying trick shots and recording them to post on Instagram while he waited for his usual session with Dana.

Years before, when Stosh was still in high school and YouTube itself an infant, Major started his own channel to showcase Stosh's prowess, but the most viewed video on the account was one in which Stosh hit a ball that ricocheted off a tree and hit Major square in the head. Major abandoned the channel after reading the comments section, which included such poetry as, "This guy should kill himself," written by someone with the handle @popcorn_lung.

Major, like most of his generation, was not internet literate and made the mistake of getting into a pissing match with the one called @popcorn_lung. Major didn't understand the irony and nihilism the species known as the internet troll cloaked himself in, so the days-long battle in the comments section ended in Major's retreat from the internet altogether, but not before amending the record of "Jablonski" on a site that @popcorn_lung had pointed him to called Urban Dictionary. Major was appalled to see his name so defiled.

Definition 1, noun: "A Jablonski can be a male or female, of any nationality, and above the age of 10. A Jablonski is someone who fucks something up. They will make you do things twice; they are also the reason why we have so many fuck ups in the world in many different aspects of life. Jablonskiism is a term used to describe exceptional feats in

Jablonski behavior. To spot a Jablonski in its natural habitat, you have to look. Everyone in life has experienced a Jablonski at one point in time. To deal with a Jablonski requires great patience and skill. Sometimes you have to become a Jablonski to deal with a Jablonski effectively. To de-Jablonski, someone is to teach them a lesson so that they will learn not to repeat the same mistake. I coined the observational term Jablonski and Jablonskiism back in 1994 when I first experienced them in high school." Used in a sentence: "Smooth move, Jablonski. You Fuckin' Jablonski." Submitted by MuddySock89, February 3, 2011.

Definition 2, noun: "When someone has a lack of skill in a certain subject." Used in a sentence: "Look, he can't drive a truck, what a Jablonski!" submitted by Gareth_of_Omega_Fame, March 26, 2009.

Definition 3, verb: "When you drink so much alcohol, you can't walk anymore." Used in a sentence: "Dude, you got so jablonskied last night we almost had to bring you home in a wheelchair!" submitted by Bigdog7777, January 13, 2008.

Definition 4, noun: "Huge ball of crusty jizz in your jizz bib." Used in a sentence: "Man, when I rub my Jablonski, it's like Christmas!" submitted by popcorn_lung, October 26, 2006.

So, Major wrote an entry himself— "A person who can do anything and inspires people. His morality is strong, and he's as dependable as a rock. A guy you can count on." Used in a sentence: "Jablonski knows how to push through the god damn shit no one deserves," and signed the submission, @majorsaint-jablonski1957.

Stosh went back to hitting his trick shots, deleting most of the takes without posting them, thinking back to Major's experience on social media and fearing the same fate.

He was a bit anxious about Dana's lesson that evening, but it was all for not, as she never showed. She didn't call, didn't text, just stood him up.

GATOR WAS at the door when Stosh and Al got home. He ran right past Stosh and to Al, who bent down and scratched him behind the ears.

"He's sure taken to you," Stosh said.

"Someone's got to take care of him."

"What's that supposed to mean?"

"Feels like I only see you on our way to work."

"Feels the same to me," Stosh said.

There was a loud clank outside, like a shovel hitting pavement.

"Duty calls," Al said, taking Gator into his room.

Stosh went out back and saw Fred's straw planter's hat peaking above the line of forsythia on the other side of the parking lot. Then Stosh smelled smoke. He saw flames lapping up between the shrubs and ran over, seeing that Fred had dug a hole in the lawn and started a small bonfire.

"Not you," Fred said.

Stosh's stomach rolled and bloated with anxiety. He wiped his palms on his pants. He was built for leisure, not confrontation.

"I'm going to have to ask you to put that out," Stosh said with the authority of a hall monitor. "You're gonna burn the whole place down."

"Go tell it to your mother."

"What does that mean?" Stosh said. "Look, the siding is starting to melt."

"That was from last time."

"You've done this before?"

"Controlled burn."

"Come on, Fred. Work with me."

"Suck on a pig's tit," he said, throwing another handful of newspapers on the fire.

Stosh cleared his throat, said, "If you don't put it out, I'll have to."

"Give it a try, carpetbagger, see if you don't lose more than what you've got for sale."

"I'm not sure I know what that means either."

"Shove it."

Stosh had no reply. A small group of owners had gathered to watch the show.

"Should we call 911?" someone asked, losing confidence in her president's ability to take control of the situation.

Stosh looked around, his vision constricted by the weight of his own fecklessness. His spine was a rubber hose. He needed to do something to prove to these people that he could handle himself and the duties of the presidency without doubling over into a pool of anxious sweat and stale vodka.

A rubber hose, you idiot! He heard Major's voice. He ran to the side of the building, grabbing the garden hose. He unraveled it and made his way back to the fire. Fred stood there with his cane outstretched.

"You'll get this thing to your head if you come any closer," he said.

"This gives me no pleasure," Stosh said.

From his hip, he blasted Fred with a solid stream, aiming first at his face then down to the flames and back at him again. Fred swatted at Stosh with his cane, but he was no match for the stream.

Cletus arrived as the sirens rang closer and tried to calm the old man down.

"Kick his ass, Stosh!" someone hollered.

"Fred's an old man," someone else said. "It's not a fair fight."

"Kid's damned if he does, damned if he doesn't," another

owner chimed in. "He's either gonna be the kid who kicks an old man's ass, or the kid who gets his ass kicked by an old man. Kid's screwed."

"Cops are here," Amy said sadly.

She stomped out her cigarette and walked away before the cruisers pulled up. Stosh had just about put out the fire, so the firefighters had little to do but stand in the evening heat, fully geared up.

After Cletus had calmed Fred down, the cops questioned Stosh.

"What happened to Tara-Lynn?" the cop asked.

"You know her?" Stosh asked.

"She must've had us on speed dial," the cop said. "She retire or something?"

"Or something," Stosh said.

"Fred was at it again?" the cop asked.

"He has his bad days, Billy," Cletus said.

"How'd you get involved?" Officer Billy asked Cletus.

"I live around the corner."

"Do you wanna press charges?" Officer Billy asked.

Cletus looked at Stosh.

"I'd rather not," Stosh said. "I know he's got his problems, but what would happen to him if we did?"

"He set a fire within ten feet of a dwelling. It's a pretty serious offense," Officer Billy said.

Cletus shrugged and stole a glance at Fred as he was being carted into the ambulance for his mandatory psyche evaluation.

A voice squawked over Officer Billy's radio. It was all gibberish to Stosh, cop-talk, but Cletus and Billy exchanged glances.

"Looks like we've got to take him in anyway. Outstanding warrant," Officer Billy said.

"I guess we're off the hook," Stosh said.

"For now," Officer Billy said.

Officer Billy walked over to the ambulance, where the EMT

was still working on Fred. After a brief discussion, Officer Billy cuffed Fred to his gurney.

"My name is Frederick Amos LaPierre," Fred said as they wheeled him away. "Date of birth, May eighth, nineteen-forty-six, and I demand to be treated as a prisoner of war."

"I don't want to be like Tara-Lynn," Stosh said to Cletus, "fining people for every little thing, but I don't want people worrying about if Fred is gonna peek through their windows or set a fire outside their door."

"He's not our only problem either," Cletus said. "I've been seeing Gail McKitch's kid, Adam, hanging around again. He and his little band of jolly junkies have been traipsing down to the brook, to their little camp."

"What do you want to do about it?"

"What's the ROE?"

"The what?"

"Rules of Engagement."

"Observe and report," Stosh said.

"Well, that's no fun."

By the time Stosh finished with the cops, it was nearly eight o'clock. He walked past Zyvalia's unit and saw the bathroom light on. He could see her silhouette in the shower, behind the window's frosted glass. He felt warm and perverted, but he kept looking. He kicked at the dried mulch in the neglected flower bed and pulled out a few weeds to look busy while he watched her in the shower. What a loser. He tossed the weeds back into the bed and went home, feeling as though he needed his own shower to wash away the shame.

Al was still in his room with Gator, so Stosh poured himself a shot and packed a bong. He sat there on the couch, stoned and hot, scrolling endlessly through Instagram. He and Bambi weren't friends, but her account was public, and in those moments, he couldn't help himself. He searched her name and meandered through her life. There were many pictures of her daughter. Stosh examined them, tried to see himself in the child's chubby cheeks and round, blue eyes, but there was no relation. He had the sunken cheeks and low jowls of his people, of someone from east of the Elbe. Bambi seemed happy, but we all *seem* happy on social media, whether we are happy or sad, or competent; it was only an appearance. The reality beyond the edges of the screen is far more complicated than what the image suggests.

The ability to remain so viscerally connected to one's former love was a wholly modern affliction, and one that Stosh was suffering from. It was strange and alienating—modern self-flagellation.

Maybe he should just sign the divorce papers, let her get on with it, release himself and her from the prison cell of his nostalgia, but would it change anything if he didn't also renounce social media? Would isolation be his only solution, his only way forward? And what lay on the path ahead for a man like him? Was it a family, marriage, or kids? A corner office? A house in the suburbs, or better, in a place like Palm Ridge? It wasn't that Stosh didn't want some version of that life, but that it now seemed beyond the pale.

Al, too, dreamed of that middle-class life, but found himself exactly where Stosh was—stuck, burdened by a generational failure their parents couldn't or wouldn't take responsibility for. Al hadn't grown up with the kind of luxury that Stosh had, but his inability to obtain even the simple domesticities and pleasures of his childhood—a house, a lawn, maybe a dog—was to him, even more depressing than Stosh's inability to obtain the excess of his childhood. Or maybe their problems weren't social, but personal. Maybe they simply didn't deserve that kind of life. Maybe Stosh should've gone to school for finance. Maybe he should've worked harder. Maybe this was their lot.

Halfway through his bong, he got a direct message from Sara Wilson. They'd been going back and forth on Instagram for about a month. He was bored and lonely one night and commented on one of her posts, which was suggested to him as he got lost in Instagram's mosaic of desire they call their algorithm. After Bambi left, he had trained his feed to serve him a steady diet of Cryptid content, OnlyFans models, and self-improvement coaches, pitching everything from mindfulness meditation to abstinence as a cure for male loneliness and isolation. According to his algorithm, nearly half the world was trying desperately to cum, while another portion preferred to retain their dignity through public displays of chastity.

Sara was one of the latter.

"Do you want to annihilate your yearnings through the power of the holy spirit?" Sara asked in her post. "Do you want the key to true happiness on earth!? Comment 'Annihilate' in the comments section for a DM with the answer."

"Annihilate, annihilate!" Stosh exalted in the comment section.

She said she was a member of some church called Alpha and Omega House Ministry and lived across the country, in the desert outside of L.A. She DMed Stosh, not with any answers but rather asking him about his beliefs. She asked if he'd ever heard about her church. He hadn't but was familiar with the general tone of American Evangelism.

She was as nice as any salesperson he'd met while working at Dreamy's. Even when he messaged her drunk, she responded with a kind answer. It began a horrible pastime of his—catfishing rightwing evangelicals on social media. They were just so nice to white guys looking for salvation. It was like free companionship. Better than the dating apps, and despite their decades' long friendship, Al wasn't much of a talker, preferring to communicate in a series of grunts and hisses, representing everything from satisfaction to contempt, but Stosh could come home and unload his troubles on Sara. She might not be Bambi, and their relation-ship might not be what he imagined for himself, but their chats, no matter how holy—or unholy—were as close as Stosh got to flirtations.

"Given any thought to my offer?" Sara asked.

"I think I might drink too much for your church."

"We all have things we need to work on."

"But didn't Jesus turn water into wine? And not, like, a little bit, either? I remember a priest saying that Jesus turned something like one hundred and thirty gallons of water into wine."

"Of course, but we find alcohol to be the cause of a lot of modern problems, especially in the family unit."

"What do you consider 'the family unit'?"

This, Stosh believed, was how these types flirted.

"Genesis Twelve: One through eleven," Sara replied.

He looked up the verse in the Bible Major had given him for his First Communion. The verse goes something like this: Lot welcomes two angels, hunky-dude-angels—again, the vulgarity of these angels and their horrid wings and cocks!—to town and let them crash on his couch. Then some Sodomites show up and ask about the two hot angel-hunks that're staying with him. Lot—an absolute savage, apparently—begs the Sodomites to leave the two angel-hunks alone, and instead, offers them his two daughters, both of whom he assures are virgins. Then the two hunky angels pull Lot back into the house and smite the Sodomites.

"If that's how you treat family, I'm a little concerned," Stosh responded to Sara after reading the passage.

"Sorry, Wrong verse! Try Genesis one twenty-seven through twenty-eight," she said. "We're planning a mission to your area, and I'd love to meet up IRL and have a chat!"

Stosh found her oscillation between biblical prose and online slang confusing. It seemed to be the native tongue of Evangelicals, this amalgam of new and old language. Stosh found it off-putting: their embrace of technology and modern fashion somehow spoiled the heir of ancient ritual, and even though he considered himself lapsed, he wanted the full sugar, hundred-proof Catholicism when his soul was thirsty, not the diet light colloquialisms of a digital age Jesus.

Stosh scrolled through Sara's posts. Most of her pictures were from New Age-looking ceremonies and drum circles, all of which featured her in modest but fashionable streetwear, and often with a tall, bleached-blonde man who may have been her boyfriend, or some other soul she'd taken pity on through her online mission.

He left her on read and went to bed.

The Second Letter of Saint-Jablonski Minor
to the People of The Association

Hello, neighbors,

I know everyone is disappointed that we're still unable to open the pool, but we must urge you to NOT go in it. It was brought to our attention that some owners have continued to use it, and we must warn you that, because we are unable to determine what the sludge is, bathing, swimming, and even dipping your toes in it could be unhealthy. Please bear with us as we attempt to resolve the issue.

Most of you are aware of the recent incident involving me and Fred. Although we understand why some in the community have a great deal of mistrust of the board, we want to remind you that we are a kinder, gentler board; less concerned with meticulous order and obedience and more focused on the quality of life we can achieve through cooperation, not coercion.

We will update everyone as more details emerge about the black sludge, or goo, as some of you prefer to call it.

Please also join us for the upcoming board meeting if you have any questions or concerns, or if you wish to get more involved in our community.

Lastly, we want to thank everyone for paying their dues on

time. It has allowed us the continuity we desperately need in these trying times.

Your public servant,
Stanislaus (Stosh) Saint-Jablonski
President

CHAPTER EIGHT

STOSH TOOK a few days off for condo business. They filed new documents with the state's Attorney General, officially making him the president of the association. He and Birdie reviewed the financials and attempted to prioritize which bills to pay and which projects to start. It was a real slog, but they were fast approaching the first board meeting since Tara-Lynn left, and he wanted to be ready.

By Friday of that week, Stosh was ready to tie one on. Al was in good spirits after having fixed much of the damage caused by the tournament. He'd gotten some new pot for the occasion, and Stosh picked up a fresh handle of Tito's. Even Cecelia and Cara were going over after their evening round at the Ridge.

The girls wanted burgers, so Jocko's it was, but Al didn't eat meat. He wasn't a vegetarian, though. He didn't eat vegetables, either. He ate bread and cheese. Only bread and cheese. Grilled cheese, string cheese, fried cheese, though he complained he couldn't find a good mozzarella stick in central Florida if his life depended on it. He was also a fan of mac and cheese, but he didn't like Jocko's mac and cheese, because he said it wasn't *real* mac and cheese, though what he really meant was that it *was* real mac and cheese and that he only liked the boxed stuff.

The girls picked Stosh up and drove to Jocko's while Al assembled his cheese-slop and rolled a few joints.

"We saw your girl, Dana," Cara said in the car. "She was getting a lesson from Ketch."

"Better keep an eye on your woman," Cecelia smirked.

"I don't think I have to worry about that," Stosh said. "Little Jablonski wasn't too keen on her."

"Ew," Cara said, "I don't wanna hear about your little anything."

"At least you're honest about its size," Cecelia said.

"Anyway, with everything going on at the condo, I don't have the time for it," Stosh said. "But I'd like to think I could still be professional with her. I mean, I would have been happy to keep teaching her."

"Why is the condo your problem?" Cecelia asked.

"The responsibilities of the president," he said.

"Ah, yes," Cara said, "heavy lies the crown."

They pulled up to Jocko's, got out of the car, and stepped in line. Stosh turned and observed the crowd as Cara and Cecelia each stared at their phones.

Across the parking lot, sitting alone at one of the picnic tables was Zyvalia. She, too, was on her phone, mindlessly sipping on a milkshake.

"Who's that?" Cecelia said, noticing his stare.

"My new neighbor."

"She's hot," Cecelia said, glancing up from her phone.

"Go talk to her, see if she wants to hang out," Cara said.

"I don't want to be a pain," he said.

Stosh remembered going to dinner with Major, who would inevitably leave Stosh at the table to go chat up any woman he suspected of being single, and even when they weren't single, he'd try his best. Sometimes he'd even bring them home. Stosh would be in the backseat, shy and quiet, and Major would be up front with some random woman, singing along to his favorite Willie Nelson or George Jones. On those nights, Major would have Stosh go to bed early. When Stosh got to be a bit older and knew what was going on, he'd sneak down the stairs and watch Major in the living room with the woman. Those moments always made him miss his mother, even though he'd never met her. He wanted for nothing as a kid, with the exception of a family, or something closer to one than he had.

There was one time when the woman was still there in the morning. Stosh was in high school. He went downstairs to get ready for school, and she was there, in one of Major's day-glow construction shirts. She was making coffee, some eggs bubbling in a pan on the stove.

She had the kind of rough sophistication and oblivious confidence of a college student. She was pretty and small and thumped around the kitchen cooking breakfast with bare feet. It reminded Stosh of a commercial or TV show, the way families always sat together for breakfast, bustling about, briefcases and backpacks slamming, bacon sizzling, and the parents trying to enjoy their coffee amidst the domestic chaos. Those scenes were always in stark contrast to Stosh's mornings with Major, the two slurping at their bowls of cereal in front of the TV, watching Sportscenter in their undies like a couple of frat boys.

Stosh looked back over at Zyvalia. She was tall, too, like that woman who was still there in the morning. She wore low-rise linen pants and a smock-like top that revealed her midriff, still glowing with the hue of a fading sunburn.

They placed their orders and stood to the side. Zyvalia looked up from her food just as the cashier called Stosh's name. She smiled and waved at him as she gathered her trash and made her way over to where he was standing, but before she reached him, a shot rang out.

At first, Stosh thought it was just some kids firing off roman candles, but then he heard the shouting and saw him, the crazy guy, the analog man.

"Jocko's is people!" he screamed; his rifle held high in his hand in the style of Charlton Heston. "I come from the end!"

He fired the rifle again, this time at the restaurant, blistering the building's wood frame and spraying splinters into the air.

Cara covered Cecelia's head with her purse.

Stosh moved, too: first toward Cecelia's car, then to Zyvalia who was completely exposed in the no-man's land that was the parking lot. They embraced each other in a panic just as the analog man fired another shot at the broadside of the squat building.

People fled like buckshot from the restaurant, dropping their milkshakes and condiments on the pavement and fleeing for cover.

After a few more shots, someone much braver than Stosh brought the analog man to the ground.

He continued to harass bystanders, including a man in a pair of Mickey Mouse ears and Bermuda shorts, as Jocko's staff evacuated the building. "Deep state agents!" he yelled at them. "Omega won't spare you!" he said, seemingly at the man with the mouse ears and Bermuda shorts.

Zyvalia and Stosh had found refuge behind the dumpster, where they waited for the police to arrive.

He knew they were safe and in good hands when he saw Officer Billy arrive on the scene. Stosh peeked over the dumpster and saw that Cara and Cecelia were safe, too.

The veins in Stosh's face throbbed. He was still holding Zyv. He looked her over and brushed some dirt and broken pavement from her knees. He slicked the hair away from his face and rubbed his eyes. His brain was struggling to keep up with his movements, but he was proud of his reflexes. He always figured he'd be the first one to get popped in a mass shooting.

The cops took the analog man into custody and rounded up

witnesses. Stosh texted Cecelia from across the parking lot and told her to leave before she was sequestered.

"I really wanted the rest of my milkshake," Zyvalia said with a traumatized smile.

Stosh looked over to the counter, where their food was waiting, unscathed. He could feel every drop of blood in the spidery tributaries that were his veins.

"I'll buy if you fly," Stosh said. He sprinted to the counter, grabbed every bag of food he could carry, along with a tray of milkshakes, and ran to Zyvalia's car. She turned it over, and they got out of there before they were made official witnesses to what would later be referred to in the media as "Burger-gate."

Zyvalia drove carefully away from the scene to evade suspicion. Stosh talked the whole way home. He was nervous, and his blabbering was involuntary, much like his scrolling, which he did between rants, his blood pressure lowering with each flick of his thumb.

For her part, Zyvalia chimed in only when Stosh paused to take a breath, but she said very little. Her eyes were wide and expressive, just as they'd been when Stosh first met her. After several minutes, she interjected in Stosh's rather lengthy diatribe about how he could see Fred pulling a similar stunt to what they'd just witnessed, and said, "This may seem strange, but I need to breathe for a minute."

"Were you not breathing before?" Stosh asked in earnest as they stopped at a traffic light.

"I mean, like, really breathe," Zyvalia said. She closed her eyes and took a deep breath.

Stosh stole glances at her, watched as the constellation of freckles on her pink chest heaved—in through the nose, out through the mouth, he thought as he saw the dim glow of the association's sign in the distance.

After they arrived home and parked, Zyvalia exhaled one last time and started screaming. Stosh jumped. He blocked his ears and reached for her, but she continued to scream and chant nonsense. As abruptly as she started, she stopped, took another deep breath, and said, "That's better."

"Are you sure?" he asked, concerned that whatever madness afflicted the analog man might have been contagious.

"Yeah," she said with a smile. "It's good to scream."

Cara and Cecelia were already parked.

"That. Was. Crazy!" Cara said, climbing down from Cecelia's car.

"I'm, like, still shaking," Cecelia said.

Zyvalia moved to her and took her by the hand.

"You're OK," Zyvalia said. "Just breathe. That's all there is. What happened has happened, and now you're here and you're safe."

Cecelia's pants relented to something more rhythmic and balanced. She wiped away the tears that were forming in the corners of her eyes.

Zyvalia then introduced herself to the girls—"Zyv for short"— taking the time to hug each one. She said, "I don't know about you, but I could use a drink."

"I have Tito's and some pot, if that's more of your thing," Stosh said.

"Let me just get changed," Zyv said.

Inside Stosh's condo, the girls relayed what happened to an incredibly stoned and increasingly paranoid Al, who could do nothing more than light another joint. Stosh went to the bathroom and regarded his shaking hands. He splashed some water on his face and took a deep breath, but his chest wouldn't loosen. The analog man's voice was still ringing in his ear, punctuated by the awful crack of his rifle. He dressed the scrape on his elbow and pulled out a few splinters from when the bullet hit the shack. He turned them over in his hands. They began to wiggle and slither like worms. Stosh dropped them and splashed more water on his face, thought about messaging Sara for guidance, but figured she'd only offer thoughts and prayers. He looked at the splinters on the floor, and they were inanimate again. He took a deep breath but knew that what he'd witnessed that night would stay with him for a long, long time.

He gathered himself as best he could and returned to the living room when there was a knock on the door.

"Birdie?" Al said, pulling the joint from behind his ear.

"You haven't met Zyv?" Cecelia asked.

"The influencer?"

"She's an influencer?" Cara asked.

"You'll learn all about her, I'm sure," Stosh said.

He went to the back door and opened it. Zyv was there in a spaghetti strap tank top and a pair of baggy sweatpants. Her eyes were two different colors, and her magnificent red hair was pulled back into a bun that looked like a peach on top of her head, with shades of yellow and orange glinting in the light of the moon.

They each took a shot and chased it with a handful of Mike and Ikes in the kitchen before moving to the living room, where Al, Cara, Cecelia, and Gator sat around the coffee table. Al was lighting one of the joints as Cara and Cecelia went in on their burgers.

Stosh was feeling a bit of a buzz about his head after the empty-bellied shot he'd taken and the weight of the evening's events. Al offered him a joint, and he ripped it. Then he devoured his burger as if it were his last meal on earth.

The burger coagulated the booze in Stosh's gut and kept him alert enough to keep smoking. Zyv sat next to him, her laugh as regular as the hands of time, clucking away in a consistent rhythm, washing away the night's trauma.

Al got to talking about buying a stump-grinder, which, on most nights, was nothing but wishful thinking, but that night he'd decided it was time to make Stosh a proposal, perhaps thinking that his near-death experience had sparked a sense of urgency in him.

"We got the money," Al said, toking on the last of a dying joint.

"We don't got the money."

"Take it. Take it like that bitch, Tara-Lynn did," he suggested.

Zyv had gotten up and joined the girls in conversation. Al inched closer to Stosh, the seeds of desire speckling his glossy eyes.

"Come on," he said. "None of these people do their own yard work around here, and we can work year-round."

"I don't need any more jobs," Stosh said.

"What about a podcast?" Al said. "I need something in my life, man."

"And you've narrowed it down to a stump grinder or a podcast?"

"I have stories," Al said. "I'm interesting," he reassured himself.

"You could tell the story about Lola Costello and that box of Banana Boat you..." Stosh said.

"We don't talk about that," Al cut him off, hocking up a snot and clearing his throat.

Stosh stole the roach from Al's rheumatic hand. He didn't have much to say after that. It seemed he could only open one eye at a time, and to look at the world through both would have sent him into another dimension.

Zyv was reading the girls' natal charts. She was asking questions about their times and dates of birth, the cities they were born in, and the number of parents they had.

Stosh was fading fast—the grease, the carbs, the pot, the liquor, and violence all catching up with him. Gator reached his fore-hooves onto the couch by Stosh's head. Stosh grabbed him underneath his pits and lifted him up. He nestled down on the other side of the pillow where Stosh's head was. He reached behind Gator's head and scratched his ears as the star talk continued on the other end of the couch. Al was dead on his ass, nodding in and out of his drink, then Stosh was gone, chasing birdies on courses unknown.

He woke up to Zyv rubbing his head. He came to, his vision blurry and askew. The girls were gone. He could hear Al snoring in his room and Gator snorting at the door.

"What does that mean?" Zyv asked, nodding toward the hog.

"He's gotta go out," Stosh said.

He righted himself on the couch and tried to shake the buzz away from his head, but it was a heavy one.

"Take these," Zyv said, handing Stosh a couple of Advil.

"Why don't I walk you home?" he said, choking down the pills.

"You don't have to," Zyv smiled. "I can take Fred if he tries anything."

Stosh stepped into his slides that were sitting by the door. He called Gator into the kitchen, opened the back door, and they walked out.

Stosh had slept through the rain. It was cool, but the humidity was already brewing, fermenting the air.

"You don't want another drink, do you?" Zyv asked as they approached her door.

"I got an early tee time with Thelma and Louise tomorrow morning."

"Seriously, that's your excuse?"

"I didn't say it was a good one."

"It certainly isn't," she said. "I didn't realize you were one of the girls."

"You're not challenging my masculinity by making fun of my alcohol tolerance, are you?"

"Is it working?"

"Maybe."

"Come on in," she said, unlocking her door.

She threw her keys on the kitchen table and pulled out a

handle of Tito's. She had to cradle the bottle in the crux of her arm to pour the shots.

"So, who are Cara and Cecelia again?" she asked with a hint of suspicion in her voice.

"It's kind of a weird story."

"I love weird," she smiled.

"Cecelia was married to one of my best friends. They have a couple of kids together. They broke up and he started dating Cara, then he died, and now they're friends."

"That's not weird," Zyv chuckled. "They endured a terrible trauma together. It's actually quite natural."

"You have a point."

"I know."

"Now that I'm waking up, can I get another?"

Zyv poured them each another shot and suggested they move to the living room.

"So, the wife and the mistress?" Zyv said.

"More than what I could handle," Stosh said.

"Ever been tempted?"

"Not by them."

"Mighty noble of you," she said.

"No one has ever accused me of that," Stosh said.

"They're both very pretty."

"Do you want their numbers?"

"I've never been in a relationship with two women before. Could be fun."

"Are you implying you've been in a relationship with two men?"

"If I had been, would that change the way you feel about me?"

"How do you know the way I feel about you?"

"Your pupils dilate every time we talk..."

"I'm an alcoholic."

"You invited me over for drinks."

"We were trauma-bonding."

"You insisted on walking me home," she said.

"I'm a gentleman," Stosh said as she scooched her way down the couch toward him.

"That sounds tiresome," she said.

"I'm in atrophy."

She kissed him then. She felt drunk, but he was drunk, too; too drunk to use his head and too stoned to stop thinking.

"I'm hot," Zyv said, peeling away from him after a few moments.

She stood up and walked to the bathroom. She closed the door and turned on the shower.

Stosh wasn't sure if he was meant to follow, and he wasn't confident enough to assume he was welcomed to walk in on her, so he went to the back door, ready to make an Irish exit, but then took a moment. Frogs, bugs, and animals unknown croaked and squawked in the distance. It didn't sound all that different from the summer nights back home, but he still felt like a foreigner. He walked back into Zyv's kitchen and nosed around, peaking in the half-empty cabinets. A stack of mail sat on the kitchen table. He didn't need to touch it to see who it was addressed to—Zyvalia and David Anders.

His chest tightened; his head sobered. What the hell was that all about?

The Third Letter of Saint-Jablonski
to the People of the Association

My fellow members of the association,

Following the annual meeting, we would like to remind everyone of some key rules. Although we pride ourselves on our accommodating spirit and wish not to jam anyone up but rather create a more cooperative community, we ask that you still follow the rules, and specifically the following:

1. Please park in your assigned spot. If you own more than one car, please feel free to park a second car in a visitor spot; however, visitor spots are always available on a first-come, first-served basis.

2. Please drive no more than 25 MPH through the neighborhood.

3. Please respect your neighbors' peace. Be mindful of your TV and stereo volume. Although subwoofers and surround sound systems are not prohibited, we ask that you consult with your neighbors before installing them.

4. Please report any suspicious activity to the office, but if you feel the safety of the community or yourself is in immediate jeopardy, please call the police.

5. Shoot all solicitors and bill collectors on sight...JUST KIDDING!

In addition to these rules, we have also created a unit owners' Bill of Rights to ensure the appropriate checks and balances:

1. You have the right to view all association records, including the financials.

2. You have the right to participate in all association business, board meetings, and decision-making.

3. You have the right to run for any position on the Board of Trustees.

4. You have the right to privacy and protection from any intrusion into your unit by the association or other unit owners.

And lastly, we have an update on the pool. Although we are still unaware of what the black sludge/goo is, our board member, Cletus Wriggle, suggested that we reach out to the Air Force base to see if they have any ideas or if the goo might have originated from their cleanup efforts. As some of you may know, the base was closed after it was discovered that massive amounts of PFOAs were present in the groundwater, so we must ask all unit owners to refrain from using the pool. We hope to have the issue addressed as soon as possible and will update everyone if and when we receive a response from the base.

Sincerely,

Stanislaus (Stosh) Saint-Jablonski

President

CHAPTER NINE

THE NEXT MORNING was a rough one for Stosh. His head convulsed from dehydration, all gnarled and stressed, and his chest felt pickled with guilt. And that was just from thinking about what happened with Zyv, never mind burger-gate. Like most Americans, violence was a second language to Stosh; it was something he understood but rarely spoke. Thinking about the crazy analog man and the crack of the gunfire only amplified his hangover, but he was happy to have escaped safely and without being sequestered by the cops.

Before his round, he lurked on Facebook. In addition to learning that Zyv was a certified "Scream Coach," he confirmed that Zyv and David were married. He scrolled through her posts and pictures, traced her life back to her moment of online conception. She listed her hometown as La Brea, Honduras, though her ginger hair and nearly translucent skin tone suggested she was not native. She had no history of employment but had a linktree in her Instagram bio. He clicked on it and found the array of services she offered as a board-certified Scream Coach. They varied from natal charts and astrological readings to advanced trauma recalibration, intuitive design, and astral engineering. It was clear that Zyv had gone through something similar to Stosh's own spiritual journey after his career ended, when he spent countless hours researching the divine connection between Source and the Grays, but unlike Stosh, whose material needs had subsumed his spiritual desires for purpose, Zyv went all in.

He continued scrolling in the bathroom but had to pull himself out of the rabbit hole to meet the girls at the course. They were both putting around the practice green when he arrived. He really just wanted to play by himself. After last night, he wanted some time alone to process everything, but there they were, and there he was, so they got on with it.

Before they could even get to the first tee, they both leaned into him.

"We *love* Zyv," Cara said.

"We're just gonna ignore what happened at Jocko's?" Stosh asked.

"Zyv made me feel better about it," Cecelia said. "She has a gift."

"She has something else, too," he said.

"How'd you screw it up?" Cara said.

"What's that supposed to mean?" Stosh asked.

"You may be good at golf, but women..." Cecelia said.

"She's married," Stosh said.

"What?" Cara asked.

"But she was all over you," Cecelia said.

"Her husband is in the Air Force, waiting to transfer here or something, but it's Facebook official."

"Maybe they're separated," Cara said.

"They're probably separated," Cecelia said. "I'm a good judge of character, and she doesn't seem like a cheater."

Cecelia said this in a way that almost seemed to be as much a compliment to Zyv as it was an insult to Cara.

He supposed Zyv and David could be separated. Maybe that's

why she didn't say anything, but David was just there; they'd just bought their condo. Why would a couple on the outs buy a new place together only to split up? Maybe it was an economic decision? Something close to what he and Al had. Everyone has their plotki, after all.

Stosh spent most of that week trying to avoid Zyv. Al was nice enough to take Gator out and even picked up their takeout, though Jocko's was no longer an option as it was still an active crime scene. Stosh knew he'd eventually have to face her, but that Wednesday was the first board meeting since Tara-Lynn had left, and he couldn't be concerned with anything else.

IT RAINED the morning of the meeting, so he left work early to prepare. Birdie helped him print out the agenda for the night, and they made copies of the financial documents for everyone who wanted to review them. He knew there would still be a lot of hostility, but he was hoping that the more prepared he appeared, the fewer questions his neighbors would ask.

Stosh had assembled a real crack bunch—Birdie stayed on as Secretary. Cletus agreed to take a clerk position, and Ray Limon, the retired attorney, took the other clerk spot. They were just missing a Vice President, but Stosh was hoping to recruit another owner to fill the position.

Birdie was already in the office when Stosh arrived for the meeting, and Cletus and Ray showed up shortly thereafter. He officially appointed both Cletus and Ray to their positions, tapping them each on the shoulder as if knighting them, though Cletus didn't appreciate the pageantry.

They reviewed the financials. Cletus all but glazed over as they went page by page, line item by line item and even Stosh had a hard time making sense of the report, but thankfully for the community, Ray seemed competent enough to understand it.

"Any word from the wicked witch?" Cletus said after they finished with the books.

"I've given up trying to reach her," Stosh said.

"Figures," Cletus said.

"Pretty impressive that everyone paid their dues on time," Stosh said. "We should be pretty proud of that."

"I know we have a lot of work to do, but it appears that, for now, we're making more than we're spending, so that's good," Ray said.

"I bet she's down there, laughing at us, sipping a goddamn MY-TIE," Cletus said, drawing out the word.

"Not much we can do about it now," Stosh said, trying to keep their focus and attention toward the positives, toward the future, and not on Tara-Lynn or his own involvement in her scheme.

"And we have new controls in place so this can't happen again?" Ray asked.

"Absolutely," Stosh said.

"Been talking to a lot of people, and they still want heads to roll," Cletus said. "That bitch really did a number on you people."

"Revolutionary justice can be cathartic," Ray added, his head still buried in the books.

"I think it's important that we look to the future, and let karma take care of Tara-Lynn," Stosh said. "But if it was up to me, we'd drag her back from wherever she is and make her face the communal firing squad."

"Oh," Cletus said, "you don't have to convince me. I'm just passing along the information."

"Stosh is right," Ray said, "this is year zero of the association. Time to imagine a more beautiful future."

Stosh smiled at that.

"I will give credit where it's due," Cletus said, "Tara-Lynn was a real head-breaker, a good law-and-order gal, even if she didn't apply it to herself."

"What do you mean?" Ray asked.

"Gail's kid has been hanging around again. Fred saw him by the pool the other day, and I saw him and his junkie friends walking up and down the street in broad daylight. I thought we had a no-trespass order against him."

"We do, but they disappear before the cops can get here, and that brook they hang out at isn't on our property, so there's nothing we can do when they're down there," Birdie said.

"No offense, but Tara-Lynn knew how to keep them out," Cletus said. "She let me, you know, jam him up a bit when I first moved in here, when I still had some favors with the department."

"Jam him up?" Ray asked.

"It was just a reminder," Cletus said. "We always thought him good for a string of burglaries at the Ridge."

"A reminder?" Stosh asked.

"I mean, they don't make batons like they used to," Cletus said.

"What're you getting at?" Stosh asked.

"Well," Cletus said, leaning back in his aluminum chair, "with your blessing, I'd like to send him another reminder."

"That's exactly the kind of *gangsterismo* we're trying to get away from," Ray said.

"But they seem dangerous," Birdie chimed in.

"So, that's two votes yes, and two votes no," Cletus said. "Looks like we need to get someone to fill that VP position so we can make a decision."

"I'm confused. Are you asking for us to deputize you?" Ray asked.

"I don't think it'll be a bad idea to have some kind of neighborhood watch. I could get some of my fellow Big Boys to patrol the area, especially with all these Antifas and Black Lives Matter people over in Kissimmee," Cletus said.

"I hate to be blunt," Ray said, "but aren't those the same

people you were suspended from the sherif's department for associating with?"

"Whatever happened to innocent until proven guilty?" Cletus scoffed. "The Big Boys of the Bygone Day is a fraternal order of patriots. Most of us are proud veterans and first responders. And I went to that counter protest as a civilian, not a cop."

Ray put his hands in the air. "Just a question. Meant no offense."

"Once we get someone to fill the VP spot, we can vote on a neighborhood watch, but until then, we'll have to shelf it," Stosh said, trying to cap the conversation before it descended into partisan bickering. "And please, if you see Gail's son, or anything else sketchy, just call the cops. It's all we can do."

"Well, that's no fun," Cletus said.

After finishing with the financials and budget, they adjourned the meeting.

Stosh would have to say it was a success, or at least not a total failure, but he feared inviting Cletus onto the board may have been a mistake. Stosh knew about his history, about the scuffle he'd had at a BLM protest for which he was suspended, and he feared that now, with nothing to do but walk the neighborhood in between rounds at the local municipal course, he'd take the law into his own hands.

As menacing as Gail's son may appear, Stosh had a soft spot for addicts, considering his relationship with Christian. Somehow, Stosh and Al had avoided the pills even though their hometown nearly drowned in them when they were in high school, but they both had known plenty of people who'd suffered from the affliction. Al's little sister had spent most of her adult life in and out of rehabs all down the east coast, including in Florida, and is now MIA in California somewhere, last Al knew.

Stosh figured if Gail's son continued to be a problem, the new, kinder and gentler administration could talk to him before cracking a baton over his head.

It had rained while they were in session, and Stosh could see the moisture evaporating from the asphalt when he left the meeting. These moments—after a brief storm, when the humidity broke and there was a bit of fresh coolness in the air—reminded him of home, if only for a few minutes.

He could smell a frozen pizza cooking as he approached his back door. Al was in the kitchen, dressing his pie with fresh mozzarella and a few bits of American cheese, to cream it up, as he'd say.

"Take a slice or two," Al nodded toward the pizza when Stosh walked in.

"You're a lifesaver," Stosh said. "You need anything washed? I got to do a quick load."

Al rubbed his stomach. "No, but I'm working on my own load," he said, wincing.

"Charming."

Stosh grabbed his laundry bag and the detergent and headed downstairs. He loaded the washing machine, and as he turned around, the door opened, and there stood Zyv.

"If it isn't Houdini," she said.

"I'm here, so I'm not that good," Stosh said, forcing a smile.

She moved toward the machines, holding her hamper against her hip protectively. Stosh was frozen, a part of him wanting to avoid the situation altogether, and another part of him wanting to be close to her again, to smell the vodka and Mike and Ikes on her breath. And didn't she look ethereal, like something out of an enchanted forest, with her copper jewelry and earth tones contrasting her pale skin.

She shot Stosh a glance and said, "Was it the hair?"

"The hair?"

"It's chased some guys away before," she said. She lifted her arm and revealed her unshaven pit, though there wasn't much hair, just a few elongated strands that Stosh wouldn't have noticed if she hadn't made such a spectacle of it.

"It wasn't that," he said, noticing what he should've seen when they first met—the skinny tattoo around her left ring finger. "It was that," he said.

She raised her hand and regarded her finger.

"I forget about it sometimes," she said.

"Your marriage?"

"It doesn't make me a bad person," she said. "It's just complicated."

"I'm not here to judge, but it would've been nice to know."

"If I say I was drunk, will you forgive me?"

"Even if you weren't, I would."

"I knew you were a gentleman," she said. "But I don't want you to think differently of me. I'd like to explain it to you, maybe over dinner? Maybe somewhere that doesn't traffic children, or whatever that crazy guy said about Jocko's."

"Your husband saved me from the hoard at the annual meeting. I don't want to, you know, get involved."

"What if I told you he knew about it?"

Stosh's face flushed. He felt a great jolt of panic run up his spine. It was an ancient feeling, a prehistoric rumbling—akin to the fight-or-flight response.

"He and I have kind of an open thing," she said. "Let me explain. Seriously, it's nothing nasty, it's just different."

Stosh didn't need the trouble, he knew that, but there was something about Zyv's confidence, about her presence that muffled all the puzzling demands of the condo, a welcomed reminder that he was still young and curious and in need of affection, and although he could have gotten that from Sara or the dating apps, it was Zyv who was standing in front of him, breathing the same air, tethered to him by more than a USB cord and a million miles of fiberoptic cables. After all, his life had been all but burned to the ground—his marriage, his family, his dreams, all singed. Maybe it was time to embrace another way of thinking, of living.

"OK," he said, "Friday night?"

"Perfect," she said.

He gathered his things and started for the door but then stopped and turned to her.

"You have any interest in joining the board here?"

She laughed, "I'd rather get a root canal."

CHAPTER TEN

CHARITY TOURNAMENTS at the Ridge were raucous affairs, typically ending with Cara or one of the other bartenders calling on Stosh to haul a drunk hack out of the clubhouse and down to the visitor's lot. They were the only occasions that nonmembers could play the course and were usually filled with overweight insurance salespeople or other members of the middle-management class. Their companies would sponsor a hole or two and send their highest performers to play. Hacks, all of them, it was the only time in their lives that they would be paid to play the game.

Their scores were dismal, with many players abandoning their scorecards in their golf carts. The only thing worse than the scores—the best being in the low hundreds—were the pickup lines, but Stosh never got tired of seeing the hacks' swollen faces melt when he kindly informed them that Cara was still mourning the loss of her one true love.

The bartenders always cleaned up, though, with every golfer tipping as if lived at the Ridge and weren't just visiting. During the bigger tournaments, Cara would give Stosh a cut of the tips. He was there mainly to keep the peace, though he wasn't much of a bouncer, so he'd wash dishes and hump ice up from the freezers to keep busy.

That night was relatively calm, with prolonged thunder showers sending most of the golfers home early, and the rest into the clubhouse for their free Denver steak and domestic swill. Stosh watched from behind the bar as the murder of drunk married men ripped shots of well whiskey and chased them down with low, deep-bellied laughs you could hear all the way from the first tee box.

Henry, the security guard, was coming in from his post.

"Everything's locked," he said with a smile, "You just need to close the exit once they're out of here."

He shook Stosh's hand, as he always did when he left for the day, and Stosh went back to cleaning.

Toward the end of the night, Stosh went out back and lit a cigarette. He'd been trying to quit since he started in high school, but it was a losing battle.

Cara brought out the trash, threw it in the dumpster, then went over and sat next to him. The rain had stopped, leaving the pavement looking like glass in the light of the decorative lampposts.

"Did you hear about Dan?" Cara asked of the course Ranger.

Stosh shook his head, "Haven't seen him around."

"Cancer," she said. "They gave him three months, and he was gone in one."

"I thought he beat it."

"Came back."

"I don't think he really liked me all that much," Stosh said.

"Those cigars finally got to him," Cara said, "but he always seemed in good shape, even after he got that voice-box-thingy. Cecelia and I are going to the wake if you want to join."

"I suppose I should make an appearance."

The two went back to work, cleaning up the mess at the bar, then closed for the night.

THE NEXT DAY, the Ridge held a little memorial service for Dan Malloy, who hadn't liked Stosh, not because of anything Stosh did but because he was friends with Christian, who was always holding up the pace of play or otherwise disturbing the peace. As the Ranger, it was Dan's job to make sure players were moving at an appropriate pace, but there was little he could do with Christian. Dan kicked him off the course a few times, but when Cecelia moved down and bought a place at the Ridge, Christian became a full-fledged member, so there was no punitive action Dan could take against him. All he could do was yell, and not very loudly, after he had his laryngectomy. He'd be hollering in that robot voice, and Christian would reply with something like, "I can't hear you, Dan! What? What are you saying? Sure, I'll fuck your wife if you want me to. Kind of weird, but OK. Whatever you want!"

It really drove the old man crazy, and Stosh felt bad about it.

Ketch unveiled a little plaque they planned to set beneath the large willow up on the little knoll above the tenth hole tee box, where Dan liked to sit in the shade.

"This is the only time I'll be six under," the plaque read in honor of Dan's humor, or lack thereof.

The plaque paled in comparison to the bronze, full-scale statue of the course's designer and local hero, Aldous Fairchild, that stood in the clubhouse entryway, but we're all remembered not based on merit but net worth.

Stosh left work early so he could take a shower before attending the services. Cara and Cecelia picked him up, and they drove over to the funeral home.

Stosh didn't have much experience with death. He was one of the luckier people of his generation in that sense, with many of his friends having to attend what seemed like countless funerals, almost all of which were for young overdose victims. It wasn't that he didn't know these victims, he just didn't know them well enough to see them off to the ever-after, but he remembered the endless streams of condolences and obits that peppered his feeds and the mothers and brothers and sisters and cousins and friends who posted to the departed's walls as if they were digital prayers.

He'd only ever been to one other funeral before Christian died. His Jaju's. He was the original Saint-Jablonski. The fleer of Poland, changer of names. He went the way of Dan—some kind of cancer. Stosh's Baci, Judith Saint-Jablonski, had died shortly after childbirth, and so he came from a long line of single fathers with little knowledge of child-rearing.

Christian's funeral took the wind out of everyone. Stosh was a bit numb at first, having never really experienced that kind of loss before. He was only twelve when Jaju died, and he had been the kind of hard and emotionally distant man common to his generation. Stosh supposed that when you see a couple of world wars and survive a genocide, the whining of a spoiled American boy seemed unworthy of concern, even if that boy was your grandson.

It wasn't until Stosh saw Christian's dead body that he really felt it. The undertaker—or whatever they're called—did a good job, though. Christian looked just the same as he did when he was alive. He was so fresh his tan was still intact, and his hair was perfectly styled. Stosh's grief, however, was overshadowed by Cecelia's. She left her spot in the receiving line several times to view the body.

Stosh watched from his aluminum chair in the gallery as she leaned into the casket, all but climbing into it. The last time she did this, Christian's mother had to physically remove her from the casket and walk her outside to get some air. All the while, Cara sat with Stosh, watching after the kids as best she could. They were unfazed, not yet old enough to understand the totality of death and believing fully in their mother's promise that their daddy had ascended to a place much better, much higher and fluffier than the one where they lived. Several times, Cara had to wrangle them from the gallery as they played tag and jumped off chairs. At one point, Sasha even stood up on the kneeler in front of the casket and nearly pulled the whole thing to the ground.

Now, Cara, Cecelia, and Stosh waited in line for Dan's funeral. He'd been a cop and served in one of the country's many police actions somewhere in Asia, so they pulled out all the stops, and the line stretched out of the funeral home and into the late evening sun, still hot and hazy.

They crept forward, one inch at a time, as old ladies shuffled out of the parlor behind creaky walkers.

"It's hot hell," Stosh complained.

A few of the older ladies turned and looked at him with a kind of disgust he'd noticed was native to the south.

He bowed his head in contrition.

It took them nearly an hour to get into the parlor, where they were at least greeted by the cool relief of the air conditioner, though it seemed to be pumping out as much vaporized formaldehyde as it did cool air.

"I'm going to be sick," Cecelia said and went to the bathroom.

"What is it about the smell?" Stosh noted. "I've only been to two funerals, but I remember the smell being familiar even at the first one I went to."

"I don't know, but I hate it," Cara said.

Cecelia returned, her face as white as the casket's ruffled lining. They inched toward the body, and there it was. Stosh could only see the old man's large, sloped nose from where he was standing. When it was their turn to pay their respects, Cara only stopped briefly at the body before carrying on down the receiving line. Cecelia and Stosh knelt before the body and blessed themselves, the good Catholic kids they were. Stosh recited the Lord's Prayer, though his soul wasn't in it. He looked upon dead Dan, his gaunt face having been drained of life by the cancer before he passed.

In that moment, the connection was lost, only clicks and buzzes between Stosh and what kings sat in judgement above.

Stosh stole a glance at Cecelia. Her eyes were closed, and some tears muddied her mascara. She seemed deep in prayer. Stosh waited as long as his knees allowed, then stood up and made his way down the receiving line, nodding and smiling politely, whispering "sorry for your loss" all the way down. He looked back and saw that Cecelia was still at the kneeler, sobbing heavily now.

"Should I go get her?" Cara asked.

"The family might get suspicious," Stosh said. "Maybe old Dan still had some lead in the pencil, if you know what I mean."

"You're sick," she said. She walked over to Cecelia and helped her to her feet. Cecelia didn't say anything to the family; she just kept crying, even as they walked out of the funeral home and to Cara's car.

Stosh lit a cigarette as Cara got Cecelia situated. He noticed a group of young people at the funeral home's entrance who were not there when they'd arrived. They were handing out pamphlets to the mourners as they came out of the service. They carried with them the awkward humility of recovering drug addicts.

One of the young women was a short blonde. She looked familiar, but Stosh couldn't place her. He walked over to the ashtray to punch out his cigarette when she looked up at him and smiled.

"Stosh?" she said.

Stosh's jaw fell open when he realized it was Sara Wilson, his Instagram Evangelist.

"This is the fate of our world," she said with a bright smile.

"Omega's road," her cohort said in response.

Some of the mourners waiting in line heard their bright tone and looked over at them with that southern disgust.

"Oh, gosh, I'm sorry," she said. "Did you know the unalived?"

"I worked with him," he said with a curious smile, the way one does at coincidence, no matter how strange or morbid. "Looks like you made it to Florida, but what's the deal?"

"We're offering grief counseling," she said. "We'd love for you to join us."

She handed Stosh one of their pamphlets and smiled belligerently. He looked at it.

"Location 'TBD'?" he asked.

"Unfortunately, we don't have much of a presence around here yet, so we've been renting out conference rooms at different hotels," she said.

"Plenty of those around."

"If you're interested, I can message you the details."

"Yeah, let's, uh, keep in touch," he said.

"You have to admit, running into each other like this has to be a part of His plan," she said.

"You don't have a copy of that, do you?" Stosh asked.

Sara looked at him with dull confusion.

"It was a joke," he said. "I was asking for a copy of 'His Plan'."

"You know *HIM*?" Sara asked, her eyes screaming with excitement.

Stosh tilted his head like a confused dog.

"Oh, well, soon enough," she said and hurried back to her tribe.

Stosh looked at the pamphlet as Cara drove. On the last page, in small letters at the bottom, it said, "Distributed by Ω House Ministries... Ω: Your Friend at the End." This had never happened to him, not even on the dating apps. He had never met someone from the internet in real life. He once saw Steven Tyler perform the National Anthem at a Patriots game, but that was it, and he could barely make out the very strange-looking man from where their seats were in the stadium. It was a bit unnerving, though still intriguing to see someone emerge from the screen and occupy a shared space. He shrugged, opened the car window, and threw the pamphlet into the breeze.

THAT FRIDAY NIGHT, Zyv met Stosh outside his place. She was wearing her usual linen pants, a pair of well-worn cowboy boots, and a top that revealed the constellation of freckles on her chest. They drove to Lido's. It was an Italian place that Stosh had driven by several times but had never been to. They were both silent on the way over. Stosh wasn't sure what to say, a part of him feeling that what crumbs of passion and desire they'd shared had been wiped off the table, and the other willing to get on his knees and lap them off the floor. After a few minutes, Zyv pulled two nips of vodka from her purse.

"Maybe these will help," she said.

It was as if she could read his mind. They took their shots as they turned into the restaurant's parking lot. In their booth at the back of the lounge, Zyv regarded the décor.

"I thought this place was Italian," she said. "Is that guy wearing a sombrero?"

They laughed at the painted men on the walls, tending to their fields of maze.

"And that one has a poncho on," Stosh said.

They ordered their drinks, and Stosh began to settle into himself.

"How's the scream business these days?" he asked.

"I don't like to think of it as a business," she said. "At least not yet."

"I saw you had a pretty big following online."

"I do all right, but there's a lot of competition," she said. "Everyone is broken, and I'm just trying to help who I can make sense of the pieces they leave behind."

"Maybe I should try it," Stosh said.

"I'm not sure you're ready for it," Zyv smiled slyly.

The waiter refilled their waters and brought more bread.

"So," Stosh said, "you wanted to explain something?"

"At least buy me dinner first," she said.

"It's on its way."

"Don't make fun of me," she said. "Promise?"

"I promise."

She looked at him, her face red and suspicious. "It's just that most people don't get it. They think we're into orgies and key parties, but it's not like that at all."

"You don't have to convince me. I get it," he said.

"Do you?"

"Not at all."

She laughed, said, "It's cool. It's about loving without boundaries, without all the possessiveness and petty jealousies that come with traditional relationships."

"What is?"

"Polyamory."

It was one of many new words Stosh had heard but knew little about. Though somewhat traditional, he'd found himself navigating a whole new world of sexuality, gender, and orientation on the dating apps and was curious.

"So, you see other people?" he asked.

"We're allowed to."

"But do you?"

"It's still kind of new to us," she said. "Our policy now is more like *don't ask, don't tell* when he's deployed."

"He's deployed now?" Stosh asked, the liquor high and warm in his cheeks. "I mean, he was just down here, so I don't want to..."

"He came down to close on the condo," she said. "He has three more months on his current assignment before he moves here, or at least I think that's the plan."

Their food arrived just in time for Stosh to catch his breath and think about his next move. He didn't want to sound like a square, but he was definitely out of his element.

"Are you seeing someone else?" he asked.

"No, not yet."

"Is your husband?"

"Not that I know of," she said.

"And you don't ask."

"And I certainly don't tell," she smiled.

Stosh squirmed in his seat and tried to settle his nerves.

"Seems easy enough," he said.

She laughed, tried to put her hand in front of her mouth to hide the pasta.

"This is the worst veal I've ever had," he said. "How's the eggplant?"

"Tastes like a dish rag."

"I guess we should've been alarmed by the sombreros."

"I'm not scaring you away, am I?" she asked.

"No, but I'm curious—if neither of you is seeing anyone else, why even put a label on it? Why give it a name?"

"Because it's not just about seeing other people, it's about increasing your capacity to love."

Stosh smiled as the waiter dropped off their bill.

"Well, if we're throwing traditions out the window, why don't you pick up the tab?" he said.

"Good try."

Stosh shrugged and pulled out his wallet.

"By the way," she said, "I thought about it, and I'll be the VP."

Stosh smirked, thought about the look on Cletus's face when he learns that his baton-wielding days are over for good, and that the association would grant him no immunity.

Zyv went back to Stosh's place that night, and they watched a movie. *Beneath the Planet of the Apes* was playing on one of the bootleg stations they beamed in off the internet. It was another one of Major's favorites, even though Heston isn't quite the main character. Stosh had always thought the movie campy, but that night it was a nice warm shot of nostalgia.

At first, Zyv and Stosh sat on separate ends of the couch, but after a while, she crept over to him, picked up his arm, and put it over her shoulder. She snuggled into his chest. He stole a glance at the tattoo on her ring finger but tried not to think too much about it. It felt good to be close to someone again, Stosh thought, but he was still a bit apprehensive. He figured that's what love is all about, though. It will always ask, *what will this cost you, and is it worth it?*

CHAPTER ELEVEN

TALKING to Zyv was like having a relationship with a prisoner. There was something daring about it, forbidden, but still safely at a distance.

He teetered between excitement and moral apprehension for days after they went to dinner. One minute he vowed to keep their relationship professional, and the next he was spiraling into fantasies of tantric bliss and ecstatic cahoots.

But who would someone like Stosh turn to for advice in such a situation? A father? His was still locked up. A friend? The girls had their own complications about relationships and infidelity, and Al had only ever loved Lola Costello and a case of Banana Boat.

Who did Stosh have but a priest?

He had been an irregular parishioner at St. John's in Kissimmee since he'd moved down there, but he knew confession was every Saturday afternoon from precisely 3:30 to 3:45, just before evening Mass. He supposed fifteen minutes was enough time to relieve those who could recognize their sins in this swamp, himself included.

It had been years since he'd had any kind of genuine, heartfelt faith in the Church, but he liked the discipline. And the language of the Church was the only one he had to interrogate his conscience, to speak to that weird part of himself we call the soul, though he had to admit that the language was a bit archaic, and the prayers he'd learned and recited since he was a boy didn't make sense to him. This led him to write his own prayer, the Psalm of Saint-Jablonski: "Although I may not know Your name, I have faith that You know mine." It was simple and honest and absolved him of speaking holy words in vain.

Stosh took a seat in the pew closest to the confessional and waited for Father Mulvaney.

"Didn't take you for the church type," Stosh heard a voice say from behind him. He turned and saw Ray standing there with a stack of newspapers under his arm.

"I can say the same thing about you," Stosh said.

"Just here to drop off the latest Catholic Worker," Ray said.

"They still make that?" Stosh asked. "My dad always told me it was commie trash."

"I'm no theologian, but I think Jesus would've leaned left," Ray said. "You should come to our meeting on Friday. We have some great ideas that could help the community."

Stosh smiled nervously and looked back at the confessional as if to make sure Father Mulvaney wasn't listening.

"Free beer and pizza," Ray added.

"I'll see what I can do."

Ray dropped the newspapers by the donation boxes and left. After a few minutes, Father Mulvaney came out, looked around, and nodded at Stosh.

Father Mulvaney was a small man, somewhere in his seventies, though priests seem to age better than the rest of us.

Stosh followed him inside the confessional and took a seat on the other side of the patrician.

"Forgive me, Father, for I have sinned," Stosh started.

"Monsignor."

"What?"

"I'm a Monsignor now."

"Oh," Stosh said. "I'm sorry."

"It's fine," he nodded behind the partition, his head's shadow lurching forward and back again.

"Congratulations, though."

"Thank you."

"Does it come with a pay raise?" Stosh joked.

"What are your sins?" Monsignor asked. "I haven't seen you at Mass lately."

"I suppose I could start there: I haven't been keeping holy the sabbath," Stosh said.

"In this busy world, such a commandment can be the hardest to keep."

"It's hard to find the time," Stosh said. "I work most weekends, and things at home have been tense."

"And that's why it's so important that some things remain sacred," Monsignor said. "I hear Saint Cecelia's has started to live stream their eleven o'clock Mass on Sundays, but I won't allow it here."

"Not a fan of the tube?" Stosh asked.

"Do you know what the word sacred means?" Monsignor asked. "At least one of the meanings?"

"Holy?" Stosh said sheepishly.

"Set aside," Monsignor said. "I tried telling Father Henry that when he told me what he was planning, but he'll have to learn for himself that some things need to be kept sacred. After all, if the language of God is silence, you won't hear it amongst the noise of the internet."

"No wonder you got that promotion," Stosh said.

"I'm sorry. This isn't about me or Father Henry," Monsignor said. "Please continue."

"There are probably more sins than I can remember, but the one I've really been struggling with is pride," Stosh said.

"All too common in this world," Monsignor said.

"But should I be so proud as to turn my nose up at the love God has given me?"

"Can you be more specific?" he said.

"I mean, if a woman were to have romantic feelings for me, and I were to have those same feelings toward her, but I were to deny those feelings, that love, would that make me proud?"

"Is she a woman of faith?"

"In a sense," Stosh said.

"It's a simple question."

"Jesus wants us to be happy, right?" Stosh said. "You said that in a homily once, about the wedding in Cana and the hundred-and-thirty gallons of wine."

"He wouldn't have died if he didn't want us to be happy," Monsignor said.

"Well, what if I met someone who made me happy, but she happened to be married?"

"Jesus isn't in the business of matchmaking," Monsignor said, "but if he were, I doubt he'd be introducing married women to single men."

The Monsignor laughed to himself.

"But what's worse? Pride or adultery?" Stosh asked.

"Why must you choose between the two?"

"I suppose I don't, but for the sake of the argument..."

"If you want my blessing to date a married woman, you are gravely mistaken," Monsignor said, his voice like a gavel.

"Didn't Jacob have two wives?" Stosh wondered aloud.

"Let's stick to the New Testament," Monsignor said.

"I'm sorry for even bringing it up. I guess it does sound ridiculous."

"And sinful."

"Of course, very sinful."

"Seems you have something to confess," Monsignor said.

"Well, that's the thing, I haven't, you know, done anything with her."

"Have you coveted?"

"I was always fuzzy on that definition."

"Have you thought about her in sinful ways?"

"Will no one rid me of this turbulent priest?" Stosh snorted, thinking once again of ecstatic cahoots.

The Monsignor cleared his throat and said, "I believe you have something to confess..."

Stosh apologized again and went through his most recent list of offenses. Monsignor, for his troubles, gave him a penance of two Acts of Contrition and ten Hail Marys, which Stosh ignored in favor of reciting his Psalm of Saint-Jablonski a dozen times.

THAT WEDNESDAY, after work, Stosh met Zyv outside her place, and they walked together to the meeting.

He hadn't told her that he'd gone to see a priest, or that he was struggling with what she'd said. He didn't even know what they were, if there was a "them." He was embarrassed to bring it up. Not only did he fear overthinking the situation, but she seemed to have all the words she needed to discuss her feelings and those messy things like love and relationships that the Catholic Church had taught him required no such language beyond what had been written in the Catechism.

The rest of the Saint-Jablonski cabinet was already in the office when they arrived, with Cletus sitting at the head of the table.

"I hope you don't mind," he said, "but those aluminum chairs kill me."

"You could just switch chairs," Stosh said.

"Work smarter..." Cletus winked. "And who is this?" he said, looking at Zyv with that crooked, incestuous grin.

"Zyvalia has agreed to come on as VP," Stosh said.

"Don't we have to vote?" Birdie asked.

"Sure," Stosh said. "All in favor of electing Zyv to Vice President, raise your hand."

"Are we in session?" Birdie asked. "Should I be taking minutes?"

"Yes, we are now in session," Stosh said. "Let's vote."

And with that, all voted in favor of making Zyv VP.

Cletus insisted on immediately voting for a neighborhood watch. Stosh smirked, thinking Zyv was a sure thing. He hadn't spoken to her about the issue, but he'd assumed she would be against it, too. He figured, as a Millennial, she shared the same vague liberal politics as him, but when it came time for her to vote, she did so in favor of establishing the watch.

"I knew I liked you," Cletus said.

Stosh looked at her, but she just shrugged and said, "I've seen those homeless guys walking in and out of here at night. It can't hurt, especially with those BLM protests still going on."

"I don't think we need a police force," Ray said.

"Think of it as outreach," Zyv said. "A chance to engage with them on a spiritual level."

"I was thinking more of a physical level," Cletus said.

Stosh and Ray laid out the ground rules for Cletus—observe and report, absolutely no Big Boys of the Bygone Day, and nothing more lethal than a flashlight. Stosh wasn't happy, and Ray seemed distraught, having long distrusted the police since his days in the Civil Rights movement.

"I want to go on the record as being vehemently opposed to this," he said. "We need more mutual aid, especially for those of us on fixed incomes."

"We don't need handouts," Cletus said. "And weren't you a lawyer? Shouldn't you be playing golf at the Ridge?"

"Golf is the epitome of bourgeoisie," Ray said. "We need to

earn people's trust back, and I don't see doing that with a private police force."

"Any time you want to chime in, Mister President," Cletus said.

"Ray's right, but majority rules," Stosh said, looking at Ray, though he felt somewhat personally attacked by the golf comment. "But maybe once we get our reserve funds back in the black, we can talk about creating some kind of relief fund for people who need it."

"I suppose now is as good a time as ever," Birdie said. "We have a five-thousand-dollar tax bill."

They all went silent and turned to Stosh.

"What?" he asked. "For what?"

"The church," Birdie said.

"We own that?" Stosh asked.

"For some time," Birdie said.

"Shouldn't it be, like, tax-exempt or something?" Stosh asked.

"It's the religion that's exempt, not the building," Ray said.

Based on what they were able to piece together from some old files on the office computer, and Birdie's memory, the Seventh Congressional Church of Central Florida had owned the property. A preacher they called Killroy had been the pastor there when he married Tara-Lynn. When the church went belly-up and listed the property for sale, Tara-Lynn used Association funds to purchase it, allowing Pastor Killroy to keep on doing the Lord's work, at least until the divorce.

"And you all went along with that?" Cletus scoffed.

"We loved Pastor Killroy. And Tara-Lynn said we needed a church. Said it was a pillar of the community. Said it would increase our property values. Said we'd get a tax break," Birdie explained with a defeated sigh.

Sounded like something Major would come up with, Stosh thought, but it was true; Tara-Lynn amended the condo's master deed to ensure the church could only be used for "religious purposes" and any sale had to be to a "church, religious order, or group for the benefit of the community's spiritual health," which was exactly how the amendment read. But after her divorce from Pastor Kill-roy, the church stood empty, the Association's soul in atrophy, with the back taxes to prove it.

"We can either amend the bylaws or get another church to operate in there," Ray said. "But that doesn't save us from the back taxes."

Cletus shrugged, said, "Should we get a schedule working for neighborhood watch? I know some folks who'd be interested."

"I'm a little more concerned with the tax bill than a few vagrants," Stosh said.

"Broken windows, my friend," Cletus said. "If we let people break the windows, the community will be up in flames in no time."

"Fine. Do whatever you want," Stosh said.

"I'll leave you all to crunch the numbers," Cletus said and left.

"Fascist," Ray said under his breath.

"Is the meeting adjourned?" Birdie asked.

"No, we have to figure this out," Stosh said. "Amending the bylaws is probably our best option. Then we can sell the property to whoever we want."

"The only reason we agreed to use Association money to buy the property was to ensure we'd always have a church," Birdie said. "If we get the votes needed to change the bylaws, who would we sell it to? Whoever it is will raze the hallowed grounds and build what? A parking lot? Another Jocko's? With their sick perversions and *fast* food."

"We may not have another choice," Ray said.

They tossed around ideas for a few minutes to no avail. It pained Stosh to think that they'd survived Tara-Lynn's reign only to be bankrupted by an empty chapel, though maybe it was a sign from God.

Stosh adjourned the meeting in worse shape than they'd been in when he called it to order.

"We can ask my friends for ideas at the meeting on Friday," Ray said to him after the others had left.

Stosh looked at him blankly.

"Remember, free beer and pizza," Ray said. "You're welcome to come, too," he said to Zyv.

"We'd love to," she smiled.

Ray left, and Stosh walked Zyv back to her place.

"I'm not sure you know what you just agreed to," he said to her.

"Free beer and pizza," she said.

"Speaking of which, do you want a drink?" he asked her at the door.

"I'm supposed to FaceTime with David," she said. "Already five minutes late."

"Oh, OK," Stosh said. "Tell him I said hi."

"You're sweet," she said, "but I don't think we're there just yet."

Stosh watched her walk inside. He went back home feeling even more deflated than he had in the meeting. He could feel the humidity between his fingers, invading the rest of his body's pockets and crevices. He stopped by the mailbox only to find a few past-due bills and a menu for a new pizza place that was likely no better than his sombrero-wearing friends over at Lido's. He scanned the menu—unimpressed—but the glossy laminate reminded him of the pamphlet Sara the Instagram Evangelist had given him at Dan's funeral.

Back home on the couch, he messaged her.

"Hello, sister! Let's get together. I think I just got a sign from God."

CHAPTER TWELVE

THAT WHOLE WEEK, Stosh waited for Sara to message him back, but nothing came. He thought about baiting her, crying out for help, or faking possession, but she'd left him on read. He was a little miffed, his ego a bit bruised, but what was he to do?

He soldiered on.

Stosh was looking forward to going out with Zyv that Friday—even if it was to a Catholic Worker meeting—but he still hadn't talked to her about them, what they were, if they were anything at all. Nor had he talked to her about her FaceTime call with her husband, or why she voted to establish a neighborhood watch. He tried to hang onto what hope he could grasp.

Zyv stood waiting by Stosh's car when it was time for them to leave. She looked like Sarah Connor, fresh from the asylum and ready to crack a few metal skulls.

"I got the Mike and Ikes," she said, opening her purse and pulling out a fresh sleeve.

"Nips are in the glovebox," Stosh said as they got in the car.

She pulled out two of the little bottles and handed one to Stosh. They each took a shot and popped a handful of Mike and Ikes to chase it.

"Everything OK?" she asked as they drove.

"Why?"

"You're quiet."

"Just worried."

"About what?"

"All of it."

They were stopped at a red light. Zyv touched his chin and turned his face toward her. She smiled, and the liquor settled in his stomach with a warm breath.

"Do you want to scream with me?" she asked.

"I thought you said I wasn't ready," he said.

"There's only one way to find out," she said.

Stosh gripped the steering wheel.

"It's not about anger," she said.

Zyv counted down, and on three, Stosh let out a throaty screech.

"No," Zyv said. "From deeper."

He touched his belly, but again, she said no. "Deeper than that."

Stosh closed his eyes and reached down below his belly and let out a scream that did not sound like his own. He caught his breath and screamed again. Zyv joined in, and if you didn't know any better, you might have thought they were summoning a pack of wolves.

Stosh screamed so loudly he had tears in his eyes, but the mix of emotions he did not know by name. He fumbled for the right words, he'd settle for a sign, but he found neither. Nothing in his Catholic lexicon or its collage of icons could he conjure to make sense of this feeling. Surely there was a Yiddish phrase, or some Polish-American amalgam that would suffice, but even those failed him. His tongue fluttered in the dark pit of his mouth, a flurry of wet clucks and snaps—nothing but a scream.

"All that condo stuff is not now," Zyv said softly, taking his face in her hands. "Be in your body. Breathe."

She kissed him, and he tried to keep that moment forever.

"I love you," he said, his eyes closed, his face still in her hands.

"I know," she said.

He opened his eyes and looked upon her freckled face. He did not believe in love at first sight. He'd known Bambi since they were kids, and it wasn't until their sophomore year that they started dating. It took him nearly a year to say those words to her, but he was just a kid back then, who didn't know what he was saying. Now here he was, a grown man, telling a married woman he'd known only for a few weeks that he loved her. But this felt different than anything that had come before it. Maybe it was because of what happened at Jocko's. Maybe it was just trauma-bonding, but he didn't regret saying it. He wished she'd said it back, but her smile said it all, or at least that's how it felt.

The light turned green, and they each took another shot after passing through the intersection.

The scene inside the VFW was mixed—a nineties cover band played to a crowd of young locals and pickled Vietnam Vets on the bar side, and Ray and his comrades sat at particleboard tables in the banquet hall.

"I think they're communists," Stosh said to Zyv.

"Politics isn't really my thing," she said. "I'll be on the dance floor."

Stosh took note of the other comrades, many of whom seemed to be in their twenties and absent the usual markings and utilitarian fashion of the working class or young radicals. Not a Che Guevara shirt in sight. Ray approached and didn't even greet Stosh before pitching him on the idea of using the church as a Catholic Worker Community. Stosh waffled. Owners won't go for it, no matter how he spun it, even if they were a religious organization as defined by the bylaws. No, the community wouldn't go for liberation theology. They needed some old-time religion, so Stosh countered Ray's offer with his own.

"And they're definitely not some prosperity gospel grifters?"

Ray asked when Stosh told him about Sara and the Last Man Ministries.

"I promise," Stosh said.

Stosh poured himself a glass of warm beer but politely refused his free slice of pizza. He thought about what his father would have to say about him going to a communist party meeting, though it seemed all these communists were interested in doing was talking and drinking cheap domestic beer, which seemed about as American as one could get. After a few minutes, he excused himself and went to the bar. He watched as Zyv danced with several boys, all of whom looked hungry and drunk beneath the flashing blue and purple lights. Zyv, at first, didn't seem to pay them any mind, but then she started dancing with one of them, doing some kind of swing. They revolved around each other, and the boy dipped her low as the band finished *A Semi-Charmed Life*.

Zyv laughed and clapped with the boys as Stosh sat at the bar, hot and defeated. He felt like a chump. He could see Al shaking his head, chuckling at him for going out with her. He looked around at all the other chumps and losers at the bar and spotted Fred at the end, scowling behind a glass of cold domestic swill. Had he seen him with Ray and the other communists? No doubt, the red-blooded, hot-dog-eating veteran of a foreign war harbored a belligerent fear of the Red Menace. Stosh looked back at the banquet hall—there were no signs or markings. There was no way Fred could've known what he was doing, not to mention it was all for the sake of the community. It wasn't like he was plotting a coup. He was, after all, already the president. He ordered a shot and tried to drown the paranoia and anxiety, but it was no use.

He looked over and saw that Zyv had joined the boys at their table and was taking shots with them. He decided to call it a night.

"Stosh!" Zyv said with a loving grin as he approached. "This is Chad, Jaxon, and Jameson."

The boys looked Stosh up and down and took on sour faces.

"I'm taking off if you want a ride, or maybe one of these kids can bring you home later."

"What's wrong?"

"I'm tired and don't feel like being here."

"Come on," she said, "don't be like that. Just be in your body."

"It's not that," he said, eyeing the boys at the table.

"Oh, stop. I'm just having fun."

"That's fine, but you can do it without me."

Stosh walked away, hoping she'd follow, but all she said was, "Get home safe," in a kind of maternal tone that stung him deep in his Freudian guts.

Gator was on the back porch when he got home. He'd gotten into the dumpster and was feasting on the carcass of a rotisserie chicken. He picked at the thing, one of its ribs getting caught on his growing tusks.

"That stays out here," Stosh said. "I'll let you in when you're finished."

Gator stood there on the porch, the chicken hanging out of his mouth as Stosh closed the door. Inside, he poured himself a shot, refilled the bong, and took a seat on the couch. He remembered this feeling—the jealousy, the hurt—and he hated it. He remembered exactly why he'd stopped dating after Bambi. But he had no one to blame but himself. It wasn't as if he and Zyv were together, and she'd only been honest with him. She was married for Christ's sake. He started feeling guilty for being salty, for leaving her at the bar.

He let Gator in after a few minutes and threw out the rest of the chicken carcass.

The pot had gotten to his head. He couldn't stop thinking of all the nightmare scenarios that could befall Zyv. He teetered between jealousy and concern. Why had he left her there? She's probably in the back seat of one of those douche bag's cars, or maybe she's in his trunk. Why did he leave her there? What an asshole.

He tried to chase these thoughts away with more liquor, but before he knew it, he was gone.

A rapping at the door woke him. It took him a minute to get his bearings. He checked his phone—five missed calls from Zyv. Panic shot like a jolt of caffeine to his brain and spiraled down to his bowels. The knocking continued. Gator woke up with shared confusion.

Stosh went to the door. Zyv was there, her big smile nearly taking up the width of the threshold.

"You still pissy?" she said, her eyes drunk and glossy.

"Sorry about that."

"It's not a good look on you," she said.

"I know."

"You'll learn," she said, walking into the kitchen. She kicked off her shoes and threw her wallet on the table, where the dried husks of various bugs—all of which were exotic to Stosh—lay waiting for some larger pest to gobble them up. She went over to Gator and patted him on the head.

Stosh looked outside toward the mailboxes and thought he saw Fred's slender frame. The figure moved away from the mailboxes and bobbed into the hedgerows.

"Who brought you home?" Stosh asked, closing the door and following Zyv into the living room.

"Fred."

"Our Fred?"

She laughed, said, "I guess you could call him that."

"I didn't even know he could drive."

"He could tonight," she smiled and took a seat on the couch.

"What's that supposed to mean?" Stosh demanded, feeling the vodka rise up his throat, the saliva thicken behind his molars.

"Now, now," she said, pulling Stosh toward her by the belly of his shirt. "This is your second warning."

She was drunk, and he was somewhere beyond that, closer to a hangover than a buzz. He forced a smile and averted his eyes the best he could without offending her, but she wasn't going anywhere.

They began to kiss, her breath sour and labored. She took off her shirt and started to unbutton his.

"I don't think this is a good idea," he said.

"That's why I'm doing it when I'm drunk."

"I don't want it to be like that," he said.

"Most men wouldn't hesitate."

Stosh thought about her husband, those boys at the VFW. Who was he to deny what little love God was willing to tip him?

"I figured that's why you liked me," he said.

"Now you're getting it."

He stood up and followed her to his bedroom. She wiggled out of her pants and sat on the bed.

They kissed. His tongue chased after hers but couldn't keep up. She pulled away briefly so he could take off his pants, then she got on top of him. They each released a sigh. He felt his had been trapped somewhere deep in his lungs.

"Stosh," she whispered as she moved up and down, sliding occasionally from side to side, their sweat slick and warm against his thighs.

"Jablonski," she said with a kind of sweetness he'd never heard his name said with before. She was gentler than he imagined she'd be, but still strong. "Jablonski," she said again, clutching the Polish chicken on his bicep. She breathed his name, like a mantra. He wiggled beneath her, her legs straddling his narrow hips. They were both so skinny that there was little flesh to shield their shuffling bones. "Jablonski," she said again, this time in a higher pitch, but still gently. It was the first time he'd heard his name spoken with such soft passion. He wasn't being laughed at or scolded; it wasn't spoken with snickering sarcasm or irony. "Jablonski," she continued until he couldn't take it anymore. He tried to think of something that would allow him to avoid disappointment—nuns! He thought of Sister Mavis, one of his grade-school teachers, but then he began to lose his erection, a fate worse than arriving too early, so he had to pivot. He thought he'd found the perfect balance when he remembered the porno DVD he'd come across while cleaning out the parish rectory as punishment for laughing during Mass—*Nuns: A Dirty Habit*, but that only brought him shame. Dead puppies, he thought to himself as he squeezed Zyv's thigh, finally finding a balance and working his confidence back. Dead puppies!

Zyv had lit something in him he hadn't felt in a long time. Maybe it was passion, maybe frustration, or perhaps desire, but it was something—something more than shame, disappointment, or regret. It was something beyond what he could describe, just more wet clucks and hisses, but whatever it was, he certainly hadn't felt it with Dana or in the wires between him and Sara.

Zyv dug her nails into his back, and they went at each other like dogs. He wanted to last forever. He wanted to kill her husband and those smug boys at the VFW. He was mad with love's inevitable grief. He knew that he would have to eventually pull out, possibly never to return. He had slipped into a rhythm, his confidence returning to him in pulses of white heat behind his eyelids. But, perhaps, he had gotten ahead of himself when, now in another position, he smacked his head against the headboard in a mad thrust.

"Fuck!"

She laughed, her teeth a string of pearls in the darkness. He, too, wheezed with delight.

Her laugh returned to her belly, then she went quiet, save for a few whimpers, until she finally tensed up and squeezed him tightly across the back. She squirmed away, shaking and sticky with all that their bodies had to offer.

He rolled away from her and didn't bother to clean himself off. She breathed heavily. Neither of them said a thing. After a minute, she put her head on his chest, and the world was again small and simple and everything he could have ever worried about was now nothing more than a pestering mosquito to be swatted away and squashed underfoot.

"Jablonski," she said one last time, her voice heavy with liquor and exhaustion.

She fell asleep, but he was still vibrating. After a few minutes, he slipped out from beneath her and went to the living room for a cigarette. He opened the window and lit one. The blue smoke hung like lace curtains in the thick air. He could hear the dew forming on the grass, the crickets and bull frogs in their nightly debate, and the exhausted clicks and groans of his neighbors' labored air-conditioners. Across the street, Cletus's *Thin Blue Line* lamp glowed blue behind his living room window, then flickered out.

Stosh puffed slowly on his cigarette, his lungs warm and raw. From across the room, he saw his phone light up.

He walked over, pulled it from the charger, and looked at it— one new message from Sara Wilson.

"*He* was right about you!" it read.

CHAPTER THIRTEEN

THE HEAT COVERED Stosh like a blanket. The air conditioner groaned on in his room, but it didn't seem to be working, and the heat that radiated from Zyv's body made it impossible for him to fall back to sleep once the sun cracked through the window.

He pulled his arm out from beneath her head, but she barely moved. He was sweating, dehydrated, and felt as shriveled as the dead bugs that littered the kitchen. He swung his legs around and righted himself. His head was still heavy with alcohol, and he didn't want to be alive in that moment.

Zyv huffed and rolled over as he stood up. He chased the fireflies from his vision and made his way to the bathroom.

Al was sitting on the couch.

"I was just about to wake you up," he said.

"Take the truck. I'm not going in."

"Jesus, man. You look like shit."

"Imagine how I feel."

"Stosh," Zyv groaned from the bedroom, "can you get me some water?"

Al perked up, raising his eyebrows. "Are you serious?" he whispered.

"Please, not now."

Al shook his head. "I suppose you want me to take Gator out, too."

"You're a lifesaver."

Al didn't say anything. He just grabbed Stosh's keys from the hook, whistled for Gator, and walked out the door.

Stosh filled two glasses of water, but before he could make it back to his bedroom, he had to hit the head. What came out was nothing but a slur of hollow barks and a string of yolky bile.

After he'd cleaned himself up, he called Ketch and told him he wouldn't be coming in.

Zyv was lying in bed, scrolling on her phone, when Stosh returned to his bedroom.

"I'll never get used to this heat," he said.

"This is nothing," Zyv said. "I grew up in Central America. Dad was with the State Department. You try doing wind-sprints in a Nicaraguan summer."

"No wonder you're in such good shape."

"Yoga helps, too, and I'm on an ancestral diet," she said. "Berries, nuts..."

"And Mike and Ikes," Stosh smiled.

"Everyone has a vice," she said.

Stosh watched the video on Zyv's phone. *Evangeline Sorenson Channels the Galactic Counsel.*

"Far out," Stosh said in a nasally southern Californian accent.

"Laugh all you want, Evangeline saved my life," Zyv said.

"That so?" Stosh asked, leaning back on his elbows.

"I went into a deep depression after the trial, and it wasn't until I found Evangeline's page that I was able to find my truth, to speak it in the most powerful tongues I'd ever heard."

"Trial?" Stosh asked.

"You didn't check out my Instagram after I accepted your follow request?" Zyv asked, seeming slightly embarrassed.

"I skimmed it," he assured her.

Zyv took on a serious look, her bright eyes dulled by her sudden shift in mood. She took a deep breath and said, "I was responsible for killing a girl."

Stosh held his breath until his cheeks warmed and his face felt swollen. The way she said it, so legalistically, made it sound rehearsed, as if lawyers had coached her to recite it time and time again in this specific way.

After a minute, he asked, "What exactly does that mean?"

"A girl I went to school with killed herself, and I was held responsible. Involuntary manslaughter," she said matter-of-factly. "I was in high school, and you know how kids can be, especially girls. You might have heard of her—Adeline Richards."

"You were part of the Fairview Five?" Stosh asked.

Zyv hung her head. Stosh's face turned red, and he felt sick again. The case had made national headlines. He was in high school back then and remembered sitting through an assembly on cyber-bullying and harassment after it happened. From what he could remember, Zyv wasn't the only person involved, but she was the only one who faced charges. She was dating a guy who cheated on her with a lower classman. Zyv and a group of other seniors harassed the girl online, catfishing and doxing her until she finally snapped and killed herself on a live stream. His stomach churned and gurgled. His throat warmed, and his scalp turned slick with regret. Zyv didn't seem like the type to act out of spite. Such jealous behavior didn't square with her open relationship, but maybe the ordeal was why she was non-monogamous. It'd make sense, he thought, someone who went through such an incident rejecting traditional relationships for something more fluid and understanding. I mean, he'd done plenty of stupid, hurtful things when he was a kid. No, he wasn't a bully, and he'd never harassed someone to the point of suicide, but he'd lied, he'd cheated on his homework, and stolen cash from Major's wallet. But involuntary manslaughter? The words stuck between his teeth like gristle. Sounded worse than regular old murder. His stomach contracted. The sweat pooled behind his knees.

Zyv curled into a little spoon. She took Stosh's hand, pulled it over her body, and settled it between her breasts. "I was young and stupid back then. We had just moved back to the States, and I was trying to fit in. There's so much more to the story than what the lying mainstream media said, but all that's in the past. Evangeline taught me to use the internet for good, to empower people. It's only love now," she said, tapping her heart with his hand, then settling back on her left breast.

Who was he to judge another's experience? To do such a thing was to question someone's whole identity and purpose, and because he was someone who owned nothing but his story, who was in the middle of his own redemption arc, he wasn't going to undermine the power of narrative, for if through the alchemy of an origin story, Zyv could build something beautiful from the rubble of her own tragedy, then Stosh was OK with it. After all, everyone has their plotki.

They lied like that for a while until Zyv fell back to sleep, Stosh waking her only when his arm went numb and he could no longer wait to use the bathroom. Stosh watched her get out of bed and gather her clothes.

"I hope this doesn't change anything between us," she said as she pulled her hair back up into a messy top bun, her bare breasts rising and falling with the motion and a coy smile blossoming on her face.

"I don't think anything could change this feeling," he said.

After she left, Stosh went to the bathroom where he doomscrolled and hoped to exercise his hangover through his lower intestine. He looked up Evangeline Sorenson's Instagram account. He scrolled through it, watching old videos and reading the many memes, pithy and positive proverbs that she posted, all of which were written in beautiful calligraphy and superimposed against vistas of green pastures or fields of elegant flowers. "Sadness," one of them read, "is caused by the trauma of non-consensual birth." Stosh wasn't sure what that meant, but it sounded elevated. She claimed to be an ambassador for something called the Intergalactic Association of Channelers, which sounded like his own position at the condo—just banal enough to be believed. Stosh remembered all those abduction stories he'd listened to on the Apeus Dei channel and countless other podcasts. Again, who was he to judge, especially if she was preaching self-love.

Stosh exited her profile and got back to business. He messaged Sara about the church. She said they were still looking for a building. Said they were interested, but he didn't want to make any promises until he spoke to the other board members.

Ray was willing to meet with them to discuss it, and Zyv was as well.

Cletus, however, was a hard no.

"I know guys who were on the job in Clearwater when those damned Scientologists started moving in. They own the town now," he said on the phone. "Crazy Cult."

"These are Christians, not Scientologists," Stosh said.

"You met them online?" Cletus asked.

"That's kind of the way the world works now," Stosh said.

"I've done my fair share of online dating and let me tell you something—what you swipe for is not what you usually get," he said. "You guys agree to this, and you'll have a fight on your hands," Cletus said.

"Is that a threat?"

"It's a guarantee," he said before hanging up on Stosh.

Birdie was uneasy about it, too. "I've heard rumors about these people," she said.

"What people? You haven't even met them."

"They're called the Disciples of the Last Man, or something like that," she said. "Sophie Saltus, over in twenty-nine, her husband, Wrecks, joined them and went crazy. He was the one who shot up Jocko's. Sitting in some federal prison up north as we speak."

The back of Stosh's neck warmed at the thought of that night. He looked at his hands and thought he saw those splinters again, crawling beneath his skin, but he swatted the hallucination away.

Birdie sucked her teeth, said, "They can hack your soul."

"I'm not sure I know what that means," Stosh said.

With few options, Stosh, Zyv, and Ray planned to meet with Sara and her leader that Monday.

Sara showed up first, chaperoned only by an Uber driver, who dropped her off by the office door.

"Let's wait down in the office," Ray said. "Get out of this heat."

"She looks familiar," Zyv whispered to Stosh, who could only offer a shrug in response.

"Brother Roland will be here shortly," Sara said, taking a seat at the table and pulling a notebook from her bag.

Moments later, the office door opened, and there came a tall white man in the kind of streetwear more common to mumble rappers and skateboarders—baggy pants, dark sunglasses, and a ridiculous tie-died bucket hat—than to a man of God. And he had a small cross tattoo beneath his right eye that suggested an air of narcotic violence, and his teeth glowed an unnatural shade of ivory.

The man took off his hat as he entered the room, revealing a shock of gold hair, and with great, Biblical strides, he approached the board's ceremonial poker table.

"Kadoosh, Kadoosh, I say to you," the big thing said. "I am Brother Roland."

Stosh ignored the babble and introduced the board. Brother Roland did little to hide his wandering eye as Zyv took her seat.

"I spoke to Sara, and she said you're looking for a church," Stosh said to him.

"We already have a church," Brother Roland said. "We're simply looking for a place to put it."

"You probably saw it on your way in," Stosh said.

"It needs some work, but not bad," Brother Roland said.

"Do you think it'll hold your congregation?" Ray asked.

"We don't have in-person services," Brother Roland said.

"How do you mean?" Ray asked.

"The Spirit of the Lord is all around us," Brother Roland assured the board. "He's in the fiber optics, the Wi-Fi! Like the Kingdom of Heaven, nothing ever dies on the internet."

Stosh did what he could to hide his smile and then asked, "But do you think the building is a good fit?"

"Of course," Brother Roland said. "We hope to use it for our studio."

"I'm sorry, Roland...," Stosh started to say.

"Brother Roland," Sara corrected him, lifting her head out of her notebook.

"Are you taking minutes?" Stosh asked her.

"Transcribing the words of our prophet," she said.

"I really don't follow," Stosh said, looking at Ray.

"You see, our ministry is not corporeal," Brother Roland said. "We have an online presence, and we hope to rent the building to record our services."

"It's completely online?" Ray asked.

"We have thousands of followers on Instagram, don't we, Sara?" Brother Roland asked her.

"Eighty-two thousand," Sara said, peeking at her phone.

"And what about TikTok?" Brother Roland asked.

"Another thirty thousand," Sara said. "Up five hundred followers from last week."

Stosh and Ray stole a glance at one another.

"But you're a *real* church?" Stosh asked. "Tax-exempt and everything?"

"Of course," Brother Roland said. "Once we're in here, it'll all be official, both spiritually and judiciously."

"What do you mean, 'once you're in here'?" Ray asked.

"In order to gain tax-exempt status, a church needs a physical location," Sara said. "A house of worship."

"Sara speaks the truth," Brother Roland said.

"Can't you see, we're a part of something new, something better," Sara said, looking up to Brother Roland's pale face.

"I think what Sara means is that we are not directly affiliated with any specific denomination," Brother Roland said. "We're neo-fundamentalists."

"Sounds like an oxymoron," Ray said.

"Sadly, most have strayed from the Lord's true teachings, the Kabbalah Incarnate, the roots of which still feed our trees of wisdom," Brother Roland continued. "We are something of a revival, like the old tent churches, but our roads are not paved."

"The internet is our highway, and social media is our tent," Sara said. "The universal road to Damascus."

"That all sounds fine, but we have certain obligations on our end," Ray said. "That church is a part of our property, and a tax-exempt religion must occupy it."

Brother Roland then produced a wad of cash, hundreds mostly, and placed it on the table.

"We have the first three months of rent right here, and I'm confident we'll qualify for tax-exempt status as soon as we move in," he smiled. "Is the building being used for anything now?"

"We use it once a year for our annual meeting," Ray said.

"And some AA groups use the basement for meetings," Stosh said.

"That might have to change," Brother Roland said.

"It's only once a year, and typically at night," Stosh said.

"Your annual meeting shouldn't be a problem," Brother Roland said. "We would have to ask the AA groups to go elsewhere or utilize our own healing programs."

"Those groups have been there for a long time," Ray said.

"They're very popular," Stosh added. "I've heard they do a lot of good."

"They think they do a lot of good, but like a lot of churches, it seems AA, too, has lost its way," Brother Roland said. "They were founded and rooted in Yeshua, but have since relented to secular pressures, requiring their participants not to relinquish their wills to Yahweh but to a 'higher power'."

"Whatever that is," Sara said, her head still buried in her notebook.

"And you offer some kind of alternative?" Stosh asked.

"Of course," Brother Roland said. "Many of our followers are in recovery. We actively seek them out, but we believe it's a problem of the soul, not of the flesh."

Zyv poked Stosh's leg beneath the table. He looked at her and then at Ray and nodded.

"Well, we really appreciate you meeting with us," Stosh said. "We still have to run it by the other board members, but can we get back to you later this week?"

"Of course, my child. You can reach out to Sara," Brother Roland said, standing up and placing his bucket hat back on his head. "Until next time, kadoosh onto you!"

Sara closed her notebook, put it in her bag, and followed him out the door.

"What choice do we have?" Stosh lamented. "I mean, that wad of cash would have taken care of the tax bill, and everything on top of that could go into rebuilding our reserve fund."

"I say we bring it to the community, lay out our options, let them choose," Ray said.

"Wash our hands of the decision?" Stosh said.

"It worked for Pontius Pilot," Ray said.

The Fourth Letter of Saint-Jablonski
to the People of the Association

Dear community members,

The board hopes you're all enjoying your summer, despite the pool remaining closed. Rest assured, we're still working on finding a solution to the ooze.

We regret to inform you of further bad news, specifically regarding the church.

We find ourselves in a difficult position, having to either find a new religious organization to operate in the church or amend our bylaws to sell it to a non-religious entity. We know that many of you want to keep the church, and the board agrees it can be a useful and vital part of the community, so long as the right people are operating in it.

With that said, included in this letter is a QR code that's linked to a survey. We ask that you scan the code and vote on how you'd like us to proceed and provide any comments or feedback you'd like. The surveys are completely anonymous, so please be honest. And for those of you who would rather discuss the issue in person, we'll be holding special office hours all week.

We can't wait to hear from you.

Your public servant,

Stanislaus (Stosh) Saint-Jablonski

President

CHAPTER FOURTEEN

THE SURVEYS TRICKLED IN, and although everyone had an opinion, there were few constructive comments. Stosh went down to the office every morning to check the results. A week after he'd sent out the letter, he was in the basement, reviewing the most recent batch of responses, when he was greeted by such poetry as, *Circumcise your heart of sin! Repent now!,* and *I don't care what we do, as long as Saint-Jablonski eats glass and shits blood!*

Stosh didn't think Fred knew how to use a smartphone, let alone a QR code, and although that first message sounded like something Sara or Brother Roland would say, he hadn't heard from them since their meeting, leading Stosh to believe he'd inspired such passionate responses from yet even more disgruntled and violent community members.

He continued scrolling through the results, telling himself they hated the position, not the man.

The computer was an old HP that lagged whenever you had too many tabs open in the browser and was only used to keep the books, but Stosh navigated to a file on the desktop labelled "Personal" and opened it. Inside that folder were several other folders, one labelled "Insurance", another "Divorce" and one labelled "Damn Dirty Ape." Stosh immediately heard his father reciting the famous line from *Planet of the Apes* in his best Heston impression. Stosh clicked on the file and was greeted by a dick pic of his father's uncut member, Major's Polish eagle tattoo visible in the picture, too, along with the bottom half of his stubbled face.

"Jesus!" Stosh winced, looking away from the screen.

He wanted to bleach his eyes. He always had a feeling Major and Tara-Lynn had a fling, even if they both denied it. Cold Springs was a small town, with an even smaller population of single grifters with a thirst for petty crime—it would have made sense—but based on Tara-Lynn's lackluster responses to the innumerable dirty pictures Major had sent her, it appeared he was in a long-distance relationship with himself, rifling off one poorly lit and unrequited full-frontal after another and stopping only after he convinced her to help Stosh move to Florida, his digital abstinence a condition of the deal. Stosh scanned through their email threads, fearing that Major had somehow played a role in the missing money, but found no evidence that he had aided or abetted Tara-Lynn in her scheme.

A barbed chill ran up Stosh's spine at the thought of Major and Tara-Lynn, and he all but lost what little was in his stomach when he thought about the possibility of Bambi being his stepsister.

The office door swung open and Zyv and Ray entered the room, momentarily relieving Stosh of his morbid daydreams. He shut the computer monitor off and spun around to greet them. He did his best to bury his disgust and filled them in on the most recent surveys but spared them the blood shitting comment and his father's penis.

They counted the votes, but they were still miles away from a quorum. Stosh was occupied with images of his father mounting Tara-Lynn when Zyv chimed in.

"Maybe we're thinking about this all wrong," she said. "The

language in the bylaws is pretty vague. Why are we limiting ourselves to Christianity?"

"It doesn't matter who takes over the property so long as they're tax-exempt," Ray said.

But before Zyv could respond, Cletus came barreling in, the letter in one hand and his phone in the other.

"Stupid thing doesn't work," he said, pointing to the QR code. "I vote no, to all of it."

Stosh pulled at his wiry hair. As if the morning couldn't get any worse, this buffoon comes clomping in.

"Maybe you can help come up with a solution instead of marching around here like the Gestapo," Ray said.

Stosh cleared his throat and tried to compose himself. He nodded in agreement with Ray and then turned to Zyv.

"As I was just about to say, maybe we can get some of my collaborators to rent the church," she said. "I know a lot of people online who'd love an opportunity to run IRL retreats out of there."

"I don't know what any of that means, but it sounds like something I don't like," said Cletus.

Stosh threw his hands in the air. Zyv touched his arm and shook her head. "Embrace your power," she said quietly.

"Taking advice from your mistress now?" Cletus asked.

Stosh turned red and averted his eyes.

"Yeah, I know all about you two," Cletus said. "Fred told me he dropped her off at your place late one night. Sleeping with your neighbor's wife. A serviceman on duty. Shows who you are. Makes me think you're not all that different than your father with all your schemes. Didn't take me too long on the Google to find out all about him. Seven years. Fraud. Conspiracy. Seems like the apple doesn't fall too far from the tree."

Sweat pooled beneath Stosh's eyes. He thought about his father's penis on the computer behind him, his scalp again slick with regret, but Zyv touched his arm, lifted her chin in defiance and smirked as if she'd just seen a future in which grotesque men like Cletus were not welcomed.

"I had my doubts about you," Stosh said to Cletus, "but I was really hoping you'd prove me wrong."

"And I thought you knew what you were doing," Cletus said. "Weren't you the Vice President? I mean, what the hell were you doing these past few years, other than being Tara-Lynn's little puppet?"

"I'm trying here," Stosh said. "If anyone else thinks they can do a better job, they're welcome to try."

"In that case, I nominate myself," Cletus said.

"You can't be president. You're a renter, not an owner," Stosh kindly reminded him.

"Then I propose a vote of no confidence," Cletus said.

"You can only do that if you're on the board," Stosh said.

"What, you're kicking me off?" Cletus asked.

"Seems like you have your hands full with the neighborhood watch and your arbitration case with the department."

Cletus shook his head violently, his jowls flapping and making a sound like that of someone vigorously stirring a pot of mac and cheese.

"I'm done with all this talk," he said, "but I can guarantee if you try any more cockamamie ideas, you're going to have a mutiny on your hands."

Cletus stormed out of the office and slammed the door behind him.

Ray took a seat at the computer, pulled the glasses from his nose and rubbed his eyes.

Stosh stood there, his fingertips pulsating, his palms sweating and his face flushed with adrenaline. His scab from the splinter wound itched. He felt his vision constrict, and for a moment he couldn't catch his breath, but then Zyv placed her hand on his chest and his lungs filled with relief. She smiled, her confidence wafting off her and filling the air like pollen. She need not say anything for Stosh could feel her pride.

Brother Roland and Sara wouldn't save them, and Cletus and his Big Boys of the Bygone Day were nothing but a liability, but Zyvalia Anders and Stanislaus Saint-Jablonski might just have the magic!

Stosh smiled, but his victory was short lived as Ray swung around in the swivel chair and reached for the computer.

"No!" Stosh said, his shriek causing Zyv to jump, but it was too late, and the three of them were greeted by Major Saint-Jablonski's penis.

"Stosh!" Zyv said, stepping back.

"It's not what you think," Stosh stammered. "It's not porn," he said, taking a deep breath before adding, "That's my father's penis."

Ray, who often wavered between stern contemplation and solemnity, recoiled in disgust and confusion.

"What the hell are you talking about?" Zyv asked.

"I mean, I just found that," Stosh said, but Zyv was inching toward the door, and Ray had stepped away from the computer in fear of being implicated by what was on the screen.

After attempting to Gish gallop his way out of the dick pics and the nature of his relationship to Tara-Lynn, it was apparent neither Zyv nor Ray had any appetite for word salad, so Stosh had no choice but to confess his crimes. He told Ray and Zyv that he'd signed the paperwork that allowed Tara-Lynn to take the money, and that he was only able to move to the association because his father had negotiated a deal in which she'd lend Stosh the money for a down payment in exchange for his loyalty and, apparently, a moratorium on dick pics. But getting this all off his chest brought him no relief, just more shame.

Ray looked at him, opened his mouth, but then paused.

"I don't remember doing it, but my signature's on the paperwork," Stosh pleaded. "I was a patsy, I swear!"

Ray folded his arms and stole a glance at Zyv.

"Think about it. Why would I put up with all this if I was in on it, if I had the money to leave?" Stosh said. "You have to believe me!"

"And what Cletus said about your father?" Zyv asked.

"It's all true. Had this whole scheme about flipping 'eco-friendly' houses and green tax breaks," Stosh said, the sweat now so visible on his face you might have thought he'd been water-boarded. "And it's like every day I'm here, I'm repaying his debts. I'm trying to cover the bill for the life he gave me off the backs of others. And I truly believe we have an opportunity to create something beautiful here. Something that would put all that phony hope and change to shame. Something real and working."

Stosh looked back at the computer before locking eyes with Zyv, whose face had relaxed, her eyebrows no longer sharp and menacing, and said, "I don't know what all that is on the computer. I guess my dad was banging Tara-Lynn, or trying to bang her, or sexually harassing her, but whatever it was, I had nothing to do with it, not that part, and now he's locked up, and she's gone, and I have no one but you guys to help clean this mess up."

Stosh was sweating again, the tips of his ears smoldering with guilt and panic.

Ray and Zyv exchanged glances, their doubt still obvious, their disgust with the penis on the screen behind Stosh still palpable, but their anger was now replaced by something close enough to sympathy that Stosh felt comfortable wiping the tears from his cheek.

Ray moved over to Stosh and placed his arm around him, said something about a John Berryman poem that went over Stosh's head, though he appreciated the sentiment all the same. It was a kind gesture, certainly one that Stosh didn't deserve. The embrace of a parent forgiving their child. Not mad, just disap-pointed.

After a moment, Zyv felt compelled to join in and she too embraced Stosh, the three of them in their little struggle session, eating the communal sin so that they may start again. After some back rubs and generic affirmations, they went about negotiating the terms of their own agreement. In exchange for his discretion and continued legal services, Ray would use Tara-Lynn's old condo to set up a local Catholic Worker Community; and for her secrecy, Zyv would organize a spiritual program for the church, so long as Ray's research proved it to be legal, though she now seemed less than enthusiastic about the idea.

"You OK with that?" Stosh asked her.

"Mmhmm," she said, mindlessly picking at a fingernail.

Stosh smiled nervously and rubbed her shoulder, but it might as well have been cold as ice.

"I'd usually suggest getting all this in writing," Ray said, "but considering the nature of our plan, I'd have to recommend forgoing that formality, though we should memorialize it in some way."

Lacking the proper instruments or intestinal fortitude required of a blood oath, Stosh recommended that, as a sign of good faith and camaraderie, they go to the computer and delete the cache of dick pics from the hard drive. They gathered around the monitor, each placing a finger on the mouse, and then dragged the file to the recycle bin before wiping it from the computer altogether.

CHAPTER FIFTEEN

FOURTH OF JULY brought the hottest week of the summer, and although Stosh now had a plan for the church, and he was looking forward to seeing Calvin, who was in town visiting Cecelia, he was still restless.

He and Zyv hadn't talked about what happened in the office. Zyv said she wasn't mad, but she was noticeably silent the few times they'd hung out since that day. Stosh wanted to do something nice for her, but she hadn't seemed impressed with the hydrangeas he'd bought her, though she still agreed to go to the party with him.

They were driving to Cecelia's when Stosh stopped abruptly to let Gail McKitch's son cross the street.

Adam had all the trappings of a homeless addict—the backpack, the plastic bags full of God-knows-what, and the labored gait of someone whose body was failing him. Even from a distance, you could see how the needle had bloated him.

"Our very own Boo Radley," Stosh said to Zyv. "Cletus worries too much, though. We need more sympathy, not foot patrols."

Zyv didn't say anything. She just nodded and popped another Mike and Ike into her mouth.

"How are those hydrangeas doing?" Stosh asked. "They used to grow wild in our backyard."

"You don't have to hide anything from me," Zyv said abruptly.

"I know."

"Then why did you?"

"I don't know. I guess I wasn't ready."

"And now you are?"

"I don't have a choice," Stosh said.

Zyv turned and looked out her window as the Ridge came into view.

"I was embarrassed," he said. "I was afraid. I didn't know what people would do if they knew I allowed Tara-Lynn to take the money, and if they learned that she had loaned me the down payment to buy my place, and that my dad was in prison for fraud and apparently had some kind of relationship with her, I figured no one would believe that I was innocent, or even ignorant of what she was doing."

"You need to embrace your power," Zyv said as they pulled up to the Ridge's security gate, where Henry was stationed in the kiosk.

"There's the kid," he said. "Who are we going to see today? Dana, Cecelia and the kids?"

"The latter," Stosh said. "I thought you were off on Saturdays."

"This is my last overtime shift," he said. "My son is about to graduate from college. Never thought he'd put down those stupid video games and finish his degree, but he'll be taking care of me soon enough."

Stosh smiled as Henry opened the gate.

They drove up the Ridge's main road. Those gaudy red GOOP (Glory of Our Past) signs still littered the lawns as if the president hadn't won.

"Dana?" Zyv asked. "Van Ronk?"

"You know her?"

"She came to a few classes when I was teaching yoga at the Y," she said. "How do you know her?"

"I gave her a few lessons."

"At her house?"

"It's a small community," Stosh blushed.

"Something else you were going to tell me about eventually?"

"I'm sorry," Stosh said. "You can't blame me for hiding what I did. Everything was happening so fast. I didn't know who I could trust."

"It's called intuition, Stosh," Zyv said. "I'm starting to think mine might be off."

"Don't say that," Stosh said. "I'm trying my best for the community, for you."

"I don't want you to think this is just some summer fling."

"I know," Stosh said, taking her hand in his. "It won't be. I promise. What we're building is going to be too good to abandon."

Zyv was still mulling over Stosh's proposal to rent the church for her online collaborators. She hadn't brought it up again since that day in the office, and he was starting to think that maybe she was reconsidering the idea altogether. But the deed only stated, "religious organization." It didn't specify what kind of religion, though Stosh was sure Cletus and some of the others would be in full revolt if they learned Stosh had decided to turn the church into a New Age scream therapy retreat. But no one else was offering any alternatives.

And if Zyv did take over the church—if she even still wanted to—it would only complicate whatever she and Stosh had. It'd make them business partners, or something close enough to marriage that it couldn't be undone so easily if their circus tent collapsed.

THE WHOLE NEIGHBORHOOD WAS ALIVE, vibrating red, white, and blue. Kids played in the road, breaking away from their street hockey and basketball games as Stosh drove by. Parents sat outside, drinking and laughing. Columns of smoke rose from the backs of houses, curling up from grills and barbecues and folding into the day's hazy air.

Stosh parked, and he and Zyv walked around the back of Cecelia's place. The kids were in the pool. Cecelia and Cara sat on lounge chairs in their bathing suits, sipping hard seltzers, their skin a radiant brown, their faces half-hidden by large sunglasses that made them look like insects.

Zyv took a seat next to them, and Stosh rushed over to where Calvin was manning the grill.

"You already boozing?" Calvin asked as the two went in for a hug.

"I sweat the stuff."

"I'm guessing that's the famous Zyvalia," Calvin said, looking to the pool. "All the sex, none of the commitment, Christian would be proud."

"It's a little more involved than that," Stosh said. "We really have a connection."

"Do you have the same connection with her husband?"

"Very funny."

"Just enjoy it while it lasts," Calvin said. "But, speaking of marriage—Bambi called me again."

"Just when I start to get over her, she pops back up," Stosh said. "She haunts me."

"Sure seems like it's the other way around."

"Why, what's she saying?"

"She's not saying anything."

"Oh," Stosh said, a little disappointed.

"You have to sign the papers, buddy."

"She wouldn't take my last name, but now she wants my signature."

"Sign the fucking papers," Calvin said.

"It's bullshit, man. It's unfair," Stosh said. "You know, everything fell right into place for her just as my shit was falling apart."

"That's why you won't do it?" he asked. "Because she's happy?"

Stosh shrugged.

Calvin shook his head, said, "And what's this I hear about you being the president of the condo association? I know you had issues with the last one, but why would you ever want to take on something like that?"

"I have a civic duty," Stosh said.

"So did Caligula," Calvin snorted. "Look at you, the Caligula of the condo association."

"Good one."

"Hell, if you're happy," Calvin said, nodding toward Zyv, "then I'm happy for you."

Stosh took a sip of beer and looked over at Zyv.

"Al didn't want to come?" Calvin asked.

"He doesn't get out much these days," Stosh said. "We're barely talking."

"Take it easy on him," Calvin said in his usual older-brotherly wisdom. "And tell him I said hi."

Stosh finished his beer and grabbed another one from the cooler before going to find Zyv.

She had wandered down to the snake rail fence that separated the house from the course. Stosh lit a cigarette and watched her staring off into the sunset, the light throwing shadows over the course. Further in the distance, he could make out the dark ruffles of a thunderstorm brewing.

"Such a waste," she said as he approached. "I could think of a million different uses for this much land."

"Now you're starting to sound like Ray," Stosh said. "Are you now or have you ever been a member of the Communist Party?"

She smiled, but it was subdued, a polite gesture, not the full-teethed celebration of her usual grin. His intuition was telling him he'd lost her, like he'd lost Bambi, but Zyv was still close, could still smell the incense in her hair, the booze on her breath.

"Fore!" someone yelled from the course.

Stosh shrank and covered his head, but the ball landed just on the other side of the fence. Zyv took out her phone and walked away, saying she had to take a call. After a moment, a golf cart crested the horizon, coming slowly over the hill in the distance and picking up speed on the downslope toward Stosh. He waited to see if it was anyone he knew, but Stosh didn't recognize the man, though his bright green Bermuda shorts seemed familiar.

Stosh pointed to the ball and said, "Easy to overshoot this hole. Try a three-wood next time."

"I guess you're right," the man said. "It's these little subtitles that give a course its character. Wouldn't you agree?"

"Sure thing."

"Having a party, huh?" the man asked, nodding at the American flag that hung from Cecelia's second story deck.

"Yeah, might as well."

The man had taken out his seven-iron and was taking a few aggressive practice swings, bringing the club violently through the second cut like a scythe, some leaves of grass popping out of the ground and dancing in the subtle breeze before fluttering to the ground.

"I'd take your medicine," Stosh said. "Just get yourself back into position. No way you're going to make it over that tree with a seven."

"God hates a coward," the man said in the middle of his backswing. He held the club above his head for an awkward and unnatural amount of time before coming down on the ball and hitting a miraculous high fade over the large sycamore tree that stood between him and the green.

Stosh clapped softly.

"You live here?" the man asked.

"Just visiting a friend," Stosh smiled.

"You know Mo Van Ronk?" the man asked. "Lives around the corner there. Works for a software company. Ascension."

"I hate to be the one to tell you this, but he went missing on that Malaysian flight."

"Did he?" the man asked. "That is a shame, huh?"

The man knocked his cleats with his club before climbing back into his golf cart. "Take care of yourself, Stosh."

Stosh waved and didn't think much of the fact that the man knew his name until after he'd driven off toward the green, disappearing somewhere beyond the sand traps. Must be a member, Stosh shrugged.

Calvin finished cooking and dumped another case of beer into the cooler. They ate hot dogs and hamburgers, staining their shirts with ketchup and mustard as the neighborhood kids launched Roman candles somewhere down the street. Sasha and Quentin squirmed with excitement every time one of them popped off. The adults drank domestic beers, and when their hands had warmed the last sips, they used the bottles to launch little rockets from them. Their skin was hot and sticky from sunscreen and bug spray. They tossed a football, played one inning of whiffle ball, and drank until the sun went down, and then they lit sparklers that hissed and burned in their hands, dropping them in the emerald grass only when they became too hot to hold. And when it became full dark, they walked up to the cul-de-sac where they could see the club's fireworks, and later, the extinguishing tips of Disney World's own display.

Zyv, though somber, smiled, too. She played with the kids, chased them with sparklers, and drank beer, but when they all got up to the cul-de-sac, she had disappeared. Stosh looked around and saw her back in Cecelia's yard, on the phone.

Stosh hung back for a second, letting families walk ahead so he could rip the joint he'd brought with him. He took his time, dragged his boots across the lawns of strangers, spat smoke into the air, and watched it rise as the cherry pulsed with each drag.

He felt as close to the future he'd envisioned for himself as he'd ever had. Close to Bambi and the life he thought he'd inherit. He felt a strange and exciting familiarity with it, this domestic dream. For all his training, success on the golf course never felt this close. It had always felt like a mirage, something forever in the distance, constantly moving away from him. But in this moment, he felt close to success, close to this other dream of a thirty-year fixed mortgage and Saturday morning errands. He now yearned for it, the kind of life that so many teenagers and poets and rock and rollers rebelled against—the familiar mediocrity of suburbia. It was a life he was only ever allowed, at least as an adult, to peek in on with the hungry voyeurism of a peepshow regular. It was always behind glass, teasing him and melting like ice cream between a child's fingers. He remembered watching the girls across the dance floor in middle school, and while the other boys discussed the things they thought they should do to them, he was busy, lost in a dream, wondering which one would look best in the passenger seat of the many SUVs he'd surely own.

How naïve of us to think we deserved what our parents had, what they told us was our birthright.

But dreams have a funny way of tethering us to reality, to who we think we are going to become, and although he knew he'd never own a home in Palm Ridge, he believed what he'd told the owners at the association's annual meeting—they could build something beautiful, and that was his dream now, and one that he thought Zyv was destined to be a part of.

"I can't see," Sasha said to him as he rejoined the pack.

"Elevator going up!" he said and placed her on his shoulders.

The fireworks began gently in a rolling epiphany of light. Slowly, they became louder and bigger. Stosh flinched from the noise, the smell of grilled meat, and the barrage above, sending him back to Jocko's parking lot that fateful night. He looked at his hands again, for those squirming splinters, but was relieved when they didn't appear. But then he looked at his elbow, where the scars from the shrapnel were. The three red marks wiggled and assembled on his arm to form a Ω. He went to brush it off and nearly dropped Sasha in the process, but when he looked at the scars again, they were normal.

After the display, Cecelia took the kids back home, where Zyv was still on the phone, now pacing across the front yard, arguing, her free hand conducting a wild orchestra of frustrations.

Stosh moved away from the crowd to smoke a cigarette.

"Did the kids have fun?" a voice said from behind him.

He turned around and saw Dana standing there with a beer in her hand.

"You seem good with them," she said.

Stosh smiled, said, "How's the swing?"

"Good, not great."

"That's the game of golf for you."

"Guess so."

"If you ever want another lesson," he said. "I consider myself a professional."

She laughed. Disney's fireworks cracked and sizzled in the sky, their light sending streaks of blue and red across Dana's face.

"Maybe we can try it again," she said.

But before Stosh could respond, Zyv appeared beside him.

"Brought you a shot," she said, her tone lemon bright once again.

"Zyvalia," Dana hissed.

"Small world," Stosh smiled nervously.

"How're you, Dana?" Zyv asked.

Dana's eyes narrowed, and her lips tightened. She zipped up her hoodie and folded her arms across her body.

"We better get going," Zyv said, taking Stosh by the arm and leading him away. He turned and looked at Dana and said, "See you around," but Dana didn't say anything. She remained frozen, her silhouette growing taller as he walked further away.

Stosh followed Zyv back to Cecelia's house, checking out her butt the whole way. Dana must just be sour. Her jealousy went to his head, the grotesque cyst it was becoming.

Back at Cecelia's, they said their goodbyes and the adults took one last shot in honor of the nation before parting ways.

"You're right," Zvv said to Stosh on their drive home. "We are building something very special together."

Stosh reached over the center console and squeezed Zyv's thigh as they pulled into the association and passed the church that stood guard atop the street, the neon seahorse on its sign glowing in the dark night.

"And we're going to put it right there," Stosh said, stopping in front of the church.

CHAPTER SIXTEEN

CALVIN THOUGHT they were gathering for Quentin's birthday, who, with every year that passed, resembled his father more and more, and not just the looks, but the bitter rage behind his piercing blue eyes.

They were staying at Palm Ridge, but not with Cecelia, though she had the room. Calvin, his wife, and his mother rented another condo in the community for the week if only to give them a place to soothe the baby when she got fussy.

The night before the party, Cecelia invited everyone over for drinks in observance of Christian's upcoming anniversary, or at least that's what she'd said.

"Did you remember to bring something of Christian's?" Calvin's mother asked him before walking down to Cecelia's.

"One of his chains," he said.

"It's not *just* a chain," Calvin's wife, Evelyn, said.

"That was Christian's?" his mother asked regarding the crucifix.

"I'll explain later."

Evelyn rolled her eyes and smiled at her husband, who she knew would be happy to get rid of the thing.

"What're you gonna do with it anyway?" Calvin asked.

"A time capsule?" Evelyn said.

"Something like that," Calvin's mother said.

They made their way down the street.

Cara, Stosh, and Zyv were already there, drinking around the kitchen counter as the kids played in the living room.

Calvin put the baby down in Quentin's old crib that Cecelia had set up in her room. In the kitchen, Evelyn poured herself and Calvin a glass of wine.

"Kind of surprised you'd come to something like this," Stosh said.

"What do you mean?"

"Your mom didn't tell you?"

"Tell me what?"

"I'll get you some more wine," Stosh laughed.

Calvin pulled his wife aside.

"Do you know what's going on?" he asked.

"That's always a difficult question when those two are involved," she said, looking back at the kitchen counter where Cecelia and Cara were giggling at their phones like school children.

Before Calvin could respond, the intercom system clicked on and the security officer at the front gate called for Cecelia.

"We have an Evangeline Sorenson here to see you. She's not on the list," he said.

"Oh, shit," Cecelia said. "She's good to come up."

"You got Evangeline Sorenson to come?" Zyv asked, her eyes wide with excitement.

"I'll meet her out front," Cara said.

"She wasn't cheap, but it will be worth it," Cecelia said.

"Who's Evangeline Sorenson?" Calvin asked.

"You didn't tell him?" Cecelia said, looking at Calvin's mother.

"I can't believe I'm about to meet Evangeline freaking Sorenson. I have to freshen up," Zyv said, standing to go to the bathroom.

"I didn't think he'd come if he knew," Calvin's mother said.

"If I knew what?" Calvin asked.

"You said he agreed," Cecelia said.

"Agreed to what!?" Calvin demanded.

"Not exactly," his mother said.

"What in God's name are you talking about?" Calvin asked.

"Evangeline's a psychic medium," Cecelia said.

"She's more than that," Zyv said, coming back into the room. "I follow all her accounts."

"You know how I feel about that stuff," Calvin said.

"She said we'd have a better chance at contacting your brother if everyone was here," his mother said.

"You guys have taken this way too far," he said.

Calvin was a skeptic, his heart belonging to Evelyn and their daughter, and his head to reason, but his soul was still on the market. His mother on the other hand—she, Cara, and Cecelia had fallen for all this esoteric nonsense after Christian died, visiting various readers, seers, tellers, and channelers with the regularity of nuns to a chapel, spending God knows how much in the process, and discussing their lineups with the same criticisms and intricacies as they did their favorite *Bachelorette* contestants. "Think of it like fantasy football," Evelyn once tried to explain it to Calvin.

He shook his head and walked down the hall to get the baby.

Evelyn went after him. "What's the harm?" she said.

"Not you, too," Calvin said.

"You don't have to believe it. It's for them."

"Haven't I done enough for them, for my brother?" he said. "I've been dealing with his shit since I was seventeen. He's still tormenting me from the grave."

Evelyn rubbed Calvin's back.

"The baby's not even baptized yet," he said.

"Worried the spirits will possess her?" Evelyn said with a smile, poking Calvin in the ribs. "Maybe we can have a photo-shoot afterwards—Baby's First Séance."

Evelyn let Calvin vent before finally convincing him to grin and bear it.

In the kitchen, Calvin inspected Evangeline from his peripheral vision as he poured another glass of cabernet, this time right to the brim. He couldn't tell how old she was, maybe in her thirties or early forties, but she dressed just like Cara and Cecelia, looked like someone he'd see them with on Instagram or even up at the clubhouse for brunch. She wore her brown hair straight and long, and her forehead had the same rigidity as his mother's own Botoxed face. She wore a tank top with a shawl wrapped around her shoulders and a pair of black yoga pants. She carried her Louis Vuitton bag in the crook of her arm, at the elbow, very stylishly. She didn't match the picture in Calvin's head of what a psychic was. He'd imagined one of two things—an old Black woman with a thick Creole accent and a string of bones around her neck or a gray-haired, long-nailed white woman with turquoise rings on each finger.

He'd never met a psychic before, or a medium, and certainly never a psychic medium, which he imagined was something equivalent to a Bishop or Cardinal in their ranks. The closest he ever got to meeting one was back home, in Cold Springs. There was a squat house next to Turnpike Liquors. It had a sign in the window that read "Psychic Readings: Five Dollars." Judging by the Louis Vuitton bag, it seemed to Calvin that the rates had gone up. The house also had an open sign in the window that appeared to always be on, no matter the time of day, glowing in welcoming strobes of neon. One night, when Christian was still living back home, he and Calvin tied one on at the Dugout and then stopped at the liquor store for a nightcap to finish in the privacy of their mother's Volvo. It was almost midnight, but the open sign was still on.

"You scared?" Christian teased his older brother.

"Looks like a meth-house," Calvin said.

"Fuck it," Christian said, strutting across the liquor store's parking lot drunk with confidence.

He rapped on the screen door. The wooden frame rattled, its hardware jangling like strange wind chimes.

A man opened the door, his face tanned, almost burned; his V-neck t-shirt stained with some kind of oil or barbecue sauce.

"We want a reading," Christian said. "I got ten for me and my brother."

"Carol's not here."

"Is she the psychic?"

"Sure."

"And she didn't see us coming?" Christian joked, looking back at Calvin.

"How about you get off my porch before I put your head through that window?" the man said.

Christian and Calvin walked away, but not before Christian looked back, pointed to the open sign that hung in the window, and said, "That's false advertising, buddy!"

The man took an aggressive step onto his porch, but Christian and Calvin were already running back to the car.

CECELIA WELCOMED Evangeline and walked her to the living room, where she took a seat by the fireplace.

"Shall we get started?" Evangeline asked.

Cecelia nodded.

"My name is Evangeline Sorenson, and I'm a psychic-medium, meaning that I can sense things that have yet to happen, and I can also contact those who have passed. From what Cecelia has told me, we're trying to contact Christian."

"My husband," Cecelia said.

Cara adjusted herself and took a big sip of wine.

They went around the room, introducing themselves and describing their relationship to Christian.

"By the way, I'm a huge fan," Zyv said when it was her turn. "I follow you on everything."

"That's very sweet of you," Evangeline said. "That reminds me —you can get ten percent off your next session if you like and subscribe to my YouTube channel."

"Incredibly generous," Calvin snickered.

Evangeline ignored his comment, having heard it all before and having successfully shielded herself from such comments by relentlessly and meticulously blocking such trolls online that it was easy for her to translate the practice IRL. She then looked at Cara and said, "And you are?"

"Um," she started, but Cecelia cut her off. "My good friend."

Cara downed the last of her wine and inched away from Cecelia.

"I ask because the more people who knew him, the better chance there is he'll come through," Evangeline said.

"I see hawks a lot," Cecelia blurted out, her face flushed from the wine, "and someone told me that it was Christian."

Evangeline shook her head and smirked. "People don't turn into birds," she said.

"Duh," Calvin said.

Evelyn nudged him to be quiet.

Cecelia deflated a bit, but she'd always been close to birds and resigned herself then and there to believe what she'd previously been told, regardless of Evangeline's expert opinion.

Evangeline then instructed everyone to place their items in the center of the room. Cecelia stood up and placed Christian's wedding ring on the ground, followed by Calvin's mother, who had brought his tattered baby blanket, held together more by a string of precious memories than any series of threads. Next, Stosh got up and placed a golf ball on the floor and said, "He tried to hit this out of the trees the first day we played the Ridge together. The thing ricocheted and knocked me in the head."

Everyone laughed a muted laugh, though something about the energy in the room had become heavy, serious in a way that made Calvin regret taking the time off from his young practice to be there.

Zyv went next and placed a copper wire on the floor. "It has telluric properties," she said, looking at her guru. "It can ground alternate timelines to our own."

"That might be a little advanced for this group," Evangeline said. "But I love your enthusiasm."

Zyv blushed.

When it was Calvin's turn, he stood up, pulled the crucifix out of his pocket, and placed it on the floor before quickly returning to his seat.

"Where did you get that from?" Cecelia asked, leaning in to get a better look at it. "I didn't buy him that."

"It's a long story," Calvin said.

"And now you, Cara," Evangeline said.

"I have to get it from the laundry room," Cara said and stood up.

After a moment, she returned with Christian's motorcycle jacket, the expensive one with his name embossed on the sleeve, the one Cecelia had given him on the last birthday he'd lived to see. She placed it on the ground and took a seat back on the couch, this time a noticeable distance from Cecelia.

"I didn't know you were bringing *that*," Cecelia said, a bite in her voice.

"I have to remind you that it doesn't matter where you got the item or why it's important, just that it reminds you of Christian," Evangeline said to the girls.

"Oh, this is gonna be good," Calvin whispered to Evelyn.

She nudged him in the ribs and tried to hide her smirk.

Evangeline took a deep breath, raised both arms, and clasped her hands together above her head. She then quickly drew her arms down and into her stomach, as if stabbing herself. After taking several more deep breaths, she opened her eyes and went about regarding each item, picking up first the baby blanket and then the motorcycle jacket, rubbing the cloth and leather between her fingers. Then she picked up the golf ball and rolled it between her hands like a pitcher getting ready for a new inning. Next, she picked up the wedding ring and rubbed her thumb against its gold. And finally, she picked up the crucifix and regarded Christ with a defiant intensity. Calvin almost flinched, hoping she wouldn't discover the USB drive hidden in it.

Evangeline rearranged the items in front of her and closed her eyes. Calvin, for all his doubt, found himself holding his breath, waiting for something to happen. He was willing to be persuaded; he might have even wanted to be, though he would never admit it.

Evangeline then picked up the crucifix and held it in her palm. She began to hum, the sound soon deepening to a groan, rising up from her belly and rattling in the back of her throat before echoing through her sinuses and out her of her mouth. She started to pant and whimper. Calvin looked on but remained silent.

She smiled and blushed. "He was very charming, wasn't he?" she said.

"Jesus, is he hitting on her from beyond?" Calvin said aloud.

Stosh let out a hearty laugh, but Evangeline kept going.

"He misses *you*," she said.

"Who?" Cecelia said, "Me or Cara?"

Evangeline didn't answer. "He says he loves *you*."

"Who is he talking about?" Cecelia demanded.

"Jesus, it's not a competition," Cara said, rolling her eyes, though she, too, wanted to know.

Evangeline opened her eyes and looked at Calvin. "He says you know the answer."

"Me?"

"Who is he talking about?" Cecelia now demanded of Calvin.

"How the hell would I know?" Calvin said.

Cara looked at him, and he remembered the time Christian had brought her up to Cold Springs for Thanksgiving. Calvin was happy to see how well his little brother was doing. He was sober and had bulked up a bit since moving to Florida. They ate dinner, and then Calvin stepped out onto the deck for a whiskey and a cigar, happy to see his brother was only drinking Red Bull.

"She seems nice," Calvin said about Cara.

"She's the best," Christian said. "But I still don't know what I'm going to do about Cecelia. She's driving me crazy. I think she fucked her yoga teacher."

"Didn't you cheat on her first?"

"Not the point," Christian said. "All we do is fight. Even now that I'm sober, she can't help but remind me that getting clean is the only thing I've ever done for myself."

"Maybe you just need to learn to co-parent," Calvin suggested. "You know, separately."

"What're you talking about, dude?" Christian said, offended at the thought. "I love her."

Calvin rolled his eyes. "I know, what was I thinking?"

"But Cara doesn't judge me. She doesn't remind me of all the bad shit I've done. And she didn't fuck me until the third date!" Christian said. "I mean, what kind of mind game is that?"

"Seems you're in quite the conundrum," Calvin said, sipping his whiskey, the ice cubes log-jamming against his lips.

"What do you think I should do?"

"I think you should be with the person you can see yourself fighting for, not fighting with."

Christian shrugged, said, "That's cute, but I was gonna try to get them on board with a sister-wives kind of situation."

"For heaven's sake."

"Everybody's doing it," Christian said. "Poly-armory or something like that."

"If anyone could do it, it'd be you," he reassured his brother.

That was the same night Christian gave him the necklace. He didn't tell him there was a USB drive hidden in it. Calvin still wasn't sure if Christian knew about it. He was hesitant to accept it at first, figuring it was stolen, but he always had a hard time saying no to his little brother.

"Calvin knows the answer," Cara said, still staring at him. "Don't you."

"It was nothing. I don't know," Calvin said. "Ask the medium."

Cara huffed, stood up and went to the kitchen.

"Maybe we should take a break?" Calvin's mother said to Evangeline.

Calvin nearly snarled at her, coming in here and stirring things up. She would shortly collect her fee and fuck off to dimensions unknown. She didn't have to sit there and mediate between the sister-wives like he would.

He got up and went to the bathroom, but as he was coming out, he was confronted by Cecelia.

"Why did Cara say that you knew who he was talking about?" she said.

"Cecelia, it doesn't matter, OK? He's gone, and I know he loved you."

"But who was he talking to?"

"Why does it matter? You were married to him. Cara can't say that."

"Real nice," Cara said from the end of the hall.

"I didn't mean it like that," Calvin said.

"So, are you going to tell her, or should I?" Cara said.

Calvin sighed, said, "All I know is that he loved you both. In his own, fucked up way, he really thought he loved you both."

"Thought?" Cecelia said.

"Maybe we should give Calvin some space," his mother said.

Cara turned and marched away, grabbing her purse from the counter and walking out the front door. Cecelia retreated to her room and slammed the door, only to reappear with the baby in her arms. She walked to Evelyn and handed her over with a grimace.

Calvin picked up the crucifix from the floor and put it back in his pocket.

Evangeline didn't move through the whole incident. She just sat there, checking her phone and picking at her nails in apparent boredom.

"I'm sorry about all this," Calvin's mother said to her.

"It happens quite often," she said. "I know people come to me for answers and comfort, but it doesn't always work like that."

"I understand," Calvin's mother said. "My medium back home says the same thing."

"'Trauma doesn't stop at the grave'," Zyv said, quoting one of Evangeline's most popular and pithy Instagram posts. "Your live sessions helped me through a very dark time."

Evangeline smiled politely and bowed her head in appreciation.

"Is there any chance we can finish this another day, maybe tomorrow, after the party?" Calvin's mother asked.

"I could probably do that, but my manager would kill me if I didn't charge an additional fee," Evangeline said.

"Oh, of course," Calvin's mother said. "I hope a check is OK."

"I prefer Venmo," Evangeline said. "Taxation *is* theft."

"You're telling me," Stosh said.

Evangeline collected her fee and thanked everyone before finishing her wine and leaving.

Outside, Calvin sat on the front porch, staring out at the neighborhood.

Only my brother could fuck up a life like this, he thought to himself, regarding the perfectly kept lawns and quiet homes.

Evangeline appeared on the porch and threw her shawl around her shoulders.

"So, that's it?" Calvin asked her.

"The truth is rarely convenient," she said, rather coldly, Calvin thought, considering the pipe bomb she'd just dropped in the living room.

"Truth?" Calvin asked. "Seems you traffic in realities."

"One person's reality is another's fantasy," she said, sounding off like an inspirational desk calendar.

"What makes you an authority on this stuff anyway?"

"I derive my authority from those I surround myself with."

"What does that even mean?" Calvin asked.

"Have you ever heard of Joan Quigley? She was Nancy Regan's astrologer," Evangeline said. "She was like the American Rasputin. Nearly every major decision the administration made went through her first."

"I'm sure you're a barrel of laughs at dinner parties."

"I have business leaders from around the world, actors, and two state senators who have standing appointments with me," Evangeline said.

"Plenty of sinners in that bunch."

"Don't be so rigid," she said. "Religion's no good. It makes too many promises. Claims to answer questions that don't really have them."

"And how are you any different?"

"I don't promise anything. People bring to me their anxieties and fears and desires, and I take them all. I don't give them anything they don't already have, they don't already know. We're perfect beings, perverted by an imperfect world, and I show them that. I'm not special. Religions, in return for the promise of answers, ask for devotion. I don't ask that of anyone. I take their baggage and ask nothing in return."

"You take their baggage and their money."

"A girl's got to live," Evangeline said, peaking into her Louis Vuitton to make sure she had all her things. Satisfied with its contents, she turned back to Calvin and said, "Religion tends to stifle the very thing it supposedly wants to nourish—the soul—

but how can anyone understand their soul if it's caged like a veal calf?"

Calvin didn't say anything.

"I break down those barriers and set what's behind them free," she said.

Calvin was frustrated, not just with Evangeline but himself— here he was, arguing with a charlatan, though he agreed with her on one thing: she sure didn't provide any answers. He felt stupid and angry. Angry at his mother, Cara, and Cecelia. Angry at his dead brother, who was still finding ways to torment him from beyond the grave.

Stosh came outside then and asked, "You good, man?"

Calvin looked up, but Evangeline was gone, and only his thoughts lingered in the stifling air. Some animal hissed in the distance, drawing him away from the porch for only a moment. He looked to Stosh and said, "Yeah."

"Weird night, huh?"

Calvin looked at Stosh and wanted to hurt him for saying something so obvious.

"Evangeline leave?" Stosh asked.

"I don't see her broom parked out front," Calvin said.

Stosh lit a joint, first puffing in the flame through the mouth-piece and then turning it around and blowing on the cherry to get it going.

"Partake?" Stosh asked.

"You remember the last time I smoked?"

"That was a funeral," Stosh said, "this is different. It's for fun."

"What about *that* was fun?" Calvin said.

"You have a point."

"I have them often," Calvin said, taking the joint from Stosh.

Stosh giggled and clapped quietly as Calvin puffed on the joint.

"Tell me something," Calvin said, talking through a hit as he passed the joint back to his friend, "do you believe in all that shit?"

"I don't not believe," Stosh said. "Even though I got enough to worry about in this timeline, I was craving spirituality."

"Not going to mass anymore?"

"Sometimes, but everything about it is so old," Stosh said. "I needed something beyond myself that I could still make sense of. Something from this century."

"It just seems predatory."

"Wait until you get into cryptids," Stosh said, taking a big toke. "The skunk ape—now that's a predator."

Calvin laughed, said, "I miss you."

"That's the weed talking."

"Doesn't always feel like it, but I miss him, too," Calvin said, now taking in only the humid air.

"Where's he again, Island Pond?"

"Christ the Redeemer."

"Is that irony or a coincidence, considering what happened tonight?"

"Irony, I think," Calvin said, stealing the joint from Stosh's fingers.

He took a pull, coughed a bit and felt young again, felt himself folding into memories, the days spent in basements, silly and young, Christian often being the butt of his and Stosh's entertainment; like the time he glided around Al's basement, stark naked, save for the roller blades, all the while taking a yard stick to his pre-pubescent pecker in order to relay his measurements to the girls on AOL Instant Messenger.

"I wanted to cremate him, scatter the ashes," Calvin said, "maybe set up a memorial golf tournament in his name, donate the purse to a sober house or something."

"I bet we can make that happen," Stosh said. "Between me and Cecelia, we should have enough connections to work something out with the Ridge."

"I think I'd like that," Calvin said.

"What's on his headstone?" Stosh said.

"A picture of him and the kids," Calvin said. "The funeral home director tried selling us on a new trend. I guess it's big in Japan to have QR codes stamped on headstones with a link to a song or video."

"Christian probably would've had a link to his favorite porn," Stosh said, chuckling with the joint between his lips.

"Imagine that," Calvin said, looking up to the stars, to the place where he hoped his little brother was, "walking into Christ the Redeemer while all the other families stand, listening to their loved one's favorite songs, only to be interrupted by *Petite Cum Shots, Volume Three.*"

"It may not be polite, but it'd be honest," Stosh said.

"You sound like Evangeline."

"I know it's strange, but you should check out her Instagram. She's helped a lot of people."

"That Zyv's got a hold on you, huh?"

"I think I might love her," Stosh said.

Calvin looked at his friend and saw the dulled eyes of a man who'd forsaken his character for a piece of ass. "Maybe it's just a rebound," he said.

"It's more than that," Stosh said. "I was dying, man, just wasting away, and she brought me back to life, shifted my energy."

"Energy?" Calvin said, twirling his finger above his head, coo-coo.

"It feels good to believe in something again, especially when everything in this world is going to shit."

"More trouble at the condo?"

"Speaking of which, I have a legal question for you," Stosh said. "What would happen if we can't pay our bills? Could I be sued?"

"Why would you be sued?"

"I was technically the one who signed over our finances to the old president," Stosh said. "Couldn't I be held liable?"

"Doesn't sound like anyone over there has the money or patience for a lawsuit, especially if you're keeping the place above water."

"Wouldn't be able to do it without Zyv," Stosh said. "She grounds me somehow."

"Not sure how someone can be grounded when their head is in the clouds," Calvin said.

Stosh laughed and Calvin shared in his friend's belligerent smile but was quickly reminded of reality when he heard the baby crying inside.

"There's my cue," Calvin said. "Still don't know what I'm gonna do with this," he said, showing Stosh the crucifix.

"Only your brother would have something so obnoxious."

"You know anything about this?" Calvin said, pulling the crucifix apart and showing him the USB drive.

"I remember seeing him with the necklace, but he never showed me that."

"Christian gave it to me last time I saw him," Calvin said, handing it to Stosh.

Stosh turned the crucifix in his hand and read the inscription —Property of Ascension.

"Jesus Christ," Stosh said, showing Calvin the name, a shiver crawling up his spine. "This was Mo Van Ronk's company. The guy used to live here. That's his house over there."

"Perfect," Calvin said. "You can give it back to him."

"He went missing on that Malaysian flight. Someone broke into his house a few months after that."

"Safe to say we know who that was," Calvin said.

"The company was supposed to sponsor me before I quit playing," Stosh said, thumbing the letters on the necklace in awe.

"Sounds like fate to me," Calvin said.

"Now who sounds like Zyv?" Stosh said. He paused and looked

over at Dana's house. "Mo's wife still lives here. She's probably looking for it."

"Then give it to her."

"I don't know, man, she's not my biggest fan, and I got enough legal issues."

"It's a gift. You can't say no," Calvin said. "Sell it for the platinum. Consider it payment for setting up Christian's golf tournament. Hell, use the money for the condo."

Stosh took the necklace and felt the weight of coincidence in its cool plating. "I guess I'll figure something out," he said.

The two hugged before Stosh left Calvin to regard the stars for another minute. Somewhere off in the distance, a motorcycle screamed, its muffler laughing out in pops and hisses, and Calvin hoped that, if his brother wasn't in heaven, he was at least moving in the right direction.

CHAPTER SEVENTEEN

DANA DIDN'T LIKE REFERRING to herself as a widow. After all, the plane had never been found, and her husband was only presumed dead. She was too young to be a widow. The word tasted like potpourri whenever she said it, and even though her neighbors had stopped whispering when she passed them, the hollow pain of a sailor's wife remained.

The only person who kept in touch was Cam, her husband's business partner, but she preferred he didn't.

She couldn't tell you exactly what her husband did, but she knew it had something to do with software, and that he made enough money to buy the condo in Palm Ridge and liberate her from the toils of labor for the foreseeable future.

The last time Cam visited, he wanted something more than her forgiveness.

"Could he have been wearing it on the flight?" he'd asked in her kitchen.

"I don't know, Cam," she said. "What does it matter anyway? Wasn't it a joke?"

"Yeah, kind of, but we were gonna hang it in the office, you know, as a kind of memorial," he said. "But only if you're OK with that."

"I may be doing better, but I'm not ready to go through his things."

"It could be therapeutic," he said.

"I don't want to do it, OK?" she said.

"All right. You're right," he said. "Sorry."

"You know how I feel about that word."

"My bad," he said, lowering his head. "Still volunteering at the Y?"

"Five nights a week."

"And yoga?"

"When I have the energy," she said.

"You know that girl, Zyv? I think she teaches a few classes over there."

"You slumming at the Y now?"

"I follow her on Instagram," he said. "She's done wonders for me."

"It's not just because she's cute and thin?" Dana asked.

"That helps, too," Cam said. "But if you get a chance, talk to her. She really helped me with all this stuff."

Dana nodded.

"You know what I mean," Cam said. "He was my business partner, my best friend. I'll never forgive myself for booking that flight."

"We're not having this conversation again."

"You're right," he said. "I'm sorry."

"Language."

"Shit," he said. "But seriously, Zyv does this scream regiment therapy. I think it'll do you some good."

"Scream regiment therapy?"

"Don't knock it 'til you try it."

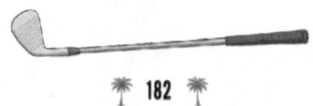

DANA LIKED volunteering for janitorial work. It made her feel important in a necessary and satisfying way. That night, she was on bathroom duty. She pulled her hair back into a bun, grabbed a handful of vinyl gloves, and went to work. By the end of her shift, she was sweaty and dizzy, having finished in the pool's locker room, the humidity and chemicals wafting in every time someone opened the door. She knew she should hit the 6:00 PM class. It always made her feel better, but she was tired. She just wanted to go home and shower, make a little dinner, and watch reruns of *John D. Wolf: Bounty Hunter* that would surely be on one of the innumerable streaming platforms she subscribed to. But with those small comforts of home came a gaping loneliness she could only chase away with a bottle of red ever since the accident, so she grabbed her mat from her car and went to the gym. She found a space in the back and warmed up.

Zyv walked in and set up her mat in front of the class.

Dana looked at her phone, She turned to the woman next to her and said, "I thought Kat taught this class."

"Usually," the woman shrugged.

Dana looked at Zyv and admired her beauty. She was a good instructor, but her beauty was intense, her poses formidable, and despite her height, intimidating. She reminded Dana of the popular girls who'd bullied her as a kid, but she tried to enjoy the class all the same. She closed her eyes and postured accordingly, and at the end of the session, she felt a clean and invigorating fatigue.

Dana took her time packing her things as Zyv cleaned up. Dana noticed she worked with an intensity that she herself had yet to master when scrubbing the bathrooms. She thought of what Cam had said about the scream therapy and was curious, but what a strange thing to ask someone about. She pulled out her phone and looked up Zyv on Instagram. Her account was full of the kind of content she'd trained the algorithms to feed her after the accident. Platitudinous slop promising to unveil hidden truths and sacred powers. She'd never been religious, having grown up like many young Americans with a vague Christianity that paralleled her secular world but was never in full focus. She'd gone to church at Christmas and Easter but never understood the whole story. The eating of bodies, the masochism and scandal; Dana didn't get it, but then the accident happened, and she found herself groping for meaning. Meaning and community. She'd only ever had Mo in Florida. They went to dinner dances at the clubhouse and made nice with the neighbors, but she didn't have friends in any real sense. She wasn't part of a community, and the steady drip of esoteric content gave her something to hold onto, and the bubbly characters who whispered affirmations, incantations, and light languages became something close to a tribe. But then the algorithm started giving her a slow drip of darker content. Most of the theories were old enough for her to ignore—the New World Order, 9/11 was an inside job. The kind of stuff her best friend's older brother used to talk about after facing a blunt, but then she found theories about the accident, about her husband. The plane went missing over the ice wall. It was abducted by aliens. It was a ruse to scare people from flying under the false flag of climate change. Ridiculous, all of them, but the vilest of them all was the one that claimed the plane was full of pedophiles and was shot down by so-called white hats in their war against the deep state sex traffickers. The deep state? Her husband was a software engineer. He still played with Legos. Strange, maybe, but nefarious? It was just a hobby. He was a grown man allowed to do with his money whatever he wanted. But why hadn't he played golf or taken up fishing? Why a child's pastime? She went through her husband's things, looking for hidden files on his computer or evidence of grave transgressions, but found none. That's when she packed up all his stuff—computers, hard drives, clothes, and Legos—and put it all in the basement. She knew his most recent contract was with the Defense Department, but no, it couldn't be. It was just an accident. A faulty wire or human error. No way her nerdy husband had anything to do with something so menacing as a cabal. He was just a guy with a job. Not everything had to make sense for it to be real. She went about scrubbing her algorithm after that, liking and following only cooking and baking accounts, trying to retrain it to keep the vile slop from her feed, but occasionally one slipped through, and she had to swipe away the filth before it stained her mind once again.

She scrolled through Zyv's account, admiring her beauty. It was strange to see her, a "creator" in the flesh. She thought about sending her a message, asking about the scream therapy, believing such an exchange would be easier if dulled by a DM. But then she looked up and saw she was the last student left, and Zyv standing before her, smiling.

"Shit," Dana said. "I'll get out of your way."

"You're fine," Zyv said.

Dana fumbled with her things.

"Take a breath," Zyv said. "Don't lose the cool you just got."

"Yeah, OK," Dana said, taking in a deep breath, the pool chemicals still clinging to her nose hairs. "I was wanting to ask you about something."

"We can scream," Zyv said.

Dana was speechless.

"I'm not that good," Zyv smiled. "Cam messaged me, said a beautiful woman might be gracing the six o'clock class with her presence and in need of something beyond a stretch."

"I don't mean to put you on the spot," Dana said. "Can I make an appointment?"

"How 'bout now?"

"Here?"

"My car."

Dana followed Zyv to the parking lot.

"Just push that shit aside," Zyv said as Dana opened the passenger door.

Dana sat down, kicked the bags of Jocko's wrappers and empty nip bottles aside, and had second thoughts.

"It's my first time," she said.

"It's everyone's first time with me."

"So, how does this..." Dana began to ask, but before she could finish her sentence, Zyv started screaming.

Dana instinctively covered her ears, the column of noise and air billowing out of Zyv, seemingly without end.

"Louder than I thought," Dana said once Zyv had finished.

Zyv took a deep breath and said, "I can't help you if I don't help myself first."

"Do I just let it out?" Dana asked.

"Do you know what it is you're trying to let out?"

"My husband has been missing for over a year," Dana said.

"That's a fact, not a feeling," Zyv said. "What is it that you're trying to get out? What's its name?"

"Sadness," Dana shrugged.

"Then go cry about it."

"Loneliness?"

"I doubt you'd have a problem getting laid," Zyv said.

"I'm not sure what to say."

"Let's see what it wants us to call it," Zyv said, placing a hand on Dana's back.

They each took a deep breath, and then Zyv said, "Tell me its name," and Dana screamed as loudly as she could. Her throat ached, and the blood pulsed behind her eyeballs. She took a breath and screamed again, this time with her eyes open. She thought she could see the windows vibrating from her might. She screamed until she cried. She caught her reflection in the windshield—she'd popped several blood vessels in her eyes.

"Now you know what to call it," Zyv said.

Dana wept. It didn't make sense. She didn't really know what Zyv was talking about, but she felt better, even lighter than she had after yoga.

"I'll teach you how to make those feelings your bitch," Zyv said.

CAM WAS NOT one to panic. He hadn't panicked when the company nearly lost the bid for the contract; he hadn't panicked the several times they were short payroll while they developed the software; and he didn't panic when he heard his business partner, Mo Van Ronk, went missing on that Malaysian flight. But now that Big Brother was calling, he was beginning to panic.

He was meeting the client at Palm Ridge for a business round. He was trying to buy himself some more time until he could find the necklace. Mo hadn't liked that the client insisted the software be put onto an external drive, thought it was dated and insecure, but that's how these government guys operate, Cam said, somewhere between the analog and the digital, briefcases full of nonsequential bills, and foreign wars orchestrated over the course of casual lunches at the club house. But if Mo didn't like the idea of an external drive, then he really hated that Cam put it in something so gaudy and expensive; but that was Cam for you—gaudy, expensive; the brain-rotted product of a VC career in Silicon Valley.

"We couldn't even make payroll a week ago, and you're pulling a stunt like this," Mo had said when Cam presented him with the necklace. "And what does Jesus have to do with it?"

"This deal is our *savior*," Cam said with that stupid smile.

"Fuck, Cam."

"Stop worrying. They just paid their last invoice. We're officially a part of the military-industrial complex, my friend," Cam said. "It doesn't get any better than this."

"I didn't get in this business to sell surveillance equipment to the state," Cam recalled Mo's lament.

"If only your morals had market value," Cam remembered responding.

But now that was all in jeopardy, with Mo scattered to bits across the Pacific Ocean and the software possibly missing or buried in a pile of tchotchkes in Dana's basement.

In the clubhouse, Cam went into the locker room and got changed. He swung open a stall door and came face to face with a young man pulling a needle from his arm, the tourniquet still strangling his blue bicep.

"What the fuck, man?" the guy yelled. "You don't knock?"

Cam muttered something like an apology but quickly shut the door and made his way to the pro shop. He thought about telling someone, but decided against it—he was a guest, and he didn't want any more trouble than what he was sure to get with the client.

"Caddies are waiting for you and your partner on the first tee," the pro said.

The client was waiting on the tee box, his neon green Bermuda shorts in stark contrast with his long-sleeved Oxford shirt and plaid slouch hat. He looked like a toddler, or some bizarro Payne Stewart up there.

"Why does a guy from Alexandria need a membership to a course in central Florida?" Cam asked him.

"That's classified," the client said.

Cam subdued his smile.

"I'm kidding," the client laughed. "But seriously, don't ask questions."

"I guess I won't ask how your wife is," Cam said.

"Now you're getting it," the client said. "As much as I could use some work on my short game, I'm hoping you have some good news for me."

"I'm working on it."

"The speed you move, I'd think you were the one who worked for the federal government."

"You know, there were extenuating circumstances," Cam said.

"That's the line of business I'm in," the client said.

The caddies approached with their clubs. Cam turned to get his driver and saw the guy from the bathroom with his bag.

"You got two hundred yards to the trap on the right," the guy said.

Cam nodded and took the club. He slapped the ball a measly one-hundred-and-twenty yards firmly into the palm trees on the left of the fairway.

"I didn't tell anyone," Cam said to his caddy as they walked to his ball.

"Didn't tell anyone what?"

"If you're gonna be like that, maybe I will."

"No cameras in the bathroom," the guy said. "And my wife lives up at the Ridge. It'd be my word against yours."

"Your wife lives up there, but you're caddying?"

"Filling in for a friend," the guy said.

"Depending on what you were doing, maybe I'm interested in some."

"Nah, man."

"Fair enough," he said. "My name's Cam."

"Christian," the guy said. "You got a seven iron from here."

"Let's see how good you are at this," Cam said, standing over his ball and eyeing the green.

Cam swung nearly out of his shoes and watched as his ball apexed and landed with a plop twenty-five yards short of the green.

"I can only do so much with a swing like that," Christian laughed.

Cam kicked at some grass in frustration but appreciated the banter, considering the shit he was in with the client, whose name he didn't even know. The client was not the man with whom Cam negotiated the contract. He had never met that man and had only spoken to him on the phone and through emails. This man, whose name Cam didn't know, was sent to Florida to retrieve the software after Mo went missing. Cam only knew the financial parts of the deal. The specs of the product were negotiated by Mo and yet another representative of the Pentagon's Division of Perception Management team over several months. Cam didn't know shit about software, algorithms, or why the Pentagon was interested in their rinky-dink Human Capital Management software startup, but he wasn't going to say no to those sweet, sweet DOD duckets. And so now he found himself playing golf with a nameless government agent, assigned to retrieve the only copy of a software that he couldn't find, thanks to Dana and her bellyaching. Shit, he was mourning, too, and he was going to be a lot worse off if he didn't get that stupid necklace, which, like Mo, the client would likely find ridiculous. He knew it was in bad taste and wasteful to spend all that money for a joke, but shit, isn't that what Silicon Valley has brought to corporate America? A sense of humor? Foosball tables in the break room and a cooler, sleeker style of feudalism?

"You play often?" Cam asked the client on the fifth tee box.

"It's a requirement of the job," the client said. "No deal in the history of human commerce has ever been closed in a bowling alley."

"That's really profound," Cam said. "I like that."

"I majored in poetry in college."

"I guess you have to be a romantic if you want to work in espionage."

"Espionage?"

"Division of Perception and all. I mean, I don't even know your name," Cam chuckled nervously.

"Mann, Guy Mann."

"OK, keep your secrets, danger-man," Cam ribbed the client.

"Eighty years of clandestine operations have left the alias pool pretty shallow," the client, Guy Mann, said.

"So, you are a spook!"

"Say God Forbid!" Guy Mann snapped. "You wouldn't call a

nice young woman a broad, would you? Or a gay man, a fag? I won't even ask if you're a frequent user of the N-word."

"I didn't mean anything by it," Cam said.

"This is why the Division of Perception Management was established," Guy Mann said. "We, too, wish to be seen, which leaves us in a precarious situation—how do clandestine agents achieve accurate and appropriate media representations without blowing our cover?"

"I always liked the Jack Ryan flicks."

"Tom Clancy was a bootlicker," Guy Mann said. "And don't get me started on James Bond. We need the American people to know that we're not all reckless, womanizing 'danger-men,' as you so poorly put it. We're men of great integrity, subtlety, and monogamy. That's why we contracted your firm."

"I bet you're wishing there was another copy," Cam said.

"As I'm sure you are," Guy Mann said. "But we couldn't risk the technology being duplicated or falling into the wrong hands."

"But you didn't consider it getting lost?"

"Listen, we're trying, OK?" Guy Mann said. "Operation Real Love is about winning back public support for the national security apparatus, and the men like me who've devoted their lives to returning this country to the glory of our past."

"Operation Real Love?" Cam snorted. "What, did you guys create your own dating app?"

"That's classified."

"What if—and I'm not saying this is going to happen—but what if I can't find it?" Cam asked. "Would I need to repay the money?"

"If you think the United States of America's Department of Defense, Division of Perception Management hasn't allocated the appropriate contingency funds for such a monumental undertaking that has become Operation Real Love, then you haven't been paying attention for the last eighty years," Guy Mann said. "But yes. You'd need to repay the money or face the wrath of a far more dangerous division than that of Perception Management."

"Black ops?"

"Accounting."

Cam deflated, then asked, "What if I could find someone to make a new one for you?"

"You ask too many questions," Guy Mann said. "But could the United States of America's Department of Defense, Division of Perception Management buy or otherwise procure the appropriate software—by whatever means we deem necessary—to execute Operation Real Love? Of course, we could, but I've made this my pet project, and by God, I won't only see it through, but I'll make everyone else involved see it through, too."

"You're talking about me, right?"

"Damn right, trooper!" Guy Mann said.

Christian approached the two and said, "Cara wants to know if you guys want anything off the cart. She didn't want to interrupt you."

"Never drink in the sunlight," Guy Mann said as if giving Cam advice.

"I'll take a double of whatever brown liquor she has," Cam said.

Christian returned to the cart girl, and Cam watched the two flirt. Christian reached into the cart, but the girl shook her head. It looked then as if the two were arguing. Then the cart girl reached into the cash box and handed Christian a fistful of bills.

Cam turned to Guy Mann and said, "I'll have the hard drive by the time you leave."

"I appreciate your confidence and find it utterly attractive," Guy Mann said. "Now watch me drop this piss-missile down the middle of the fairway."

Guy Mann did, in fact, uncork a piss missile straight down the fairway, and Cam watched in what he could only assume was some kind of cucking.

Cam did not particularly like golf, but they'd offered it as an elective in business school, so he took it figuring it would be a good skill to have in the world of finance, but he never thought he'd be hitting the links with an agent—secret or otherwise—from the Department of Defense's Division of Perception Management.

"Strange guy," Christian said, handing Cam his three-wood as Guy Mann marched down the fairway to his ball.

"You don't even know the half of it," Cam said. But then he got to thinking. "You actually might be interested in what we were discussing."

"You trying to get me to do some faggot porn or something?"

"You don't get to talk to me like that!" Cam belched. "You're my caddy."

"Until you fix that swing, I can talk to you however the fuck I want."

"Ah, fuck you," Cam said. "What I'm trying to say is, habits like yours come with certain requisite skills, right?"

"If you wanna watch me fuck the cart girl, it'll cost you."

"Listen, you little shit, do you wanna make some extra money or not?" Cam asked.

DANA SOON HAD a standing appointment with Zyv every Thursday night after yoga. They'd meet in Zyv's car and scream, but Dana noticed the effects of their sessions often wore off as soon as she returned home, where only emptiness greeted her. The feeling of being alone in the house she once shared with her husband was something like restlessness, but more distant.

"Like a ghost story, but instead of being haunted by my husband, I'm the one lurking around the house," Dana told Zyv after one of their sessions.

"Have you tried sage?" Zyv asked.

"Twice."

"Masculine energy?"

"Feels too soon."

"Even for your golf instructor?"

"He's cute and all, but not a lot of masculine energy, you know?"

"You don't have to fuck him," Zyv said.

Dana blushed at the thought.

"See," Zyv said. "I knew you liked him."

"He's a little awkward, but he's sweet and patient."

"So, he doesn't have big dick energy," Zyv said. "Who cares? He could still be useful."

"I'll think about it."

"Would you be open to trying something different?" Zyv asked.

"I've been screaming in your car for the past six weeks. I think I'm open to almost anything," Dana said.

"I've been working with some colleagues on new modalities," Zyv said. "A manifestation tool."

"Sounds very Silicon Valley."

"I'm still learning, but the people I've been working with have been doing awesome things," Zyv said.

Dana shrugged. "I'll try anything at this point."

"In the meantime, get laid," Zyv said. "Never underestimate the power of sex magic."

A week later, Dana was waiting in her living room for Zyv to arrive with her online collaborators—two experts in manifestation therapy. Zyv said they should do the therapy in Dana's home, the source of her blockage, as it were.

Zyv arrived first. She came into the house with a motorcycle helmet under her arm.

"New ride?" Dana asked.

"This is the tool I was talking about," she said. "Don't worry, we'll ease into it."

The helmet looked like a standard motorcycle helmet, except the visor had been blacked out, and several slots had been drilled into it at various angles.

Dana had provided all of Zyv's requirements—twelve blankets (or large towels), two belts, and a table large enough for Dana to lie on. Zyv went about arranging the blankets on the table before telling Dana to lie on them.

"I consider myself pretty unassuming, but this is a little odd," she said.

"You trust me, right?" Zyv asked.

"Yeah."

"Then get your hot ass on the table."

Dana laughed nervously and complied. Zyv began wrapping the blankets around her, making sure she was covered from the tips of her toes to her chin. She only started to feel slightly claustrophobic when Zyv used the belts to secure her to the table.

"Let's do some breathwork," Zyv said.

The two began breathing in unison, in and out and in and out, until Dana was comfortably lightheaded.

"I'm going to put the helmet on now," Zyv said. "If you panic or need to stop, just say the word Gack."

"Gack?"

"From now on, only say it if you need to stop."

Dana nodded, and Zyv fixed the helmet on her head. The light was completely shut out. After a few seconds, she felt like she was floating. Zyv's voice was muffled, coming through like ambient surround sound.

"I'm going to slip several magnets into the helmet," Zyv said. "Each one corresponds to a specific set of lobes in your brain."

Dana heard the magnets click into place.

"The pain you feel is only a sensation," Zyv said. "A product of that lump of flesh that is your brain. Your consciousness is trapped in those lobes. It's caged by them. With each magnet, a bar is broken, a shackle unlocked."

Dana felt the muscles in her back loosen, and if it wasn't for the weight of the helmet, she wouldn't know her head was still attached to her shoulders.

"I'm going to ask you several questions, but don't answer aloud," Zyv said. "When you mourn, who do you mourn for? When you pray, who do you pray for? When you yearn, who do you yearn for?"

Dana responded to these questions in her heart; her husband the answer to each one.

"I know you miss him," Zyv said, "and that's why we are going to manifest the timeline in which he never got on that plane. We must be careful, though. We don't want to manifest the wrong timeline, one of the many in which you two never meet." Zyv breathed deeply. "Focus on that timeline, on the morning of the flight. He's late, I can see it, can you? He's late because you make love, and he misses his flight. He's here now."

Dana was smiling through her tears, lost in this fantastic timeline. She was there, on the morning of the flight, and so was he. For the first time since the accident, she could imagine his face—the strap of plucky stubble on his chin, the radiant green eyes; she could even see his receding hairline. He had the money for transplants, but he didn't care, and neither did she. He had the confidence of a man much more attractive than he was, and she loved him for it. He was there, in that moment, still alive and twitchy; worried about things that only existed in the space behind our world, in the cloud, where he always told her the essence of our reality was trafficked and exchanged; every interaction, transaction, and movement collected, collated, repackaged, and sold. He described a world that existed parallel to ours but completely out of sight. He spoke about this world the way Christians speak of heaven. She could never understand that anxiety, what with the real world in the state it was, but he spent so much time worrying about this cloud world that he may very well be a part of now.

In the darkness of that manifestation helmet, she was whole again and happy, but then the light started to creep in, and Zyv pulled the helmet off.

"Don't move," Zyv said. "Enjoy your moments in this timeline."

Dana opened her eyes and saw a man standing there, completely naked and fully erect, wearing only a manifestation helmet.

"Welcome your husband home, in this timeline and in every other one in which you can only feel his spirit," Zyv whispered.

"What the fuck!" Dana yelled, struggling against the belts.

"Miracles of manifestation often appear unbelievable," Zyv said.

The man in the helmet approached.

"Get the fuck away from me!" Dana yelled, struggling to get free.

Zyv just stood there, her smile that of a medieval devil. "Relieve yourself of the trauma of your husband's absence," she whispered encouragingly.

"Fuck you!" Dana cried, hyperventilating as the man in the helmet started to climb the table.

"Gack!" Dana finally yelled, and the man in the helmet stopped moving as if the word had magical powers.

"Is everything OK?" Zyv asked.

"Get these fucking belts off me and get the fuck out of my house!" Dana said.

"This is a normal reaction," Zyv said. "Right, Gareth?"

The man in the helmet nodded, his penis bobbing with the motion as if in agreement.

"Maybe we take a break?" Zyv asked.

"Get me out of these now!" Dana demanded.

Zyv shrugged and complied.

As soon as Dana was free, she slapped Zyv across the face.

"This is normal," Zyv said, nursing her cheek.

"Nothing about this is normal," Dana said. "Get out of my house before I squeeze the gack out of your fucking skull!"

CHAPTER EIGHTEEN

STOSH HAD DONE his research and believed he'd conceived a foolproof plan to start his own religion.

On their website, the IRS states that it "makes no attempt to evaluate the content of whatever doctrine a particular organization claims is religious, provided the particular beliefs of the organization are truly and sincerely held by those professing them and the practices and rites associated with the organization's belief or creed are not illegal or contrary to clearly defined public policy." There were other requirements, too. They needed regular services and practitioners trained in specific rites and traditions, which is where Zyv came in. She was a board-certified Scream Therapist and had obtained affiliation status with the Highest Plane School of Enlightenment to train and certify others in the modality.

Stosh didn't bother running the idea by the board. The process would only frustrate him and result in the usual deadlock, so, with his research complete, he and Ray showed Zyv around her new church.

Zyv stood in the sanctuary, staring up at the crucifix that hung from the ceiling.

"We can do something about Him," Stosh said.

"He's fine," Zyv smiled.

"Just got to come up with a name," Stosh said.

"And decide whether or not you want your roommate to remain a director," Ray said to Stosh.

"Al?" Zyv asked.

"Non-profits are required to have three directors," Ray said.

"And we didn't have a lot of options," Stosh said.

"He was OK with that?" Zyv asked.

"I'm sure he won't mind."

"I'll buy him some mozzarella sticks," Zyv said. "But maybe we can find someone else who's interested."

Stosh took a seat in one of the pews and watched Zyv inspect the place. Ray took a seat next to him.

"I held up my end," he said. "Everything is above board, so when can we have our first meeting?"

"I think it's a good idea, but are you sure the owners are going to go for it? I mean, isn't that what the board is for? I'm not sure how they'll feel about a deep state operating behind the scenes."

"It's not a 'deep state'," Ray said. "Think of it as another branch of government. We need checks and balances; you said so yourself."

"I know but maybe think of calling it something other than the politburo," Stosh said. "You know how the owners are."

In addition to letting Ray use Tara-Lynn's old place as a Catholic Worker Community, Stosh agreed to let him set up a second branch of government in the association—a kind of congress. Ray would divide the community into eight separate sectors, all of which would have representatives in this new body. In Ray's imagining, the president and his board would act as the executive branch, and the new congress as the legislative, proposing new policies and deciding where to allocate surplus funds, if there ever were any. Ray even hoped to create a judiciary to review fines and bylaw violations. Stosh thought it was a good idea, but he didn't believe it was a priority. He only agreed to the plan so Ray would file the appropriate paperwork for the church and keep his secret about Tara-Lynn and the money. Stosh didn't have time for Ray's utopia, but he would entertain the dream so long as it proved politically advantageous.

Ray left Stosh alone in the pew. He looked up to the crucifix, reached into his pocket, and pulled out the necklace Calvin had given him. He sat there for a moment and wondered what to do with it. It was heavy, the platinum likely worth the trouble of pawning it, but its mystery was too intriguing, the splinters shivered at the coincidences too perfect to be ignored, and so long as Dana remained in the dark, he had no reason to return it.

Stosh looked around the church, but the place failed to inspire the same awe as the Catholic churches he'd grown up in. There were no paintings on the ceilings, no cherubs with their grotesque wings and cocks flying around, no ornamental molding around the cubistic stations of the cross. This place had the styling of an Elk's Lodge built in the 70s—real shag-carpet chic, except the stained-glass windows, whose radiant colors seemed at odds with the rest of the place's earth-tone décor. He wasn't sure which biblical stories they were depicting, but their bright lights confused the aesthetic and made the place feel more like a flea market than a house of worship. He inspected one of them more closely—a woman in a modern pantsuit stood proudly, the heel of her pump impaled through an alligator's head as a man seemed to cower behind her. Stosh typed the Latin inscription into Google Translate: "Our Lady of the Royal Palm."

Fucking Tara-Lynn. Stosh couldn't help but smile.

Zyv threw a light switch that lit up the left side of the sanctuary, revealing a small wooden cupboard tucked in the corner by the baptismal font that appeared to be whatever the Protestant version of a tabernacle was. Stosh walked up to it. He was somewhat offended by the simplicity of the hutch and the plastic jars full of wafers that gave the communion about as much spiritual authority as a cheese-doodle. Regardless, he was tempted to pop one in his mouth, if only for nostalgia's sake, but thought better of it (they had desecrated the grounds enough). He went to put the necklace inside when Zyv approached him.

"That the necklace from the other night?" she asked.

"Calvin asked me to look after it. I'm not really sure what it is," Stosh said, showing Zyv the USB drive hidden within it.

She regarded it in her small hands.

"Might want to wipe your fingerprints off it," Stosh said.

"It's stolen?"

Stosh shrugged. "Guess so."

"Don't hide it here."

"It's just until I get the courage to give it back to Dana," he said. "I think it belonged to her husband."

"Then I can only imagine what's on this thing. He was in the CIA," Zyv said, looking at the necklace.

"I thought he was a software engineer," Stosh said. "Owned a company called Ascension."

"It was all deep cover. Why do you think he was on that flight? Who knows if he's even dead?" she said.

Stosh thought about it. He'd heard conspiracy theories about what happened to the flight but figured it was either bad luck or alien abduction. But with the way that summer was going, he couldn't be sure of anything.

"What happened between you guys?" Stosh pivoted. "Dana seemed upset when she saw you at the fireworks."

"She was a student of mine, and it didn't work out," Zyv said. "She was low vibrational."

"What's that mean?"

"The opposite of you and I," she said and kissed him.

Stosh put the necklace in the tabernacle as Zyv continued with her inspection. He could see her mind spinning, envisioning how she was going to set it up and what she was going to call it. "The Millennial Temple for the Universal Celebration of Life and the Triumph over Trauma" was what Stosh suggested over drinks on his back porch later that day, but Zyv thought it was too wordy.

After going back and forth with ideas for nearly an hour, Stosh went inside and poured them another round of vodka and Twisted Teas. Neither of them felt the teas alone had enough alcohol, but they didn't want to be ripping shots in the middle of a Wednesday afternoon, so Stosh introduced Zyv to Dana's Super Tea, (mix one peach Twisted Tea with one original Twisted Tea and two shots of vodka) which was damn good and refreshing in the afternoon heat.

It was Stosh's day off, and Al had taken his vacation that week, though he spent most of it held up in his room, smoking endless bongs and playing Call of Duty or watching reruns of *John D. Wolf: Bounty Hunter*. He was in the kitchen as Stosh mixed another batch of Super Tea.

"Want one?" he asked.

"A bit early," Al said, curtly, Gator grunting about his feet.

"You're on vacation."

"Still."

"Come on, man, why don't you come hang out?" Stosh asked. "We're trying to come up with a name for the church. It's kind of fun. I mean, how many opportunities are you gonna have to name a church?"

"I'll pass," he said.

"At least let me take Gator out," Stosh said, bending down to pet him.

"Gator does what he wants," Al said, giggling at his phone.

"What's up?"

"Nothing," Al said.

"Bullshit," Stosh said, leaning over his shoulder and stealing a glance at his phone. "Is that supposed to be me?"

Stosh looked at Al's Facebook feed, at the picture of himself in full golf attire taken when he was a senior in college. It was superimposed in front of a medieval cathedral, some gaudy shards of stained-glass flanking either side of his face; his eyes had been replaced by those of an anime character's—oversized, the pupils disproportionately smaller than the sclera. He stared sadly toward the sky, a halo floating above his head. The words "In Stosh We Trust" were written in white impact font below the image.

"It's just a meme," Al laughed.

Stosh read the comments section. Cletus had posted, "The false prophet!" Fred, whom Stosh was surprised even had a Facebook account, posted, "Cocksucker." And another post simply read, "Kill yourself."

"That guy doesn't even live here," Stosh said of the last poster.

Al shrugged, still smiling.

"Who posted it?" Stosh asked.

"Amy from across the street."

"What a bitch," Stosh said, a little impressed, flattered in a strange way. "What did I ever do to her?"

"Same thing you do to everyone."

"What's that supposed to mean?"

Al had always had a stick up his ass, but lately he had become an unbearable grouch, moping around and giving Stosh the silent treatment. Al didn't know Stosh had listed him as a director of the church, and Stosh wasn't going to tell him then. He didn't have time to unpack all his roommate's misery, or that meme, so he went back outside to where Zyv was still writing in her notepad, scribbling a few lines, only to cross them out in frustration.

"Everything is either too much or not enough," she said.

"I think Palm Ridge has its own yoga studio. I wonder what it's called," Stosh said. "Who knows, we might give them a run for their money."

"What do you mean?"

"What do they have that we don't?" Stosh chuckled. "We have a pool, and now a community center/church of enlightenment. We're pretty much a resort."

"Our pool is full of toxic sludge," she said. "Keep dreaming."

But the idea kind of stuck, and a moment of pride washed over Stosh. It may have all been held together by chewing gum and duct tape, but they'd held it together, and that was worth celebrating. It might not have been like how he envisioned it for himself, those years scraping it out on the mini tours so that he and Bambi could someday build a life of domestic bliss in a place like Palm Ridge, but this seemed to be as close as he'd ever get to that dream. He still felt on the peripherals of society, as though access to the mainstream was something he'd lost many years ago, if he ever even had it, and he still worried about what would happen with Zyv when her husband returned. He tried to conceive ways to preserve these moments—when they were drinking and talking, relaxing in each other's company—for the days, and weeks, and months, and years to come, but in that moment, he was proud and happy.

"Home," Zyv said then. "*Home: A Place for Spiritual Growth and Healing*. Because, like, we all want to be at home."

Stosh nodded, took a sip of Super Tea. "Home," he repeated with a smile.

He leaned over then and kissed her, tasted the peachy vodka on her lips. A couple of monarchs in their own little kingdom.

"I wonder what's on that USB drive," Zyv said.

"Calvin told me it was encrypted, so we may never know."

"One of my collaborators is an IT wizard," she said. "Maybe he could help."

Stosh shrugged. "You know where it is."

Zyv smiled. She stood up and took off her shorts, revealing her bikini bottoms.

"Time for some telluric rays," she said as she pulled off her shirt.

Stosh looked at her and reached for her butt, but she shooed him away, playfully.

"I want it too, but we need to retain," she told him.

He wasn't sure what that meant exactly, but he agreed if only to avoid embarrassment.

No one was at the pool, the residents having little use for it since the ooze arrived, but Stosh had dragged the old lounge chairs out from the shed and had been enjoying the sun there with Zyv when they found the time.

"Want some?" Stosh asked, showing Zyv the bottle of Banana Boat he'd brought with him.

"I never use the stuff," she said. "Full of micro-toxins."

"Micro-toxins?" Stosh said, reading the label's endless ingredients, none of which he could pronounce.

"The sun would never hurt her children," Zyv said.

"Gave Al's dad skin cancer."

"Not likely," she chuckled.

"You really don't believe sunscreen works?"

"It works to keep big sunscreen in business," she said. "You watch, let that sun hit this pool long enough, and whatever that sludge is, will be turned to water so pure you can drink it."

"I'll stick to the super tea," Stosh said, shutting his eyes. He was greeted by vague but pleasant dreams of birdies and eagles and great victories on tour, but there was a part of him that was still tethered to the waking world, a vague understanding that the dream wouldn't last, and he was OK with that. For once, he didn't mind waking up. And when he did, it was to Zyv's dirty foot digging into his ribs.

"Your phone's ringing," she said.

Stosh lifted his head, already heavy from the liquor, and looked at his phone. It was another email from Calvin, who'd been busy setting up the charity for his brother. Stosh should have known Calvin wasn't just spit balling when he mentioned the idea, but Stosh didn't think he'd actually put him in charge of the operation—even after he tried to refuse the duties and access to the newly formed 501c3's bank account, citing his position at the condo and his history of financial mismanagement. But that was

Calvin for you. Like a dog with a bone when he put his mind to something, and Stosh figured it was the least he could do, not only for his friend, but for Cecelia and the kids too.

"I think I'm going to ask her to be the inaugural presenter at Home," Zyv said, pulling Stosh from his phone.

The sun was cutting through the trees at a late angle. Its light seemed foreign. It was almost August, and the sun's arrows shot down in a way that made Stosh feel regretful, his eyes puffy and already hungover. Shadows listed across the ground and leaned against the world like drunks slumped at a bar.

"Who?" Stosh asked.

"Evangeline Sorenson."

CHAPTER NINETEEN

ZYV COLLABORATED with Evangeline for a series of posts promoting the event and put up flyers around the community, though that certainly meant trouble with Cletus and the others.

The night of the event, Stosh got held up by Calvin, who'd called him to ask how the planning for Christian's charity tournament was going.

"I'm sorry, man," Stosh said. "I've been so busy with this condo stuff, I haven't had a chance to ask the Ridge, but I'm sure they'll be able to work something out for the offseason."

"All right, well, get on it," Calvin said. "Because Cecelia already donated ten grand from her family's company, so if the course needs a deposit or anything, you have access to the account."

"Wow, that's great. I've been pounding the pavement down here, too," Stosh said. "I'll deposit it in the bank when I get a chance."

In reality, Stosh hadn't thought much about the tournament, though he had put out a mason jar with Christian's picture on it at the Ridge's bar, but last he checked, it only contained some loose change and a half-dozen broken tees.

Stosh hung up just as he was getting to the church. People gathered outside and started to file in around sunset. They were mostly the younger people in the community, including Amy, and a gaggle of youths Stosh didn't recognize but assumed were either from the neighboring trailer parks and daily-rate motels, or followers of Zyv's Instagram page.

They filled the sanctuary, anxiety and anticipation eclipsing their eyes as they took seats far from one another in the damp wooden pews. It was almost too much for Stosh, their hope palpable, suspended like cobwebs from the wooden gambles. He stepped outside for a cigarette just as Evangeline showed up, her designer bag in hand and her large sunglasses shielding most of her bronzed face.

"Anyone here yet?" she asked as she approached.

"Got a good crowd if you ask me, considering the mixed bag of beliefs people have down here," he said.

"And what about you?" she asked. "I know your friend didn't take the last reading very seriously."

"I have an open mind."

"But what about your heart?"

"A two-car garage," he smiled as Zyv came outside.

"We can do a one-on-one reading if you'd like," Evangeline said, then followed Zyv into the church.

Stosh punched out his cigarette to follow them, but a tall figure across the street caught his attention. The man was about a hundred and forty yards away—a pitching wedge—but Stosh could tell it was Brother Roland if only by that goofy bucket hat. Stosh waved, but Brother Roland didn't return the favor. A panther screamed somewhere in the distance, pulling Stosh's attention away, and when he looked back to where Brother Roland had been, he was gone.

Inside, Zyv addressed the congregation from the pulpit.

"I just want to say thank you to each and every one of you for coming," she started. "I know we've been through a lot these past months, and not just those here at the condo, but all of us, because our shifting timelines and the angle of the stars actually. I'm so honored to be given this opportunity. We don't care what or who you believe in, who you pray to, or what your sign is as long as you have the same goal, and that is to understand yourself better, better love the world, and live life with bigger smiles and abundance."

Zyv then introduced Evangeline, referring to her as an "expert in human tragedy," to which Evangeline kindly corrected her. "Human trauma." Zyv blushed and sheepishly ducked away from the pulpit.

Evangeline stood up and went into her preamble, explaining the differences between a psychic and a medium and how she had been blessed with both gifts, as well as her affiliation with the Intergalactic Association of Channelers, but was soon interrupted by a few latecomers.

"Is this the Friday Night Social?" a bearded man asked, his face red from the sun's relentless presence in his life.

"AA is downstairs," Stosh said.

The man nodded, looked around, and then walked to the basement door.

Evangeline went around the room, probing everyone with the same questions, making assumptions, and getting lucky. Stosh took a seat in the back and tried to see exactly how she did it. He was a Millennial, suspicious and doubtful by design. He'd seen so many institutions fail as soon as his generation leaned upon them for support that seeking the help of a psychic medium in a dilapidated church seemed totally reasonable. Like those in the crowd, he too hoped to find a new system of beliefs; new institutions, popes, and presidents who could provide the clarity and guidance that the old guard had failed to do.

Was his curiosity and hope the sign of a rising soul, of

someone reaching a higher stage of consciousness? Was Stanislaus Lech Saint-Jablonski ascending to a new astral plane? Or was he still groping around in the dark, reaching for something that was never there? The truth was it didn't matter. He was beginning to embrace this new life in such a way that made the questions irrelevant, for it wasn't the local Bishop or preacher up there beneath Christ, but Instagram poet- -philosopher, Evangeline Sorenson, with the clout of her one-hundred-thousand Instagram followers.

Some of the attendees hung around after Evangeline's reading. Some had their natal charts read by Zyv, and the whole scene was just too strange to make sense of, but Stosh supposed it was the vision Zyv had for the place, for her ministry as she'd called it, though he believed practice would have been a better word, considering the copays she and Evangeline were charging.

Evangeline approached Stosh as the last of the patients left.

"How about that one-on-one?" she asked.

"I'm not sure I can afford your rate," Stosh said.

"It's on the house."

Stosh had never said no to anything that was free. "In this world, that's the dumbest thing someone can do," Major used to say.

"Forgive me, Mother, for I have sinned," Stosh snorted.

"You use humor to protect your soul," she said.

"I guess."

"And you've lost someone," she said. "Someone close to you."

"He was hitting on you from beyond the grave."

"I'm not talking about Christian."

"My grandfather died when I was young."

"I'm picking up serious feminine vibes," she said. "Where's your mother?"

"You're probably better equipped to answer that than I am."

"She's not dead."

"That's a relief."

"You've never met her."

"Correct."

"Siblings?"

"None."

"An aunt," she said. "You were very close to your aunt."

"My father's an only child."

"What about your mom's side?"

"I wouldn't know."

"It was a woman you were close with," she said.

"There's a soon-to-be ex-wife," he said.

"This is different, kind of maternal, but controversial," she said.

"I believe you're feeling the omnipresent vibrations of our former tyrant, Tara-Lynn," he said.

"She was a bitch, huh?"

Stosh snorted again.

"Is there anything you want to ask me?" she said.

"Will Zyv and I stay together?" he barked.

"Petty, but if you want to be with her, you will be. Anyone can see she's in love with you."

Stosh smiled but thought that surely this line of questioning would inevitably coax enough information out of him that Evangeline could surmise the correct answers. But he had to admit there was something about her that made it feel more elevated than educated guessing. It was hard to explain. It was a feeling that he did not have the language to describe, but that his heart understood. Maybe it was her confidence, her air of authority, but either way, he felt as if she had tapped into the corners of his consciousness in a way that only Zyv had done.

Before he could say anything else, he heard a loud bang coming from outside, followed by the unmistakable voice of one Cletus Wriggle, who led Fred and a mob of owners into the sanctuary.

"Please," Zyv said, with a smile, "this is a place of peace."

"This place is a scam," Cletus said, looking at Stosh. "I thought the Jesus freaks were bad, but this? This is just insanity," he said, holding the flyer Zyv had placed under his door.

"We need the money," Stosh said. "But I suppose that doesn't matter much to you, considering your mom still pays your HOA fees."

"Please take this outside," Zyv said, now taking on a look of concern. "I don't care who or what you believe in, this is still a place of worship."

"Is that the witch?" Fred said, pointing to Evangeline.

"Please," Zyv said again, "take your petty arguments somewhere else."

"The young lady is right," Mrs. Bronski said, waving her hand and shuffling in front of Cletus and Fred. "I may not agree with what's going on here, but as long as He is still up there," she said, pointing her cane to the crucifix, "this is still a church."

"I thought you agreed with us," Cletus said, but Mrs. Bronski held her hand to him and said, "outside."

Cletus deflated and led the mob outside, where they stood waiting for Stosh.

"Take Evangeline out the back and call the cops," Stosh said to Zyv.

"You don't have to go out there," she said.

"I'll be fine."

Stosh almost reached for the last nip in his pocket, but he didn't want to give Cletus any more reason to hate him, so he went out there more sober than he'd like to be.

"I don't know where you get off," Cletus said as Stosh walked outside, "but you got a lot of nerve."

"No one else had any ideas. We're drowning here."

"And who's to say that's not your fault?" Cletus said. "After all, giving a church to your girlfriend—a married woman, at that— seems a lot like something Tara-Lynn would do."

"Do you speak for all of them?" Stosh said, turning to the

mob. "What's more important, the roof over your head or your beliefs?"

Some in the crowd grumbled.

"I'm trying my best with what little we have. We'd gladly take donations from any of you, hell, even a productive suggestion, but here you stand, silent, save for this brute," Stosh said, pointing a dainty finger at Cletus.

But before Stosh or anyone else could say a word, Fred took his cane and smashed one of the stained-glass windows.

Everyone flinched.

"Fred," Cletus said, as shocked as the others.

Fred didn't respond; he just lifted his cane high above his head like Abraham held the knife, but instead of God, it was Officer Billy who intervened.

The mob scattered and dragged themselves back to their condos. Cletus and Stosh hung around to give their statements to Officer Billy as the other officers put Fred in a cruiser. This time, Stosh agreed to press charges, though he had little hope they would result in anything but another mandatory psych evaluation.

The police lights danced across the church, shimmering against the remaining stained-glass windows, and standing across the street was Brother Roland, his chin raised in righteous defiance and his ridiculous bucket hat glowing in the dark. Stosh wondered what holy storm he was bringing with him.

Al was sitting on the couch with his chin in his chest when Stosh got home. Assuming he was passed out, Stosh tried to be quiet, but Al perked up at the sound of the door shutting. He lifted his head, his eyes swollen and red but not shot with vodka's bloody veins.

"Gator's gone missing," he whimpered.

THE PASSION OF SAINT-JABLONSKI

A Letter from Vice President Zyv
to the People of the Association

Greetings, friends, star-seeds, humans:

Most of you are probably aware of the incident we had at Home the other night. Violence is the lowest form of consciousness, and I know we can do better, which is why I want to invite everyone to come check out our community, your community!

We're here for you, after all, and we want everyone to take part in what we have to offer at Home. I know what we're doing might seem a little odd, because it is! We're oddballs, like you!

We're not scary, just weird, and at Home, we think that's great. We want you to be yourself so that we can be better selves.

And we're open to ideas, so if there's anything you want to explore, why not do it where you're comfortable, at Home.

As for the incident with Fred, although we should forgive, we will only do so when Fred learns to embrace a higher vibrational frequency, a level of consciousness I know we can all achieve.

Please, come get to know us, but even if you don't, Home is there for you, working for you. Our presence in the community will alleviate the association's back taxes and be a vital source of income.

We look forward to seeing you here, there, and everywhere!

With great love, abundance, and beautiful spirit,
Zyr
Vice President of the Association

CHAPTER TWENTY

AL WAS UP ALL NIGHT, moving about the kitchen, coming and going out the back door. Stosh could hear him stalking around the patios, trampling over the perennial grasses that lined the little parcels of earth they were allotted, whispering the things we whisper for our friends to return to us.

He was already lacing up his boots when Stosh got up the next morning.

"It's not like he can't survive," Stosh said, following him out the door. "He's a wild animal."

"That's not the point."

"Then what're you all dithered up about?"

Al shook his head and hollered for Gator.

Stosh grabbed him by the shoulder, "We'll find him, all right?"

"Jesus, man," Al snapped. "I'm sick of picking up after you."

Stosh stepped back.

"I told you not to bring the pig into the house, but you insisted, and who's taken care of him?"

"I've been busy," Stosh said. "You know we're holding on by a thread here."

"Why didn't you ask me to be the Vice President?" Al said. "I mean, you asked Zyv, and you don't even know her. I feel like your fucking butler sometimes."

"I didn't know you wanted to be on the board."

"I don't."

"You're impossible."

"It's the principal. I moved down here with you, and what have we done? Nothing. We're doing the same things we did in high school—we get drunk, smoke weed, and eat fast food."

"How is that my fault?"

"I don't know. I guess it's not," Al said. "I'm just sick of sitting around. Sick of missing my dad, and I'm sick of this goddamn heat," he said, lifting the belly of his shirt to his forehead to dry the sweat. "I know you gave me a choice, but it doesn't change the fact that I have nothing, and that Gator is missing, and that I love the little shit."

"I suppose now's as good a time as ever," Stosh said. "But we needed another director to make the church tax-exempt."

"You're kidding me."

"It's not the Vice Presidency, but you're on the board of Home: A Place for Spiritual Growth and Healing."

Al looked to the heavens, the veins in his neck pulsing blue.

"Listen, we'll go play a round somewhere, just me and you," Stosh said. "Somewhere we've never played. Hell, I'll even take you to Disney if you want. I've never been. Whatever you want to do," Stosh said. "You know how much I appreciate all you do around here. Just don't hold this shit in. We've been through too much not to talk about it."

"Yeah," Al said, swallowing the rock in his throat. "But what happens if this whole thing—whatever it is you got going up there at the church—doesn't work? What the hell do we do then?"

"If the pig can survive, a couple of feral boys like us will be just fine."

The two split up then, with Al heading off to look in the thickets that separated the condo from the air force base, and

Stosh starting down toward the brook that ran along the back of the property.

Stosh was a little concerned to go down there alone, with the homeless encampment and all, but it was daylight, and he figured they were harmless enough, as harmless as any other addict, just looking for money and relief. The worst thing they could do was rob him, and he didn't have much they could take. But before he could reach the brook, he saw Cletus standing with a Black man in the back parking lot.

The two seemed to be in conversation until Stosh saw Cletus place his hand on the Black man's shoulder and turn him around, as if to arrest him.

"Mind your business, Jablonski, let me handle this," Cletus said as Stosh approached.

"This dude is crazy," the Black man said. "I'm just doing my job."

"And what job is that?" Cletus asked, "Trampling on our civil liberties?"

"Jesus, Cletus, let him go. You don't have the authority."

"You're not a cop?" the Black man asked.

"Not anymore," Stosh said.

"Get off me, man," the Black man said.

Cletus released him but remained in his face. "He's with BLM," he said. "Look at his shirt."

Stosh looked at the man's shirt embossed with the letters BLM.

"I'm an intern with the Bureau of Land Management," the man said.

Stosh couldn't help but smile. "I think you're confused," he said to Cletus.

"I know what it stands for," Cletus snarled. "The Bureau of Land Management is far more dangerous than any gang of Antifa thugs. But now that you mention it, I found this on him..."

Cletus held high a device that, to the untrained eye, looked somewhat like a hand grenade, but that Stosh easily recognized as a vape.

"Could be some kind of false flag operation," Cletus said. "What better cover for BLM than, well, BLM."

"It's just nicotine," the man said. "I'm trying to quit smoking."

"Let's see some ID," Cletus demanded.

"I'm an intern, man, I'm lucky I even got the shirt."

"Well, what the fuck are you doing here?" Cletus asked.

"I'm surveying the area," the man said. "We got reports of some kind of runoff leaking from the base, and I'm trying to find out what's going on."

"The black ooze?" Stosh asked.

"Ooze, sludge, whatever it is," the man said.

"Where's your car?" Cletus continued his interrogation.

"Just let him get on with his business," Stosh said.

"I walked."

"Walked? What kind of government agent has to walk?" Cletus asked, looking at Stosh with that smug smile of his.

"I told you, I'm an intern. I was told to go to the brook and see if the ooze was down there. Busy work. My dad works up at Palm Ridge, so I went in with him this morning and walked down here."

"Your dad works at the Ridge?" Stosh asked.

"Yeah," the Black man said, "Henry Adams."

"The security guard?" Stosh asked.

"And how were you going to get back?" Cletus asked. "It's getting damn hot out here to walk all that way across all those tarmacs."

"I was gonna call an Uber from the main road up there," the Black man said.

"Why don't I give you a ride back to the Ridge?" Stosh said. "It's the least I can do."

"Hell no," Cletus said. "I don't care who your dad is; this is all too convenient."

"I have some paperwork in my dad's car from the agency," the Black man said, "but I don't know why you won't take my word for it."

"If that's the case, I'm coming with you," Cletus said.

"Let's just get you out of here before you sue us," Stosh smiled at the Black man, who seemed even more skittish than before. "You OK?" Stosh asked him.

"I don't know how I feel about getting in a car with you," he said.

"I know your father. I work at the Ridge, too," Stosh said. "Just trying to do the right thing."

"I guess I don't have much of a choice," he said, looking at Cletus.

"Are we leaving or what?" Cletus asked, leading the way.

"He doesn't have to come," Stosh said.

"No. He's coming, and he's about to look like a real asshole."

And with that, they piled into Stosh's truck and drove up the road.

"I thought you got rid of those crazies," Cletus said, looking out the passenger window at the church parking lot, where Brother Roland and his disciples stood silently in what looked like prayer, a few of them holding signs.

"Damn, what kind of place are you people running here?" the Black man asked.

"Don't ask me," Cletus said, shooting Stosh a glance.

"You in charge here?" the Black man asked Stosh.

"Here I stand," he said. "I can do no more."

"Martin Luther?" the Black man asked Stosh.

"Maybe," Stosh said. "Yeah, I think so."

"I was developing an RPG about his life," the Black man said.

"You're making a video game about Martin Luther?" Stosh asked.

"I'm so sick of this Woke culture," Cletus said.

"Martin Luther the monk, you scrambled egg," Stosh said to Cletus.

The Black man cracked a smile.

"Still a strange topic for a video game," Stosh said.

"He lived an exciting life. He was in constant danger. My church was funding the development. They funded a game based on King David's life. Sold really well," the Black man said. "But Dad doesn't see a future in the gaming industry, not for Black people. Made me get a degree in environmental engineering."

"Black ooze, huh?" Cletus eyed the Black man suspiciously.

"Part of the Air Force cleanup of the base. They don't tell me much, but the bureau got complaints, and so now I'm here."

Cletus scoffed, saying, "Just like the federal government to invade private property."

"I wouldn't consider one man an invasion," Stosh said. "And wasn't it your idea to call the base about the sludge in the first place?"

"Classic government overreach," Cletus said.

They had come to a complete stop. Traffic on the strip was usually stop-and-go, but that day it was at a standstill.

"That's right—President's in town!" Cletus said as if he would be joining him for dinner that night.

"That guy is such a fraud," Stosh said.

"Sorry, he's not some blue-haired, poly-globalist Marxist like you," Cletus said.

"I'm not any of those things," Stosh said.

"Neither am I," the Black man said.

"Whatever you say," Cletus said.

"I'm an accelerationist," the Black man said.

"I don't know what that is, but I know we need a serious change in this country," Cletus said.

"It means I believe our society is no longer sustainable," the Black man said. "We need to break everything down, blow it up, start over."

"See, even the kid agrees with me," Cletus said.

"I wouldn't go that far," the Black man said. "People like you have had your time. You've benefited from the current system until recently. And my name's Angel."

"Well, Angel, who did you vote for in the election?" Cletus asked.

"I don't vote," he said. "It doesn't make a difference."

"What about you?" Cletus asked Stosh.

"Not him," Stosh said, nodding at a GOOP sign on the side of the road.

"Figures." Cletus rolled his eyes, said, "We need limited government. Big business, and a lot less whining."

"Government jobs have been some of the best avenues to the middle class, especially for Black people," Stosh said, stealing a glance at Angel, who ignored him.

"The President is going to drag the deep state from the shadows, pump the septic tank, and return us to the GOOP."

Stosh was starting to get a headache. "What do you have against government?" he asked. "You were a cop. You *were* the government. And that pension of yours probably wouldn't be worth half of what it is if it weren't for your union."

"That's local government," Cletus said. "Totally different."

Stosh rolled his eyes, looking at Angel in the rearview mirror for camaraderie, but he just stared back blankly.

"All I know is that not everything is about race or gender. It's not like how it was when I was a kid," Cletus said.

"And how was that?" Stosh asked.

"There used to be KKK rallies right in the town square," he said.

"Like what happened in Carlsville last summer?" Stosh said.

"That was a false flag," Cletus said. "It's changed. People like him," he said, nodding to Angel in the back, "could get killed just for walking the wrong way back then."

"You mean people like J'Davious Wallace?" Stosh asked.

"He was high!" Cletus argued. "A rap-sheet as long as my leg."

"And that gave the cops the right to give him the death sentence?" Angel asked. "You sound like a cop."

"Not just any cop. He's Cletus Wriggle," Stosh said. "A proud Big Boy of the Bygone Day."

"You're *that* guy?" Angel said. "Jesus, my father would kill me if he knew I got into a car with you. Always told me to stay away from cops, I can only imagine what he thinks of you."

"Really?" Stosh said. "Doesn't seem like something your dad would say."

"You don't know Dad," Angel said. "He talks to you like that 'cause you're white and probably make more money than him. You think he's gonna be honest with you?"

Stosh thought about that for a moment and felt bad, as if he'd done something wrong. He considered himself an ally. He posted a blacked-out screenshot on Instagram after J'Davious Wallace was killed. He voted for the lesser of two evils once and hope and change twice! He felt he had more in common with Angel than he ever would with Cletus or the President. But maybe he didn't do enough. After all, he had the privilege to wait for his confusion and disgust to pass after the president was elected. His life—he knew—would go on almost the same as it ever had.

Stosh always said the right things, bought the right products and watched the right movies and shows, but he never actually did anything, and when faced with racial inequalities or fascist politics in the wild, he was revealed to be at worst a reactionary, and at best just another a lily-livered liberal inching ever closer to the right if only to preserve his own position in the national corporation's org chart.

"Nothing means anything anymore," Angel said. "Everything is stripped of any real meaning, you know? Makes me almost miss the bygones Dad talks about, when you knew who the racists were, when they burned crosses and branded themselves with Swastikas. They were proud. They acted in good faith. At least you knew who you were dealing with, but now I wonder what that thin blue line really means."

"You don't know what it's like," Cletus said. "I put my life on the line every time I put my uniform on. Put it on the line for everyone. Whoever needed me. And I know you two are too young to remember, but I turned state's evidence against the sheriff's department in the eighties."

"What'd they have on you?" Stosh asked cynically.

"Nothing," Cletus said. "The department was corrupt back then, and I did something about it, but you wouldn't understand, because now we have every blue-haired SJW harassing us in the comments section. I was ostracized after I testified. Distrusted by the community I patrolled and hated by the department that was supposed to have my back."

"All right, Serpico," Stosh said. "I'll take your word for it."

"You think you could do a better job?" he asked Stosh.

"No, and that's why I'm not a cop," Stosh said.

They were still stuck in traffic, inching along at a speed Stosh's speedometer couldn't even register.

"Hey," Cletus said, perking up in his seat, "I think that's Fred."

Stosh looked across the street and saw the old man stalking toward them, not on the sidewalk, but on the shoulder of the road, peeking into every car he passed with that snarled look on his face, his back as twisted and barbed as the walking stick that held him up.

"Pick him up," Cletus said.

"What? No," Stosh said.

"It's gotta be over a hundred degrees out there," Cletus said. "He's an old man."

"He's on his own," Stosh said. "He's caused me nothing but trouble."

"Man, you're ice cold," Angel said from the back.

"You don't understand, this guy is a menace," Stosh said.

"Seems like you got a lot of them around your neck of the woods," Angel said.

"You have no idea," Stosh said.

"You say that as if you're not one of them," Angel said.

Stosh's throat tightened, but even if he could speak, what would he have said?

"I mean, you may not be the problem, but what have you done to be a part of the solution?" Angel said. "Let me guess, you posted some shit on social media, put BLM in your Tinder profile, and went about your life. 'Likes and shares are the liberal version of hopes and prayers,' Dad always says. But what he thought could be fixed through good jobs and political action, just needs to be demolished, then maybe we'll have better luck in whatever system comes next."

Stosh sank deeper into his guilt.

"Hey, Fred!" Cletus said, hanging out the passenger window and waving at him. "Hop in!"

Stosh ate what choice words he had for Fred. Angel was right —he was becoming icy, impatient. He'd forgotten the opportunity he had at the condo—the opportunity to change what he could, to control the controllables, and build a better community. Most of us lack the means and opportunity to effect change in the world as it so benevolently does upon us, but he had an opportunity to make a difference at the condo. He had never thought too deeply about his politics. Maybe he was an accelerationist, too. After all, he'd done away with most of Tara-Lynn's old system, and in its place was building a system that worked better for everyone, Fred included. Or maybe that made him a communist, or maybe Zyv was right—maybe we can only change ourselves and hope everyone else does the same. Either way, Stosh needed to keep his cool, so he unlocked the back door as Fred approached.

"Where've you been?" Cletus asked.

"VA hospital," the old man said. "Cops sent me for a mandatory hold. Fucking thought police."

Stosh thought about saying something, but the nicest thing he could do at that moment was keep his mouth shut.

"I saw the President's limo up there," Fred said, "but couldn't get close enough to see him with all the security."

"Who did you vote for in the election?" Cletus asked him.

"Not him."

Stosh nearly choked on his own laughter.

"Why the hell not?" Cletus demanded of Fred.

"President's a chicken-hawk," Fred said. "Lied his way out of the draft. Can't respect a man who does that."

"That's the first thing I've ever agreed with you on," Stosh said.

"Don't think they'd have much use for someone like you in the service," Fred said.

"What's that supposed to mean?" Angel asked.

"Kid's a fag," Fred said.

"I'm not gay," Stosh said. "Didn't you accuse me of sleeping with another man's wife?"

"That was me," Cletus said.

"Like I said, you're cold-blooded," Angel said to Stosh.

"It's not like that," Stosh said. "She's polyamorous."

"That's some soy-boy cuck shit," Angel said.

"Unnatural," Cletus added.

"Or is it monogamy that's unnatural?" Stosh asked.

"Fag has a point," Fred said.

"What, you believe in that shit?" Cletus asked him.

"What does it matter what people do in their own bedrooms?" Fred said.

"I just figured you for a Christian man," Cletus said.

"For what it's worth," Fred said, "but how can loving as many women as possible be a sin?"

"Well, Angel's with me on this," Cletus said. "Aren't you, Angel?"

"I hate to admit it," he said, "but I'm a traditionalist in that regard. Polyamory is a feminist construct to keep betas simping over low-value women."

"Yeah, what he said," Cletus said.

Stosh went silent. Alliances had shifted, and with the looming threat of Cletus and now Angel, he had to be prudent.

Traffic began moving again. They were finally on their way to the Ridge, certainly now more confused than ever.

They pulled up to the service entrance and into the employee parking lot.

Angel opened his door and walked over to his dad's car.

"Are you seriously whistling Dixie right now?" Stosh asked Cletus as Angel walked across the lot.

Cletus chuckled, "I don't even realize when I'm doing it."

"Well, can you whistle something else?" Stosh asked.

"What would you like to hear?" he asked.

"Just shut up or whistle something else," Stosh said.

"Well, I can't very well whistle the double bass intro to *Hot for Teacher*, can I?"

Stosh let his head drop onto the steering wheel.

Angel returned to the truck and slapped an offer letter—with the Bureau of Land Management seal on the top—against the passenger window for Cletus to see.

"That good enough for you?" he asked.

"I kind of like him," Cletus said with a smirk as Angel walked away.

"Let's hope he doesn't sue us," Stosh said.

Back at the Association, the sun was setting, the light streaking through the pines in bright shards. Stosh dropped Fred off at his unit, but he just turned on his heels and started walking back toward the main road, where he was going, only God knew.

Stosh parked in his spot, and Cletus got out of the truck.

"I still don't know what the hell you were thinking," Stosh said to him.

"You know," he said, leaning across the truck's hood on his

elbows, "you may not be a crook, like I thought you were, but you're naïve and immature. I don't trust you. You're soft, and all your little schemes are gonna come back to haunt you."

"Really? I thought we were finally turning a corner," Stosh said.

"I'm gonna do everything in my power to get you out of here," Cletus said.

Stosh composed himself and bit right back. "Are you treading on me?"

"Cute," he said, walking back toward his place. "Don't get too comfortable."

Al still wasn't back when Stosh got home.

His head hurt. His eyes couldn't adjust to the strange light still leaking in through the blinds. He was tired and needed a drink. The shots warmed his belly and eased the muscles in his neck and shoulders. He took a seat on the couch and lit a cigarette. The smoke danced blue in the jaundice light. He turned on the news, and there was Cletus's face. The anchor said the Sheriff's Department might reinstate him as an auxiliary officer if a deal with the union could be reached.

Fucking unions.

CHAPTER TWENTY-ONE

STOSH AND AL spent several weeks looking for Gator in between their respective shifts at the Ridge, but by mid-August, they'd all but given up. Al was coming around to the idea that Gator was gone and that all parties were likely better off because of it, though he wished he could've said goodbye. But that's the way it goes.

Stosh never said goodbye to Bambi, not officially. Didn't even say goodbye to his dad before he got locked up. He tried with Bambi, in the days and weeks after they broke up. He called her relentlessly, begged her to meet up, and when she finally relented and met him for coffee, he thought he'd get some closure, but it ended in vague pleasantries, like the kind you wish upon your high school classmates at graduation.

Then there was the time she came back to Cold Springs for Thanksgiving. Who she was there to see was never clear—her mother was already in Florida, and Major was on trial, so Stosh was staying with Al. The two went to the Dugout the night before.

It was the usual high school reunion. Stosh thought it was nice at first, seeing the people he hadn't seen since the night before Thanksgiving the year before, but everyone kept asking him about his career, saying they were rooting for him, and some even asked him for swing advice. It was pathetic, and for his sins, he gave it to them.

Stosh spotted her first and tried to play it cool. He waved politely. Fantasized about ripping her collar bones out with his teeth. They exchanged smiles from across the bar several times before approaching one another, and when they spoke, they spoke about nothing in particular. There was some reminiscing and laughter. He told her where he was staying and how to get in through the back door, and they laughed some more, and he no longer looked at her collar bones, but he went to the bar alone and took a shot before going home with Al.

Stosh was starving, but it was the early hours of a holiday morning, and even McDonald's was closed, so he made Al drive him to the Cumby's on East Street. He got a steak, egg, and cheese from the case beneath the heat lamp, and Al looked at him with disgust as he devoured the rubbery thing.

They smoked a joint when they got home. Al went to bed soon after, but Stosh lost consciousness on the couch, still in his winter coat, Alkaline Trio's '97 playing through the broken speakers of his phone.

An hour later, his phone woke him up.

"The back door's locked," she said. "I'm freezing."

Stosh was silent, a dreamy film about his head.

"It's me," Bambi said.

Stosh gathered himself as best he could and greeted her.

"So much for the backdoor," she said.

It was exactly as he'd wanted. He couldn't believe it, the way he led her down to the basement, and the way they got right down to it, like the way they used to get right down to it, but he was drunk and full of bad food. He hadn't moved like that since the last time they'd gotten down to it, so afterward he righted himself, grunted in a strange way, and then vomited all over the floor.

"Was it *that* bad?" she asked.

"No, no," he said, pulling at the rope of snot hanging from his nose. "It was the sandwich. I promise."

"I'm gonna go."

"Bambi."

"This wasn't good for either of us," she said, stealing a glance at the vomit on the floor.

But Stosh kept calling, kept wanting one more time, one more chance to cauterize the wound, but every time they talked, it was just like ripping the scab off again. This continued until she stopped taking his calls and eventually sent him the divorce papers, but that only gave him an excuse to keep holding on, gave him a thin fishing line of hope that would tether them together for just a little while longer. That's the thing about the last time— you don't know it's the last time until much later, when your memories have coagulated into nothing but a mirage of pleasant nostalgia that you mistake for hope.

The last time they looked for Gator was a hazy Sunday morning, and by noon, they'd given up. Al dragged himself back to the condo, and Stosh walked up to the church. He'd been spending a lot of time there, even without Zyv. It was a good place to reflect, a place separate from everywhere and everything else. It wasn't his home, which had become nothing but a headache, with Al's moping and the problems with the condo, and it wasn't work, which always made him feel inferior and ashamed. And it wasn't a bar where most go to complain and whine about their problems. It was a place to work on himself, to soul search and practice his breathwork, and if he kept it up, Zyv said he'd be ascending in no time, though he'd settle for sleeping with her again.

Brother Roland and his merry martyrs had continued their protests at random, showing up spontaneously to perform various foreboding rituals and cautionary Biblical tales, so Stosh was happy at their absence when he arrived at the church that day.

Zyv was talking with a young couple as Stosh entered. A small man in a motorized wheelchair drove about the sanctuary, spinning wires to and from monitors and speakers that had been set to the walls.

"Hi, love," Zyv said to Stosh with a gentle smile. "This is Gareth and Alexandria Jubenville."

Stosh smiled and noted Gareth's height and slim frame. He was wearing a large black T-shirt, skinny jeans, and a pair of immaculately white Nikes. His slick look and sculpted arms suggested Silicon Valley by way of Austin and stood in contrast to his wife's dreadlocks, septum ring, and lotus peddles dripping from the tattoo on her chest..

"And that's Dill, the tech wiz," Zyv said, pointing to the man in the wheelchair who continued his rounds.

Gareth stood and stuck his hand out, said, "Gareth Jubenville, Chief Spiritual Officer of Jubenville Whole-istic."

"They're very popular on Instagram," Zyv said.

"We have a similar community to the one you have here, but virtually," Gareth said.

"An affordable condominium complex?" Stosh smirked.

"No," Gareth laughed, "like Ascension."

"Ascension?" Stosh asked, looking at Zyv. "Like, the company?"

"We saw it on the side of the USB and thought it was perfect," Zyv said.

"*Home* was a little too vague," Alexandria said.

"And then we were thinking *The Whitman House*, you know, because he's my favorite poet," Zyv said.

"But that kind of sounds like a halfway house, right?" Alexandria said, looking at Zyv.

"Isn't *Ascension* a bit too Christian?" Stosh asked.

"I was a little hesitant, too, but it's a stronger brand," Zyv said.

"And it doesn't have to mean ascension to heaven. It can just mean, like, elevating to a higher plane."

"Exactly," Alexandria said.

"I suppose it has a nice ring to it," Stosh said.

"After all," Gareth said, "Jesus was an influencer, had followers, a brand. I'm not wrong."

"He's not wrong," Alexandria said.

"Gareth and Alexandria are interested in a partnership," Zyv said.

"And in that love algorithm," Gareth said.

"It's the algorithm *of* love," Zyv corrected him.

"Yeah," Alexandria agreed, "the love algorithm sounds like a reality show."

"You guys have an algorithm for true love?" Stosh asked.

"I'll tell you all about it," Zyv said, jingling the crucifix with the USB in it.

"Zyv says it really works," Alexandria said, glancing over at Gareth, her eyes bulging like an addict staring at a hot spoon.

"This place might be the hinge on which the new world meets the old again," Gareth said. "This might be where we find our Apostles."

"I don't know much about technology, but the algorithm of true love sounds like science fiction," Stosh said.

"Think about it," Gareth pondered, looking out from the sanctuary at his imagery congregation.

His wife moved then, her phone at the ready, and started recording him.

"If you could turn vibes into lines on a map, they'd all point here, right, babe?" he said, craning his neck.

"A very high frequency," she said from behind her phone.

He smiled and looked at the vaulted ceiling. His wife circled him, recording from every angle.

"It's a pitch like none other, vibrating from a continuum of alternate timelines. Hope echoed," he said.

"That's beautiful," Alexandria said.

"OK," Gareth said, taking a deep breath, "That should be good."

He stepped down into the nave, and his wife showed him what she'd recorded.

"Good, good," he said.

Then he said, "We'll be back for the service tomorrow, but Dill's gonna hang behind to finish setting up."

"Can someone show me to the basement?" Dill asked. "I need access to the modem."

"And remember to face the books toward the door. Probably want to set them up somewhere in the front, and maybe put a few on the altar, where everyone can see them," Gareth said before leaving the church.

"Books?" Stosh asked.

"Alexandria is a poet," Dill said, pointing to a box of books in the corner by the door.

"And what the heck is Gack?" Stosh asked, reading the label on a second stack of boxes.

"It's their supplement," Zyv said.

"Gareth's proprietary blend," Dill said, scooting toward the basement door. "I'll find a way to get myself down there."

"Sounds almost as interesting as the algorithm of love," Stosh said.

"I haven't had a chance to tell you," Zyv said. "Dill was able to decrypt what was on the USB, and I have to say, it's pretty wild."

She smiled like a hyena.

"What is it, like, *Tinder* or something?" Stosh asked.

"It's so much more than a dating app," she said. "You input someone's ideal partner specs, like eye color, height, weight, and whatnot, along with any personality types, cultural interests, and political views and then it uses AI to create a unique profile on the blockchain, like out of thin air, and then searches the internet for the best possible match."

"I guess that blows your theory about Dana's husband being in the CIA," Stosh said. "I don't think they're in the business of matchmaking."

"I don't know," she said. "Think about it. What better psyop is there than love?"

"Whatever the case, you should probably think about changing the name or at least limiting who knows about it," Stosh said, pawing at a phantom vibration from the splinters. "I'd hate for it to get back to Dana."

"I told you, she's low vibrational; she wouldn't know what to do with technology like this."

"Well, if it really works, what does it say about us?"

"We already have each other," she said. "This is for people looking for *their* Zyv," she winked.

"What're you going to do with it?"

"I'm gonna use it."

"And the Jubenvilles?"

"I've worked with them before," Zyv said. "They have, like, two hundred thousand followers, and I figured we could collab, you know, Gack and Ascension, total brain, gut, and soul health."

"Why is it that color?" Stosh said, regarding a jar of Gack.

"It's just dye," she said. "You poop blue after you take it. That's how you know it's working."

"Can you say that more slowly?"

"Don't worry about," she said. "It's wicked popular, and I have a chance to be a brand ambassador for it."

"Is that what you want to be, an *influencer*?" Stosh said.

"Don't make it sound so dirty," she said, "but sure, I mean, I could start making real money doing what I love. If tonight goes well, they might even buy some of my shares."

"Shares of what?"

"Gareth is a savant," she said. "He sold shares in his future to a bunch of venture capitalists. He made a fortune on his IPO."

"His company is public?"

"No, his Initial Personal Offering. He sold shares in himself, in his future," she said. "Investors will see a return on everything he does, and he might want to do the same with me. Says my potential is wild."

"That's one word for it," Stosh said.

"I don't need your cynicism right now," she said. "This could be a great opportunity for me, for this place."

"Sounds like new age slavery."

"You need to think bigger," she said. "More money for me means more money for you and the condo. But it might not even matter if those crazies come back."

"I didn't see them out there," Stosh said. "It is the sabbath after all."

They went to work setting up and merchandising Jubenville's books and Gack. Stosh picked one of the books up and regarded it. It looked and felt cheap, smelled like the inside of a cardboard box, different from the musty comfort of the books he'd filed away and cared for in the university library.

He cracked one open and read a few lines.

> *"Pleiadians plant all that we grow,*
> *They bring the light, the rain, and the snow.*
> *What splendors they provide and what wonders*
> *But the Reptilians come to rape and plunder.*
> *Star-seeds germinate all that you see*
> *Rise up, sweet seeker, awaken to what you're meant to be!*
>
> *Ha-la, ha-la, lamin-la-la-linking,*
> *Nasa say-ba-lay, low-lana, la-maia!*
>
> *Rise up, sweet seeker,*
> *Light language is sweeter.*
> *Rise up, star-seed,*
> *Heal yourself; you is all you need.*

Rise up!
Rise up!
Rise up!
The world is big and scary, but our souls are ours to
carry!"

Stosh was no wordsmith, but he knew what he liked, and although he may not have understood the poem, he like that last part. A new mantra. A new prayer for his new religion.

He put the book away and went back to unpacking the Gack from their boxes. But just as he and Zyv were finishing up, they heard Brother Roland return.

This time, the Last Men were all walking in a circle around the perimeter of the parking lot, moaning and chanting like the Israelites at Jericho. They were in white robes, with Brother Roland leading the way, his floral-patterned bucket hat perched high on his head. Sara followed directly behind him, wearing angel wings, like the kind you find at one of those Halloween shops that squat in whatever vacant storefronts lie available around October, like hermit crabs occupying a discarded shell.

For a group of only about a dozen people, they sure made a lot of noise.

"I'm calling the cops," Zyv said, taking out her phone.

"Wait," Stosh said, "I don't think that's a good idea."

"Why?"

"They were just here for the Fred incident, and now with the Bureau of Land Management poking around after Cletus's stunt, the last thing we need is more attention."

"But they're trespassing," Zyv said.

"I don't want to risk it."

"Risk what?"

"The algorithm *is* stolen," Stosh said.

"They'll have no reason to think we have it."

Stosh looked outside and saw the zealots filling up a kiddie pool with jugs of store-bought water. Brother Roland continuously blessed himself as the waterline rose in the plastic pool, his disciples working like an old fire brigade, passing along the bottles to one another and dumping them into the impromptu baptismal font.

"I have an idea," Stosh said, straightening out his collar and brushing off the front of his shirt as he made his way outside.

"Ahoy, Satan! Here comes the ringleader of the devil's own circus," Brother Roland announced at Stosh's appearance. "Don't look now, brothers and sisters, the time is too close. Like Lot's wife, you will suffer the Lord's wrath if you look back!"

The disciples continued to fill the pool, all the while chanting in indiscernible tongues—a full-on revival moment.

Stosh approached Brother Roland, but he only looked away and said, "See, brothers and sisters, he tempts me, the heretic blasphemer of the Greater Orlando area!"

Stosh stood there like an idiot as the troop went on with their ritual. Their chants had a lulling effect, a kind of sirenic melody, dragging Stosh toward the rocky cliffs of redemption.

"I wish to be saved!" he proclaimed.

With that, the moaning and chanting stopped. The disciples looked to Brother Roland for answers, but even he looked surprised.

And after a moment, he took off his hat, ran his fingers through his bleached hair, and said, "Like God, Satan, too, works in mysterious ways," he said. "Let us not be tempted by false faith!"

"You brought that pool here for a reason," Stosh said. "You must have prophesied this."

"I can wet your head, but that does not cleanse the soul," Brother Roland said.

"I'm ready, Brother," Stosh said, bowing his head in reverence.

"He's ready! He's ready!" the disciples sang out.

Brother Roland looked displeased. He moved his jaw in the

way Stosh did when he sniffed Al's Adderall, grinding his teeth and sucking at his cheeks with a wicked fury.

"What do you say, Brother?" Stosh asked.

"Keep praying, brothers and sisters!" Brother Roland said, grabbing Stosh by the shoulders and moving him away from the war party. "Pray for this man, and for his salvation!"

They were now on the side of the church, away from the theatrics out front.

"What the hell was that?" Brother Roland asked Stosh.

"I'm trying to make a deal with you," he said.

"This will not be my crossroad moment," Brother Roland said. "Too many have sold their souls, but mine is not on the market!"

"Listen, I don't care what you believe in, but I need you to leave."

"Or else?"

"Or else we'll call the cops, and you can continue your ministry in county jail," Stosh said with his meager secular authority.

"I suppose you would've done that already if you intended to do so," Brother Roland said.

"Baptize me," Stosh said.

"What would it matter?" Brother Roland said. "I know you don't believe."

"But wouldn't it look good on a live feed. All those Instagram followers of yours would be mighty impressed if you convert the likes of me," Stosh said. "I've got viral written all over me!"

Brother Roland looked back at his disciples who were still marching about the church's parking lot.

"But what happens to this place?" he said, looking at the church.

"That won't be your problem anymore."

Brother Roland peered back at his disciples before once again looking toward the sky. "Do I get to dunk you?" he asked.

"Sure," Stosh said.

"Clothes and all?"

"I'll swan dive into the kiddie pool if it means you leave us alone."

"You have yourself a deal."

The two shook on it, the way mortals do.

They moved back to the parking lot where the disciples continued to moan and chant in rhythm until Brother Roland raised his right hand. "Brothers and sisters," he started, "what if I were to tell you that Lot's wife had a second chance? What if I told you there is an alternate timeline in which she listened to Lot and kept her head down?"

Stosh tugged at Brother's shirtsleeves. "Are you talking about me?" he whispered.

"Inhale the holy oil," the disciples chanted. "Cleanse the wicked lungs of blasphemy!"

Brother Roland took out a vape pen from his pocket and took a large pull. He held in the smoke and then screamed it out over Stosh. "Cleanse your lungs with the holy vape..."

"I'm an indica guy," Stosh said, waving the smoke from his face.

But the prophet ignored him and shoved the vape to his mouth. "This vape has been on one percent since we left California, and yet it continues to bear juice. May it cleanse your wicked lungs and fill them with the spirit of the Lord manifest!"

Stosh took a reluctant drag and immediately began coughing. It tasted like burnt copper and spent batteries.

"Yahweh has brought Brother Stosh to us," Brother Roland continued during the ceremony. "Has brought him to admit his own sin, and so, in communion with the Lord, and His Holiest Spirit, the Last Man..."

"Omega!" the disciples sang out in chorus with the Lord.

"...He brings Brother Stosh into the waters of salvation."

Brother Roland lowered Stosh into the pool, drenching him with the holy and purifying water of Poland Springs. Stosh held his breath, felt the cool and suffocating presence of water in his nose before Brother Roland picked him up.

"For the Father," he said, dunking Stosh again, catching him off guard.

"And the Son!" Stosh heard Brother Roland say before going under once more.

"And the Holy Spirit!" he said, finally lifting Stosh out of the pool and holding him up toward his disciples, Stosh's clothes sucked tight to his body.

"Sons and daughters, brothers and sisters," Brother Roland said, "Yahweh has blessed us with a very unique opportunity."

Stosh's ears were full of water, but what he heard was something closer to the gurgled squall of a demon than the tender voice of God.

After another prayer, for which Stosh lowered his head, the Last Men emptied their kiddie pool and piled into their van.

"No hard feelings," Stosh said.

"Not yet," Brother Roland said.

Sara looked sadly back at Stosh, but Brother Roland redirected her, and the two joined their cohort in pilgrimage.

Stosh walked back inside to where Zyv was standing, her hand over her mouth, the peaks of her smile still visible.

"I've been saved," Stosh said, dripping wet.

CHAPTER TWENTY-TWO

THERE WAS a line of people waiting to get into the church the next night to see the Jubenvilles. The congregation had more than doubled since the first service, when Evangeline Sorenson had come. Stosh didn't like to use that word—"congregation"—but his light language was still contaminated by that of Catholic Mass.

When Zyv finally opened the door, Stosh filed in with the others and took a seat in the back pew next to where Dill had parked himself. Zyv and the Jubenvilles were up front. They'd set up what looked like a dentist's chair just below the crucifix. Behind the chair on the altar was Zyv's laptop, with the platinum USB containing the algorithm of love jabbed into its side.

After the last of the parishioners took their seats, Zyv stepped up to the lectern and introduced the Jubenvilles.

"As I mentioned in my post, they're here to perform one of their more popular services. Magnetic Manifestation Therapy," Zyv said. Stosh perked up in his chair. Zyv hadn't told him what they were doing, but he was intrigued.

"But before we get into that, let's take a moment to settle ourselves," she said, taking a deep breath. "With this breath, you purify the world, like the way a plant purifies the world with its breath."

After a moment, she raised her hands and said, "Exhale your telluric wind!"

Everyone exhaled in unison.

Gareth stood up then and approached the lectern. He kissed Zyv on the cheek before taking to the microphone.

"You see, friends, that two-pound lump of fleshy lobes between your ears that you call a brain is nothing but an operating system, and we're here to give it the latest update."

"Like autotune for the soul," Alexandria added.

"Exactly," he said. "This is a tool to fine-tune what you're already capable of."

Gareth looked at Zyv, who was now sitting in front of her computer, and asked for the name of the first participant. She punched a few keys and waited a moment. "@emily_wholler92," she said, calling the first participant.

The young woman approached the altar and sat in the dentist's chair. Gareth placed a reassuring hand on her shoulder and explained the process.

"We'll start with some breathwork," he said, taking a deep breath. "We want to become a column of air."

"Telluric air," Alexandria added.

Gareth then began to quickly breathe in and out, as if he was panting, breathing harder and harder until Stosh couldn't tell if he was inhaling or exhaling. @emily_wholler92 followed suit, panting, nearly hyperventilating until she began to tremble.

"Now I want you to think about what it is that you want in your life, what you'd like to manifest. I like to think about this as the *Amazon* method. You know, like when you order something on *Amazon*, you know it's on its way. You never think it won't show up. You know it will arrive, and what this is..." Gareth said, pulling a motorcycle helmet from behind the dentist chair and putting it on @emily_wholler92's head. "...This is a *Prime* membership, here to ensure near immediate delivery of whatever you want."

"We will now place the magnets into the slots of the helmet," Alexandria explained, handing the magnets to Gareth as if he were a magician.

"These slots correspond to the neocortex and thalamus parts of the brain, the parts that stimulate imagination," Gareth said, sliding the magnets into place.

Once the magnets were set, he closed his eyes and Zyv shut off the lights.

Gareth called for silence and for a unified breath. Stosh closed his eyes and joined in, the lungs of everyone in the church working and wheezing like accordions.

"Manifest the timeline in which everything you want is present," Gareth said. "But be careful not to manifest the timeline in which *you* are not present."

Unlike his father, Stosh tried not to judge what others needed to survive. If it helps, it helps. Who was he to cast the first stone? Hell, he thought, Christian had tried just about every kind of therapy there was before he finally took too much. He was never one for religion—or any ethos for that matter—but he found God in AA, though he said you don't have much choice when you're going through the steps.

Stosh always felt it was strange that the first step is to relinquish your will to a higher power. People go their whole lives trying to do that. You'd think that'd be the last step, not the first. But Christian did it, or said he did, and he lived the good AA life for a while.

He'd tried everything to cure himself—methadone, Suboxone, cold turkey; ninety-day detox, six-month rehab, sober homes and halfway houses; smoking weed and magic mushrooms; psychotherapy, anti-depressants. But maybe he could have manifested his perfect sober life with the Magnetic Manifestation Therapy.

"That's it," Gareth said. "I can feel it!"

"It's coming!" Alexandria cried.

"The clocks won't tell you what your body already knows!" Gareth proclaimed.

The lights flicked back on, and Gareth pulled the helmet off @emily_wholler92. She looked pale and was short of breath. Gareth and Alexandria helped her upright, rubbing her back until she had enough strength to stand. Then they walked her to the first pew and sat her down before calling the next participant.

The synapses in Stosh's brain felt frozen. Gareth's act was something between an Apple product launch and the revivalist stylings of Brother Roland. He was uncomfortable and kind of embarrassed, but his curiosity kept him solemn, matching the energy in the room. He was not there to judge, and as Gareth spoke and entered the magnets into the helmet that now sat upon another participant's head, he closed his eyes and tried to manifest his own desires. But what were they?

His first instinct was to picture Bambi, and the life he'd wanted with her—he saw the brick house by the golf course and the large SUVs parked in the driveway. He imagined breakfast. Whenever he thought of his perfect life with Bambi, it was always breakfast, never lunch or a romantic dinner, but the chaotic rhythms of a morning routine spent scrambling eggs and dancing around the marble kitchen island, tending to the baby, and laughing at the burnt toast.

But this time, he couldn't get the image right. He couldn't fill the house—not with Bambi or their baby or even himself. He took another breath as Gareth continued with the therapy. He tightened his eyes, wrapped his hands around destiny's throat, and tried manifesting his ideal life once again.

This time he found himself on the fairways of Augusta National, on the seventy-second hole, a pitching wedge in his hand, Al in the white coveralls standing next to him, and the scoreboard showing his five-stroke lead. Zooming into the green, he saw Bambi with their baby in her arms, awaiting his inevitable win. Fast-forwarding, he shed a tear as Tiger Woods placed the green jacket on him. But he couldn't taste the pimento cheese, and when he looked back at Bambi, her face was obscured, and their baby was gone from her arms.

Error 404: dream not found. Manifestation failed. Stosh closed his eyes once more and tried to clear his head. He softened the edges of his imagination in hopes of manifesting through osmosis. This time he saw Zyv in the church, her posing beautifully beneath Christ's feet, a line of acolytes out the front door waiting for her. She paid them no mind, and instead looked to Stosh, her smile so bright her lips couldn't contain her teeth.

Blades of golden light cut through the stained-glass windows, their images no longer of martyred Christians or Tara-Lynn but of the great many victories he'd won for the condo: extinguishing the petulant blasphemer, Fred; being baptized in the parking lot; saving a lowly Black intern from Cletus's fascist hand. This time the dream stuck. It didn't fade. It rose like dough into a warm and fluffy reality he could bite into right then and there.

Gareth took the Magnetic Manifestation helmet off the patient's head, with Zyv standing off to the right, proud and resolute. Stosh was surely on his way to the only destiny he now had.

Feeling light-headed, Stosh snuck out the back for a cigarette. It was a hazy night, the moon nothing but a fingernail in the sky. He didn't know much about what happened up there, but what he'd believed about it—the realm of God and bestial fairies—seemed to be dissolving, being replaced now with something new, seemingly old, perhaps as ancient as anything else, but still new. He was confused, hopeful, and tired, but it was pretty to look at, up there, and maybe that's all it was. He found himself surrounded by zealots. He wished, too, to be a zealot, to be enraptured by a cause, something he'd willingly lay down his life in service to. It seemed like such an easy life. Good versus evil, light versus dark. It's easy to be on the right side when there is no nuance, no room for confusion or complication, or questions. But the wisest thing he'd ever thought was that he didn't know anything at all, and that brought him peace. Perhaps that is what it truly means to relinquish oneself to a higher power.

His current peace, however, was interrupted by the whirring of a small motor. Stosh looked and saw Dill coming down the handicap ramp in his wheelchair.

"What were you doing in the basement?" Stosh asked, noticing several garden hoses running into the open hatchway.

"That was part of the deal," Dill said. "That's where the servers are."

"Servers?" Stosh asked. "Wait, what deal?"

"With you and Zyv," Dill said. "And me."

Stosh stared down at Dill blankly.

"We're mining crypto, and my library is down there, too," Dill said. "Come and see."

So, Stosh went and saw. He followed Dill and found the basement had been filled with rows of servers, the hoses running through their stacks as a kind of makeshift coolant. Stosh heard murmuring. He peeked around one of the stacks and saw two men sitting in aluminum chairs, each with a Styrofoam cup in his hand.

"Who are you?" Stosh asked.

"We're Sunday Night Sober," one of the men said.

"Who're you talking to?" a voice said from the other side of a server stack.

"The guy, you know, the one who runs the place now," the man said to the disembodied voice.

"Ask him if we can get some A/C down here," the voice said back. "It's hot as balls!"

"I didn't see a reason to kick them out," Dill said. "My father was an alcoholic."

The AA meeting continued as Stosh followed Dill through the rows of servers, each one containing one or two AA members sitting in their aluminum chairs, nested by a labyrinth of wires and bright green garden hoses.

"I know he likes to talk a lot of shit, but he's right about crypto," Dill said, still leading Stosh down the rows. "And it's not just about the money, it's about freedom."

"Freedom to do what?"

"Freedom *from* banks, the government..." Dill stopped and looked at Stosh. "...You know, tyranny."

"Sic Semper my ass," Stosh said, regarding the machines and their wires and little green lights. "The electric bill is going to be through the roof."

"Mining takes a lot of energy, not to mention powering that algorithm of love, or whatever it is."

"Was that part of the deal?"

"I guess Gareth and your girl have it all worked out," Dill said. "If I were you, I'd ask for whatever they pay you to be in crypto. Bitcoin is a sure thing, but NFTs are going to the moon right now."

"I didn't realize the basement was this big," Stosh said, now following Dill farther into the stacks. "Where is this library of yours?"

"I guess it's all around you," Dill said, stopping and spinning around to address Stosh.

The heat from the servers boiled the air, making the temperature above one hundred degrees.

"I catalog abandoned podcasts," Dill said. "I spent the better part of my life online, playing games, shit-posting, trolling, but eventually that got old, so I started this project."

"But why are you showing me?" Stosh asked.

Dill then scooted to his laptop that was sitting on a small poker table, pressed a few keys, and turned up the volume. Stosh immediately recognized the voice—it was Greg, of Dreamy's fame, but it was his own voice that brought forth a bout of déjà vu.

"Life on the road can be fun," Stosh heard himself say, "but it's lonely, and I wanted to buy a house, start a family..."

"But, why?" Stosh asked Dill.

"Don't you want to be remembered?" Dill asked. "It's like, if I don't, who will?"

Stosh listened to himself describe the end of his golf career.

"Each one of these podcasts was a dream," Dill said. "I came across this one and showed it to Gareth, who, I guess, had already been in touch with Zyv. He made the connection and believed it to be fate."

Stosh got chills, the splinters writhed with glee. He felt a part of some great narrative but tried to subdue his percolating curiosity. He wasn't yet ready to drink the Kool-Aid, though he was holding the cup.

"I should get back upstairs," Stosh said.

"Don't be a stranger," Dill said, returning to his laptop.

Stosh nodded in disbelief. He made his way through the basement, passing the rows of servers and the AA attendees laced between them, but his head remained stuck between stations.

Back upstairs, the Jubenvilles were finishing up with the last participant. Gareth was at the pulpit again.

"Wow," he said, "It's not just a word. Not just a palindrome. It's what we believe: We. One. World. It starts with us, a group of sovereign individuals, motivated and fit for service, who go out and change the world."

Everyone clapped. The air was thick, the mood tender with hope. Stosh joined in the applause.

"We'll be around for a little while if anyone has any questions," Alexandria said. "And don't forget to follow us and Zyvalia on social media."

Gareth shot her a look. "Oh, and Gack, our organic spiritual supplement, and my book of poetry, *Mining Your Precious Stones*, is available for sale at the back door."

"Like and subscribe for better vibes!" Gareth proclaimed.

Stosh began breaking down the aluminum chairs and hauling them to the storage closets in the entryway. When he went back into the sanctuary, Zyv was sitting with the Jubenvilles, her computer on her lap.

"Everything OK?" Stosh asked.

"The numbers, my friend. The numbers are good," Gareth said.

"But it's not just the algorithm, it's Zyv," Alexandria said. "Without her, it was just code. She's a conductor, our copper priestess."

"This is the new world," Gareth said, now smiling, "We have crypto, and NFTs, and now the algorithm of *true* love! But what about the now? The now is a valuable asset. We can gamble on futures, but to capitalize on the now, on the present earth, that is to be rich in more than just money."

"Should I record this?" Alexandria asked.

"Yeah, there's good lighting beneath Jesus," Gareth said.

They moved to the light.

"This is just another step. We are so close to becoming the community we dreamed of," Gareth said. "A real community ascending to a plane of abundance. Manifesting a timeline in which we own the majority shares..."

He went on like this for a few minutes, and Stosh tried to follow, but Gareth's authenticity seemed to be rooted in his incoherence, though it was intoxicating all the same. After the shoot, Gareth pulled Stosh aside.

"Jablonski, is that Jewish?" he asked Stosh.

Zyv and Alexandria were in conversation on the other side of the altar.

"Polish, but it's a bit fuzzier than that."

"You into crypto?" Gareth pivoted.

"No, but I saw you have quite the operation downstairs."

"Stosh, you're young still!" he laughed. "It's the future, and not just of money, but of everything. I know you, and I know me, and

I know we both want what's best for this community, and in turn, the greater community, that is this world. We both want what's best for the world, right?"

"Sure."

"Then you've got to get into crypto, man," he said. "We try, Stosh, we really do. We try to be holistic and *environmentally friendly,* but at the end of the day, this place, this world, is going to shit. If a plague doesn't take us out, then nuclear war surely will. Do you know why we came to Florida?"

"The tax breaks?"

"Fate," Gareth said. "Dill must've told you about the podcast."

"Always strange hearing your own voice."

"People down here are free, and their freedom, their relentless self-reliance has prepared them for the end of the world, so, when the end comes, and we're trapped in our homes, connecting to one another with things like NFTs and the algorithm of love, when humanity is leveraged as B2B SAS, you'll wish you'd have taken me up on this offer. Crypto, my friend, it's the future. A totally vibe-based economy. It's where we're going, there's no doubt about that, so why not start now?"

"Back to the operation in the basement," Stosh said. "I'm not sure what the agreement is between you and Zyv, but I hope it involves picking up the utilities."

"We'll work something out, maybe I'll even buy some of your shares," Gareth said.

"I don't think there's much money in my future," Stosh said. "My best days are behind me."

"Nonsense!" Gareth said. "You not only have the future right here, in this place, in Ascension and Zyv," Gareth said. "But your dreams—that's really what I would be investing in—your ability to see the future and manifest it."

"I don't know," Stosh said. "The community here doesn't have the luxury of futures."

"Hesitancy is a sign of fear, and you don't strike me as fearful," he said. "You're not fearful, are you? Your anxiety isn't rooted in the failures of your past, is it?"

"That's a bit complicated."

"You know, I often put the Manifestation Helmet on and sit alone, in the dark, without the magnets, and just sit there, blind and in the dark, because that's how we should see the future—dark, a black canvass where we can sow the seeds of abundance anywhere we'd like. Because the past is so vivid, so easy to fall into its pools of nostalgia, which is why I envy the blind—they go out into the dark world, day after day, seeing only possibilities, so I will ask you again: are you a fearful man?"

"No," Stosh whimpered.

"That's what I thought. Digital currency, digital art, digital faith, digital love," he said, "this is the future, and it's not a very good one. I would know. I was a part of that digital world, spent the entirety of my teenage years online, and it nearly ruined me. And I know what you're thinking, but stop thinking that way. We can all sense this future, and that's why this kind of community is so important to people *now*. It will be their last chance to have a real connection."

"Speculation might be another luxury we can't afford," Stosh said.

"Don't be silly," he laughed. "Buying futures, speculating, and acting upon that speculation is a divine form of quantum time travel, you follow? To speculate correctly is to see the future, and the future is bad, but that doesn't mean it won't make us rich."

"OK," Stosh said, feeling as though a targeted ad for Adderall had just cornered him.

"It's analog social media," Alexandria said, approaching them.

"Because in the world of the digital, it's the corporeal that is most valuable," Gareth said. "Just like I was telling Stosh, there'll come a time when our souls will be tethered to each other only by a thin fiberoptic cable, so now is the time to buy the now!"

The Jubenvilles said their goodbyes, each of them kissing

Stosh on the cheek, a practice he'd never been fond of, though he reciprocated the gesture and almost giggled at the touch of another man's stubble on his face.

Zyv and Stosh locked up the church and headed back to her place.

She poured them each a drink, and they took a seat on the couch.

"The Jubenvilles were so impressed with the turnout that they're gonna make me a brand ambassador for Gack. I just have to save up a little more money, and then I can buy in."

"How much are they asking?"

"Two grand."

"Not nothing, that's for sure."

"It's kind of like a franchise."

"I guess so."

"Everything costs something," she said. "And if I bring in more ambassadors, I can earn bonuses, but I'm a little short on cash at the moment."

"I thought there was a cover charge tonight," Stosh said.

"Everything we made went to the Jubenvilles," Zyv said, taking down her hair, the amber locks falling gracefully over her freckled, sun-kissed shoulders. "As a feminist, it pains me to ask, but is there any way you could front me the money?"

Stosh almost snorted. He was flattered that she thought he had that much money, but she was out of luck.

"What about the charity fund?" Zyv asked. "Didn't you say Calvin gave you access to it?"

Stosh felt his throat tighten. He didn't like disappointing anyone, which is why he accepted Calvin's offer in the first place, but this was beyond the pale.

"I'll replace it, of course," Zyv said. "I'll make the money back in no time."

Stosh smiled nervously, said, "Zyvalia..."

"Please?" she said, batting her long red eyelashes.

"It's a slippery slope," Stosh said, now reminded of the many times Christian had asked for money, begged for anything Stosh could spare so he could buy some relief.

"What, you don't trust me?" Zyv said. "After all we've been through."

"I do, I do," Stosh said, now feeling as though he was begging for her forgiveness. "But do you trust the Jubenvilles?"

"They sure trust you."

"Why do you say that?"

"Gareth wouldn't stop talking about you," she said. "He was really impressed with how you're able to wield power."

"I don't have any power."

"Sure you do," she said. "Look at all you've done around here. You've kept this place afloat, turned this church—a liability—into an asset. And you got me," she winked.

Stosh smiled, said, "I thought tonight was pretty cool, but I don't feel very powerful."

"That's what we want to show you—your inherent power. You just need to believe in what we're doing," she said. "I know you were raised Catholic, but what do you believe now?"

"I don't know. But I guess I can admit that. I can admit I don't really know anything."

"That's not faith. Humility is passive. Faith requires action, asks something of us," she said. "And you've never asked me exactly what I do, in my sessions."

"Astrology and stuff," Stosh said.

"And I've developed a new method, something similar to what the Jubenvilles did tonight," she said. "Want me to show you?"

Stosh shifted on the couch.

"I promise not to insert magnets into your head, if that's what you're worried about," she said.

"OK," Stosh said. "What the hell?"

Zyv stood up, kissed him on the forehead, and then turned off the light. She lit a candle and had him sit on the floor, facing her.

She directed him to put his hands on the top of his head, his arms and head forming a triangle, the most powerful shape, she said.

"Close your eyes," she said, her voice taking on a quiet rasp.

Stosh complied. She had a calming presence, a way about her that felt familiar and comforting. She could disarm anyone with her voice as quickly as she could cut them with it.

"Now breathe with me," she said.

Stosh inhaled and exhaled with her as she felt for his pulse on his wrist. They went on like this for some time, all the while Stosh tried to clear his head of all the anxieties and meandering thoughts that crawled into it—the trouble with the condo, Bambi, his father. He had to constantly swat them away like flies on shit, until finally, Zyv began to speak.

"We close our eyes, not to ignore the world, but to look inwards, to better understand ourselves. The world is big and scary, but my soul is mine to carry. Say it with me."

"The world is big and scary, but my soul is mine to carry," they said in unison.

"How do you pray?" she asked.

Stosh opened his eyes, but Zyv quickly redirected him, "Don't answer out loud," she said. She took a deep breath in. "Who do you pray to?" she asked, speaking through a prolonged exhale.

Her breath occupied the space between her mouth and Stosh's. He could feel it curling like cigar smoke in front of his face.

"What do you pray for?" She continued.

Another deep breath.

"What do you mourn?" she asked. "And who do you mourn for?"

Stosh twitched in the dark room and adjusted his breathing, trying to remember its rhythm.

"Who are your dead, and how do you talk to them?" she asked.

Stosh thought about these questions but had no immediate

answers. His prayers had previously come in the shape of poems, and though he recognized the beauty of their tradition, the words meant little to him. As for the question of who, well, he'd prayed for himself nearly every time he took up a golf club, and later, he prayed for his marriage, and after that for his father, at first to be freed and later to be damned. As for death, it was a distant relative, reaching out and into his life only once in any meaningful way when Christian died. Perhaps, he thought, he should pray for his friend's soul, but had he ever mourned for him? Not really. He'd spent more time mourning the loss of Bambi and his father than he had Christian, but he figured they were all his dead, and he longed to speak to each of them.

"Clear your mind," Zyv said. "If you were a time traveler, where in time would you go?"

"What?" Stosh blurted out, but Zyv placed her finger on his mouth.

"What would you do?" she asked. "Would you save your marriage, your father from jail? Would you meet your mother?"

Where *would* he go? There were countless tournaments he'd like to return to, and although he wished he could, he had no idea how he'd save his marriage or his father if given the opportunity.

She placed her hands around his face and pulled him toward her. She kissed him on the forehead and then leaned him back into her lap, and they stayed like that for some time.

Maybe Gareth and Zyv were right—maybe he had all he needed to be his authentic self. Maybe he was powerful, but he just needed to harness it. Maybe what was happening to him wasn't random or even bad; maybe it was his destiny.

"So, where would you go?" she asked.

"I think I'd stay right here," he smiled.

"That's just what I wanted to hear."

They kissed, and he agreed to loan her the money from the charity fund.

Back at home, he found Al passed out on the couch. He was

sitting upright, his chin to his chest, a warm, almost curdled white Russian on the end table. Stosh emptied the ashtray before waking him up.

He was really out of it, his waking eyes wide and confused. He looked at Stosh first as a strange threat before finally realizing who Stosh was.

Al coughed and reached for his drink. He rubbed his neck where it turned scoliotic at his shoulders, the same ones that carried Stosh's bag for so many years.

"Thanks for everything," Stosh said.

"Fuck you," Al grunted.

"I'm serious."

"In that case, you're welcome," he said, walking into his room, "and also fuck you."

Stosh took a seat on the couch, cracked the window, and lit a cigarette. He thumbed through Instagram and Facebook, bouncing between them in a kind of nervous boredom that always seemed to inspire his scrolling.

Stosh went to punch out his cigarette on the windowsill, and as he did, he saw a great beam of light coming from the heavens. It appeared to illuminate the pool area. Then Stosh saw a ghostly figure walking down the street. He could only make out the wings and the white dress at first, but then the figure took on a more corporeal shape.

"Sara?" Stosh asked.

"I've been waiting for you, Brother Stosh."

CHAPTER TWENTY-THREE

"YOU REALLY DON'T RECOGNIZE ME?" Sara asked Stosh after he let her inside. "I thought that's why you followed me."

Stosh shook his head but couldn't admit that he started following her on Instagram solely for sport and companionship.

"Do you remember the show 'John D. Wolf: Bounty Hunter'?" she asked.

"Do I?" he said, and then quoted the show's tagline, *"It's Not His Bark You have to Worry About."*

Sara turned over her right forearm to reveal a tattoo that read, *"It's Not MY Bark You Have to Worry* About."

Stosh looked at her and squinted.

"I'm Baby Sara," she said.

Stosh smiled, but his excitement was quickly replaced by suspicion. He looked at her and could vaguely see the remenance of the girl he watched time and again on one obscure channel or another—often stoned—riding shotgun with her father as he chased petty criminals down dirt roads and through trailer parks.

"But I thought your last name was Wolf," he asked.

"Our real name is Wilson. Dad thought Wolf was a stronger

brand," she said. "You really didn't recognize me?" she asked again with a tinge of disappointment in her voice.

"You were pretty young when the show was on," he said.

"Seven when it started, sixteen when it was cancelled."

"I don't remember you having a brother Roland, though."

"Popcorn Lung," she hissed.

"Who?"

"We're not related, and that was Brother Roland's handle online; @popcorn_lung," she said.

Stosh supposed it was as good a username as his own AOL handle—Killerbasa420x69.

"You know this whole Last Man thing?" Sara asked. "Well, Dad and Brother Roland met online after Omega started posting. Dad didn't know what to do with himself after the show got cancelled. He couldn't understand the world. It was like he'd been trapped inside the TV for so long that when the show ended, and he had to return to reality—*real* reality—he didn't recognize it. But then he became an early supporter of the president, thought he'd return us to the GOOP. It was as if the president was his avatar, but after a year in office and still no change, Dad started to lose hope, and then he found Omega, and it all made sense. The president was fighting a shadow war against the deep state, just like *he* was fighting a war against the Hollywood elites to get the show back on."

"Wait, who's Omega?"

"He's a time traveler," Sara said. "Someone from the future, posting memes."

Stosh thought about what Zyv had asked him—where he would go and what he would do if *he* could time travel, and posting memes never crossed his mind.

"He's a whistleblower, someone from inside the future New World Order, warning us about the fate of our country if we don't do something to fight the deep state," Sara said.

"But what does that have to do with us?" Stosh asked. "Why here?"

"Burger-gate," she said.

Stosh shuddered at the memory of that night. He'd never been that close to a gun before, never mind someone shooting one. He scratched at the splinters in his arm, felt them slithering beneath his skin—pale maggots on spoiled flesh.

"Dad and Wrecks met here when we were shooting the pilot for *Hog Wild with the Wolfs*," Sara said.

"I didn't really like that one," Stosh said, shaking away the sentient splinters.

"Major flop," Sara said. "America preferred Dad tasing humans more than shooting pigs."

"Me too," Stosh said, shamefully.

"Omega had posted that the restaurant, Jocko's, was serving people."

"Like *Soylent Green?*" Stosh asked.

"What's that?"

"Never mind."

"Dad sent us down here after Wrecks shot the place up," she said. "To keep his cell alive."

"And all this started on the internet," Stosh said.

"We *are* the internet," Sara said. "We've just found a way to crack through the screen."

Stosh listened with a mix of empathy and fear. That summer had taught him to withhold his judgment and never underestimate the power of belief. He felt a phantom vibration and reached for his phone. He looked at its black screen, the same color as the ooze in the pool, and wondered what else was leaking through the pixelated prison.

"Popcorn Lung thought I was special, gave me my own origin story about how the show was cancelled because I refused to be indoctrinated into the cabal," she said. "A part of me always knew it was wrong, that Omega was probably just some kid trolling from his mom's basement, but I'd be lying if I said I didn't like the attention from everyone online. I mean, I'd spent my whole life with a camera following me around, with fans, so I went along with it, said I knew all about the cabal, all about the Hollywood elites. I said Tom Hanks was a cannibal. I met him once. He was so nice!"

She stopped for a moment and wiped her eyes.

"Popcorn Lung," she said through her teeth. "And you know who his father is? The Sultan of Sleep himself, Casper Sugarheard."

These awful coincidences wrapped their conspiratorial hands around Stosh's neck—the emoji's jaundice tentacles breaking through the screen and squeezing tighter and tighter. Hideous is the human community, gristly are the tendons that connect us to each other. Surely, we must be heaven's favorite cringe content.

These scenes of madness, of wild boars and alligator sightings, of late-night therapies, manifestation sessions, and psychic readings were taking their toll on Stosh. Before that moment, he could still make an argument that it was all mere coincidence, that he was experiencing a kind of psychosis, but a time-traveling cult led by his favorite reality TV star and his former boss? Not to mention Gareth and Dill's podcast project. Surely, it must all mean something. He was powerful. He wielded the telluric winds and guided his fate through the labyrinth of time to lead these people all to him. All to the association!

"I just wanted to be a part of something bigger than myself," she said. "Like what you have here."

She may have been onto something. Stosh had lost many a brain cell keeping the community afloat, and he was proud of that, but it was still under threat. What he and Zyv were building was still fragile.

"We've spent a lot of time creating this community," he said. "We have to be vigilant. It's not just Brother Roland whom we have to contend with, but subversives within our ranks."

"In a weird way, I think Omega would be proud of what you've done, even if Brother Roland thinks it's an abomination."

Stosh changed the sheets on his bed and let Sara crash there for the night. After she settled in, he went to the couch and took out his phone. He tried connecting all the dots, shoving all the round pegs into the square holes, and making them fit. It was uncanny. Unsettling, but still empowering. He looked out the window. The night's silence was periodically interrupted by the burps and squalls of animals, all crying, like us, at the dark sky, confused and lost, hoping something from above would shout back or send us a sign—a shooting star, a coincidental shadow, a sliver of light between dark trees. Something, anything beyond our own tragic coincidences to witness. He locked his phone and tried to relax, but he couldn't help but wonder if maybe Brother Roland had sent Sara there to work as some mole.

He called Zyv to get her take.

"Either way, he's sure to return now," she said. "You should bring her to Ascension."

"Why would I do that?"

"She's still kind of a celebrity."

"B-list at best."

"I'm looking at her Instagram now," Zyv said. "Twenty thousand followers. I could make the charity money back in a day if I could get her in my downline."

"Don't you think she's been through enough?" he said.

"Exactly," she said. "We'll heal her."

Stosh hung up and kept watch for a few hours before finally relenting to his heavy eyes. It would be good publicity, he thought, having a celebrity endorse Ascension, and with her onboard, Zyv could make their money back and some. After all, Sara owed them. She brought Brother Roland to the community. Yeah, he might have invited them, but she could have at least told him about the time-traveling shit-poster stuff before he had. Didn't she have to repent? Wasn't he due some reparations for his troubles? Surely, he was.

The next morning, Stosh woke up to his phone vibrating off the coffee table. He threw the blanket off himself, his legs damp with sweat.

"I need you at the church," Zyv said.

"Popcorn Lung?" he asked.

"Who?"

"Never mind. I'll be right there."

Stosh heard clanking from the kitchen, but Al's door was still shut.

Sara poked her head around the corner and said, "Is it him?"

"No," Stosh said, eyeing her suspiciously. "Not yet."

"Who the hell are *you*?" Al asked, coming out of his room.

"I'm Sara," she said, a flash of that reality star charm in her voice. "Breakfast?"

"I don't eat eggs," Al said. He turned to Stosh and asked, "Who the hell is *she*?"

"Another star in the constellation," Stosh said, walking with him to the door.

Al looked back into the kitchen, said, "She looks familiar."

"You remember Baby Sara, from *John D. Wolf?*"

"Get the fuck out," he said, craning his neck to steal another glance. "That's really her?"

"She was part of Brother Roland's group."

"Jesus, man," he said. "First Gator and now this nut? What're you adding her to your haram?"

"She'll be on her way in a day or so."

"Whatever you say," he said. "You ready to go?"

"I'm off today."

"We have a tee time at Champions Gate," Al reminded him.

"Shit," Stosh said.

Al rolled his eyes and dropped his shoulders.

"I just have to stop at the church, and then we'll head out. Let me get changed."

Stosh ran to his bedroom and changed out of his day-old clothes. He smelled sour, the small of his back a constant pool of sweat. He told Sara to make herself at home, and then he and Al hopped in the truck and drove up to the church.

Zyv was waiting in the parking lot, a group of people standing behind her holding signs that read "Black Lives Matter" and "Down with Wriggle".

"Leave the keys," Al said. "I'll go by myself."

"Listen, man, I had no idea..."

"Save it."

Stosh wanted to say more, to apologize, but he didn't have the time. He got out of the car, and Al slid across the bench seat to the driver's side.

"I'm all for racial justice," Zyv said to Stosh as he approached, "but the Jubenvilles are supposed to be coming by."

"You think they'll have an issue with people protesting?"

"If they're protesting us, yes," she said. "This is horrible for our brand."

"I'll handle it."

"That's getting old," she said.

"What is?"

"This whole machismo, *don't worry about it, baby* thing."

"I don't talk like that."

"But you sound like it."

His eyes hurt. His mind was nothing but wandering buckshot again, spinning and twisting around his head. It was all too much and too soon, but he was acting on instinct, swimming with a current that was moving too quickly to fight.

"Just give me a few minutes," Stosh said.

Zyv sucked her teeth and relented.

Stosh walked over to the group and approached the guy with the bullhorn.

"Hey, buddy," he said like an idiot.

The guy ignored him and continued shouting, "Down with Wriggle! All cops are bastards!"

Stosh winced at the sound. "Cletus deserves all of this," he said, "but is there any way you can take it across the street?"

"Cletus doesn't live across the street," the guy said.

"But this is a church," Stosh said. "Cletus lives in the condos."

"From what I hear, it's a stretch calling this place a church," the guy said.

"How did you even find out where Cletus lived?" Stosh asked, figuring such information was protected.

"He got doxed."

Stosh paused. "Angel," he whispered.

"Here I stand, I can do no more," the guy smirked.

Stosh smiled nervously. He had to give Angel credit—it was more creative than the lawsuit Stosh feared he was going to file.

"Come on, man," Stosh said, "I support the cause. Black lives matter. I've got no problem saying it."

"The *cause*," the guy laughed. "You can *say* whatever you want, but what have you *done* with all your power?"

Stosh's cheeks warmed, and saliva gathered beneath his tongue.

"That's what I thought," the guy said. "Now get the fuck out of my face."

Stosh stepped back and tried to hide his shame. He'd been cruising by on dumb wit and a kind of beggar's luck, but that wasn't going to work here. Until that moment when Cletus placed Angel under a redneck citizen's arrest, it'd all felt small to Stosh, his troubles and the troubles of the community contained to their petty little fiefdom.

After that encounter, Stosh went home and watched hours of J'Davious Wallace news coverage online. He watched the bodycam footage of the killing, the officer stopping the young man and chasing him. He watched the pixelated execution. He watched opening statements and firsthand testimony, the questioning and cross-examination of friends, neighbors, and cops. He watched the officer—the hulking white, buzz-cut, Moby Dick looking motherfucker—testify that he feared for his life and had no choice. He watched clip after clip, falling into the rabbit hole, always relenting to the algorithm's next recommended video.

And in between videos, sometimes right in the middle of one of them, an ad would pop up. The most common of which was for a male performance supplement called "Shore Leave" that promised its users a vigorous libido with absolutely no side effects. And soon, the videos got weird. No longer was he watching impartial news coverage, but hot takes about the trial, and some that presented alternate versions of the events.

In one video, a man with heavy jowls and an abominable forehead, claimed that the whole thing was a false flag, and that Wallace was not only a convict, but had actually been sentenced to death. His method of execution—suicide by cop. Smith said the deep state used him as a martyr to sow unrest.

At first, it seemed ridiculous to Stosh, so ridiculous that he was entertained by the absurdity and clicked on another video in the series. Next thing, it was three hours later, the sun was coming up. Stosh's eyeballs felt singed, and his face tanned by the glare of his phone. After that, Stosh felt part of a much larger, far more grotesque world than that of the association.

He walked back to Zyv, shaking his head.

"I'm calling the cops," she said, taking out her phone.

"I don't know," he said. "It just seems wrong to kick them out, and we really don't need the attention."

"It's too late to avoid that," she said as the protest continued.

Stosh kicked at the broken pavement.

"It's private property, Stosh," Zyv said. "They're welcome to stay, but this isn't how we get what we want here."

Stosh shrugged. He figured that in the absence of action, he could at least feel the appropriate level of guilt.

"This isn't how you change anything. You have to change your-self before you change the world," she said. "Remember: the world is big and scary..."

"...But my soul is mine to carry," Stosh responded.

"You could've complained when Tara-Lynn disappeared. You could've blamed someone else, but what did you do? You took action. You didn't throw a fit. You realized you had the power to change your own world, and you did. It's that kind of mentality that Gareth finds so promising in you," she said. "Don't you want to make the charity money back?"

Cars drove by the protest, some honking in solidarity and others in opposition. Zyv dialed 911 as she locked eyes with Stosh. He wished he had the luxury of solidarity, but all he could do was help himself. Like he told Sara the night before, they had fought too hard for what little peace they had, and he wasn't going to let Brother Roland or anyone else disrupt it.

"All right, but let's get out of here," he said. "I'm sick of dealing with cops."

Stosh walked home as the sirens rang closer. Cletus was sure to hear about the protest, but Stosh didn't have time to worry about him. He had to check on Sara and figure out what he was going to do with her before Brother Roland showed up.

"Everything OK at the church?" Sara asked as Stosh walked inside.

"Par for the course," he said.

"That woman who runs it, is she your girlfriend?" Sara said. "She's very pretty."

"We don't talk much about what we are," he said. "We have kind of an open thing."

"Oh," she said, recoiling a bit.

"We just believe in loving without boundaries," he smiled.

Though she tried, she couldn't hide her apprehension. He still wasn't sure if Brother Roland had sent her there, but he figured asking her to endorse or post something about Ascension would be a good test of her loyalty. After all, not only had she brought Brother Roland's fire and brimstone to his front door, but now she was sleeping in his bed, watching his TV, eating his food. The bill was adding up. The association might have been a non-profit, but they were no charity.

Stosh spent that night on the couch again, smoking bong after bong until there was nothing but resin in the bowl, his lungs seared and raw from the pilly black tar.

Sara stayed up with him for a while, wafting the dank smoke away from her face until she couldn't take it anymore and retired to Stosh's room. He put the TV on but was greeted by a *John D. Wolf* marathon. He watched only briefly as the bounty hunter whose daughter was in the other room twisted the heel of his boot into some bail-jumper's neck.

Stosh changed the channel to *Ancient Aliens* and then checked in on Sara. He watched her from the doorway, and when he was sure she was sleeping, he took her phone and tried to unlock it, hoping to confirm whether she was still working for Brother Roland, or Popcorn Lung, or whatever his real name was.

He thought about that one time he'd stolen a couple of pillows from Dreamy's. They were floor models, so there was no record of them in inventory. The company couldn't have known. He considered them his severance. He was due at least a couple of memory foam pillows, right?

They were the same ones Sara was sleeping on now. *Shit. Was Dreamy's actually a psyop?* Was she reporting this back to Popcorn Lung and, in turn, his father? Were his dreams really safe with the Sultan of Sleep?

He tried again to get into her phone, but no luck.

He went back to the living room where he stayed awake, scrolling relentlessly through social media, tracing the origins of the Sugarheard family until the sun came up, the dark reality behind his screen illuminated by its rays.

Stick to the plan, Stanislaus. Get her endorsement before you do anything. Maybe she was being honest and just needed to get away from the Sugarheards the same way he needed to get out of Dreamy's, out of his hometown altogether. He had been in her shoes, and he was lucky enough to have that bitch, Tara-Lynn, to help him get out of dodge.

He texted Zyv, and the two came up with a pitch for Sara. Although they really just needed her clout, they agreed that it would be a bonus if she actually got some benefit from one of their modalities.

"She'd be a great witness," Zyv said. "Her testimonial is priceless."

Stosh walked Sara up to the church later that morning. The air was thinner than it had been all summer, and a gentle breeze swept the palm leaves aside, revealing plump green iguanas, spying from their clandestine knots.

The cops had removed the protesters without further incident the day before, and the church was again peaceful and quaint beneath the sun.

"I was thinking about what you said the other night, about how you wanted to be a part of something bigger than yourself," Stosh said. "So, here's your chance."

He walked with her through the front door. Zyv sat before the altar with her laptop.

"Hi, Sara," Zyv smiled graciously. "We know the world is big and scary…"

"But our souls are ours to carry," Stosh finished.

Sara smiled nervously.

Stosh stepped up to the altar and kissed Zyv. The two turned and looked at Sara standing below them in the nave.

"We wondered if you wanted to be a part of what we have," Zyv said.

"Oh," Sara said, taking a step back and crossing her arms. "I'm not sure I'm into that."

"I know it sounds strange, but you've seen the proof," Stosh said. "Just look around and see all we've accomplished."

"And we have a lot more to offer," Zyv said. "We want to show you our Algorithm of True Love."

"Oh God," Sara said. "You people really are sick!"

"What? No," Stosh said. "I think you misunderstood."

"I know you were watching me sleep," Sara said. "And now you want me to use your love algorithm and *join* you two. I'm not like that. I don't want to be in your *open* thing."

Stosh heard chanting coming from outside. He went to the window and saw Brother Roland leading his disciples in the parking lot. Sara heard his voice and started to inch closer to the back door.

"Get her to the basement," Stosh said to Zyv.

"I'm not going in your pervert den!" Sara yelled. She ran out the back door the whole time yelling, "Now it's my dad's bark you have to worry about!"

Stosh started after her but saw Brother Roland outside and paused.

"Goddamn, Brother Roland," Zyv said, dialing 911 once again.

"Hesitation is a sign of weakness," Stosh said, making his way out the back door just as Cletus and his Big Boys of the Bygone Day crossed the street and approached the church across from the BLM protestors who had also returned.

All three groups now occupied the parking lot, all with signs and posters, the most graphic of which belonged to Brother Roland's people. It was hard to tell what was being depicted, but the painting reminded Stosh of those by Hieronymus Bosch, with the dark reds and various shades of charcoal—scenes, no doubt, of great retribution.

The BLM group had their signs, too, including a Gadsden Flag, which Stosh thought was strange, considering it was more often associated with the political right, though it kind of made perfect sense. After all, what is more unconstitutional and depriving of liberty than the execution of a private citizen at the hands of a state official?

Across from them Cletus was carrying the same flag, the rattlesnake coiled and ready to strike at whatever invisible monsters occupied his paranoid fantasies, all the while singing, "Good boys, good boys, whatcha gonna do, whatcha gonna do? Back the blue!"

One of Brother Roland's people also carried a Gadsden Flag, but the snake was in the shape of the Ω symbol. It seemed to be coiled around a rather poorly drawn effigy of Stosh—a sign of his fate, no doubt.

"Kadoosh! Kadoosh! I say to you!" Brother Roland proclaimed.

His followers chanted in tandem, "Kadoosh! Kadoosh!"

"It seems we are not the only ones who've found evil in this place, brothers and sisters!" Brother Roland said, motioning to the other groups. "Give us back our disciple, Sara. Release her from your Gomorrah. We won't let you traffic a child of God!"

Cletus piped up. "This place isn't evil, it's him," he said, pointing at Stosh.

"What, you're on his side now?" Stosh said.

"He's on the side of the righteous!" Brother Roland said.

"Even his name is blasphemous!" Cletus said. "Isn't that right, *Saint*-Jablonski?"

"Shove it, pig," one of the BLM people said.

"Who said that!?" Cletus demanded. "Fucking Thugs!"

"Listen, my Black brothers and sisters," Brother Roland said, as tone deaf as Cletus. "I know most of us are so cynical these days that we wouldn't recognize an angel if its wings beat upon our faces, but we cannot be so naïve as to ignore the devil when he is so obviously present as he is in this man, this Saint-Jablonski!"

"Fuck you!" someone said.

"Don't tread on me!" someone else hollered back, but from which camp, no one could be sure.

The various groups began shouting and pushing closer together until a bottle was thrown, followed by a volley of rocks, one of which hit Stosh on the head, followed by nothing but chaos. Stosh was pushed to the ground, his hands taking the brunt of the damage as he landed on the broken pavement. He crawled away, the sirens now screaming closer and closer.

He lay there on the patchy lawn and looked up. The sun was just above the statue of the Risen Christ that was suspended on the façade of the church. He looked at his hands—twin wounds in the center of his palms. *Stigmata*, the sentient splinters whisper. He wiped the blood on his shirt and shook the visions from his third eye.

Once the cops had cleared the scene and arrested whoever they could, Officer Billy approached Stosh for a statement.

"Who started this bullshit?" he asked.

"Can I plead the fifth?"

"Just say BLM and make my life easier," Officer Billy said.

"Can I speak to an attorney?"

"You're not under arrest."

Stosh remained silent.

"Well, we've got the preacher fellow on an outstanding warrant, so I guess I can put the whole thing on him."

An ambulance came up from the condos with its sirens on.

"I hope no one got seriously hurt," Stosh said.

"That one," the cop nodded toward the ambulance, "was for something else."

"Someone in the condo?"

"Not a good day for Fred," Officer Billy said, dragging the tip of his forefinger across his throat and sticking his tongue out. "Done-zo."

CHAPTER TWENTY-FOUR

STOSH THOUGHT about going to Fred's funeral but decided against it. He couldn't risk leaving the condo or running into Cletus at the service, but he'd gotten as far as trying on his suit to see if it still fit. It was the same one he'd worn to his father's trial. Major had insisted Stosh buy a new one, something nice, he said. Stosh remembered the way his father had handed him the money in the living room after Major made bail. The dollars were crinkled and soggy, but the old man acted as if they'd just been printed.

Instead, Stosh spent the night of the funeral on his couch, keeping watch and smoking nearly a whole pack of cigarettes to keep his hands occupied and his head sober. He looked out at the quiet neighborhood. A part of him expected to hear Fred's walking stick clicking out in the distance, but no sound greeted him.

He checked Sara's Instagram account to see if she'd posted anything. He figured there was no such thing as bad PR and was disappointed to find she'd gone dark. Not even a negative comment or disparaging post about Ascension.

Al came out of his room and walked into the kitchen without

looking at Stosh. He was great on the course, always knew what to say as a caddy, but as a friend, he was incapable of expressing anything but anger and disappointment. That's how Stosh remembered his father—quiet, solemn, and disgruntled: masculine in all those grotesque and nostalgic ways.

"Wanna shot?" Al asked, peeking from around the kitchen door.

"A peace offering?"

"It's a yes or no."

Stosh got up and joined Al at the kitchen table. He poured them each a shot and pulled the ashtray from the cabinet.

"Cheers," Stosh said.

Al nodded, his knee bouncing beneath the table, rattling the glass ashtray.

"You good?" Stosh asked as they lit up. "I hope you're not catching my paranoia."

"Birdie came by looking for you earlier. Said something about the pool."

Stosh looked at his phone, said, "She didn't call me."

"I told her I'd pass along the information."

"She corner you taking out the trash or something?" Stosh asked.

"She came to the door," he said, ashing his cigarette.

"And you answered?"

Al averted his eyes, said, "I thought it was my pizza. It sounded pretty urgent."

"God only knows what it could be," Stosh said. "Wanna take a walk? I could use the backup."

"I was just about to hop on *Call of Duty*."

Stosh took another shot to ease his frayed nerve endings, but the cops seemed to have cleaned up most of the trouble, so he put on his slides and then walked out the front door. The air was warm, but the wind was twisting and grotesque again, cutting across the tarmacs at the air base and swirling into the swamp that was the association. The community's tension tugged at the low-hanging limbs of the palm trees and made the dark patches of grass in between the streetlights seem impenetrable. Thunder rang out in the distance, a vocal reminder of potential violence.

The pool was an old metal one, and it often had leaks in the spring, especially if the winter got cold enough. Stosh didn't know much about its maintenance, but he'd picked up a few things at those god-awful board meetings Tara-Lynn used to run, though he feared the issue to be one of esoteric doom or toxic waste, considering the ever-present black ooze.

At first glance, it looked the same as it had all summer—black and sludgy—but it seemed to be at the right level. Before he went back home, he followed the skimmer lines that ran from the pool, beneath the fence, and to the filter on the other side.

The brook wasn't far from there. He looked toward it and saw a small fire winking where the homeless encampment was. He inspected the filter with the light on his phone but couldn't find anything obviously wrong with it.

Satisfied, he turned around to leave, but there was a shadow blocking his way back.

"I've given you enough chances," Cletus said, cartoonishly cracking his knuckles.

Stosh stood up straight. He could feel his pulse thumping in his fingertips, swelling like the drumhead court-martial in his ears.

Cletus puffed his chest, said, "Just came from Fred's attorney —he left me his condo. Soon enough, I'll be an owner and can run for president, and you'll be gone."

"Seems I'll have my work cut out for me at the polls," Stosh said, taking a step back and checking his six for an escape route.

"Why wait until then? I've talked it over with almost twenty owners, and they've agreed to withhold their dues until you step down."

"Are you seceding?"

"Stop wasting everyone's time and just appoint me president

now," Cletus said. "I know you had something to do with Tara-Lynn taking the money, but I'm not sure what. You make this easy, I promise not to audit the books."

"Why don't you come to the next meeting and discuss it with the board?" Stosh said. "After what happened at the church, we need to find a solution to all of this."

"The time for talk is over," Cletus said. "Time for me to do what I must to return us to the GOOP."

Stosh's cheeks warmed. His palms were as moist as the leaves above him. Like many a scrawny boy, he had fantasized about such an encounter, when he would finally face his bully, and in those fantasies, he always came out victorious, somehow harnessing his adrenaline in lieu of strength to rain blows upon his foe, but that fantasy quickly disintegrated at the sight of Cletus twisting one fist into the opposite palm.

Stosh looked up, figuring he might be able to avoid his fate by climbing up the nearest pine tree, but the bark was slick and the saplings at the bottom of its trunk too small to hold even Stosh's scrawny ass.

"Ah hell," Cletus said. "Don't make this harder on me, or yourself. Let's do this like men."

Stosh took a step back, looked for a clearing he could bolt through, but he was wearing slides, and his bare feet couldn't survive the thickets of scrub brush, let alone the snakes they housed, blocking his nearest exit.

"Don't even think about running," Cletus said. "Don't you watch *John D. Wolf?* That's the worst thing you can do to a cop."

Stosh felt the trees above him close in, his vision tightened. Was this how it all ended? Had he spent the entire summer dodging every calamity imaginable, including those of his own making, just to meet his fate at the meaty end of Cletus' fist? Stosh felt a weight lifted from his shoulders at the thought, relieved but fearing that whatever fight he had left would surely be easily subdued by Cletus' years of experience beating on people smaller than him. But then Stosh felt Zyv's presence, her voice in his ear. He'd worked too hard, sacrificed too much building what they had, what they were sure to have, so long as saboteurs like Cletus were held accountable. He was strong. He could wield power, just like Gareth believed he could. He began to breathe. He closed his eyes, drew in the dewy air, and centered himself. He tried to manifest the timeline in which he was six foot two and played football instead of golf.

"Did you shit your pants?" Cletus asked.

Stosh ignored him and continued to snarl, but he could smell the skunk, too.

"Enough of this woo-woo bullshit," Cletus said, but then Stosh screamed as Zyv had taught him.

And in return, an animal screamed out in the distance, and the skunk's smell thickened.

Stosh screamed back and opened his eyes, but Cletus was gone. Stosh looked first to his fists—which he thought might have done all the talking for him—only to find them as clean and small as he'd ever known them. Had he manifested a new timeline? Had he, through sheer will, manipulated the universe's quantum material to shift dimensions?

"Ask him for cigarettes," a voice said from the darkness.

Shadows began to appear around Stosh, the trees seeming to drop them from all sides.

"You OK?" one of the shadows asked, approaching Stosh.

He tried to take inventory of himself, the moment, but he couldn't bring it all together.

"Let's bring him to the water," another voice said.

Stosh felt faint, the glow from the campfire by the brook growing bigger as the shadows led him to it.

"That guy was always an asshole," one of the figures said.

Stosh looked at the man. His face was gray and torn up by acne scars, but he smiled.

"Stosh, is it?" he asked. "My mother mentioned you were in charge now. Said you were nicer than Tara-Lynn."

Stosh looked around and saw plastic bags dancing in the trees like Halloween decorations, and blue tarps—the likes of which Major once used to winterize his boat—hanging from shallow branches, forming little wigwams.

"I'm Adam McKitch," he said. "Gail's son."

"Thanks for your help," Stosh said, still trying to get his bearings and feeling vindicated by the irony of Cletus being scared off by the very person he so violently wanted to get rid of.

"I was friends with Christian, too," Adam said. "Hate to say it, but we used to use together."

The splinters giggled with delight beneath Stosh's skin. He heard what Adam said, but he couldn't believe it.

"My condolences," Adam said. "Anyone ever know what happened to that necklace he copped from Palm Ridge?"

"The algorithm of love?" Stosh asked.

"Whatever was on that USB, I doubt it had anything to do with love," Adam said. "I have a feeling that stupid thing is what got him killed."

"You must have heard it was an overdose," Stosh said.

"So they say," Adam said. "It's a little too convenient for my liking."

"What do you mean?"

"Some tech-bro paid Christian to rob that house," Adam said. "Tried to get me to help, but no way I'm messing with the Division of Perception Management."

Stosh had never heard of such a department, though he was about as far away as someone could be from the machinations of the federal government.

"I thought it was random," Stosh said. "I assumed he stole the necklace for drug money."

"Christian said the guy who hired him was working for the

Division," Adam said. "Something to do with a dead guy on a flight to the Pacific and that necklace."

The pieces were all there. Dana's husband, Christian, the algorithm, the deep state, but Stosh couldn't see the picture the facts were painting.

"Agents have been all over our shit down here since the base closed," Adam said.

"Bureau of Land Management has been poking around the condos, too," Stosh said.

"Those guys aren't from BLM. They're Perception Management," Adam said. "It's getting harder for them to hide the DUMB beneath the base."

"There's a deep underground bunker beneath the base?" Stosh asked, remembering the many episodes of *Ancient Aliens* on the subject.

"See, you know more than you think," Adam said. "You'd appreciate what we do here."

"I'm trying to figure out what exactly that is."

"You into crypto?"

"Currency?"

"Zoology."

"Oh," Stosh said. "Yeah."

"We are Apeus Dei," Adam said.

Stosh's eyes went wide. Adam was no reality TV star like Sara, but Stosh was star-struck all the same. "I'm a huge fan," he said.

"Appreciate the follow. We were looking for that Skunk Ape you heard back there. We've been tracking him for a long time. We were even there the night you found that peccary." Adam said. "Commonly referred to as skunk pigs. I believe you call him Gator."

Stosh felt concussed. Everything made just enough sense to pique his interest and keep him asking questions.

"But what's the connection?" he asked. "Why would the government want Christian dead? Couldn't they just arrest him for the burglary? And what does it all have to do with a DUMB and the cryptids? Gator?"

"This has nothing to do with the government," Adam said. "This is deep state shit."

Adam leaned back on the milk carton he was sitting on and took off his left boot. He fixed a shot and brought it to the vein between his little piggies and took a deep breath as the dope hit him in the face like the gentle beat of an angel's wing.

"It's cool," Adam said, rubbing his face. "I wouldn't believe me either. But think about it. Conspiracies are all around us, orchestrated by the highest authorities and most respected and celebrated leaders of society. You've heard of the Sacklers? OxyContin was a conspiracy. They told us we couldn't get addicted, that it was safe. Now look at us. We have track marks for our penance, shoot up as self-flagellation, but our story is proof of their conspiracy, so what would make any other conspiracy theory unbelievable?"

Before that summer, Stosh would have written all this off as crazy, just like he would have written off an algorithm of true love or a time-traveling agent of the New World Order as the rantings of insane people on the street corner.

He often had to talk sense into his father in the days after he was arrested, when Major was willing to grasp at and embrace any number of wild theories about why he was charged, and his co-conspirators weren't. All this would have, just a few short months ago, been a bridge way too far for Stosh, but having witnessed all that he had that summer, he couldn't dismiss these claims. Or rather, to do so would be to admit his own folly.

It was all happening so fast: the theories, the takes and opinions flying at him at a speed he'd only ever experienced while scrolling social media. The age of information.

Maybe it was all true. Maybe he had slipped into another dimension, one which had been veiled only by circumstance and decorum, just like how the truth about his father was veiled by platitudes of hard work and honest living. Maybe Christian was assassinated by the deep state; maybe there really was a time traveler posting about our doomed future; and maybe there were skunk apes and a government conspiracy to cover up a deep underground military bunker in his backyard.

But doubt still tugged at the better angels of his heart. There was still a faint voice in his head that said, *Or maybe we're all just stupid little blips in a Jurassic lineage of suffering and loss, dating back millennia, back before the sun had a name and we could tell stories to define our struggle, but who now, endowed with narrative power, weave together fantasies in which we can affect the world as it so benevolently affects us.*

Stosh's mind was racing, his thoughts gurgling and rattling in his skull. He had Cletus and the BLM protestors to deal with, not to mention the usual condo bullshit to sort out. He stood up to leave and thanked Adam again for saving him.

"Got any room at that church?" Adam asked.

Stosh thought about what had happened with Sara, about the money he still needed to replace from the charity fund, and asked, "How many followers do you have?"

"Sixty thousand on YouTube alone," Adam said.

"Come by any time," Stosh said. "I think you'll like what you find."

THE LIGHTS WERE off when Stosh got home. He stared at his reflection in the living room windows, wondering what was on the other side. Paranoia lapped at the hair on the back of his neck. Was there a deep state agent waiting on the other side of the glass, or a cryptid chomping at the bit? Anything was possible.

But it was just Al, sitting on the couch, stoned and bleary-eyed.

Stosh took a seat, too tired to make himself something to eat but feeling light-headed and empty.

"You got any of that pizza left?" He asked Al.

Al shook his head, his face turning a different shade of red than that made by his usual vodka consumption, and said, "I made a grilled cheese."

Maybe Stosh was losing track of time, the days dissolving into confusion as soon as the sun came up and spiraling into paranoid fantasies by the time it set, but he could've sworn Al said he'd opened the door for Birdie, thinking it was his pizza.

"Et tu, Little Bert?" Stosh whispered as he watched Al go cross-eyed, hitting the bong.

CHAPTER TWENTY-FIVE

WHAT LITTLE SLEEP Stosh got that night brought him no relief. He lay awake in bed, nothing to keep him company but the chaos of his algorithm's content, now an unholy orgy of piss-drinking, star-worshiping freaks. He couldn't even enjoy a golf video or a kind word from an online evangelical.

Every swipe manifested new questions and more confusion, but he tried to piece it all together in spite of himself. Dark room. Bright screen. Sore fingertips. Red veins like spindly threads across yellowed eyes. He found himself leaping across the internet like a schizophrenic; the cookies he left behind all but ensured a visit from the Division of Perception Management or whoever was tasked with keeping official state secrets and esoteric delights. But he kept scrolling, every click a shot fired against enemies both foreign and domestic, online and IRL, personal and global.

Paranoid delusions, he occasionally thought as he pawed at his swollen eyes, but the coincidences mounted quicker than his doubts. And the mystery black ooze: *could it be Adrenochrome?* That's what Wrecks Saltus thought according to one of his last Facebook posts before he shot up Jocko's. The splinters quivered as he read that Wrecks believed the DUMB beneath the base was manufacturing the substance for the elites at Palm Ridge.

Stosh immediately thought of Cecelia and Dana, the only two people from Palm Ridge that he knew personally. He never would have considered them "elites," though they were both wealthy beyond comprehension—and now that he thought about it, he wouldn't put it past the ladies of the Ridge to experiment with whatever serum promised a tighter forehead or plumper lips. And was the plane disappearance that took Dana's husband really just an accident? Could anything the Division of Perception Management was involved in be a simple coincidence? *Bullshit!*

Restless was too good a word. He jumped at every squawk, chirp, and screech; cowered as the headlights strobed through his broken blinds every time a car passed. Not even his bed provided comfort, the memory foam seemingly melted from the heat and sweat of his body, and Al in the next room, plotting, snoring.

Al was no usurper. He certainly didn't want the presidency for himself, but maybe he did it for the money. Stosh hoped Cletus had at least made it worth his while, but whatever the reason, there was no doubt Al had set him up.

Stosh's eyes felt like they were vibrating in their sockets by the time dawn broke and filled his room with purple light.

He heard Al in the bathroom hacking up the White Russians from the night before. If there was anyone he should be able to trust, it was his caddy, but he'd sent him into the woods to get his ass beat by Cletus. So much for all that stuff about caddies being like counselors.

"Our very own Fredo," Stosh said as Al came out of the bathroom.

"The fuck man," Al said, grabbing his chest.

"I hope Cletus gave you your thirty pieces of silver."

"What?"

"Birdie didn't tell you about a leak in the pool," Stosh said, approaching Al.

Al stared at the floor, said, "I don't know what you're talking about."

"You gave yourself away!" Stosh said with great bravado. "Do you prefer the term pizza-gate or grilled cheese-gate?"

"Fine, you caught me," Al said. "But I had good reason."

"What low vibrational excuse is it this time?" Stosh asked.

"Listen to yourself," Al said. "You've been marching around this place like the mad king ever since Zyv showed up. I was out of options."

"I knew it," Stosh said. "You're jealous!"

"Oh, please. You're delusional," Al said. "I knew you wouldn't listen to me. You haven't listened to me all summer. Someone had to talk some sense into you."

"So you send me to the woods for Cletus to break my kneecaps?"

"I thought he'd scare some sense into you, but that obviously hasn't happened."

"How much did he pay you?" Stosh demanded. "What does he have on you?"

"You serious?" Al asked. "Nothing, man. I'm tired of your bullshit. I'm not just your caddy. I'm your friend. But what do you care? You're off cosplaying as a fucking shaman."

A car horn beeped outside.

"Who's that?" Stosh said, taking a step back, paranoia lapping at his neck.

"My ride," Al said.

"You're not working today," Stosh said, looking at the date on his phone.

"I went in on a stump grinder with one of the other maintenance guys," Al said. "Not that you care, but I have to start worrying about myself."

"And Cletus didn't give you any money, huh?"

"You've lost it," Al said, taking a step towards the door.

"Listen," Stosh said, grabbing Al by the shoulder. "Something big is happening here. Something bigger than you and me and your stump grinder. I can forgive your betrayal, but I need to know whose side you're on. I need to know if you're worthy of abundance."

"Jesus, man," Al said, pulling his arm from Stosh's grasp. "Look at you. You're acting like a dope fiend. You smell like shit, you look like roadkill. You need more help than what I can give you."

"But you owe me!" Stosh said.

Al sighed and shook his head. "Remember that?" he said, pointing to the lone picture that hung in the condo. It was taken at a junior club championship at Stoney Hill. Calvin, Christian, Al, and Stosh stood shoulder to shoulder, their drivers outstretched before them, like knights swearing an oath. "We still had a chance back then. Still cared about the future, but now look at us, at you, crashing out over some crystal mommy and her troop of merry grifters. A fucking shame."

Al grabbed his wallet and keys from the coffee table and then walked out the front door.

Stosh followed him outside, not yet satisfied with their argument, but saw the man in the green Bermuda shorts and Mickey Mouse ears, the same man who knew his name at Cecelia's July Fourth party, standing in the parking lot, talking to Amy. Al climbed into his friend's truck and drove away as Amy pointed in Stosh's direction.

Stosh scurried back inside. He peeked through the blinds, thought he felt the faint quiver of his phone vibrating, but it was nothing. *It's never nothing* he thought. Who is that man in the green shorts, and how, or better yet, why, did he know Stosh's name? There was no such thing as a coincidence. Not anymore.

Stosh paced the living room, thought about packing a bag and leaving, but where the hell would he go? Surely, he was too deep in whatever this all was to flee. There was no jurisdiction he could hide from the long arm of the security state apparatus. And what about Zyv? He needed to warn her. She'd know what to do. She'd help piece everything together, but before he could make a move, the air conditioner in the living room window shuttered out, announcing its death with a series of gaseous sighs before clanking to a halt. It was deathly quiet in the condo. Stosh felt as though he was underwater. For a moment, he thought he might be having some kind of episode, maybe a coronary or panic attack, but then the silence was cracked open by the television turning on, and his phone vibrating and flashing, its screen illuminated in a kaleidoscope of pastel colors. The lights above flickered, and the air conditioner screamed back on, now spitting out a black mist that began to envelop the room. He backed away and made to run but tripped over the coffee table. John D. Wolf was on TV, pressing the heel of his boot into the neck of an unsuspecting Skunk Ape. Stosh righted himself, turned to leave, but was greeted by that lone picture on the wall. Christian grinned with delight and said, "Make sure the tournament has an open bar, OK? It's what I would have wanted." "Yeah, man," Calvin added. "Spare no expense. We're trusting you." Stosh stumbled back before getting up and ripping the picture from the wall. Stosh thought he heard a helicopter panting above. He peered out the window and saw that man with the green shorts approaching his unit.

Stosh ran through the kitchen and exited through the back door and into the parking lot.

A loud cackle broke his pace as he stumbled across the broken pavement. He took cover behind a gaunt palm tree and looked around. *What now? Another Skunk Ape? The Nephilim returning for the rapture?* Then he heard an orchestra of laughter. It was coming from Tara-Lynn's old place. He skulked over and looked through the window and saw Ray speaking with several people in the kitchen.

Stosh heard a helicopter's propellers echoing in the distance, and his phone was vibrating again, but this time it was an unknown caller.

"Hello?" he answered quietly.

"Hi, we've been trying to reach you about your car's extended warranty," the friendly voice said.

"And I'm supposed to believe that!?" Stosh said before hanging up.

He ran into Tara-Lynn's place, where he was greeted by a bunch of people lounging around the living room. Some were on the floor, reading, while others were in the kitchen baking bread and cleaning.

"What is this," Stosh asked Ray. "An indoctrination camp?" he said, noting several people on the couch reading Marx.

"It's what could have been," Ray said. "A commons. A place where people can get what they need."

Stosh shook his head, the helicopter outside thumping away, matching his heart's BPM. This wouldn't do.

"I'm just trying to give these people what we promised them," Ray said.

"The time for all that is over," Stosh said. "We're in the middle of something more serious than your little revolution. These people should be helping themselves, not hanging around and collecting handouts."

"Like your friends at Ascension?" Ray asked with a smug smile.

"At least they're doing something," Stosh said. "They're *making*, not taking."

"Is that so?" Ray asked. "It seems all they've done is take up your time, and now they're diverting our electricity and water. Haven't you noticed the rolling blackouts, the lights flickering?"

Stosh cleared the sweat from his eyes and was relieved but then shook his head. *No, no. That doesn't explain the mist, the TV. This is exactly how the Matrix acts when it's threatened.*

"Ascension is going to pull through," he said. "They will usher in an era of abundance. They have to!"

"They haven't paid us anything to date!" Ray scolded Stosh.

"Don't you see what they're doing? They're ripping the copper from the walls before the whole thing collapses."

"There's no need for hyperbole," Stosh said.

"No, literally," Ray said, pointing to a hole in the wall. "They said it has magical properties."

Stosh stared into the hole and saw right through to the neighboring condo. It was true; he was still waiting for Zyv to pay back the charity funds, and the crypto-mining operation had significantly increased their electricity and water bills. "But this, what you're suggesting..." Stosh stammered. "There has to be another way."

"It's this or barbarism," Ray said.

CHAPTER TWENTY-SIX

STOSH STUMBLED out of the politburo as a loud jet came rumbling across the sky. He looked up and thought he saw *Air Malaysia* written across its fuselage but couldn't stop moving to confirm. He made his way up to the church, where he hoped Zyv would have a plan, or could at least anchor him to her eternal optimism.

He walked quickly, staying close to the hedgerows, trampling over perennial grasses and fleshy plants whose elegant flowers mocked his bumbling step. He looked for Cletus, who was thankfully absent, but a figure caught his eye by the pool—the man in the green Bermuda shorts. He was standing there, leaning up against the fence the way Fred used to.

Stosh dashed up the street and into the church, where he hoped to breathe a little easier once inside, but the incense tickled his throat, filled his lungs like cheap weed smoke.

Gareth was walking around with a large man in an awkwardly fitting peach-colored Nautica polo. There was a line of congregates waiting for Zyv to administer the algorithm of love. He watched as she sat with a user and listened intently, all the while entering the user's data points and specifications into the application on her laptop. She used the broken shards of the stained-glass that Fred had smashed and some wood from the lectern to fabricate a housing for the computer, bringing an air of ancient mystery to the otherwise contemporary process.

"Stosh! Just the man I'm looking for," Gareth said, flanked on either side by a Big Boy of the Bygone Day. "These guys will be hanging around, so you might want to send out a letter to the community announcing their presence. With all the chaos happening, it was imperative that we establish OpSec."

The two Big Boys looked like they'd just finished a stint on a professional wrestling promotion, their arms double the size of Stosh's thighs.

"Stosh, you look troubled," Gareth said. "Here, take this." He handed Stosh a copper crown. "Realign your telluric bulb."

The knotted ends of the copper crown teased Stosh's scalp, bringing him sweet pain, like a tooth ache, grounding him in flesh and bone. His back was sore and his stomach gurgled with hunger. He felt real and vulnerable, tragically fucked.

Zyv gestured for Stosh to wait and then excused herself before sitting with the next user.

"Are you OK?" she asked, noticing Stosh's sun-beaten face and sour smell.

"I'm not even sure how to answer that," he said.

"New lunar cycle always puts people on edge," Zyv said.

"I think it's more than that," Stosh said, wiping the sweat from his head and stealing a glance at the line of people scanning the Venmo QR code that hung on the wall. "I'm not sure what's going on, but I think I'm starting to lose it."

"You're not losing anything," Zyv smiled. "What you're feeling is *ascension*."

"But there's so many unanswered questions. It feels like this whole thing is falling apart, and we still have to pay Calvin back the money we took from him."

"Patience, love," Zyv said, taking Stosh's hand and rubbing it in a maternal way.

"I can't let him down," Stosh said. "No matter what happens, we have to pay him back."

"You have to let go of all that doubt," Zyv said. "You need to embrace your power, your authentic self. Every decision you make, every word you speak determines your fate. Show Gareth you're deserving of his investment."

"I know, but..."

"No, Stosh," Zyv said, that signature bite returning to the back of her throat. "This is it. Tara-Lynn is gone. Your dad is gone. Ray is gone. Al is gone. Brother Roland and his little strumpet are gone. It's just us. Obviously, you haven't been manifesting the way we taught you. I need you to work on that. I need you to embrace your divine masculine. Can you do that?"

"Yeah," Stosh whimpered.

"Oh come on, you pussy," Zyv said.

Stosh took a step back.

"What, nothing to say?" Zyv asked. "Just gonna wallow, blame someone else for your problems? Gonna close your eyes and hope Adam will save you like he did from Cletus?"

"How did you know about that?"

"Shut up. I wasn't done talking, you little worm. What's the problem? Couldn't sell mattresses, now you can't even sell your own worth? Your lack of confidence is disgusting. I'm drier than the fucking Sahara. Grow a pair and manifest the money to pay your friend back and prove to me that you have what it takes to wage spiritual warfare or get to the back of the line with the others who need me to tell them what to do."

Stosh reached for her and felt the gristly tendons of her neck pop in his hands.

"That's right," Zyv said, squirming with glee.

She pulled him close and shoved her tongue in his mouth. "Now, what are you going to do?" she asked.

"I'm going to manifest my destiny."

"And are you powerful?"

Stosh didn't say anything. He just screamed, the congregants who'd gathered around now cheering, some crying and exalting him.

Stosh marched out of the church and headed straight for the condo office, his penis flaccid once again by the time he arrived to do what he should have done at the start of the summer.

He sat down at the computer, turned on the monitor, and logged into the condo's email account. Tara-Lynn always had a contingency plan. There had to be more money somewhere. He searched for passwords, secret bank statements, and buried treasure. If that failed, he'd already decided to break into the laundry machines to get the money needed to cover what he'd taken from the charity fund. *Zyv will come through*. He could feel it. They had no choice but to succeed. It was their destiny, but for now, he needed to rid himself of the last vestiges of his past life and square up with Calvin.

He was just about to get the crowbar from the storage closet when an email notification popped up. It was from a department of corrections domain to the condo account:

TL, I know you said to stop emailing you here, but you're making me nervous not responding to your personal account, so you left me no choice. I know it's bad news about the appeal, but my lawyer is still hoping I can get out of this hell hole early for good behavior. Only time in my life I've wanted to play by the rules. Your good boy will be out soon, so don't go doing anything stupid! This was my plan, and I expect you to wait. I know how you can get, but you owe me. I could've named names at trial, but I kept you safe. YOU OWE ME!!!! And don't worry about Minor. He's welcome to join us, but no more handouts. He can either get on board or fend for himself.

Your big pierogi,
Major.

Tears mixed with sweat and dirt to form a tragic paste that caked Stosh's upper lip. Rage had been a foreign word, and violence only ever a fantasy, but Stosh picked up the monitor and threw it to the floor, the screen convulsing in an epileptic fit before sizzling out. It was all so perfect, so stupidly perfect. How could he not have seen it? Where there's money, there's sex. He should've known jail wouldn't stop his father, should've known Tara-Lynn was in on the eco-friendly tax scheme, too.

And Omega! Fuck, it couldn't be. The Heston references, his father's favorite actor, his goddamn idol. But no, he couldn't have orchestrated such an elaborate plan. But who knows the kind of people he was locked up with. *Wasn't Wrecks Saltus sent up to Danbury? Could the two be in cahoots? Was it all part of the plan?*

Stosh needed answers, he needed something to chew on, something tangible to grasp, to get answers to his questions. He felt as though he had all the pieces and that he just needed to arrange them appropriately—Adam and Apeus Dei, Dana and her husband, Christian, Sara, Brother Roland, John D. Wolf, Casper Sugarheard, Dreamy's, the algorithm of true love and now his father and Tara-Lynn.

It was all there. A mosaic of human madness and absurdity too perfect to be anything but deliberate. Intelligent design. But how do you express the cosmic certainty of intuition, describe the invigorating epiphany of coincidence? Anxiety curdled into paranoia and then emulsified back into dread.

But only those worthy of it were betrayed; the only antidote to greatness, a desperate attempt to curb the march of history. He was done being a victim. He was done living as a footnote in his own story. *He* was the main character. He was not simply living through history; he was making it. He was the author of this cosmic story, but was it true? Or did people tell themselves conspiracy theories to survive, to fill the void of useless tragedy with pastel proverbs and doctored obituaries, pretending they've only ever known grace, their words and testimonies nothing but cheap spells to ward off the pestering truths and inconvenient realities?

By the time Stosh left the office, the sun was setting, the atmosphere still thick with merging timelines. He peeked out the door and made a beeline to the *Ranger*. He needed a litmus test for reality. He needed some solid ground to check his equilibrium before he did anything else.

As he drove up the association's main road, he saw the man in the green Bermuda shorts and Mickey Mouse ears again. This time, he waved to Stosh, who kept his focus on the road, flipping his visor down in hopes of covering his face.

His home was compromised. His best friend was gone. The only place he could think to go was his old third place, where all this started that day with Quentin: *Jocko's*.

If he could just get inside and confirm there was no basement, no human sausage, that Jocko's was not people, then perhaps he could start to claw his way back into reality, out of the muck of uncertainty and victimhood, regain some agency in his life, reset the current timeline he was operating in.

Stosh pulled into the Jocko's parking lot and saw a herd of children gathered behind the building. His bowels shifted, his heart rose to his throat. He heard the crack of Wrecks Saltus's rifle, saw Heston standing defiantly with a musket in his cold dead hand, and heard his father demanding the damn dirty apes get their stinking paws off him. *It can't be true.*

He parked his truck and made his way to the building. He crouched behind a trash barrel and observed the sick ritual. But something in the barrel caught his eye. It was a piece of crime scene tape. He pulled it out and read the manufacturer's name— *Stick 'Em Up Tapes and Adhesives*, Cold Springs, MA. Cecelia's family's company. The threads were now so tight he could play a tune on the corkboard. He had to act. He had to embrace his destiny!

"Jocko's is people!" he exclaimed, emerging from behind the trash barrel.

One of the adults herding the children turned and scolded him. "Too soon, too soon," she said, shaking her head.

"Stosh?" he heard someone say from behind.

He turned and saw Dana standing there. He took a step back and said, "Not you, too."

"You OK?" she asked.

"You know what this place is?" he said. "Are you in on this whole thing, too? Is this part of the script!?"

"It's the grand reopening," Dana said, the wacky inflatable man bending over the renovated building and now visible. "I'm volunteering with some kids from the Y for a fundraiser."

Stosh wiped the spittle from his mouth. "I'll bet you'll have me believe this is all a coincidence. You, your husband, the necklace. How much are they paying you?"

"What are you talking about? What necklace?" Dana asked.

"The one with the algorithm of true love in it."

"I really have no idea what you're talking about, but if Zyv is involved, I want nothing to do with it."

"You're just jealous too," Stosh said. "That's why *we* have it. Thank God Christian stole it from you. Maybe the only good thing he ever did, and it got him killed!"

"Wait, your friend was the one who broke into my house?"

"And the deep state murdered him because of it," Stosh said.

Dana sucked her teeth, brought her hands to her hips and shook her head. "That cunt, Zyv really got her hooks in you, huh?" she said. "I guess I'll have to add all this to the police report."

"Police report? In cahoots with Cletus, too?" Stosh said. "The world is not so cruel to coincide all this tragedy. It must all mean something more than how it appears."

"I don't know who Cletus is, or about any algorithm of love, but I do know that your girlfriend is under investigation for sexual assault," Dana said. "She had her *other* boyfriend, Gareth, try to rape me so that I could *overcome the trauma of losing my husband.*"

"Boyfriend?"

"Oh yeah, Stosh. I wouldn't doubt if Zyv was sleeping with Gareth's wife, too, and every other member of his polycule."

"His what?"

"I'd get out of here if I were you," she said, waving over to Officer Billy, who was eating a hamburger and talking with the man in the green Bermuda shorts.

Stosh paced backwards, finally turning around and running to his truck as they walked over. He peeled out of the parking lot and headed back to the association. The sun had set by the time he got back. The church was lit up, its stained-glass windows now replaced with various memes, including the one of him that Amy had made earlier that summer.

He drove by, seething about what Zyv and Gareth were up to. Jealousy, he knew, was close to violence on the scale of sacred geometry, but he couldn't shake the feeling; it metastasized and coagulated into cold sweat on his forehead. He drove past his condo, where a crowd had gathered. He could see Al amongst them, and he could've sworn he saw John D. Wolf's platinum mane leading the war party.

Stosh kept driving and parked in a visitor spot by the pool. A *No Trespass* order issued by the Bureau of Land Management was posted at the entrance. It said PFOAs had contaminated the area. Stosh looked it up on his phone—the forever chemicals were likely the result of firefighting foam used at the Air Force base.

"Cover up," Stosh said to himself. "This is exactly what *they* would do."

Stosh looked down at the brook, but he couldn't see any fire from the Apeus Dei camp. He thought he heard the scream of a skunk ape then, but he couldn't be sure if it was that or an engine brake from the highway. His eyes were dry and heavy. The splinters hitched beneath his skin. Was this an attempt to cover up the adrenochrome farm in the DUMB? Or was it just the horrid banality of the military-industrial complex in a decaying empire?

Was Gareth fucking Zyv? Was Zyv fucking Alexandria? Where was Zyv's husband all these months? Had he been disappeared by the Division of Perception Management? Had she killed him? Was Stosh next? Did Dana say Gareth tried to rape her?

No, no, surely these coincidences were too horrible not to be a coordinated effort, but this was beyond what his father or Tara-Lynn could've dreamt up—so who, or what was behind it? The Division of Perception Management? The Central Florida Consortium of Condominium Associations? The Professional Golfer's Association!? Were they all in on it!?

Stosh stumbled away and into the community garden that had long been abandoned and was now nothing but cattails and scrub brush.

He looked to the heavens.

"My Father, if it is possible, may this cup be taken from me. Yet not as I will, but as You will."

Stosh's woes overcame him. He'd been pilled to the gills. He tried to gather what had fallen from him, the things he'd lost, but it all slipped between his fingers again. "Surely this can't be real," he repeated the old familiar mantra. And when no answer came from his hands, he turned upward again and recited the Prayer of Saint-Jablonski. "Although I may not know your name, I have faith that You know mine." He stopped for a moment, but hearing no response, yelled at the sky, "You were supposed to know my name!"

He heard the horde that had gathered at his condo now roaming the grounds, murmuring and getting close. He went silent and hid between the cattails, their long leaves cool against his face.

Didn't these people know he did it all for them?

"Abba," Adam said from behind him. "We do it out of sheer sorrow."

"Where did you come from?" Stosh asked.

"We have to move camp," Adam said, nodding at the notice on the pool's entrance.

"Cover up, or just bad luck?" Stosh asked.

"Not sticking around to find out," Adam said. "Can I bum a cigarette?"

Stosh handed him what was left of his pack, but he was already gone, dissolved back into the darkness.

His phone vibrated. A new email from Calvin:

> I saw you withdrew some funds. Just make sure to save the receipts. I'm hoping to write all this off at the end of the year, and thanks again, man. You're like the third Kennedy brother to us.

Stosh's throat constricted. His chest felt like a Chinese finger trap. He had no other option but to seek refuge at the church as the horde stirred closer and closer.

Once again, people were milling around the grounds. White kids with dreadlocks sat on the damp pinewood benches beneath a newly erected statue of Jerry Rubin wearing a gold poncho and standing between dozens of GOOP signs. Others stood in the parking lot, talking to invisible audiences as if they were reciting Shakespearean monologues, breaking the fourth wall of their own reality shows. From the basement came forth a line of AA attendees, their cigarettes already in their mouths and in their hands, Styrofoam cups of coffee. An eclectic blend such as this surely had not been assembled since Dante dreamed it up some centuries ago.

Alexandria Jubenville was roaming about, talking into a hand-held mirror and probing the many characters that populated the once hallowed grounds.

"Kadoosh, kadoosh, I greet you, brother Stosh," she said. "I think now is a great time to get to know Stosh Saint-Jablonski," she said, still talking into her mirror.

"Who are you talking to?" Stosh asked.

"My followers," she said, turning and addressing the group of young women behind her.

"Are you fucking Zyv?" Stosh asked sternly.

"Don't make it sound so filthy," she said. "Are you sure you've ascended to five-D?"

"I shun you!" Stosh yelled at her.

"You don't have the galactic capital," Alexandria snickered. "And I don't like your tone."

"Then I block you all!" Stosh said.

"There he is!" Someone from the condo mob yelled at the sight of Stosh.

"It's not my bark you have to worry about!" John D. Wolf hollered, loading a fresh can of pepper spray pellets into an *Ed Hardy* branded paintball gun.

Stosh ran into the church, where he hoped to find refuge and be subdued by the serenity of the place, the warm embrace of the wood paneling and pews, but found no such peace. He looked to the walls, expecting to find the plaques depicting the Passion of Christ, only to see racks of yoga pants and mats hanging from those sacred spaces, and beneath them, stacks of *Mining Your Precious Stones* and jars of Gack.

In one corner of the church, Evangeline Sorenson stood, channeling the spirit of J'Davious Wallace, mumbling in light language and offending even Stosh's fried sensibilities.

"Oh no," he said aloud.

In the back corner of the church, where donation boxes once stood, was a man in a blue pinstriped suit doling out investment advice to the stream of people waiting to see Zyv. He barked about cryptocurrencies, NFTs, and digital real estate. He called himself The Pro(f)ph(it)et of Doom, but upon closer inspection, Stosh realized it was just Brother Roland now occupying a new persona.

"What if someone just copies and pastes it?" one affiliate asked him.

"It doesn't matter," the Pro(f)ph(it)et said as his laptop screen cycled through a series of images, "the original is certified on the blockchain."

"But what would I do with it?" another affiliate asked.

"Hang it on the wall of your virtual mansion," he said. "In fifty years, our environment will be so toxic that no one will leave their homes. All we'll be able to do is log in, log on, and engage. You could own what will become the next Mona Lisa, and it could be hanging in the living room of your digital house!"

"But that's *not* the Mona Lisa," the first affiliate said, "it's just a sloth smoking a joint."

"Oh, and the Mona Lisa is *so* impressive," the Pro(f)ph(it)et said, turning his attention to Stosh. "Anything catch your eye? What about this?" He pointed to a 3-D sculpture of the crucifix. "It was made using the exact amount of microplastics found in the average Millennial's testicles."

"It's me, Roland," Stosh said. "Don't you remember cursing this place?"

"I go where the money leads me," he said.

Something caught Stosh's eye on the Pro(f)ph(it)et's screen. It was the meme Amy had made of him earlier that summer.

"That's me," Stosh said.

"Ah," the Pro(f)ph(it)et said, "you see yourself in this beautiful work. It's by a local artist. I believe she's in the building tonight. She just certified it on the blockchain."

"No," Stosh said. "That's supposed to be me. *The Passion of*

Saint-Jablonski," he read from the screen. "Don't you remember? I'm Saint-Jablonski!"

"Listen, I'll cut you a deal if you're interested," the Pro(f)ph(it)et said.

"Are you trying to sell me to myself?" Stosh asked.

"Do you want it or not?"

Stosh shook his head.

"At least make sure to get branded," the Pro(f)ph(it)et said. "You can't be in here without one."

Stosh looked around; everyone had symbols seared into their forearms.

"No cell phones either," an affiliate said to him. "Until the end, we're totally analog."

"The end?" Stosh asked.

"We're fast approaching point omega."

Above them, in the choir loft, Gareth, Cletus, and a handful of Big Boys were all pissing into a jar labelled "Not for Semen."

"It's not gay," Cletus proclaimed, his jowls slapping beneath his tomato-red face.

"You can't be gay if you never cum!" Gareth said, gnawing on a piece of raw meat, the blood dripping down his chin.

Stosh looked across the church where a hog carcass hung like a martyred saint, a pair of crystals hanging from his broken tusks and his tuft of white hair purpled with blood. Beneath Gator was a young man who addressed a small crowd that sat with their backs to him, each with a mirror in their hands, watching him in the reflection. The man took out a bag of *Flaming Hot Cheetos,* dipped them in *Tabasco* sauce, and ate them. He then took a swig of *Coca-Cola,* followed by a shot of *Fireball,* and finished it off with a handful of *Listerine* strips. He consumed this all without a reaction, chewing through what must have felt like a firestorm in his mouth.

Some of the affiliates viewing his antics shouted out, "I like that!" and others disapproved, saying, "That's not even that hot," and "More like the 'Lame King' and less like the 'Flame King.'"

"I'm sorry," the man said, itching at the brand of a chili pepper on his forearm. "I haven't been the same since my ulcer!"

The crowd expressed an equal mix of excitement and disappointment as the man took out a *Volcano Burger* from Jocko's, ate it in two massive bites, and then washed it down with more *Coca-Cola* and a fistful of *Pop Rocks* before doubling over in pain.

Stosh approached one of the affiliates watching the spectacle and asked, "What is this?"

The viewer turned her back to him, her mirror still in her hand, and addressed his image in it. "His side hustle."

"I'd hate to see his day job," Stosh said.

He looked over to the line for the algorithm of true love. Cecelia and Cara were there, each with the same brand on their arms—a heart with a crack down the middle.

"You guys have to get out of here," Stosh said. "This whole thing, it's all been a part of some elaborate plan! It's all a movie!"

"We need to know who Christian was talking about," Cecelia said.

"We're gonna ask the algorithm," Cara said.

Stosh looked to the sanctuary where Zyv sat behind the altar, beneath Christ's bloody feet, staring at her computer with an affiliate opposite her. She looked up at Stosh but quickly returned to her work.

He approached her, still hoping that the algorithm that was foretold could provide some insight into what was happening, some facts that could form the contours of his reality, but she silenced him and continued with the woman.

"Let's start with your net worth, your social security number, and your five biggest icks," Zyv said to the affiliate.

"Is this, too, a lie?" Stosh interrupted her.

"Not yet," she shushed him.

"Have I not been honest enough?" he begged of her. "Shall I strip down here and show you my authentic self!"

"Stanislaus!" Zyv said as he gestured toward his member.

"You shall not say my name before you answer me!"

"This is definitely ick," the affiliate said. "Who even are you?"

"I am not ick! I am Saint-Jablonski, and I am non-fungible!"

Stosh looked back at the eager affiliates sitting in the pews, waiting for their turn with Zyv. When he caught their eyes, they looked away and stared into their mirrors, consuming their reflections.

Zyv looked at Stosh with disdain, but it didn't matter anymore.

"I am not a brand!" Stosh yelled. "I am Saint-Jablonski!"

He took first to the tables of yoga pants, tossing them in sprawling delight. An array of floral print limbs rained down upon the congregation, and as the parishioners scattered, he took to the sacred text—*Mining Your Precious Stones*. A great moan came forth from the affiliates then as he tore the milky pages from their bondage and laid upon the people their transgressions! He was a man loosed upon thee, the vile patriarch, the yoga pants and blasphemy raining down upon them all. And there he proclaimed again, "I am Saint-Jablonski, and I am non-fungible!"

"What is this ick!?" Gareth said from the back of the church, the two Big Boys beside him, rolling up their sleeves and revealing Swastika brands on their engorged biceps, their mouths stained blue from Gack.

"Stosh, not yet!" Zyv pleaded.

"Check your aura, you motherfucker!" Stosh said and continued his admonishment, flipping tables and kicking over whatever wasn't nailed to the floor.

The affiliates smiled and clapped with excitement as Stosh gleefully launched bottles of Gack up into the air and celebrated as they popped against the floor.

"I told you, not yet," Zyv said, grabbing his arm before he could throw the last bottle. "What is wrong with you!?"

"What's wrong with me is what's wrong with you!" Stosh said. "You made me. I'm your spawn, your twisted affiliate! Your reflection!"

"You're not supposed to freak out yet," she said. "Right, Gareth?"

"The timeline has accelerated," Gareth said. "We must do it now."

"Do what now?" Stosh asked as Gareth handed Zyv a jar of Gack.

"You must bear witness before you testify," Zyv said, smothering her head in the blue substance. "You will serve the brand."

Stosh pushed her aside and looked at her computer. "It's a spreadsheet!" he said. "Where's the algorithm?"

"We are the algorithm," Zyv said, now licking the Gack from her fingers.

Those left in the church bowed before Stosh as Gareth made his way to the altar, naked, except for the Magnetic Manifestation helmet, which now had Gator's head, and a crown of copper thorns set upon it.

"What's all that in the computer then?" Stosh said, backing away from Gareth as he approached.

"Their data," Zyv said, looking to the crowd. "We know what they desire, what they fear, who they are. We've cloned them."

Gareth was still approaching with the helmet on and a branding iron smoldering in his hand. He stretched out his arms to embrace Stosh, but Stosh kicked him in the balls. Then, with great strides, he made his way to the computer and ripped the USB drive from the port.

He picked up the branding iron Gareth had dropped and chased the wicked from the nave. Stosh locked the doors behind them and retreated to the sanctuary, but he had met his end.

He took out his phone, but it brought him no relief as he had no one to call. He exhaled, and not quite knowing what to do, doom scrolled through his socials and soon came across the Jubenville's Instagram page. It appeared someone had recorded the whole thing despite the phone ban. He should've known better—someone was always recording. He watched the several videos they'd posted of his tantrum, the whole thing caught in HD.

He watched as the videos racked up likes and comments with each passing second.

It was as Gareth had foretold. He had manifested it—analog social media. It was the internet cracking through the screen, the emojis reaching out from the metaverse and into the real world, their yellow pixelated hands grabbing at our throats, forever squeezing tighter.

History was now the order in which events appeared on our feeds: science merely a matter of PR; religion, nothing but a tax status; and faith a discount code for your preferred guru's online shop.

And that's the way it would be until the servers ushered us to extinction.

Stosh could hear the horde outside—Cletus and the Big Boys, Gareth and his cult of doting trolls and copper mommies.

He closed his eyes, recited the Prayer of Saint-Jablonski, and began to ascend. He rose toward the heavens, stopping only when he bonked his head on the vaulted ceiling. He began to float back to earth, stopping as he came face to face with Jesus on the cross.

"And to believe we did all of this for those people," Stosh scoffed.

"Saint-Jablonski?" a voice said.

Stosh fell to the ground but quickly righted himself and got ready for a fight as he saw the man's green Bermuda shorts.

"I'm here for the software," the man said.

"Who are you?" Stosh asked, his fists shaking.

"I'm Guy Mann," he said.

"That's not a real name."

"Neither is Stosh, but aren't we all just performing some absurd version of ourselves these days?" Guy Mann said.

Stosh regarded the platinum crucifix in his hand. "It's encrypted bullshit," Stosh said. "Clickbait."

"That bullshit is property of the United States Department of Defense," the man said. "I've been looking for it for a long time now."

"Perception Management," Stosh whispered. "It's all real."

"Real," the man chuckled. "I'm not qualified to judge such things."

"What is it?" Stosh asked regarding the crucifix.

"My salvation," Guy Mann said. "Software that allows us to search social media for those still friendly to clandestine government agencies, for job placement."

"In the deep state?"

"You watch too many movies," Guy Mann said. "Not everything is sexy. I've been stuck in a cubicle for years, creating fake social accounts and fighting with people in the comments section. It's so hard to find qualified applicants these days. You know what they call us in HR?"

"I didn't know the deep state had a Human Resources Department."

"Hopeless Rejects," Guy Mann barked. "Now, with that software, I can finally liberate myself from the horrors of the internet."

"Is this a psyop?" Stosh asked.

"No need for those anymore," Guy Mann said. "It appears people are more capable of driving themselves crazy than we ever were, thanks to freaks like Jubenville and Brother Roland or whatever he's calling himself these days."

Stosh wiped the sweat from his forehead and drew it down the front of his shirt, said, "But isn't that what you'd want me to think? Isn't that, like, tradecraft or something?"

Guy Mann shook his head and chuckled.

"Then what about the base, and the black ooze, the skunk ape?" Stosh stammered. "Is my father Omega?"

"Maybe," Guy Mann said. "Or maybe you are."

Stosh's eyes dilated. He looked at his hands. Could he have done all of this? Was he truly *powerful*?

"Don't think too highly of yourself," Guy Mann said. "Everyone has a theory. That's our most prized right these days— to choose which reality to live in. Some think Omega is a government insider, others a time traveler, and some believe it's a point in time when everyone will be so busy making content there will be no one left to consume it, but it's more than likely just another LARP, some troll living out a petty revenge fantasy from his mother's basement, pulling one over on the rubes. Or maybe it's all of those things. But the truth doesn't matter. It's just another commodity. We're all entitled to our own version of it, and now it's time for you to choose yours."

Stosh gripped the crucifix tighter and took a step back as the mob raged against the church doors.

"What do you say we get out of here," Guy Mann said, moving to the baptismal font in the corner of the sanctuary. He reached behind it, released it from the wall, and then pushed it aside, revealing a large hole in the ground.

"A rabbit hole?" Stosh asked.

"Or an old fallout shelter," Guy Mann said. "Why don't you decide?"

The mob growled outside, and judging by the serrated blade that had breached the door's wood, Al had brought his stump grinder and would be showing no mercy, the engine whining with a thousand gripes and passions. Stosh looked at Zyv's computer sitting on the altar, the cadmium and mercury of its black screen still sizzling and glowing faintly, pulsing with endless possibilities.

"I know what you're thinking, but take it from me, there's

nothing but infinite sadness in there," Guy Mann said. "It's a place where no bad idea ever dies."

"But there's nothing for me here," Stosh said.

"Don't abandon your world for the cybernetic meadow. It doesn't exist," Guy Mann said. "Just come with me before they hang you next to Him," he added, nodding toward the crucified Christ.

Stosh was wilted with fear. The splinters buzzed and rattled like cicadas beneath his milky flesh. He filled his lungs with the stifling Florida air one last time and then plunged into the void.

ACKNOWLEDGMENTS

I wrote this novel over the course of six years, so there are a lot of people to thank. First and foremost, my wife, Danielle, who had plenty of opportunities to run like hell but remains the cornerstone on which we've built our life. My daughter, Raelyn, who taught me to be a father and continues to teach me to embrace those parts of ourselves that are too often lost to age. My youngest daughter, Ava, who has only just arrived earthside but has already taught me so much. Dad loves you both. I want to thank my parents, Brian and Doreen, who have supported every cockamamie idea I've ever had with enthusiasm. Thank you, guys. Couldn't have done it without you. And I'd like to thank my father, Paul Mondry, who died without ever having sent an email. Dad, you would have hated Grok. My big brother, Matt—dude, ever since that day in our computer room when you showed me Iggy and the Stooges, I wanted to be as cool as you. Seriously, you epitomize what a big brother should be—kind of an asshole, but always proud and supportive. Love you, dude. Big, throbbing thanks to Jack Martins, whose letters and general buffoonery have always helped keep the blues away. I will forever be indebted to my mentor, Dan Bevacqua, whose now decade long guidance has been invaluable. The novel would not have happened without his encouragement. I have to thank the Williams crew—Mike, Sam, RaRa, Connor, Caralyn, Sophia, Hunter, and the Howels, Chris and Lori. Corey Bro'Skullivan and Mike Jurkowski for the good times mostly spent in basements, dodging tornados and playing *Trials*. To Alex Bramucci, for always vacuuming and providing the cool buds. All the love to my UTCA crew. Lastly, I'd like to thank my editor, Fatima Hassan for keeping me honest, and John Jarrett at Silent Clamor Press—thank you for taking the risk and for your constant generosity and guidance.

ABOUT THE AUTHOR

Andrew Mondry was born and raised in Western Massachusetts, where he still lives with his wife and two daughters. His short fiction has appeared in Jerry, The Nude Bruce Review, and Weird Lit Magazine.

You can find him on Instagram at @monjgoblin and on Substack at Comradedad.substack.com. This is his first novel.

instagram.com/monjgoblin

A NOTE FROM THE PUBLISHER

At Silent Clamor Press, we seek to illuminate the human experience with excitement, elegance, and unflinching honesty. If this work has resonated with you—offering a profound journey or a new way of seeing the world—consider sharing your reflections with others. Your voice enriches the ongoing conversation that keeps literature vital and transformative.

www.ingramcontent.com/pod-product-compliance
Lightning Source LLC
Chambersburg PA
CBHW032001130726
47903CB00012B/340